PRIYA PARMAR

A TOUCHSTONE BOOK
Published by Simon & Schuster
New York   London   Toronto   Sydney

Touchstone
A Division of Simon & Schuster, Inc.
1230 Avenue of the Americas
New York, NY 10020

First Touchstone trade paperback edition February 2011

TOUCHSTONE and colophon are registered trademarks of Simon & Schuster, Inc.

For information about special discounts for bulk purchases, please contact Simon & Schuster Special Sales at 1-866-506-1949 or business@simonandschuster.com.

The Simon & Schuster Speakers Bureau can bring authors to your live event. For more information or to book an event contact the Simon & Schuster Speakers Bureau at 1-866-248-3049 or visit our website at www.simonspeakers.com.

Designed by Renata Di Biase

Manufactured in the United States of America

10   9   8   7   6   5   4   3   2

Library of Congress Cataloging-in-Publication Data
Parmar, Priya.
    Exit the actress / by Priya Parmar.
        p.   cm.
    1. Gwyn, Nell, 1650–1687—Fiction. 2. Charles II, King of England, 1630–1685—Fiction. 3. Mistresses—Great Britain—Fiction 4. Actresses—Great Britain—Fiction. 5. Great Britain—Kings and rulers—Paramours—Fiction. I. Title.
PS3616.A757 E95 2011
813'.6—dc22
2009048703

ISBN 978-1-4391-7117-2
ISBN 978-1-4391-7118-9 (ebook)

for my mother and father
from nora who left
for plumbean's house
to see the moon
with you

Exit the Actress

By Most Particular Desire

THEATRE ROYAL, COVENT GARDEN

Audiences Brilliant and Overflowing

Are Invited to Attend the Premiere of

EXIT THE ACTRESS

This Present Wednesday, May 1, 1662

It will be repeated tomorrow, Friday, and Saturday next

PRESENTED BY MR. THOMAS KILLIGREW,

LEASEE AND ROYAL PATENT HOLDER

With: the cast as listed below

Gwyn Family

Mrs.* Eleanor Gwyn (Ellen/Nell/Nelly)—an orange girl turned actress at the King's Theatre

Mrs. Rose Cassels (née Gwyn)—Ellen's older sister

Mrs. Eleanor Gwyn (Nora)—Ellen and Rose's mother; a serving woman at the Rose Tavern

Captain Thomas Gwyn**—Nora's husband; an officer in the Royal Army

Dr. Edward Gwyn (Grandfather)—Captain Gwyn's father; a canon of Christ Church, Oxford

Mrs. Margaret Gwyn*** (Great-Aunt Margaret)—Dr. Gwyn's sister; living in Oxford

---

* a title indicating respect rather than marital status
** deceased as of 1662
*** denotes fictional character

Theatre

Mr. Theophilus Bird (Theo)—Actor at the King's Theatre

Mr. Nicholas Burt (Nick)—Actor at the King's Theatre

Mr. William Davenant—Manager of the Duke's Theatre

Mrs. Moll Davis—Actress at the Duke's Theatre; mistress to King Charles II

Mr. John Dryden—Playwright; Poet Laureate

Sir George Etheredge—Wit; playwright

Mr. Charles Hart—Actor; major shareholder of the King's Theatre

Mrs. Margaret Hughes (Peg)—Actress at the King's Theatre and possibly the first woman to act upon the London stage

Mr. Harry Killigrew—Groom of the Bedchamber; Wit; son of Thomas Killigrew

Mr. Thomas Killigrew—Patent holder; manager and major shareholder of the King's Theatre; former Groom of the Bedchamber

Mrs. Elizabeth Knep (Lizzie)—Actress; mistress of diarist Samuel Peyps

Mr. Edward Kynaston (Teddy)—Former cross-dressing star; Wit; well-loved actor

Mr. John Lacy—Actor, choreographer at the King's Theatre

Mrs. Rebecca Marshall (Becka)—Actress at the King's Theatre

Mrs. Mary Megs (Orange Moll)—Orange seller at the King's Theatre; employs the orange girls

Royal Families of England and France

King Charles I**—King of England; executed in 1649

Queen Henrietta Maria—His queen; daughter of King Henri IV of France; aunt to King Louis XIV of France

King Charles II—Son of King Charles I and Queen Henrietta Maria and cousin to King Louis XIV of France; restored to the throne in 1660

Queen Catherine of Braganza—Wife to King Charles II; former Portuguese Infanta

King Louis XIV—King of France; first cousin to King Charles II

James, Duke of Monmouth (Jemmy)—Illegitimate first-born son of King Charles II and Lucy Walker

*Henry, Duke of Gloucester***—Brother of King Charles II; died of the sweat in 1660

James, Duke of York—Younger brother of King Charles II

Anne, Duchess of York—His wife, daughter to the Earl of Clarendon

Henriette-Anne (Minette)—Youngest child of King Charles I and Queen Henrietta Maria; the Madame of France; Duchesse d'Orléans; married to Philippe, Duc d'Orléans

Philippe Charles d'Orléans—Brother of King Louis XIV; the Monsieur of France; Duc d'Orléans, husband of Minette

Royal Court of England

Sir Henry Bennet—Lord Arlington; Secretary of State

Earl of Clarendon—Chancellor, Privy Councillor, father of Anne, Duchess of York

Lady Barbara Palmer (née Villiers)—Countess of Castlemaine; Duchess of Cleveland; mistress to King Charles II, mother of their five children

Lord Buckhurst (Charles Sackville)—Earl of Dorset and Middlesex; Wit, poet

Sir Charles Sedley—Wit, poet

George Villiers—Duke of Buckingham; Wit; Privy Councillor; childhood friend of King Charles II, cousin of Barbara Castlemaine

Lord John Wilmot (Johnny)—Earl of Rochester; Wit; poet

To Be Performed by:

THE KING'S COMPANY (ESTABLISHED 1660)

PERFORMANCES BEGIN AT 3 O'CLOCK DAILY

PROLOGUE

SPOKEN BY THE ACTRESS
MRS. NELLY GWYN

upon her Farewell Performance

THEATRE ROYAL, DRURY LANE, LONDON

Prompt Copy

TAKEN BY STAGE MANAGER BOOTH

March 1, 1670

Mrs. Nelly Gwyn: (*Whispering in the wing, hands folded, eyes closed.*) Take a breath. Count three. Curtain up. *Now.*

(*Curtain rises. Enter the Actress stage left.*)

Mrs. Nelly Gwyn: Here I am. Back by request: for one night only, at *his* behest. (*Deep court curtsey to KING CHARLES II, seated in the royal box.*) What a lark and what a loss that such things are no longer fit for one such as me. How impossible is my unlikely luck: For here we are for one last night, to whirl like a dervish, and dance in delight, to look round and round at the faces bright, brightened still by candlelight. And then the curtain will fall and the thing will be done.

(*Noisy sigh.*) So if it be now: Good-bye to you and good-bye to me. To what we've loved and what we've been. To the villains punished and the good set free and love scenes played under the apple tree. There. Done it. (*Skipping.*) So off I go into the big blue swirl, to become a star, and to glitter far from home—but I will be *your* star, marked with affection, stamped and sealed. From you and of you: polished up, and good as new—well better than new; I once was a merry but meanly fed scamp but now I eat for *two.* Oh, I had forgotten how free this is. It has been many months since . . . well, you all know what I have been doing since. (*Laughter.*) And now I have a different life. I am to be an unmarried mother and devoted wife. So far a life well lived, I'd say. Turning left and left into unexpectedness I've flown through and through. Down the corridor, up the stair, over the road that leads nowhere, with candied daisies in my hair. And what did I find? A sugar-spun life of fruit and fancy shot straight through with gold. How extraordinary.

But at what cost? you ask. I'll show you. Here, over your shoulder: look closely. Look again: in the dark, there, do you see? The velvet, the hush, the eyes on me? Quiet. Back away. Disappear. It is a delicate alchemy balanced on a pin, gifted with luck, defined by illusion, brittle with fragility, but so beautiful.

Ah, you patrons and saints of the theatre . . . in the world at the edge of the world, where the king comes down from his mountain top to love the orange girl. Where reason and right run rampant and no one ever grows old. Where women are pirates and princes and wildflowers grow in the soul. The magical door will close behind me and then? Who will I be? But oh, I can live without the talk! The scandal, the chatter, the news today, and who went rolling in the hay. The who did what to whom and why? And how and when and by and by—the time is gone—and it is not life after all, this *talk*.

Still—it is fun. They say: I am charming. They say: I am charmed. They who? Ah yes . . . I know. Just remember: *They* are very powerful. Keep on the right side of They.

I gamble at the golden table, where the air is thick with time and chance and each night hundreds of scarlet slippers wear through from dancing.

Will *you* risk? Will *you* play? If you do, if you dare: wish and wish and should you win, when it is done, *if* morning comes: sneak away, snap for luck, and bless the day.

Hurry home. Fast and faster. Pull your curtains. Bolt your door. Close your eyes and wish some more. Love your neighbour. Sweep your floor. Beware. Luck can turn in a mouse's breath; before you notice, it is gone. So wish and wish for all your life to be kissed by bounty and freed of strife, and always, always for you and yours, joy upon joy upon joy—after all, it is all there is.

And as for our ordinary days: they are quicked with silver, bright and brief—and if you are snug as a beetle and free as a leaf—then shout thanks to heaven and breathe relief, for: our happiness is sewn in delicate threads. Use a thimble and *sew, sew, sew.*

But don't forget, love cannot protect the lover. It will bend but it will break. For it is not enough. Be careful what you choose.

Young girls ask how did you do it? Your cheeks are so pink? Your hair is so *red*? True, you are a stage delight, your waist is slim, your tread is light— but is that *all*? After all, you are so *small*. You are so like us. So here. So wicked. And yet, he loves you so. Why?

(*Quietly.*) And the answer is always the same: I really do not know.

(*Deep curtsey. Exit the Actress stage right.*)

I.

London Ellen

When We Live in No. 9 Coal Yard Alley, Drury Lane

May 1, 1662, one p.m. (May Day!)

Isn't it pretty? I guess I should say *"you"* rather than *"it."* Isn't that what one does in a journal, address it personally, like a friend, like a confidante? I am not sure of the etiquette, but I do know that *"you"* sounds precious and forced and not for me. Grumble. I dusted and rinsed this old sea chest twice before setting this book down upon it to write, and I have *still* managed to get grime on my sleeve. Rose will be cross. My sister, Rose, and I share this tiny back room above the kitchen, sparely furnished with only our narrow beds, a wobbly three-legged night table, and this damp sea chest pushed up to the draughty window. I only have a few minutes as I am waiting for Rose, who is dressing in front of the long mirror in Mother's room. Rose is *often* in front of the mirror. Oh, another grumble, these are *not* very auspicious opening lines, nothing of the elegant, eloquent young woman I hope to be. Never mind, ink is precious, onward.

It *is* pretty: butter yellow cover, thick creamy pages, bound with pale pink thread. It was really meant for my sister, as it is her birthday today. Rose is two years older than me and is turning fourteen and ought to be better behaved, frankly.

This morning:

Rose's friend Duncan, the stationer's son, a tall, finely turned-out young man who looks so wrong in our cramped, damp house, was wrapping his birthday gift for Rose, this beautiful journal plus: two fluffy quills, a sleek little penknife, and a heavy crystal inkpot, all stuffed in a stiff pink silk writing box. Too much for one box—the lid wouldn't shut.

"So she can record her most *private* thoughts and *deepest* desires," Duncan informed me loftily this morning, jamming the lid closed—it bulged but finally latched. We were seated on the worn rug in our tiny kitchen, working quickly to arrange Rose's gifts before she and Mother returned from church. I worried for Duncan's pale cream silk breeches on our gritty floor. I also worried that his gift would not be a success with Rose.

"Duncan?" I faltered. How to word this? Rose's deepest desire was for lady's gloves or enamel hair-combs or silk dancing slippers for her birthday—luxuries she would dearly love but cannot afford: pretty things. She has no interest in writing or reading or anything else much. If I were being unkind, I would say that Rose is only interested in beautifying Rose—but I am not *that* mean.

"Fetch over that pink ribbon, Ellen. The one edged in silver," he said without looking up from his task. I hurried to his hamper to find the right colour while he wrapped this lumpy gift in coloured paper—also pink—Rose likes pink. I handed him the ribbon, thinking that Rose will likely prefer the wrapping to the gift, and sat down again beside him. "A *perfect* choice," he gushed, wrestling with the paper and getting the lace of his frilly cuff tangled in the ribbon. "It will *perfectly* reflect my regard for her perfectly tender sensibilities." I bit my lip to keep from giggling. Duncan uses the word *perfect* a lot.

"When are they due back?" he asked, looking up at the tidy oak and brass clock Mother is so proud of. Ten to eleven.

"Soon. Father Pelham gives short sermons on sunny days."

"Lilacs or roses?" He held up generous bunches of both—good grief he came prepared.

"Lilacs." Rose detests roses—too predictable.

Two p.m. (stuffed after eating two custard tarts and still waiting for Rose to finish dressing)

Anyway, unsurprisingly, she did *not* like it, and did not take particular pains to hide it from Duncan—so rude! His face crumpled with distress when he realised his mistake. She did, however, like the new hat I gave her—grey felt wool with a wide green ribbon—the sharp, new pair of sewing scissors sent from Grandfather and Great-Aunt Margaret in Oxford, and the cake of orange blossom soap from Mother. "To get rid of the fishy smell," I chimed in thoughtlessly, trying to enliven the gloomy air. Rose sniffed, tossed her head, and ignored me. She doesn't like people to know that we are oyster girls and wishes I wouldn't refer to it aloud, certainly not in front of Duncan, who works in his father's stationery shop and smells of paper. "But people will *know* when they buy oysters from us," I am forever pointing out. A fact she chooses not to recognise—Rose does not like to be bothered with facts.

Rose just popped her head in, having changed her thick bronze hair from the simple, and I thought elegant, twist at the back to the more fashionable clumps of heavy dangling curls on each side of her head—perhaps fashionable but certainly *not* an improvement, they look like bunches of grapes. *Heigh-ho.* She scowled when she saw my sleeve. Now Rose is ready, but Duncan, who is in the kitchen eating crusted bread with butter and jam and getting crumbs on his velvet coat, is not.

Half past one a.m. (writing by candlelight)

So many people: jostling and hot and very smelly. People should wash more. Still, it was a magic day, and the freshly ribboned maypole in front of Somerset House was *enormous*. By next week, it will be a soggy grey mess, but no matter. It took us ages to pick our way through the crowded streets down to the Strand, and along the way I spoke to strangers, something Rose wishes I would *not* do, sang a May Day song with Mr. Lake, the cheesemonger, and ate sugared almond comfits until I felt ill. Too ill even to eat a slice of Rose's frosted sugar-cake (more pink), another gift from Duncan, who danced the noisy country reels over and over again with Rose. He is forgiven for the journal and has slavishly promised to make it up to her—revolting.

Mother chose not to come, no surprise. She received her weekly wages yesterday, and I'd bet she has already spent them on drink. Remember, Ellen: patience and kindness, patience and kindness.

Note—Must stop. Mother will be angry if she catches me wasting candles.

May 15, 1662 (chilly and wet)

Grandfather, very distinguished, not looking nearly as old as I thought he would (he was after all too old to fight for the old king), and nothing of the dour disapproving figure I had feared—surprising, after all he is a man of the church and aren't they *required* to be dour and disapproving?—has come down from Oxford, bringing with him his ancient, wheezing pug, Jeffrey. "He snuffles as he shuffles," Rose giggled. We have not seen Grandfather since our fortunes turned to ill and we left Oxford—and I was too small at only six years to have much memory of him. Rose says she can remember tugging his beard and watching him play cards and drink cider with Father. I cannot remember Father (who Mother calls "poor Thomas of blessed memory") at all.

Grandfather has come, he says, to guide our educations but has brought a long list of instructions from his sister, the ferocious Great-Aunt Margaret, concerning "our health and well-being," he said vaguely. I worry about that list. Unfortunately, he has already disagreed with Mother on a number of subjects, including our hygiene, dress, and vocabulary.

"You see!" Mother shrilled. "I knew you were only coming here to criticise. You have never approved of me. You think I could have done something more for him! You think I could have found someone to help poor Thomas, but I tell you once I saw that leg, I knew . . ."

"But, Nora," he said calmly. "Surely Thomas's pension will ensure more than this?" He gestured to our dreary sitting room. "After all, he died in the war, and isn't his widow entitled to the maximum amount? Yet his daughters . . ." Rose and I, sitting on the stair, held our breath.

"Yes?" challenged Mother. *Oh dear,* we knew that tone of voice. Do not push her further, or we will not have peace in the house for a week.

"They are running about London like street urchins!" Grandfather reasoned. "Why, Ellen told me that she has been wearing the same dress for a *month*! And Rose can hardly spell her name! And they both smell of fish!" Rose flinched and instinctively sniffed her fingers.

"*Oysters.* Not fish."

"Is there a difference? Is one more desirable than the other?"

Mother then launched into her familiar long litany of domestic woes.

"How am I to: clean them, clothe them, feed them, house them, *and* educate them?" she wailed. "On what? With what? There is no one to help me, now that my Thomas is gone."

With that she sank to her knees and began to sob noisily, pulling her voluminous handkerchief from her roomy bosom. Rose and I exchanged glances. *"That's done it."* Once she starts, it is difficult for her to stop. Grandfather tried tactfully to suggest that she spend less on *refreshment* (too obvious) and more on books, outer clothes, underclothes, soap, and new boots, but Mother only sobbed louder and refused to listen. She will remain like this for days.

This morning, Mother had *still* not come out of her room; Grandfather stomped off to the Exchange himself and returned with three books (used); a block of lemon castle-soap; cloth for: new chemises, summer and winter drawers, and woollen skirts for us; and a new cambric handkerchief for Mother. He laid it outside her door as a peace offering.

Friday, May 16, 1662 — Drury Lane (still raining)

Too wet to sell oysters. Instead, Rose went with Mother to the tavern, and I stayed at home and concentrated on my lessons—my often neglected lessons, as Mother is only really interested in teaching us to sing and play the violin. Today: reading, French, history, and mathematics with Grandfather—whom Mother is *finally* speaking to. The handkerchief helped. Rose told me that Grandfather had to pawn his father's gold timepiece in order to buy clothes for us. She told Mother, but Mother replied that it was only right that he shoulder some of the family expenses and we were all doing our best and so why shouldn't he? Rose held her tongue and did not tell her that spending nearly all Father's pension on drink really wasn't her *best*.

LONDON GAZETTE
Sunday, May 17, 1662
Most Deservedly Called London's Best and Brilliant Broadsheet

The Social Notebook
Volume 22
Ambrose Pink's social observations du jour

Darlings,

When I heard I became positively a-flutter, a-float, a-fizz with delight. *Grands Dieux, les possibilités les* gowns, *les chapeaux, les* boot buckles, *le scandale!* A royal wedding in London, at last, tra la la!

And then I received the news—*mon Dieu* the news:

At Lady Jemima's Tuesday evening salon—she played the virginals divinely by the by, and wicked Sir Charlie Sedley sang his own racy compositions—Lord Montagu mentioned having to take his fleet to collect the royal bride and then stay for the wedding, to be held in . . . Portsmouth. Portsmouth? Portsmouth, you say? Imagine Bonnie Charlie choosing provincial Portsmouth over chicest London? *Quelle horreur!* For shame, my darlings. I suppose poor old London will have to hear all the news by second-hand. *Dommage*, we shall have to pack our finest frippery away for another time. A royal christening, perhaps?

À bientôt, dearests,
Ever your eyes and ears,
An inconsolable,
Ambrose Pink, Esq.

*May 20, 1662—Official Notations for Privy Council Meeting on
This Day to Be Entered into the Log-book*

Notations taken by Secretary of State Henry Bennet, Earl of Arlington

*Today: A review of monies allotted for the renovation of Hampton Court Palace,
where our new Queen Catherine of Braganza and King Charles II will spend
their honeymoon. New matched daises have been built and upholstered measuring
16 feet by 10 feet. The carving about the queen's bed has been mended and regilded,
although another balustrade will have to be brought from Greenwich later in the
summer, requiring auxiliary funds. The Office of the Works will submit the proper
applications. Beyond that, all is in readiness for the queen's arrival on the 29th.
The contingency funds have already been allotted for household items, and further
funds are needed as: the palace kitchens have requested extra sugar, flour, wine,
and marzipan for the king's birthday celebration. The head valet has requested
forty-seven more pots of boot-blacking, and the housekeeper requires twenty-two
additional bath-tubs.*

*Nothing further to report.
Secretary of State Henry Bennet, Earl of Arlington*

*May 22, 1662—Drury Lane (late—but everyone
about on the streets)*

The streets are alight with bonfires. We have a new queen! Princess Catherine of Braganza, the Portuguese Infanta, now Queen Catherine of England.

What a mouthful, and a Catholic to boot. They say the queen's damask rose gown was trimmed with blue love knots, which she cut off and gave to everyone—a Portuguese custom, as I understand it, but ruinous for the dress—poor dress. They also say the new queen asks for *tea* instead of coffee or ale. Mother says that foreigners can always be relied upon to do foreign things.

Rose heard that she is small, but has huge, stiff hair—also a Portuguese custom? Best to discontinue it *now*, I would think; the English style is more unaffected and less lacquered. Rose also told me tonight that the famously overbearing Lady Barbara Castlemaine, the king's *companion* (*lover* is such an overblown windswept sort of word—and I certainly doubt that Castlemaine *loves* our king), refused to light a fire by her door. How small of her; she cannot hope to outflank the queen, his *wife*. She must give way.

Jane Smedley, who serves in the Rose Tavern with Mother and is always in a foul temper, said that I am to stay away tonight as I am twelve and no longer a child but not *ready* yet, ready for *what* she did not explain. Rose is clearly *ready* at fourteen and has gone to help Mother. Irritating, as she will only spend the extra money she earns on hair ribbons—*pink* hair ribbons that I can never wear, as my hair is impossibly red.

All the bells in town are ringing, and the city looks all lit up—the smell of burning almost covers the hot, rank London smells, so much worse in summer. With a bonfire before every door it is a wonder the night did not end disastrously.

Note—Rose just got in and was a bit clumsy on the stairs. As well her hair was all disordered—very unlike her. Could she be *drunk*? How extraordinary. Mother is still not home.

July 1, 1662 (hot!)

Rose and I slipped away to wade in the river after dinner. We left our shoes on the bank and, holding up our skirts, stood on the slimy stones and let the cool, muddy current rush around our ankles. Enjoying the falling light of the warm dusk and in the mood for mischief, I grabbed Rose's hands and began to swing us about the shallow water through an unsteady *gigue*, splashing and singing lustily as I went. Rose shrieked in soaked dismay but soon caught my mood and joined me in her sweet soprano.

Rose insisted we wash with lots of hot water when we got home; we both smelled like river rats.

July 12, 1662 — Drury Lane

Rose slept through work *again* today. She has been helping Mother and Jane Smedley serve ale in the tavern for the past few weeks and has been arriving home later and later in the evenings. Last night she did not get in until after three a.m. Once in our room she refuses to light a candle for fear of waking me and washes and undresses in the dark. Worried that she might lose her position, I told Mr. Morton that she was ill and that I was to take her share. Luckily, Mr. Bens from the Hare and Glove needed a double order of oysters; otherwise, I would not have been able to sell them all.

Walking home at nearly seven, I thought I saw Rose (pink hair ribbons) far ahead of me in Long Acre Street. She was speaking to a man I did not recognise. And she scolds *me* for speaking to strangers!

Two a.m.

Sleepy—Rose is still not home. I did *not* leave a candle lit for her tonight. Let her undress in the dark, for all I care.

VERSAILLES, FRANCE
COURT OF KING LOUIS XIV
TO MY BELOVED BROTHER, KING CHARLES II OF ENGLAND
FROM PRINCESSE HENRIETTE-ANNE, DUCHESSE D'ORLÉANS, THE MADAME OF
    FRANCE
SAMEDI, 21 JUILLET 1662

Charles,

I am so pleased! I was hoping you would choose from the royal house of Portugal instead of a cold Protestant princess from the north. From all I hear Queen Catherine is a quiet, gentle soul with an angelic face and regal bearing. And she is of the Catholic faith, which pleases our mam and, naturellement, pleases me also.

But let us not speak of things that divide us. How are your many adorable children? Is Jemmy's horsemanship improving? Mam writes that you are considering a dukedom for him. He would enjoy that honour—he enjoys any honour.

Mam also writes of the extensive and ongoing building and redecorating at her palace, Somerset House—the woodwork alone, mon Dieu, so lavish, I tremble at the cost. I know she has a tendency to find fault (the dust, the noise, the fabrics, the colours, the weather) and seems difficult to please—but you do please her in this, even if she cannot bring herself to say so.

Is it true that Lady Castlemaine is expecting again? While I cannot pretend to an affection I do not feel for her, I do welcome her children, as they bring joy and delight to you. Just be sure, my dearest, that it is you who gives shape to their unformed souls and not their mother, as she is of inferior sensibilities.

How is our darling brother James? Does he still grieve terribly for our blessed Henry? I do. I do every day, as I know Mam does, too. You must believe that she only did what she thought was best at the time, and as you know, once her mind is decided, her resolve is absolute and she is not plagued by doubt. Such determination would be a gift indeed if only her decisions were more thoughtfully considered. I hope that James has resigned himself to his marriage. Anne is a plain but intelligent girl, however unsuitable for our house. I pray for him. I pray for you and think of you every day.

I am ever your,
Minette

Note—I wish I could accept your invitation to visit England, but it really wouldn't be prudent for me to disobey my husband just now, as his temperament is growing increasingly erratic and unpredictable. As well there is so much to see to with all this building going on. Louis's plans for Versailles are truly extraordinary—there shall be nothing left of this charming little hunting lodge. Could you have your new queen's portrait painted for me instead? Une autre note—I heard that you wrote your love letters to Catherine in Spanish? Your Spanish is terrible, can this be true? And that when you had no immediate response from Catherine, you wrote to her mother as well? Oh la la!

July 21, 1662—Official Notations for Privy Council Meeting on This Day to Be Entered into the Log-book

Notations taken by Mr. Henry Bennet

Evening session:

News arrived by courier from Hampton Court:

Item: James Duke of York arrived in time to welcome his brother the king and his new queen as they entered the palace grounds. Unfortunately, the Duke of York's luggage train was delayed on the road and will not arrive until tomorrow.

Item: The Portuguese queen's retinue was much larger than expected, and the Office of the Works has allotted no rooms for their use. They must seek lodging in Kingston and are displeased.

Item: One of His Majesty's pastry cooks was run over by a furniture wagon this afternoon. They were understaffed tonight in the great kitchens.

Nothing further to report.
Sir Henry Bennet

Wednesday, five p.m. (still very hot!)

The house was too warm for lessons, so Grandfather agreed to a walk instead, on the condition that we conjugate French verbs as we go.

"Regular verbs," I specified. "Too hot for irregular verbs."

"Very well," he agreed. "To love: first person, present tense."

"*J'aime,*" I answered confidently. "Did you hear about the mess at Hampton Court yesterday? Everyone was talking about it today. People run over, carts gone missing—chaos."

"You love: familiar, past tense," he prompted, refusing to be diverted by gossip.

"*Tu aimas* . . . She must be very brave, to sail to a new country, knowing no one, and then to marry an utter stranger?" I said thoughtfully.

"Third person singular, future tense. Queen Catherine? I am sure she is very happy. After all, he is the king." Grandfather shrugged, as if a sovereign is guaranteed love and devotion.

"*Elle aimera.* That doesn't mean she will *love* him," I said. "I wouldn't do it. I will not marry where there is no love—not even a king."

Grandfather gave me a worried look. My romantic notions concern him, I know. Most girls hope to marry a man with a stable income rather than a man to love. Ever patient, he forbore to criticise and we moved on to the verb "to play."

When I Discover the Truth

Thursday, July 21, 1662—Drury Lane

I am shaking with shock and rage. There has been a tremendous row. I should insist and argue and rant, but I find I am too stunned even to weep.

After oysters I stopped at home. Finding no one about—Grandfather had gone to the Sun Tavern in Wych Street to play backgammon; Rose, I believed, was still not finished with her basket; and Mother was already at the tavern—I went to visit Duncan at his father's shop in Bow Street. I had not seen him in weeks, as he no longer calls on Rose; she is so often occupied in the evenings now. He demanded all the news of the family (meaning Rose) and politely enquired after my appetite: my *enormous* appetite. And so we went along to the cook shop on the Strand for fish pies, green cucumbers, and apple cream fritters, my favourite.

"I am glad to see you eating," Duncan said with custard cream running down his chin. "You are far to thin for your age."

I grimaced. My thinness was a frequent topic of discussion in our house—regardless of how much I eat. Rose, tall, with a long, curvy figure, has no patience for my small height or thin frame, and Mother is always quick to point out that men enjoy "*flesh,* and not *bones,* Ellen."

After a whole pie, *and* five fritters, *plus* a fruit tart—even the baker was impressed—Duncan walked me home to Drury Lane. I was walking slower than usual as my new stays—Rose insisted I begin wearing them and I have yet to adjust to the discomfort, not pain so much as *pressure*—were even tighter with a full stomach and were making it difficult to breathe. In our street, Duncan stopped short when we came upon two people embracing.

The man had his hand inside the woman's bodice, and her head was tucked inside his arm. I hurried towards our door, *mortified* that we live in such a street, but Duncan had stopped a few paces behind me. He was *looking* at them. Then, quite abruptly, he turned on his heel and left without speaking. Just then the couple disentangled. *Pink ribbons. Rose!* It was Rose! With a drunk and dirty man's hand down her chemise.

"Ellen!" She rushed towards me, wild-eyed. "How could you?" She shrieked. "How could you bring him here?" The dirty man grinned and staggered off, tugging at his breeches.

"How could *I*?" I fired back. "What were *you* doing—with *him*? What if Mother or Grandfather saw you?" I glanced up to make sure the house shutters were closed. A stripe of candlelight under the door—Grandfather was home. I struggled to open our door (it sticks), and clattered the handle.

"You really have no idea of anything, do you?" she screeched. "You think Mother did not *know* I was here. You think she did not *ask* me to be here?"

"Mother *knows* about this?" I asked, shocked. Then, all at once, the fury left her in one great puff, and she sagged against the door-frame.

"Ellen," she sobbed. "You have ruined everything. He will never, never forgive me." She turned, picked up her skirts, and ran out through the alley.

Grandfather, who had heard everything, was sitting by the fire with Jeffrey curled at his feet. Mother is still not home.

Much later (everyone asleep)

Mother did come home—late. I tried to speak to her about what happened, but she had had too much to drink and waved me away. Grandfather, in his linen nightcap, came and gently helped her to bed. Then we waited. Grandfather asked no questions, although he must have heard everything through our thin walls, but just kept quiet company throughout my agitated vigil.

Eventually, we heard Rose. I leapt up at the sound of the latch.

"Sit, Ellen," Grandfather said, and, stooping, kissed us each good night.

Once we were alone, Rose pulled at her fraying sleeve and began awkwardly, "Mother has a group of girls."

"For what?" I asked blankly.

"For men . . . to buy. To go to the alley. Or to the rooms above the tavern. To *be* with." She looked at me steadily, folding and refolding her hands in her lap. "Mother asked me to be one of the girls. You *must* understand, Ellen," she continued, catching my hand, "this is the only way. It is so difficult for her; she lost Father, her home, all her fine things. She was a captain's wife and now . . . we must do something to get it back."

"Oh, Rose, no!" I struggled to make sense of her words. "No, Rose, this will never . . ." This will *never*, ever bring that back. *This* will only bring us lower, I thought, but I did not say so. How could I explain what she ought to know already? Instead, I asked bluntly, "Does everyone know? Jane? Grandfather?"

"Yes. Grandfather knows."

That explains his bizarre lack of outrage, I thought.

"He was shocked, but then it is paying for the added expense of his board, so he can hardly object," Rose continued. "Aunt Margaret could not afford to keep him in Oxford, since he left Christ Church. But it is not all bad," she said brightly. "Haven't you noticed that we have meat every week? *And* the chocolate? *And* the extra tallow? By next month I will be able to afford an entirely new ensemble, shoes, hats, petticoats, gloves, everything, and then I shall attract customers of *quality* and really be able to earn some money. Well, perhaps not a hat *and* gloves, but certainly one or the other. It will be a step up, Ellen, I promise."

"A step up to where?" I cut in sharply. "Where does all this go? Regardless of your hats and petticoats, you will *be*, as you so gently put it, with quality people, and then what? You will *be* nothing to them."

"Not nothing," Rose challenged. "Perhaps not as high as a kept mistress, but better than an oyster girl. Anyway, who knows whom I might meet and what might happen? With good clothes, smelling of *real* perfume—not just strong soap? Mother says if we do this, all will be well again."

"*Mother* does it, too?" I interrupted, appalled.

"At first. But it works better if it is younger women. Mother is, after all, thirty-nine." Rose suddenly sounded like a woman grown worldly and not like my sister at all.

"Who are the other girls?" I asked, faintly.

"Maggie, Susannah, and Lucy mostly. A few others, but they are the regulars. Susannah has already saved enough to buy *French* underclothes. They are true white. I'm *perfectly* jealous," Rose said dreamily.

French underclothes? You give up your whole life for French underclothes? That is a bad bargain no matter how white they are, I thought, looking angrily at my frivolous sister.

"How did this happen? When did this happen?"

"Oh, some time ago. Mother wanted to wait until we were grown up before we started. Lucy just turned thirteen, but she looks so much older, because her *you know* have filled in." Rose gestured vaguely to her chest. "I was worried because mine were taking *so* long. But it is all right now." Rose has been recently blessed with a high full bosom. She looked down at my as-yet flat chest. "Don't fret, Ellen; mine took *ages*. You still may turn out all right."

"How could Mother ask them?" I shook my head as if to clear it of this nightmare. I know many girls do it, but not *us*. We are better than that, aren't we? Our father was a captain. Grandfather is in the *church*. We don't do *this*. And yet Mother . . . "How much does she take?" I asked, suddenly furious. "Her fee? After all, she is the madam." I spat out the harsh brothel word.

"I suppose she is," Rose said thoughtfully, as if she hadn't thought of it quite like that before, "but it is not like she has, you know, an *establishment*. Her fee? I don't know. I still haven't gone upstairs, so I haven't *been* with anyone yet. But I am sure I will soon. Everyone else has," Rose said vaguely. "Mother just has set the price so high to *be* with me because I am her best girl and I cost a *fortune*." She giggled. There was pride in her voice. "You would, too, if you did it—even more because you are younger. I'm sure they would overlook your flat bosom because you are so young. Some men even like that—you might find one of them? Eventually, of course, we were going to ask—"

"No," I cut her off brusquely, unwilling to hear more. "Don't ask."

Later (grey-pink sky)

I am still wakeful, wrapped in the counterpane and sitting in the window, my thoughts wound too tightly to sleep. Outside the sky was brightening in long pink streaks, but the early light had not yet touched our windows and our room still lay in deep shadow. I pulled the coverlet closer and let my thoughts swing along the well-worn track of shock and understanding. Rose wanted to become a seamstress, I thought irrelevantly. Her designs are so lovely and her hand is so neat . . . and now. What does a young whore grow up to become? Rose did not seem to share my turmoil and was lightly snoring.

"Rose," I whispered into the dark. She stirred but did not wake. I had to ask. *"Rose,"* I whispered again, "Duncan didn't know?"

She turned over to face me but did not open her eyes, "No. I hoped he wouldn't find out."

That explained her aloofness, her high-handed refusal to see him of late.

Then, when I was sure she was asleep, softly, I heard her: "I did so want him to love me."

Oh, Rose.

WINDSOR CASTLE, ENGLAND

TO OUR SISTER, PRINCESSE HENRIETTE-ANNE, DUCHESSE D'ORLÉANS

FROM HIS MAJESTY KING CHARLES II

JULY 16, 1662

My dear sister,

Escaping the heat and chaos of London, I have decamped to Windsor before moving on to Hampton Court—well, my enormous retinue and I. Do you remember Windsor? You were a baby here before you were secreted away to safety in France. It is beautiful, as only the English countryside can be. I have great plans for renovating the castle. I mean to level the skyline, modernising the structure; it has a disorganised higgledy-piggledy feel at the moment—not surprising, as it has been rebuilt relentlessly during the last eight centuries. It is currently a bellicose sort of layout, and I mean to soften the rough-hewn feel. I am planning to create a series of large airy salons adorned with painted ceilings and gilt boiseries, replant the gardens and restock the lakes, build glasshouses to grow tropical fruits never yet to be tasted on our shores, and, in short, make it the envy of all Europe— including the French—I suppose especially the French. I understand Louis's plans for Versailles are extraordinary, but they are mostly just plans, non? Has the building begun in earnest? Surely it will take him fifty years?

So to domestic business: yes, Catherine is with me, as is James. Catherine first: our wedding night was not a success, and for many reasons: timidity and homesickness on her part, and for myself an indisposition due to travel sickness being among them. I have chosen to put off my conjugal obligations for the time being and give the poor girl time to adjust.

Now James: I am trying to be patient as you suggested, but he is a difficult brother and an even more difficult heir presumptive. The least he could do after getting that poor girl pregnant and then secretly marrying her is to stand by her. But does he? No! Now, as his ardour (how he mustered ardour for that one I'll never know; she is a lethal bore) has cooled and the baby was stillborn, he wants to disavow the match and abandon the girl. She is the daughter of my chief minister—not suitable for marriage but not deserving of that sort of roguish treatment, either—I cannot think what woman would be. He is furious with me for forcing him to honour the union, and Mam (as no doubt you know) is furious that I allowed the appalling match in the first place. I do naturally point out that it was a secret marriage, and I did not allow it, but as you can imagine, it is to no avail. Without Henry, you are the last peacekeeper in our family, and you are sorely missed!

I cannot express how much I am your,
Charles

Note—What do you mean erratic? Has he forbidden you to visit your own family? Truth be told, French alliance or no, we may have made a mistake giving you to this man. Naturellement, burn this letter.

July 27 (Lord's Day)

I watch Rose at her toilette. She has new tortoiseshell hair-combs (expensive!). I won't ask her where she got them. She frowns into the cracked glass, trying them this way and that. Today she rouged her cheeks with Spanish paper—something I have never seen her do, as her cheeks are pink anyway—blew me a kiss, and left.

Later (still can't sleep)

Four in the morning and they are not home. Fretful, I crept downstairs; Grandfather in his nightshirt and slippers was dozing in his chair. Jeffrey, beside him, was softly wheezing in his sleep. How can she do this?

Six in the morning. She must have done it.

Tuesday, July 29, 1662 (sunny)

Up early and off to the market. Mr. Morton (Rose and I call him the Octopus—eight hands, fishy smell) is now doubling my share of oysters to sell. Rose sleeps late in the mornings as she is out so late at night. I do not ask her where she has been. "You could sleep, too, if you—"

"No."

August 8, 1662
Coal Yard Alley, Drury Lane, London
Dear Margaret,

A brief missive to tell you that I am happily settled here and the girls are well. I am pleased to report that both my granddaughters are beautiful. Rose (fourteen) is taller than I expected for her age and slim, with a rosy, farm-girl complexion, as befits her name, and a great mane of chestnut waves. Ellen (twelve) is small but bright and carries herself neatly. She has an expressive, heart-shaped little face, and although her hair curls beautifully, it is an unfortunate copper colour—perhaps it will darken later? She is a quick, sensitive child, and her lively antics are the heart of the family.

I wish I could tell you that Thomas's wife, Nora, is also well, but I fear she is not. She amply provides for her girls and myself, but I fear she has had to lower herself to fearsome depths to do so. I think of you, Margaret, in the snug house by the river and can hear the evening bells chiming out over the colleges. How are the chicks? Are they laying yet?

Your loving brother,
Dr. Edward Gwyn

When We Watch the Procession

Saturday, August 23, 1662 (what a day!)

It was splendid! This morning the king brought his new queen to London from the palace at Hampton Court. All of London turned out for the royal couple. It was like a feast day: a man was playing a bass violl, people were singing and leading rowdy country reels right in the road, the streets were hung with garlands and ribbons, and all the street sellers were shouting to be heard above the fray. On each corner men in royal livery with flowers in their hats liberally poured out wine. The result was drunken but good-natured chaos. Duncan and I adorned ourselves with flowers: a fat peony in my hair and a yellow rose tucked into his smart blue hat. Nowadays, we do not speak of Rose.

The crowd was so great outside Whitehall, drifting up from the river-bank, that the palace guards (also wearing flowers) were having trouble preventing the people from climbing the wall and entering the Privy Garden. Squinting into the bright sun, we saw a small group of onlookers who had climbed the rickety scaffolding and were watching from atop the great Banqueting Hall.

"Yes," I said with conviction.

"Oh no. Ellen!" Duncan called after me, but I had already begun to climb.

We scrambled up the scaffolding, and people already on top of the Banqueting Hall hoisted us up—it is much higher than it seems, but such an orderly pretty building up close, hard to imagine that this is where they executed the old king. Today, the sun was hot in an empty blue sky, and the river below us was blanketed in colour. I pushed back my cap and shaded my eyes to get a better view. Looking down, I couldn't see the water for the crush of boats and barges. Each boat was festooned with bright canopies and trimmed with ribbons and ropes of fresh flowers. One of the men who had pulled me up pointed out the king's tented barge shimmering in green and gold and behind it the queen's barge covered by a pink-and-white-striped awning.

I could see the king standing (so tall!) in the prow of his barge—not under the canopy but waving to the crowds lining the banks and bridges—but I could not make out the queen. My informed neighbour, a Mr. Peeps (funny name, I wonder how he spells it?), also pointed out Barbara Palmer, Lady Castlemaine, cutting a fierce and bright (she was covered in glittering stones—not quite right for this time of day, I'd say) silhouette on a lower platform at the edge of the river. She is dark, with a generous figure and the heavy lidded eyes that are so fashionable now but to me just look sleepy. Next to her was a nurse with a starched collar holding a baby—a red-faced, screaming baby.

"Is that the king's baby?" I shouted to my neighbour, but he could not hear me above the crowd.

The great guns on either side of the river sounded as the royal barges landed at Whitehall Bridge and the king himself handed down his little queen (she is tiny!) and led her towards the palace. I could not see her face as her head was bowed, but it was sweet the way she clung to her new husband. Rose was right—her hair is enormous, sticking out on either side of her head like elephant ears.

"Foreign," the man behind me grunted.

"Mmm, *dark* and foreign," my neighbour agreed.

"She dresses English—that's a start," a woman behind me in striped taffeta remarked, squinting down at the new queen. "But she looks like a hairy little field mouse, just the same." Others around her laughed in accord.

People up and down the riverbank must be watching, criticising, and making similar comments right now, I thought with disgust. I felt compelled to rise to this little woman's defence when the king, passing below the balcony, looked up and, with a flourish, *bowed* to Lady Castlemaine! She did not modestly cast her eyes down, but boldly kept her head up and deliberately took the squalling baby from the nurse and slowly dropped into a long, deep curtsey—displaying her expansive bosom. The court and crowds were riveted, waiting for a reaction from the royal couple. The king casually watched her rise and nodded in easy acknowledgement, and the procession moved on. The little queen looked around for explanation from her ministers and her Portuguese ladies (all in black and *not* dressed English). Everyone carefully avoided her eyes.

Later, Duncan and I wandered home, sharing a cone of sugar-cakes. He used his linen cuff to brush the sugar from my chin, and finally mentioned the unmentionable. "Is she happy?" he asked, faltering. "Doing *that*, I mean."

"Oh, Duncan." I did not know how to answer him.

Sunday, September 21 (Lord's Day)
Farm Cottage, Oxford
Dear Edward,

So happy to hear that you are comfortably settled in London. The girls sound attractive—make sure to watch them. Ellen in particular sounds the very picture of her father. He was always such an able and likeable mimic and had such tidy movements. He, too, suffered fiery curls. I am sorry to hear that Nora is not thriving, but then she has always been a selfish woman, given to melancholy and exaggeration. You must not let her influence the girls. Are they attending church? Washing regularly? Practicing their music? Minding your lessons? I am quite sure Nora did not pay the least attention to their education. You did not mention any of this in your letter. Do try to be more specific when you write next, dear.

Edward, is Nora taking proper care of you? I worry with winter coming on and your delicate health. Does she know how to make the bread and milk poultice for your cough? The Michaelmas term is starting, and Oxford is bustling again. The chickens are laying, and the calf is weaned. The cheese is heavenly.

Your loving (and worried) sister,

Margaret

Note—A don called Pressman has applied for the room. He will be teaching history at Pembroke beginning this term. He is clean and quiet and can pay the rent (a month in advance, and I was sure to check under his fingernails for dirt). I have decided to take him on, provided he is willing to bring in his own bath-water and feed the goats.

Whitehall, London
To our beloved sister, Princesse Henriette-Anne, Duchesse d'Orléans,
the Madame of France
From His Majesty King Charles II
Monday, September 22, 1662

My dear sister,

Yes, Queen Catherine is lovely and amenable and gentle and pretty, but entirely incomprehensible. I have two tutors working with her teaching her French and English, but languages are not her forte, and unfortunately, she speaks only Portuguese and Spanish. Currently, we are conversing in broken Latin, which you can imagine is tedious and worrying to my Anglican subjects. To date, I have engaged: a dancing master, a music master (her voice is exceptionally low and pretty), a riding master, and, curiously, an archery instructor—at her request. I hardly see her for her swarm of tutors. When not with them, she is attending mass with Mam at Somerset House.

What touches me is her painful shyness. Although she is twenty-three (yes, I know, ancient for a first marriage), she is so child-like it is easy to forget. I wish to protect her from the harsher elements of my court—in particular a certain lady who has been less than generous about her appearance. You understand of whom I speak. Unfortunately, Catherine's Portuguese fashions (James persuaded her to take them up again, arguing that she would feel more comfortable—silly) look frightfully homely here. I can only imagine that they would fare worse in brutally fashionable France. She has led such a sheltered convent sort of life and seems provincial and so young that I would spare her criticism if I can. Could you, perhaps, in your next letter, advise her on matters of hair and dress and deportment? I feel it would be better coming from a sister rather than a husband or, worse, another tutor. Write simply, her French is terrifying, but I will ensure a patient translator.

Yes, I have attempted conjugal duties—no, it did not go well, although I do hope to entertain her better than the Monsieur did you. Your nightmarish account of that encounter haunts me still; I cannot imagine being unattracted to women—one or two perhaps, but all? Mystifying.

Are the rumors vrai, my dearest? Does our cousin King Louis bitterly regret marrying you to his brother Philippe? My envoys tell me that le roi danced with you three times at a recent fête at St. Cloud, straining the bonds of decorum. Our aunt Anne cannot have approved of that—is it true that her hold on the young king is slipping? J'espère, for she must be a suffocating burden for poor Louis, as she, like our mam, is always one to speak her mind. And what of Philippe, your very grand Monsieur—we hear of his extraordinary personal expenditures—700 livres for a wig, mon Dieu. Has his erratic behaviour become more predictable? Again, j'espère. Marriages, as I am learning, take time to settle into their rhythm. Bonne chance!

Know that I am faithfully your,
Charles

Note—*Can it be true that Louis has already spent five hundred thousand livres on his new palace? An unthinkable sum—although I have heard that his new gardener Le Nôtre is worth every sou. I have just engaged another Portuguese cook, ah the holy state of matrimony.*

September 29— Michaelmas Day (sunny and warm)

The Octopus has taken to pinching my bottom after he fills my basket. I have become adept at outmanoeuvring him, but I have to be quick. Exhausting. "You could . . ." Rose says.

"No, I couldn't," I repeat firmly.

Rose still undresses in the dark, regardless of whether I leave a candle burning or not.

Monday, November 24, 1662 (freezing!)

"The world will end a week from tomorrow," Rose informed me breathlessly, shedding her heavy muffler. It was one of her rare afternoons at home. "I just had it from a woman in the market," she continued, hanging her icy mittens over the hearth rail. "Everyone is talking about it."

"What?" I asked distractedly. I was trying to stir the beef stew and read Mr. Pink's column in the *Gazette* at the same time.

"The end of the world, Ellen," Rose repeated impatiently, "it is *next week*."

"*What?*" I asked, alarmed, dropping the spoon. Eventually, I got the full story. A lunatic in Bedlam Hospital has prophesised this calamity, and he would be discredited but this same fanatic also foresaw the king's blessed Restoration. How like Rose to deliver such news without preamble. Just in case the end is near, Rose and I and possibly Grandfather are going to church this evening.

Later (home with Grandfather)

It was a good thing that Grandfather did not come, for the pews were overfull and he would have had nowhere to sit. Rose felt uncomfortable up front and preferred to stand near the door. Crowds make her nervous now that her reputation is growing. I squeezed in next to Mrs. Lake, the cheesemonger's wife, who had obviously been eating garlic. Lots of garlic.

Now at home: Grandfather and I are off to bed. We no longer wait up for them. There is no point. They do not return until dawn. What a quiet little household we have become.

Tuesday, December 2, 1662

Relief. The lunatic was wrong. Nothing happened.

December 25 — Christmas Day (rainy)

All of us at home today. Mother baked Christmas pies. The neighbours devoured most of them and then got sticky sugar on all the door latches. I played my guitar—Rose is mystified as to why I do not learn a more fashionable instrument. "A guitar is so *provincial*," she complained, sounding like the old Rose. I welcomed her criticism, as she has been so unnaturally quiet lately.

When We Celebrate My Birthday

Wednesday, January 7, 1663 (late—so sleepy)

This evening I attended a rousing musical lecture at Gresham College with Duncan, Grandfather, and Dr. Genner, an old friend of Grandfather's who looks just how you want a doctor to look: white beard, kindly expression, and walking stick. Rose did not come along as she is rarely at home now that she has started working for Madame Ross at her large and notorious establishment in equally notorious Lewkenor Lane. It is a step up of a kind, I suppose. Mother is angry that Rose no longer works exclusively for her, but cannot complain about the extra money. She has already found a girl to replace her.

Rose was in the kitchen, hemming the sleeve of her new bluebell blue dress and drinking a bowl of chocolate when we came trilling home—a happy, boisterous quartet. I pulled off my hat and went to stand by the warm fire. Duncan stopped at the door and flushed crimson when he saw Rose. A sad sort of look flashed across Dr. Genner's face, but he quickly crossed the room and kissed her cheek. "Lovely to see you, my dear. Are you keeping well?"

"Very well, thank you, Dr. Genner. Did you enjoy the concert?"

"It was a lecture, not a concert," corrected Duncan from the doorway, and then he mumbled his thanks for an educational evening and fairly fled out the door.

"Rose, dear, is there any of that chocolate left to offer our guest?" asked Grandfather, unfazed, "or is that the last of it in your mug?" Rose smiled at the jibe; she has a sweet tooth and always finishes off the chocolate.

"No, there is plenty in the pot. I thought you might be coming back soon."

"I can't stop, either, I'm afraid," said Dr. Genner. "Celia will start to fret." He gently patted Rose's cheek. "It was good to see you, my dear. You must stop in and see Celia. She misses you." He left after shaking Grandfather's hand and promising to thrash him in a game of backgammon on Sunday.

The three of us were left standing in the kitchen in the wreckage of the lovely night. Grandfather reached up to the high shelf and brought down two more mugs. Rose set down her sewing and poured out the thick chocolate. Once we were all settled at the table, I could no longer hold back, and my giggles erupted. "Forgive me, Rose," I gasped. "Duncan just looked so uncomfortable and pompous, and then he . . . he . . . he *panicked*."

Grandfather chuckled. "I think, my dear, he did not know quite what to say to you."

Rose smiled sheepishly. "No. No one seems to know what to say to me these days."

Thursday (icy cold!)

Even though I wore two pairs of woollen hose and stuffed my boots with paper, I still had to stomp my feet to keep my toes from freezing today. The wintry sun did little to warm me, and by two in the afternoon I could stand no more and ducked into the cook-shop for warmth and a beef pasty. What luxury! If Rose can spend money on absurd hair-combs, then I can surely buy a pasty. Regretfully, I did not have any hot cider as I need the money to buy lip salve tomorrow for my wind-whipped face. These days I am permanently pink—most unattractive.

Early—six a.m.

Rose came home at dawn this morning and, thinking I was asleep, undressed in daylight. I gasped when I saw her bruised collarbone and forearms.

Rose turned, swiftly covering herself with her chemise. "It is not as bad as it looks, Ellen," she said tersely, pouring water from the china pitcher into the basin. "Go back to sleep."

In the morning I found the cloth she had used to wash bundled at the back of the wooden washstand. *Blood.* So it is as bad as it looks.

January 19 (bitterly cold)

The news:

Fourteen people froze to death in the village of Highgate, a five-legged cow was born in Chelsea, and the king asked his new queen to accept Barbara Castlemaine as her First Lady of the Bedchamber. She refused! Bravo!

January 21

The news:

The farmer in Chelsea is charging fourpence a head to see the five-legged cow. "Less than a penny per leg," Grandfather said. "That is reasonable." The Dutch have inflated the price of lace to more than seventeen shillings a yard, and Queen Catherine relented! Mother says a wise woman accepts. Rose says the young gallants are calling it the "Bedchamber Crisis." Are those her customers—young gallants?

St. Cloud, France

To my beloved brother, His Royal Majesty King Charles II
    d'Angleterre

From Princesse Henriette-Anne, Duchesse d'Orléans, the Madame of
    France

Jeudi, 19 Janvier 1663

Charles,

Is it true what Louis tells me? Did you really install your mistress into your new wife's household? It is one thing to seduce one of your queen's existing ladies—these things are common enough at court—but to ask your wife to accept your present mistress as one of her ladies? Unheard of. Such things are not comme il faut, *dearest. These breaks in decorum threaten the delicate balance of conduct in which we live. It is said here that she is grieved beyond measure, and to speak frankly, I think it is with reason.*

I am not preaching fidelity (I well know that such things are not within bounds for kings), but I am urging prudence and discretion. Do not be ruled by Lady Castlemaine's petty spite. You cannot believe that her vengeful nature will be satisfied with only this. You set a dangerous precedent, my love!

À bientôt,
Keep well,
Minette

Note—*Louis has nearly completed the Orangerie—orange, oleander, pomegranate, and palm trees. He has also begun the Menagerie—the pelican is named Pocket.*

Une autre note—*Portuguese cuisine is said to be simple and fresh and good for digestion.*

January 30 (hungry!)

No oysters to sell. Today the whole country kept a solemn fast in remembrance of the late king's murder. Funny that now that the king is restored, it is called murder: three years ago the punishment for mourning the late king's execution was imprisonment. Grandfather, a true Cavalier, fasted despite his frail health. Twice I tried to filch some cheese from the sideboard, and twice Grandfather caught me. Unusually stern, he was *not* amused.

SOMERSET HOUSE, LONDON
TO OUR DAUGHTER, PRINCESSE HENRIETTE-ANNE, DUCHESSE D'ORLÉANS, THE
    MADAME OF FRANCE
FROM HER MAJESTY QUEEN HENRIETTA MARIA
JANUARY 30, 1663

Ma fille,

Just a brief note, my darling, to tell you that I think of you and all my fatherless children today above all days. I know I need not remind you to keep the fast and have masses said for your dear father's soul. James has joined me here for a private mass—it must be private, as Charles insists we conceal our religion. I know you pray as I do that God will also turn Charles's soul to the Catholic religion and stop all this Anglican nonsense. I know your father died in that faith, but there is no reason to follow him—he was in error.

I pray for your father, who died so bravely here in London fourteen years ago today. I think of how he said good-bye to your brother Henry and your sister Mary (so young!), bidding them to look upon Charles as their sovereign. I think of how he must have felt waking in our bed in St. James's Palace, our own home, on that cold morning and then climbing out the window of his beautiful Banqueting Hall (he loved that room) to that high platform to face that ghoulish crowd, waiting in the street. How he lay down his noble head upon that common block, forgiving the executioner, who never had the courage to reveal himself. Charles, to this day, cannot discover his identity—coward. Know that your father loved you sincerely, although you do not remember him. Know that he thought of you on that terrible morning: of the loveable baby you were and the gracious, principled woman you would become. We must keep our promise and abide by his last word to Bishop Juxon and "Remember."

With fondest love, chérie,
Maman, *Her Majesty Queen Henrietta Maria*

Monday, February 2, 1663— Candlemas (warm and cloudy and my thirteenth birthday)

Meg, who sells oranges in Covent Garden, Orange Moll, as she is known, stopped to speak to me today. I was wearing a white smocked chemise under my new yellow pointed bodice that laces in the *back,* a present from Rose. Grandfather said I looked like a field of daisies.

"Turn, turn, so I can see!" encouraged Meg. I obliged, twirling in my new clothes. "Ah, fresh and sweet and always a favourite with the customers. How do you like selling oysters?"

"They are smelly and the walk to the market is tedious and Mr. Morton is overly . . . forward." I answered candidly. Will I ever learn to be discreet?

"I'll bet he is. How would you like to sell oranges instead? I need one more girl for Mr. Killigrew's new theatre in Bridges Street." She held out a fat, round orange. "For the birthday girl."

"Thank you!" I said, pocketing the sweet fruit. China oranges are such a luxury; I would save it to share with Grandfather.

"You'd best understand," she said, catching my chin in her hand, "I sell fruit, not girls. The minute you sell yourself, you work for someone else." She looked hard at my face, her expression searching and fierce. Then, breaking into a smile, she patted my cheek. "No, I can see it. You don't have the vanity to go bad. Not like your sister over in Lewkenor Lane. She was always going to go that way." I must have shown my surprise, for she laughed a kind, enveloping laugh. "Oh yes, sweeting, I've been watching you."

So it is decided: I will give up the Octopus and become an orange girl.

Note—If Candlemas day be dry and fair—but it was cloudy, so six more weeks of hard winter.

2.

Orange Girl Ellen

By Most Particular Desire

THEATRE ROYAL, COVENT GARDEN

Audiences Brilliant and Overflowing

Are Invited to Attend the Revival of

THE HUMOUROUS LIEUTENANT

A Tragicomedy by Mr. Beaumont and Mr. Fletcher

This Present Wednesday, May 7, 1663

It will be repeated tomorrow, Friday, and Saturday next

PRESENTED BY MR. THOMAS KILLIGREW,

LEASEE AND ROYAL PATENT HOLDER

To be Performed by:

THE KING'S COMPANY (ESTABLISHED 1660)

With: Mr. John Lacy, Mr. Michael Mohun,

Mr. Theophilus Bird,

And: Mr. Nicholas Burt, Mrs. Margaret Hughes,

and Mrs. Anne Marshall

PERFORMANCES BEGIN AT 3 O'CLOCK DAILY

When I Begin to Work

Friday, May 8, 1663 (day after the opening, and my second day!)

We stand with our backs to the stage. We line up and face out, and as the audience piles in—we begin. Each girl has her own technique. Alice Winthrop tugs down her bodice until she is nearly bursting out, leans low over the young men in the pit, and, breathing in their ears, asks them if they might care for an orange. *Of course* they might—unless she has been eating onions. Lily Beale (Mad Lil) used to sell oranges at the Duke's Theatre (the Opera) and so is known to the regulars and has her patter down perfectly. She targets couples: "Go on, Mr. Weathercombe, buy your lady a lovely China orange! Don't you be too cheap to treat her to something sweet." Lil could sell water to a fish.

Meg, her skirts pinned high on her stocky frame to allow her greater mobility, is *everywhere* up and down the aisles, selling oranges, delivering messages, chatter, chatter, chatter: hats with the ladies, hunting with the men—and spreading gossip faster than any news sheet. She keeps a close eye on her girls, deciding where we stand and how many we sell, and when she feels like a pitch isn't working she invents a new one. Laughing at my inexperience, she calls from the aisles: "You don't have to do much. You've got the goods. Little bit sweet, little bit sharp: always honest, and pretty as a peach. Just get out there, and they'll flock to you!"

And they *did* flock to me. I sold my basket before the end of the first act! I also sold some of Alice's share, as she got waylaid on Jack Parson's knee in Fop's Corner through much of the second act—Mrs. Parson had stayed home with a head. I sold twenty-six oranges, ferried three love notes—one was rejected unopened by a thick-necked woman in a sour green dress—and brought a lovely girl in a lavender lawn gown a rose from a man in the gallery with a bushy moustache. Then I got to watch the third act from the footlights. It was *marvellous*.

LONDON GAZETTE

Sunday, May 10, 1663

Most Deservedly Called London's Best and Brilliant Broadsheet

The Social Notebook
Volume 73
Ambrose Pink's recollections of an evening of theatre

Darlings,

On Thursday last, London's beau-monde witnessed the King's Company's first performance in its new and delightful Theatre Royal in Bridges Street (so much better than the fragrantly cramped hard-benched ex–tennis court of old). Sumptuously cushioned boxes with thick curtains *(très privé)*, a hidden musicians gallery—somewhere under the floor-boards—ingenious but a bit muffled, a veritable constellation of wax candles (*mon Dieu*, the cost!), delicious fruit sellers, and lavish curling gilt galleries gave one the feeling of being entertained inside an enormous and very pleasant golden egg. Dear Tommy Killigrew has outdone himself. Light-footed Lacy in the title role and naughty little Nan Marshall in the role of Celia only added to the entertainment. A triumph.

In the audience: the dashing Prince Rupert (in a pink lute-string coat with silver lace), seen *tête-à-tête avec* clever Dickie Rider, the master builder of the theatre. In the centre box was the Great Mrs. Hester Davenport, old Roxelana herself (peach taffeta—rather too many ruffles, I felt); and tucked in a corner box was crafty Will Davenant, rival manager of the Duke's Company (in his habitual black silk kerchief and low-brimmed *chapeau*—surveying the competition, no doubt). Tommy Killigrew, beware!

À bientôt, dearest,
Ever your eyes and ears,
Ambrose Pink, Esq.

Saturday, May 23 — Theatre Royal (rainy)

Titania, Bottom, Helena, Demetrius, Hermia, Lysander, Oberon, Puck. Act One: Enchanted Forest. Act Two: Titania's Bower. These words are *beautiful.*

PALAIS ROYAL, PARIS

TO MY BROTHER, KING CHARLES II D'ANGLETERRE

FROM PRINCESSE HENRIETTE-ANNE, DUCHESSE D'ORLÉANS, THE MADAME OF FRANCE

29 MAI 1663

My dearest,

For shame, my darling. I know that you have been "supplementing" your wife's English lessons, for there are several filthy words that your queen included in her last letter that could have only come from you. That is terrible, Charles, to teach her such things and not tell her what they mean. However much it amuses you, you must correct this!
Bon anniversaire, my dear!

Je t'embrasse,
Henriette-Anne

Note—*The doctors say I am in good health.*

Saturday, May 30 (Midsummer Night's Dream)

Tonight, just before the audience came in, Peg Hughes, in her costume as the honest fairy Puck (deep green hose, moss-green tunic, pale golden wings), came out from the tiring rooms and, leaning down from the stage, bought an orange from me. Meg saw it and refunded the money immediately—actors, actresses, and Mr. Killigrew get complimentary fruit. *Always.* A terrible mistake I shall not make again. Still, we spoke for a few minutes, and then Mr. Booth hurried her away for places.

Palais Royal, Paris

À mon frère, King Charles II d'Angleterre

From Princesse Henriette-Anne, Duchesse d'Orléans, the Madame of France

3 Juin 1663

My dear,

Have you listened to none of my admonishments, and not only added Lady Castlemaine to your queen's household but also moved her apartments closer to your own? I was given to understand that her apartments faced the street on the other side of the Privy Garden from your own. Are they now adjoining? Mon Dieu! I know you care for your new wife's feelings. Would you treat her as Philippe treats me? He is forever parading his young men before me.

With my love,
Henriette-Anne

Tuesday—Theatre Royal (hot and sticky and smelly)

So, what I know:

The Actors

Charles Hart and John Lacy: the two great leads. Hart, a man hung on an enormous frame, with thickly waved brown hair (although he often wears a periwig), has a booming voice and says he is the great nephew of Shakespeare—but then everybody says that. Lacy, a surprisingly nimble, bluff Yorkshire man was trained as a dancer before the war and never keeps still.

Theophilus (Theo) Bird and Edward (Teddy) Kynaston: before the war, both trained in the old style to play the female parts, although Theo, with his great drifts of snowy hair, must be at least sixty and so trained a half century ago. Theo is married to comely Anne, the actor and manager Will Beeston's daughter, and she is forever patching everyone's costumes and blacking their boots. Teddy is delicately featured, sweet-tempered, and very fond of Theo.

Nicholas (Nick) Burt: also trained to play ladies but plays the hero very well (a good thing, since he is well over six feet high). He is pleased that King Charles has brought height back into fashion.

Michael Mohun: also a leading man but smaller and somewhat owlish. He is married to Theo's daughter Eliza.

Robert (Rob) Shatterell: lives quite close to us in Playhouse Yard.

William Cartwright: haven't met him yet.

The Actresses

Mrs. Ann (Nan) Marshall and Mrs. Rebecca (Becka) Marshall: sisters. Becka is the elder. Apparently, they are the daughters of a Presbyterian minister. One would never guess with their lewd talk and constant flirting. They are neither subtle nor pretty enough to make it endearing.

Mrs. Elizabeth Weaver: the eldest of the women. She takes pains to hide her enormous hands and feet.

Mrs. Elizabeth (Lizzie) Knep: small and bird-like. Teddy says she has a risqué past, but I have yet to see evidence of it. She does have an invalid husband who is always gambling away her money.

Mrs. Kathleen (Kitty) Mitchell: pretty brunette with a sweet disposition and a fine actress (specialising in doomed heroines) but softly spoken and *impossible* to hear beyond the pit.

Mrs. Margaret (Peg) Hughes: direct, popular, bright, and full of fun. And, they say, the first woman to act upon the stage—Desdemona.

Later

This afternoon, Peg and Teddy heard me on the stairs and called me in to join them in the tiring room. Teddy was having trouble fixing his wig (he swears his head is too small to carry off a man's wig, but I thought he looked splendid), and Peg needed me to help lace her into her silk wings. I did my best to appear nonchalant, but in truth I was delighted. Everything about their world fascinates me.

Note—Peg loved the new way I tied her wings (crossed over in the back with a bow) and has asked me to help her dress again tomorrow!

When I Glimpse Grandeur

June 7, 1663 (Whitsunday)

In the tiring rooms:

Theo, who tried to sit quietly while Teddy painted his face with Venetian ceruse, announced, "The queen is with child." Teddy heralded his announcement with trumpet noises and ended up spitting on Lizzie.

Kitty, applying more *crayon bleu* to her eyelids, looked up and said, "Maybe now she will settle in and stop being so . . . so . . . foreign."

"She *is* foreign," said Theo, trying not to laugh and crack his face. Teddy gave him a stern look. "It's not her fault. But she does seem to be adjusting. Still no ale but at least she has changed her dreadful hair."

"Is it true?" asked Kitty, outlining the delicate veins on her bosom. "What he said when he saw her?" She turned to me. "Too much?"

"Maybe overdone just here," I offered, wiping the harsh blue stripe off her throat—Kitty's eyesight is not good. "What who said when he saw her?"

Teddy reached for a fresh pot. "Ugh, you don't know? Bonnie Charlie. He said that instead of a beauty they had brought him a bat. Theo, honestly, if you don't sit still, I will leave you to do this on your own, and then where will you be?"

"No! He didn't! Because her hair . . ."

Theo, between clenched teeth, said, "Well, when she first arrived it did look like she might—"

"Take flight?" Teddy quipped, flapping his brushes in the air like great bat wings and getting powder on Lizzie. "*Someone* has had a word with her, thank goodness. She is wearing it *à la négligence* now—very chic."

"Bravo, Braganza!" Theo cried without moving his lips.

"And now she will have a baby," I said, handing Teddy Theo's wig and taking up my basket. "She must be so relieved."

Teddy licked his thumb and pasted the wig to Theo's head. "Oh, I think it is more than relief. I think she's in *love*."

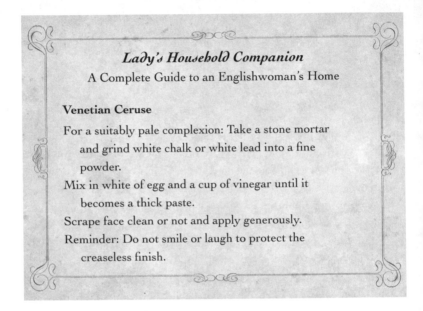

Lady's Household Companion
A Complete Guide to an Englishwoman's Home

Venetian Ceruse

For a suitably pale complexion: Take a stone mortar
  and grind white chalk or white lead into a fine
  powder.

Mix in white of egg and a cup of vinegar until it
  becomes a thick paste.

Scrape face clean or not and apply generously.

Reminder: Do not smile or laugh to protect the
  creaseless finish.

Friday, June 12 (The Committee still on)

This morning, before the audience came in, Lacy was on the stage trying to teach Peg *La Duchesse*, the latest dance in London—French, of course. Lacy says it is *magnifique*! Peg says it is impossible. She has such trouble, being left-handed, and kept turning the wrong way at the top of the figure, but Lacy was patience itself. Teddy and Theo joined in. Teddy took the lady's part (he prefers the ladies' parts—more twirling) and then called me up to make up the set with Nick Burt. My pinned skirts felt patched and shabby next to their starchy silks, and my boots were too heavy for dancing, but I leapt onto the stage anyway. Meg and Lil thumped out the rhythm from the pit. *Da, dum, dum, da, dum, dum and demi jeté and change.*

"Do it *barefoot*, Ellen!" Teddy called from stage right. "You cannot *pas de bourrée* in boots."

Although I did not know the steps, I watched closely and caught on quickly, and in the end Lacy used Nick and me to demonstrate the proper form. We would have been *magnifique*, too, if we hadn't collapsed into giggles.

Saturday, June 13 (first performance of The Faithful Shepherdess)

Theatre has been in an uproar all the morning as they put together the new scenery for *Shepherdess*. Mr. Rider, the master builder, was in, directing the mayhem and showing the managers how to work the new machinery (very expensive and very noisy) to drop the flats from above. It is all very modern, and the flats are huge although not quite dry. I caught Mr. Fuller touching up the last of the fluffy sheep just before the doors opened.

Note—The queen is not with child. She was mistaken. How sad.

Wednesday, July 1, 1663

Excitement in the house tonight: at the end of the first act of *Othello*, Lady Castlemaine in a watered crimson silk gown and tall Frances Stuart—she is a *giant* of a woman—slipped into the royal box. The ladies in the pit were pulling off their visors, the latest fashion, to get a better look at *la belle Stuart*. She is said to be the *most* beautiful woman in Europe. The king was not with them, but the audience still shouted for the play to start over. What a bore. That put us an hour behind.

Afterwards we went off to the Bear for supper. I tried to hide my excitement at the invitation. Usually Meg's girls do not join the actors after the performance. The cast still do not know their lines as apparently they haven't done *Othello* for a year and a half. They ran the words all through the meal as is their custom but still managed to carry on a conversation as well—confusing. All the non-*Othello* talk was of Castlemaine and her young rival—*la belle Stuart*.

Theo (Iago) pulled off a piece of the crusted farm bread and said, "Apparently, they arrived in the new light *calèche* that the king has given Frances Stuart. Becka saw it pull up."

Teddy, taking the jam and butter away from Theo (he is encouraging Theo to lose some weight), said, "Mmm, I saw it, dark green and ebony, *very chic*."

Nick (Cassio), piling his plate with pasty, and chicken, and stew, and bread, *and* jam, *and* butter, said, "Clever Stuart kept the coach but refused the king!"

Peg (Emilia), drinking only coffee, offered thoughtfully, "That's the way to do it, I reckon. Be the only one to say no. It'll drive him mad. He will offer her *anything*."

Teddy ordered a dish of roast carp, a fruit tart, and a mug of raspberry sack for me, and a huge slice of iced nutmeg cake for himself. He has a terrible sweet tooth.

"Eat," he commanded. The company also think I am too thin, although my bodice size *has* increased since winter. Rose measures me at least once a week.

Monday—Drury Lane

Half an inch! Rose has begun to sew me a new gown of pool-blue linen and is saving the stiff bodice for last—just in case my size should continue to *improve. Heigh-ho.*

HAMPTON COURT, ENGLAND
TO OUR DEAR SISTER, THE MADAME OF FRANCE, PRINCESSE HENRIETTE-ANNE,
　　DUCHESSE D'ORLÉANS
FROM KING CHARLES II
JULY 5, 1663

How sharp you are, my dear. Yes, Lady Castlemaine's apartments have moved, but then so have some of my own (or they will as soon as the renovation is complete). The nurseries were just too far for me to see the children as often as I like. My bedchamber is moving to the river-front adjoining the queen's apartments—unfortunately, that puts Catherine between my bedchamber and Lady Castlemaine's, but Catherine is a sound sleeper. You see, I am not so unkind as you believe. I do worry that the sound of my children would upset Catherine, but she is making a sincere effort to befriend them. My wife sends for me just now to dance, so I must end and can only add that I am entirely your

Affectionately,
Charles

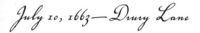

July 10, 1663—Drury Lane

Drat. I missed the excitement. I took my half-day on Wednesday, and naturally on that day the king and his bosom friend, the known rakehell George Villiers, the Duke of Buckingham, attended the early performance. Teddy reported that the king wore lavish lace cuffs, a long, narrow rhubarb-pink-striped waistcoat, high-heeled court shoes with *wired* grosgrain ribbon (*quel* glamour—Teddy swooned), and a knee-length embroidered surcoat, which he removed immediately and slung on the back of a chair. The king's hose were true white, Teddy was careful to mention—Teddy is very particular about hose. The king's thick black hair hung in long ropey curls, and he laughed loudly and freely. In the second act, Lady Castlemaine joined them in the royal box. Kitty reported that she wore an overly garish sunset-orange taffeta gown embroidered with gold thread, sat on the king's knee, and twisted her fingers through said ropes of hair. Theo says that the performance lasted an additional two hours on account of the royal visitors. He also said that Castlemaine and Buckingham are cousins . . . *close* cousins. Does that *mean* . . . ?

Later—Drury Lane (raining)

Improvement! Rose is letting out the new bodice a bit more—just in case. Tried some of Peg's rice powder this evening—awful. I looked as if I had fallen face-down in a flour vat.

When We Suffer a Terrible Rumpus

July 20, 1663—Official Notations for Privy Council Meeting on This Day to Be Entered into the Log-book

Notations taken by Secretary of State Henry Bennet, Earl of Arlington

Insufficient business was conducted this morning. The Privy Council held discourse on only items one and two of our eleven-item memorandum. The excluded nine items will be herewith attached to tomorrow's (July 21, 1663) meeting, thus greatly increasing that day's business. His Royal Majesty was much involved in writing small notes to the Lord Chancellor, Edward Hyde, Earl of Clarendon, on the matter of his journey to Tunbridge Wells. For the purposes of record I obtained the notes, and they are contained herein:

> *Lord Chancellor: I suppose you will go with only a light train?*

> *His Royal Majesty: I intend to take nothing but my night bag.*

> *Lord Chancellor: Yet you will not go without forty or fifty horses?*

> *His Royal Majesty: I count that as part of my night bag.*

Nothing further to report.
Secretary of State Henry Bennet, Earl of Arlington

July 25, 1663 (hot!)

The excitement is over. The season is done. The king *and* queen *and* Castlemaine *and la belle Stuart, and* the rest of the court have deserted London for Tunbridge Wells. Elizabeth, ever discreet, says the queen is eager to take the restorative waters there to benefit her *health*. Becka, never discreet, says she is going there to cure her *difficulty*. In *Romeo and Juliet* rehearsals this morning—the fight scene:

Lacy, choreographing the fight, said breathlessly, "I'll bet the king can cure her *difficulty*. What is he up to now? Five? Six bastards? How old is Jemmy Monmouth now? Thirteen? Oh, I need to sit a minute." He thumped heavily onto Juliet's prop bed—too heavily, as the lightly constructed bed creaked loudly.

Peg, forgetting her cue and letting her sword drop with a bang, said, "Well, it's not her fault. The king has to actually spend time in her bed to cure *that* difficulty. Yes, yes, I know, *En garde!*"

Teddy lay on the stage and fanned himself with his script. "Perhaps she does not *quite* know what is supposed to happen? After all, in that prissy Catholic country, who would have told her? Lacy, I'm not sure you are meant to *recline* on that bed."

Nick, who was practicing his footwork downstage, chipped in, "Castlemaine's in a delicate way all the time; perhaps she could give her some pointers? Is it left, parry, left, or the other way round?"

"The other way round," Lacy called without sitting up.

"Well, we certainly know that it is not the king who has a *difficulty*," Teddy said, blowing out his cheeks and turning to watch the scene. "My God, this heat! *Left!* The *other* left, Peg!"

Peg, turning the wrong way, missed her mark again.

Much later

In the interval Lizzie Knep came down with her courses and was unable to perform the last act, and Mr. Hart *himself* sent Meg to find *me*. I was whisked backstage and quickly stuffed into Lizzie's dancing costume; she is small like me, but her slippers were too big—I packed paper in the toes to make them fit. Hart came striding offstage and abruptly said I would be led out to dance *La Duchesse* but to a slow sombre beat, in the final scene, by Benvolio (Nick) and then left to stand at the back and silently feign to weep when the Prince (Theo) makes his speech and they bring in the dead lovers (Kitty and Mr. Hart).

"Remember," he said briskly, "you are playing a lady of the court: head up, languid eyes, soft fingers but a strong grip on your partner, supple neck, straight spine. Think: seduction. Do *not* make a misstep." With that, he turned and, frowning at the stage, ferociously concentrated upon his entrance. It is extraordinary how still he stands in private before launching himself into public vitality. I felt fidgety and slight next to him, and I wished he had not given me so much instruction and just left me to do it as I did the other day. Standing in the wings, I thought seriously about being sick, so great was my fear. At least it would be Nick who would partner me as I had danced with him before. Hopefully, in these fine clothes, no one will recognise me.

I waited, trying to remember the steps, when Nick came up behind me. "Ready?" he whispered. The music swelled, and out we went. Terrifying! I could not make out the faces of the audience. The dance ended, no missteps, but then most likely my spine was bent and my neck unsupple, but at least I did not topple over in Lizzie's big shoes. Nick left me behind the tomb (Juliet's bed without the coverings) to weep. From there I peeked out at the pit from behind my hands but could not see Alice or Meg. I wish Mother and Rose and Grandfather had been there! But then, I was behind a particularly robust Capulet, so I don't think they would have been able to see much of me anyway.

SOMERSET HOUSE, LONDON
TO OUR SON, HIS MAJESTY KING CHARLES II AT TUNBRIDGE WELLS
FROM HER MAJESTY QUEEN HENRIETTA MARIA
JULY 22, 1663

Charles,

Just a few things to remember:

She must avoid heavily salted foods and pickled foods of any kind. Herrings would be disastrous. She must limit her physical exertions out of doors. I do understand that she is a young queen away with her court (remember I also took the waters there), but she must remember her purpose and not overtax herself. She has told me of her passion for archery, but I do not think such strenuous activity can bring about the result you desire. In the mornings (after you have been to her chamber—which I hope you will do frequently—this is for your country, Charles, and must be taken with all seriousness), she must elevate her legs for at least two hours. James writes that she drinks water. Is it true? Ruinous. She must stop immediately. I am sending my physician, Dr. Fronard, to personally see to her health. In truth, Charles—affection. That is the key to a happy marriage and to a happy country. Just affection. Be good to her.

Maman,
Her Majesty Queen Henrietta Maria

August 1, 1663
Coal Yard Alley, London
Margaret,

So sorry that you were not able to visit us here this summer. I hope your foot is much recovered. All is well here. Rose is growing up faster than any of us could have imagined and is more beautiful each day. Ellen is still small and seems likely to stay that way. Oddly, it seems to suit her fairy spirit. I am as well as ever. I think Jezebel is a perfect name for the new goat—particularly if she has such a tempestuous disposition. Please do not allow her to eat my books.

My best love,
Edward

Tuesday, August 6 — Will's Coffee-house, one p.m.

(hot and clear)

The delicious smells of apple cakes baking and warm French macaroons drifted from the vast kitchens. I entered the famous coffee-house with some trepidation. It is holy ground reserved only for actors and writers and artists and politicians, but Meg had sent me with a message for Teddy, and I was determined to deliver it. The dark, wood-panelled interior was austere, but the scene inside was convivial, noisy, relaxed, and *crowded.* The next room smelled of coffee, new bread, and *people. Lots* of people. Men and women lounged everywhere, on everything: faded sprigged sofas and peeling painted chaise longues, spindly ladder-back chairs, stained window-seats, even on the rough plank trestle tables themselves. By the enormous open fireplace were two men sleeping in patched overstuffed armchairs that were losing their stuffing. (I have heard that Mr. Dryden keeps an armchair reserved by the fire.) Everywhere people were eating, laughing, dicing, talking, drinking, and in one corner dancing. A man played a violin but could hardly be heard over the ruckus. Dogs lay on the floor and waited for scraps. It was chaos. How would I ever find Teddy in this mess?

After some effort, I caught the barmaid's attention, and she pointed me to a corner table by an open window. Theo was drinking cold chocolate, and Teddy was fanning himself with a script against the heat. The table was heaped with summer fruit pies, sugary glazed cakes, and pots of fresh snow cream.

"Ellen," Teddy said, looking up and scooting down on his bench to make room. He has a way of always making me feel welcome.

"Oh no," I started, "I can't stay. Meg just wanted me to tell you that Lady Fenworth has come up from the country and has arrived at the theatre looking for you."

"Ugh!" Teddy slapped his forehead in an elegantly affected gesture. "I was meant to ride in St. James's Park with her this afternoon, and I forgot." He turned to me. "Is she very cross?"

"I wouldn't keep her waiting," I told him with sincerity, taking a seat beside him. I'd seen her sweep into the theatre, swathed in voluminous black silk and carrying an incongruously small dog. She probably outweighed Teddy by at least two hundred pounds and looked exactly like an impatient rhinoceros. "When I left, Lacy had found her a seat in the great foyer to wait for you. But she did not look too comfortable."

"Time to go," Teddy said, getting wearily to his feet. "It will take me half an hour to dress, at least. Thank you, Ellen, for finding me so swiftly. No, no, stay." He waved me back to my seat. "Eat something. You look famished. Theo, until this evening." With that he hurried out the door.

"He . . . rides with them, these older ladies?" I tentatively asked Theo once Teddy had gone.

"They like to be seen beside him in their carriages. He is somewhat of a favourite companion with the women of this town." From what I'd heard, he was equally a friend to the gentlemen, but I kept these thoughts to myself.

"And he wears—"

"Yes, he loves to dress up. He was so good at it, you see, and then everything changed. Not that we don't appreciate having lovely creatures like you around, my dear, but it used to be so . . . different. And Teddy, of course, he was the star. I think he must miss it, but he would never say so."

When I returned to the theatre, I encountered Lady Fenworth, now standing and calling her fluffy dog. The ferocious air about her had dissipated, and she was coquettishly giggling and girlishly fluttering her eyelashes. With her was a delicately beautiful woman, wearing a light walking gown of spotted yellow silk. Watching her fluid gait, it took me a moment to realise that it was Teddy. He winked at me as he went by.

Lady's Household Companion
A Complete Guide to an Englishwoman's Home

To Make French Macaroons

Wash a pound of Jordan almonds and then beat them
to a fine paste.

Add half a pound of finely ground sugar and dampen
with rose-water.

Add the whites of two new beaten eggs and bake until
crisped white.

SOMERSET HOUSE, LONDON

TO OUR SON, HIS MAJESTY KING CHARLES II AT TUNBRIDGE WELLS

FROM HER MAJESTY QUEEN HENRIETTA MARIA

AUGUST 5, 1663

Charles,

*A most disturbing report has reached me. Does your queen dress as a man? James writes
to say that she has embraced a peculiar new fashion, and all the young people are following
suit. She has been seen publicly in velvet breeches, an embroidered surcoat, and a plumed
hat. You must put a stop to this at once. It is neither dignified nor safe. Does this mean
she has been riding astride? As you know, I dislike strong language, but this behaviour in
a lady of rank, never mind a queen, is unthinkably disgusting. At this rate she will never
have children and the country will come to ruin, and it will be squarely on your head.
Manage your affairs better.*

Queen Henrietta María
Your (displeased) maman

Postscript: *I have heard from Queen Anne that Phillipe has been opening Minette's letters. Minette naturally dislikes her husband's intrusiveness but cannot stop his bad behaviour, no more than she can prevent his fruity choice of hats. I recommend you engage a special courier at once in order to correspond with your sister.*

Saturday, August 15, 1663—late (everyone asleep)

Cannot sleep. Rose was in the theatre tonight. It did *not* go well.

This evening:

Meg, Lil, and I were in the middle gallery counting up the day's takings, forty-seven oranges and seventeen limes (a good sum) when we heard a frightful commotion below. A woman's voice: "Harry! No! Put me down! Not here!" as the Venice lamp for the new *Claracilla* crashed to the floor. I turned sharply at the sound of the voice. Quietly, we three peeked over the gallery banisters. On the stage were a drunken Harry Killigrew, Tom Killigrew's eldest son, and an equally drunken young woman in a tightly laced pink gown. Her brown side curls had come undone, and the loose hair concealed her heavily made-up face. Harry was fumbling with her bodice but unable to manage the laces, changed his mind, and decided to lead her in a disorderly *pavane* instead, smudging the wet paint of the new flats as he went. The woman was careful to keep her dress away from the paint. Something in the set of her shoulders . . .

"Oooh, no! Mr. Fuller hasn't even finished 'em yet!" Lil whispered as Harry brushed against the fresh paint.

"Shh!" Meg hissed, intent on watching the couple on the stage.

"There we go! You've got it! *Brava!* Now bow to the audience." Harry applauded his partner. The woman, giggling overloudly, turned and curtseyed to the pit. She tipped her face up to us . . .

Rose—and her young gallant.

"*Go,*" Meg said quietly, turning to me. "Get her out of here. I won't say a word, but do it now and be quick."

"Who *is* it?" Lil whispered, confused.

"You never mind. Ellen, go *now*."

I scrambled down the back steps to the pit and ran up the side aisle towards the stage. "*Rose! Rose!*" I whispered urgently. "It's me. Come away with me now."

"*Ellen?*"

Just then the main house doors banged open behind me. Mr. Killigrew and old Samuel, the night watchman, stood framed in the light of the doorway. "God Almighty, Harry!" Mr. Killigrew thundered, squinting into the dimness and stalking down the centre aisle with his great dog Kitt trotting beside him.

Quickly, I vaulted up onto the stage. "*Now*, Rose, you *must* come with me," I half pulled, half dragged her into the shadowy wings and then pushed her out through the stage door.

"But, Harry—"

"No, Rose!" I said, manoeuvring her down the lane away from the theatre. "That was Harry's father. It's *his* theatre," I panted, pulling her down the wet cobbled street. "You two have just destroyed the new scenery for *Claracilla*, the play Mr. Killigrew himself *wrote*. Please, believe me. You cannot go back there. He could hold you for the damage, or worse, you could wind up in the clink."

"But Harry—" Rose repeated, belligerently dragging her feet.

"Harry will never say it was you," I said, impatiently tugging her along. "Don't *worry*, Rose. You won't be blamed. Rose, *move!*"

"No!" Rose turned to face me squarely, her jaw grimly set. "Harry hasn't *paid* yet. For tonight. I need my money, or Madame Ross will turn me out. It's been a whole evening, Ellen. I can't come away with nothing to show for it."

"Oh!" Instantly, I loosed her arm.

"I will wait in the alley by the stage door," she continued. "Harry won't let me down. He will come," she finished with quiet dignity. How odd: she was not drunk at all.

I watched dumbly as she smoothed her gown, straightened her small hat, and pinched colour back into her cheeks. She flashed a bright smile. Her professional face, I suppose. Composed, she turned and began walking back towards the theatre.

"Ellen"—she turned—"you have nothing to fear, I would never tell them that you are my sister."

"*Rose*—" I flushed, mortified that she had guessed my thoughts.

"I would never want to shame you, Ellen," she said softly, looking like Rose again.

In one movement, I was beside her. I squeezed her hand tightly. "Good night, dearest Rose," I said, kissing her still pale cheek.

"Good night, Ellen."

I watched her disappear up the lane. She did not turn round again.

Loyal Rose.

Watching her go, I determined, from now on, always to be proud that she is my sister.

Sunday, August 16, 1663 (exhausted)

No one but Meg knows it was Rose. Harry, bless his lying tongue, said he was drunk and alone and lost his way, and so came to the theatre in search of his father. An unlikely story, but he is sticking to it. Mr. Killigrew keeps asking *who* was with him, but Harry will not give way. I keep my head up—sally, jibe, and flirt with the audience. Just like any other day. It *is* any other day, I tell myself.

Mr. Fuller was brought in to repair his beautiful scenery. It will take him all night. Mr. Killigrew is stony-faced but silent. He didn't make his usual fuss about the cost. How could he? Harry is keeping himself scarce. I have not yet seen Rose. Say nothing. *Smile.*

Later—Drury Lane

Rose was hemming my new gown with tiny, clean stitches when I came home. "Do they know?" she asked, expertly snipping off a thread.

"Not yet."

When I Am All Alone Up There

Tuesday, August 18— Theatre Royal

"Ellen!" Alice hurried up the aisle to me. "Mr. Hart and Mr. Killigrew want to see you."

"Why?" I asked, alarmed, nearly dropping my basket.

"No idea, but they said they wanted you and Meg sent me to fetch you up to Mr. Killigrew's *private* office. You'd best hurry."

"How do I look?" I asked, anxiously unpinning my skirts to cover my dusty boots. I wished I had worn my best skirt, but no matter now. At least I was wearing my new vanilla-water scent, a present from Mr. Adams, the apothecary—he mixed too much in the last batch and saved the extra for me.

"All right," Alice said, standing back to appraise me. "If I just loosen these," she said, pulling some curls free from under my cap.

"But . . ." It takes me forever to get them all under my cap.

"No, leave it a bit undone. It's alluring." She looked at me, squinting critically. "Now, bite your lips. Good." Her gaze travelled downward. "It's your bosom."

I rolled my eyes. It always seems to be my bosom.

"Too flat. But if I just tighten these," she said, nimbly retying my laces, pushing my small breasts firmly up into two soft curves. "Better."

I paused outside the heavy oak door. My hand was trembling, raised to knock. Head up, Ellen. Heart and courage. Smile.

"Mistress Gwyn, come in," invited Mr. Killigrew, his ample figure seated behind the surprisingly delicate desk. Kitt slept on his bed by the fire; he lifted his great bear head and thumped his tail when I entered. Mr. Hart was lounging close to the window, his round face flushed. Meg, standing beside him, smiled in encouragement. I moved to the centre of the chamber and stood before him, feeling every bit like a prize goat.

"She's a pretty little thing, I'll grant you, but there is not much to her, is there?" said Mr. Killigrew after a long silence, stroking his greying beard. Looking me over carefully, he pronounced his verdict: "Red hair, not ideal. But her eyelashes are dark, and that is something." I stood a bit taller in my shoes. I was particularly proud of my inky eyelashes and darker brows, happy to have escaped that carroty look so many redheads have. "Good, creamy skin, but not enough of it to notice," he went on. "Doesn't have a shape. May as well be a boy. Pull up your skirts; let's see your feet." I obliged, quickly pulling off my boot, raising my hem, and poking my stockinged foot towards him. Kitt immediately began to sniff my discarded boot and then nose about in my skirts, hopeful of the treats I usually keep for him in my pockets.

"Shh, not now, good boy." I eased him away.

"Mmm, small, well-shaped ankles. And you say she can dance?" Mr. Killigrew asked, dropping my foot.

"Yes, Lacy has been watching her and thinks she has a natural grace, although wholly untrained, of course," Mr. Hart offered easily. I sat between them, a spectator in this exchange. Should I put my boot back on? Kitt was contentedly gnawing on it. "But she seems to learn quickly enough," Mr. Hart continued. Yes, I was supposed to put my boot back on, I decided. I stooped and retrieved it from the big dog. He promptly slurped my outstretched hand. Mr. Hart was still speaking: "She picked up *Duchesse* in half the time it took Peg, danced it better, and then remembered it well enough to fill in for Lizzie, with a tempo change. Not many can do that."

"Yes, I saw that," Killigrew said evenly, his eyes fixed on me. "But that is not enough. She didn't have to speak, and Nick is a strong partner. Can you read, mistress? Or write? Or play? Or sing?"

"*Yes,*" I answered quietly.

"Yes, to which?"

"Yes, to all," I said, meeting his gaze levelly.

"Humph. We shall see," he said, turning to Meg. "Call the company up here. No, better yet," he said, eyeing me, "to the stage. Come along, Mistress Gwyn." We all—Mr. Hart, Meg, Kitt, and me—trooped out of the room behind him.

A lute was brought. A song Mother sang. An aching ballad. An empty stage. Sing.

"Look at her up there. You can hardly see her. She'll never hold this stage," observed Mr. Killigrew from the back of the pit, loudly enough to be heard by the little clutch of friendly faces in the first row. Loud enough to reach me, up here, all alone. "Go on then, girl!" he called, louder still.

I breathe in and begin. Clear-eyed. Low and lilting, soft and strong. A woman singing in the night. A woman singing for her lover. Her lover, lost at sea. A woman calling. A woman waiting. I sing, light and full. I sing, strong and sweet. I sing. Lulling them. Coaxing them. I sing. Charming them into captivity. I am more than myself. My voice is rich and clean, my fingers are sure on the strings; my hips sway gently, my head tilts with pleasure.

> *I hold them.*
> *I hold the room.*
> *The cavernous, golden room.*
> *I am enchanting.*

3.

Theatrical Ellen

When I Learn to Sing

Saturday, August 22 (hot, everyone buying oranges)

It is decided—*finally*. I will train with Mr. Lacy and Mr. Hart, the more in-
timidating of the two, in dancing, singing, speech, deportment, French (for
the new comedies), and gesture, each morning, and still work for Meg selling oranges in the afternoons and evenings until I debut. *If* I debut. Until I
am actually given a role, Mr. Killigrew will not put me under contract. Ever
sceptical, he waits for me to fail. But I won't! *I won't!* We begin tomorrow.

SOMERSET HOUSE, LONDON
TO OUR DAUGHTER, PRINCESSSE HENRIETTE-ANNE, DUCHESSE D'ORLÉANS
FROM HER MAJESTY QUEEN HENRIETTA MARIA
AUGUST 30, 1663

*I understand your distress, my dear, but you must not weep, nor mourn. Instead, you
must remember exactly what you did and vow never to do it again. These things happen
when a mistake has been made—accept the blame and find the mistake. Did you perhaps
eat spiced foods? Take too much exercise? Breathe unhealthy air? Dance or laugh with
too much enthusiasm? One must not grieve at these events but learn from them. And you
must pray for forgiveness.*

Maman

P.S.: To lose a living child is far worse, believe me. At least you have been spared that.

*And another—I read the script of this new Monsieur Molière you are patronising. Do
you think it wise to be associated with such smut? Theatre is meant to ennoble the spirit.*

MEMORANDUM
SEPTEMBER 1, 1663

To: *Mr. Thomas Killigrew, Being the Holder of Two Shares in the King's Company of the Theatre Royal, Royal Patent Holder, and Previous Groom of the King's Bedchamber*

From: *Mr. Charles Hart, Being the Holder of One and One Quarter Shares in the King's Company of the Theatre Royal and Actor of Standing and Renown*

Concerning Mistress Ellen Gwyn's Progress as an Actress
Weekly Report

Tom,

As we agreed, Lacy is her dancing master and I her action and singing master. I will report to you weekly on both our doings with our new pupil. Mistress Gwyn (Ellen) is a sweet-tempered, biddable girl and learns quickly but is a constant surprise to us. Her mimicry is cannily precise, but when asked to strike an attitude and sing in a proper voice and tone, with proper stage decorum, she falls flat. We have yet to re-create the glorious (if unrefined) rapture of her audition. Although Lacy reports that her dancing is quite exquisite, and her feet are lovely.

Hart

Postscript: I think reviving Jonson's Alchemist *is a superb thought, considering we have not put it on since June of '61. Although with their Royal Majesties and the whole of the court at Bath, perhaps we should wait for the season to start, as it is a court favourite. Would Walter still be up to the role, I wonder? If not, consider Nick, although he makes an excellent Face. Subtle is not a part I have any particular liking for, but I would be happy to appear briefly as Lovewit.*

Memorandum
September 7, 1663

To: *Mr. Thomas Killigrew*

From: *Mr. Charles Hart*

Concerning Mistress Ellen Gwyn's Progress as an Actress
  Weekly Report

Tom,

  Frustration abounds! I am quite sick with it. She has a quick mind and is a technically able if not a truly gifted songstress, but she is cursed with an inability to justly conform to the proper action and then sing! She stumbles and falls out of key when holding her attitude. Her arm, held before her, as is right, looks stiff and childish. Her head looks pitched and askew, much like a pumpkin on a pike. Her eyes are not demurely cast down, but stubbornly wander up to look at the house directly. She altogether looks like an ill-positioned, thoroughly miserable, but uncommonly pretty doll.

  She fares better in her action tutorials, and is even picking up French with a swift ear, but again when instructed to deliver a speech of any length, she falters and fails. Although I must note that she reads rapidly and learns her lines with all diligence and speed, and her soft Oxfordshire lilt is dulcet and alluring.

  Lacy is well pleased with her deportment and dancing, which I do concede is characterised by a rare grace and delicacy.

At a loss,
Hart

Postscript: *While I understand your wish to observe our pupil's progress, I do beg you for at least a month's leave before you act upon such a notion. If you must come betimes, please do so in secret. She is terrified of your presence, with reasonable cause.*

September 7, 1663—Theatre Royal, Covent Garden, Bridges Street
Hart,

> *If she is to be an actress, she must learn to expect an audience. I am travelling briefly to the country and will attend a rehearsal upon my return. Inform her or not, I leave it to your discretion.*
>
> Tom

Monday, September 22, 1663 (finally home)

My arms, my legs, my very bones ache. My head swirls: Jonson, Shakespeare, Beaumont, and Fletcher. One two three, one two three, *un, deux, trois, plié, arabesque,* and change. "China oranges! Juicy and sweet!" I fall into my bed and sleep. *Finis. Finis. Je suis finis.*

Wednesday, September 24—early early early!

Teddy and Nick joined my lesson this morning. Ever helpful, they corrected my arms, improved my lines, and turned out my feet. "*There*, there! That's it! Now *sing*!" I sang.

"Oh dearie, no!" moaned Teddy.

"Stop! Stop!" cried Nick.

"You see! You *see* the problem!" Hart scowled.

"But her dancing, her dancing is *magnifique*!" added Lacy unhelpfully.

"Yes, but she isn't dancing at present, is she, Lacy?" grumbled Hart.

"*What* happens to you?" asked Nick, genuinely baffled.

"You look so, so . . . so . . . *wrong*," said Teddy, circling behind to check my posture. He shrugged his shoulders. "It should be right. She hasn't moved."

"She certainly hasn't. She manages to look like a marionette up there—wooden," Hart offered, bluntly.

"The arms," said Teddy, critically standing back with his slim hands on his slim hips. "I think it is the arms—too tight."

"No, it's the legs, they have no fluidity, no give—more *pliés*, definitely. That's what she needs," Nick said conclusively, dropping into a graceful *plié*.

"Not sure she's breathing," Hart said gruffly. "Perhaps she should try that."

"Ellen, what *feels* wrong?" asked Lacy, kindly changing tack and at last addressing me.

"I just feel false, and stuck, like, like . . . a statue," I said miserably. I felt tears pressing and squeezed my eyes shut to keep them back.

"But that's right, my dear, a *graceful* statue. We'll get it. Don't you worry," said Lacy, handing me his handkerchief.

"Yes, we'll all help," Teddy said, folding me into his slender arms. I blew my nose loudly.

"Yes, you certainly will," said Hart in a determined sort of tone. "All of you here at break of day tomorrow."

"Ugh!" wailed Teddy, who hates to rise early.

Nick put his arms around Teddy and me. "We are all in it together now, chickees."

Monday, September 28 (eight a.m.)

Elizabeth, Kitty, Theo, Peg, Rob, Nick, Teddy, Lacy, Hart
All in it together.

Friday, October 2, 1663 — Theatre Royal

Help help help:

> *Peg:* Turn out your feet!
> *Kitty:* Tuck in your bottom!
> *Teddy:* Pull in your tum!
> *Rob:* Bend your knees!
> *Lacy:* Point your toes!
> *Hart:* Breathe, for God's sake!
> *Elizabeth:* Take your time. Enjoy it. This is *your* moment.
> *Nick:* I honestly have no idea anymore.
> *All: No! No! No!*

When I Rehearse and Rehearse

PALAIS ROYAL, PARIS
TO MY BROTHER, KING CHARLES II D'ANGLETERRE AT WINDSOR CASTLE
FROM PRINCESSE HENRIETTE-ANNE, DUCHESSE D'ORLÉANS
FRIDAY, 2 OCTOBRE 1663

My dear brother,

I simply adored the suit of men's clothing Catherine sent to me. It is piquant, charmant, and parfait! Not suitable for the French court, naturellement (we could never relinquish our complicated gowns and feminine mystery—and Phillipe would never allow it), but I am pleased to know that Catherine has found her style in England—and it is a delightful style at that. Your queen will surely bear many healthy princes, no matter what she wears.

I am sending this letter via Monsieur de Grammont, whom you were so kind to send to me. You were right: Philippe is opening my letters. Such scrutiny is a dreadful thing.

À bientôt, chéri,
Minette

P.S.: I enclose the recipe for the burdock tooth tonic that my physician has patented, as well as a bottle of the calming spirit of lavender and white lilac parfum *that I recently discovered on my last visit to Colombes. Mam's château there is truly falling into disrepair. If Louis will not fund the renovations, could you, perhaps?*

Monday, October 5 — Theatre Royal

Rehearsal:

Everyone comes. Teddy raids Will's coffee-house and carts over breakfast: coffee, chocolate, bottles of lemony stepony, bread, cheese, and cold mutton pie. Meg often looks in, bringing oranges, of course. We gossip and breakfast, seated on the edge of the dusty stage, legs dangling. Teddy is always careful to lay down a cloth before he sits down. He insists on dressing smartly even to rehearsal. All morning before the audience arrives we have the huge space to ourselves. It is a happy time.

"She definitely miscarried last week, and then three days later was up and returned to the king's bed in Oxford," Kitty declared with authority.

"Even for the energetically wicked Castlemaine, that *is* impressive," said Teddy, sceptically. He carefully tucked a linen serviette under his chin to catch any falling bits of flaky pastry.

"Teddy, it's true!" screeched Kitty. "I heard it from someone who would know . . . *directly*," she said, wiggling her eyebrows meaningfully. Lizzie, seated next to her, rolled her eyes.

"This irrefutable source wouldn't be the dashing Lord Sedley, would it?" asked Rob, giving Kitty a sidelong glance. Kitty flushed a furious red.

"Careful, sweeting. Even among the Wits, Sedley's a wild one," cautioned Meg, handing me my heavy basket of oranges for later.

"Johnny Rochester and George Buckingham are worse," said Lizzie, yawning.

"And Buckingham's beautiful cousin, heavens, *what* a harlot," said Teddy, handing Theo a hefty slice. "*Can* we return to that topic, please?"

"Mmm, she *is* beautiful, but then so is the queen, in her way," offered Nick, his mouth full of pie.

"Did you hear that the king sacked Sir Edward Montagu just for squeezing the queen's hand?" asked Peg, putting down her coffee and standing up to begin her stretches.

"He didn't actually go out of his way to *squeeze* it; he was handing her down from a coach. More of an accidental squeeze," said Teddy, lifting his bowl of rich chocolate.

"A wife is a lovely thing," said Theo absently.

"Good morning, ducklings!" chirped Lacy, joining the group and cheerfully helping himself to some chocolate. "Ooh, slip-coat cheese! Is this from Will's? Mmm, scrumptious." Then, seeing me sitting by Teddy, he kissed my brow affectionately. "Good morning, Ellen, dear."

"Right, shall we all get started?" boomed Hart, striding onto the stage. "Ellen?" He beckoned me over. "Perhaps you should try these," he said quietly, holding out a pair of delicate petal-pink silk slippers, tiny in his vast hands. "How can we ask you to stand properly if you are always wearing those wretched boots?"

Delighted, I surprised myself and stretched up onto my toes to kiss his powdered cheek. "Oh, Hart! Thank you!"

He beamed. "Now, none of that," he said, flushing.

I had never noticed before how pleasant his features are, generous and even and, while not finely drawn, certainly not coarse. He reminds me of an absolutely enormous, powerfully built cherub.

"To work, shall we? Everyone!" Hart's loud voice sounded, and his brows knit in displeasure as he thundered across the stage—*not* a cherub then. "Clear away this mess! John, is Peg here yet? We need to rehearse her scene this morning as well. Ah, there you are . . ."

"Yes, I have been thinking about that scene . . ." I heard Lacy say as he and Hart moved downstage.

I sat down and pulled off my worn leather boots. I slid into the whisper-pink slippers. My feet arched gracefully, as if they had been made only for dancing in gilded ballrooms. I pranced in my delight, twirling in the feather-light shoes. When I stopped, breathless, I was conscious of Hart's eyes on me, his scowl replaced by a look of curiosity. I openly smiled back at him.

Thank you.

Later—after my lesson

Everyone had taken themselves off to the tiring rooms to change and make up for the performance. I took off my beautiful slippers and set them next to my crumpled boots. Flexing my cramped limbs and wiggling my toes, I luxuriated in my undisciplined stance. Bare-footed, I stood on the empty stage and looked out at the great tiered room, undaunted. The candles glowed golden in their cressets, warming the waiting rows of green baize cushions. The October rain drizzled on the blue glazed cupola above. Stretching out my aching arms in ownership, I took to the stage.

Picking up the lute at my feet, I played.
Singing softly, gaining confidence, I moved to the music, supple-spined.
I twirled, lissome, laughing and dizzy.
I felt small and limber, and giddy with song.

Monday, October 5
Theatre Royal, Covent Garden, Bridges Street
Hart,

I am now convinced that the tutelage of Mistress Ellen Gwyn is moving in an inappropriate direction as per her abilities. We may have misjudged her talents. It is an error that begs a remedy. Please come and see me early on the morrow. Six o'clock? Best to come before your lesson and rehearsal.

All best wishes,
Tom

Tuesday October 6 — Theatre Royal

Rehearsal:

Loitering and laughing on the stage, we waited to start. Teddy, in a fine mettle so early in the morning, pulled me up to dance a jig, to limber up. Theo, in his armchair in the wing, tucked under his coach blanket (he has been feeling poorly this autumn), lowered his news sheet to watch us affectionately. His wife, Anne, who had stopped in to leave some mended costumes and re-curl his periwig (he is forever unravelling), dropped a kiss on his forehead. Nick had fallen asleep, his long legs hanging off the stage.

By and by, Hart arrived with Mr. Killigrew. "Everyone, please!" Hart called out. "I would like to work with Ellen and Teddy just at present.

Would the rest of the company please clear the stage?" Seeing Theo struggle to rise, he said, "No, no, Theo, if it pleases you, stay as you are."

Mr. Killigrew, who had taken a seat in the first row of the pit, was silently watching.

"Ellen," Hart called me over softly, "you and Teddy are to sing the duet from the new Dryden: the one you have been rehearsing. Mr. Killigrew would like to mark your progress." Then, under his breath, he said, "Have faith, my girl, this will all come right for you." With a quick pinch of my cheek, he left me to the stage and took a seat beside Killigrew.

"Ready, Ellen," whispered Teddy beside me, "like we've practiced, *grace*. You can do this. Relax. I am right here."

"When you are ready, please," called Hart officiously.

Teddy began, his clear tenor voice holding the slippery notes easily, exuding an effortless charm.

My cue. Breathe in. *Now.*

I began. My voice thin, my reedy arms held before me in a poor imitation of grace. Even to me, they looked childish and silly.

"Thank you," called Mr. Killigrew, after only a few bars, "that is enough." Climbing the stairs to the stage, he waved Teddy away without a glance. "*Ellen?* Is it?" he asked in a gentle voice. I nodded, too ashamed to speak. "Ellen, I want you to sing. Just *sing.*"

I stepped to the centre of the stage and began. Trying hard to hold my pose—arms, toes, tummy, bottom—grace. *Useless.* I faltered and stopped. My cheeks flamed anew.

"Ellen, where did you learn to sing?"

"At home, with my sister and my mother. My grandfather sings as well, as did my father, although I never knew him," I mumbled, not meeting his gaze.

"Is this how you sing at home? Standing, like this?"

"No. At home it is just us. Just me. At home we just . . . we just . . . play, and . . . sing," I said miserably, unable to meet his gaze.

"Like that first day on the stage?"

"Yes."

"Like yesterday afternoon?"

I took a quick breath in, mortified. "I . . . the stage was empty, sir. I didn't know anyone was here. I certainly didn't know *you* were here. I never would have . . . I just wanted to, to . . . Oh, sir, I am sorry," I finished, finally meeting his eyes. To my surprise, there was only a look of kind encouragement upon his face.

"Would you sing for me now?" he asked softly.

"Yes, sir," I said, smoothing my cap, straightening my back, setting my shoulders, lengthening my neck.

"No, Ellen," he corrected me, shaking the stiffness from my hands. "Close your eyes. Breathe. That's it. Steady. I want you to sing as is natural to you. Sing like you did yesterday."

My eyes squeezed tight shut, my heart curled into a ball, I sang as myself. Breathing evenly, I moved into the music. The familiar rhythm and joy thrummed through me. The lyrics tripped off my tongue with clean precision. I opened my eyes, and Mr. Killigrew was smiling down at me. Joining in, he took up Teddy's part in the duet, the corner of his song lifting with delight. Breathless and pleased, we came to the end.

"Yes," said Mr. Killigrew, looking at me gently. "This is you. As you will always be. You are meant only for ease and laughter."

"Yes," I said rashly. "I fear I am unsuited to elegance."

"Ha!" He chuckled. "You are a candid little thing. I like that. I predict that you will create your own elegance and that you will be followed by joy. I wish you well, Ellen."

As he moved away towards the wings, I gathered my courage and called out, "Mr. Killigrew! Am I still to become one of your company? Or would you prefer someone more . . . more dignified?"

"Ha!" He laughed again. "Plucky as well! Good! Yes, you will remain in my company, and I will inform Hart of the change in your regime."

"My regime?" I looked at him quizzically.

"Yes, Ellen," he said, his eyes alive with mirth. "I fear you may change everyone's regime." With that, he beckoned to Hart and retired upstairs to his private office.

Theo, forgotten in his wing chair, chuckled softly. "Well, my girl, you have done it. Everything will change now."

MEMORANDUM
OCTOBER 13, 1663

To: *Mr. Thomas Killigrew*

From: *Mr. Charles Hart*

Concerning *Mistress Ellen Gwyn's Progress as an Actress*
 Weekly Report

Dear Tom,
 I am mightily pleased with this week's progress; it showing both our actors and actresses to best advantage. Ellen's easiness onstage is blossoming into an engaging style of action, and her voice, enriched with confidence, is finding a rare timbre and pitch. If she is cast in younger, ingénue roles, this new and exciting style will work very well for us as a company. I also believe that it will give us an advantage over Davenant's much vaunted novelty. I think very well on the choices we have made together.

All good wishes,
Hart

Postscript: *Lacy would like me to add, and I quite agree, that her dancing remains exemplary. She danced in her breeches yesterday and has quite the prettiest legs and feet I have yet seen upon a stage.*

LONDON GAZETTE

Sunday, October 18, 1663

Most Deservedly Called London's Best and Brilliant Broadsheet

The Social Notebook
Volume 96
Ambrose Pink's lamentable observations du jour

Darlings,

Sad news from Whitehall. Our gentle new queen is gravely ill. Her fever has not broken in five days, and if it does not abate, her physicians say there is little hope. She faces her travail with piety and grace, and according to Lord Henry Jermyn, Earl of St. Albans, His Grace the King is much moved by her suffering and is at her bedside daily despite the danger to his own health. In her fevered wanderings, according to another reliable court insider, she is said to have told the king tales of their imagined three living children and confided that she would willingly leave all the world behind but for him. This news has much afflicted His Majesty. I heartily urge you all to pray for our queen.

À bientôt, dearests,
A greatly saddened,
Ambrose Pink, Esq.

October 22, 1663 — Drury Lane (raining)

At home this evening with Grandfather. He loves to hear the theatre stories from the day. Today, during *Alchemist,* Teddy dropped an entire scene, stranding Peg onstage. Nick, playing Face, had to cover for him. Hart was furious!

SOMERSET HOUSE, LONDON

TO OUR DAUGHTER, PRINCESSE HENRIETTE ANNE, DUCHESSE D'ORLÉANS, AT
   ST. CLOUD

FROM HER MAJESTY QUEEN HENRIETTA MARIA

22 OCTOBRE 1663

Chérie,

It is so very sad and still here. In the first days of the queen's illness there was much bustling about, physicians and apothecaries and even botanists—Charles insisted. Now, there are only priests and prayers. She is beyond any of us now. Have you seen Charles's apothecary, Le Fevre? I know Charles despatched him to consult Louis's physicians with all speed.

The few times she has awoken she has asked only for Charles. Her devotion to him is sincere and touching. She will die a good Catholic; we may rejoice in that. Far worse things can happen.

I kiss you, my sweet,
Queen Henrietta Maria

Note—*Just because your husband and his brother the king are engaged in all this building is no reason for you to risk your health. Your lungs have never been strong, and the dust must be considerable. Do not spend time in places you shouldn't; you will only have yourself to blame.*

October 23—Drury Lane (theatres closed in honour of the queen)

Rose says the king has taken it very much to heart and is beside himself with worry. Rose also says His Majesty has not yet missed supper once with Lady Castlemaine during the queen's illness. Wretched man. I pray nightly for Her Majesty.

Note—The queen is so ill as to be shaved and have pigeons tied to her feet. I have been reading Culpeper's *English Physician:* that is what they try when there is no hope. The pigeons are to keep her soul from flying away.

SOMERSET HOUSE, LONDON
TO OUR SON, KING CHARLES II OF ENGLAND
FROM HER MAJESTY QUEEN HENRIETTA MARIA
OCTOBER 24, 1663

Charles,

I am not unaware of how and where you spend your time. Your queen is the Portuguese Infanta, and this sort of liberal peasant behaviour reflects badly upon us in the eyes of Europe. Show more character and discipline yourself, Charles.

Maman

Note—*There will be plenty of time to resume what must be a very compelling liaison with Lady Castlemaine next week.*

Tuesday—Drury Lane (raining)

The account of the queen's treatment in the *Gazette* this morning: blood-letting, anemone, leeches, crushed fox lung, lungwort, spider web, swallow nest, pennyroyal, cottonweed, bedstraw, foxglove, the ground skull of a hanged man? These remedies *cure* illness?

Note—Spent two days' wages on a thick woolly blanket for Grandfather and new mittens for Mother. It is already winter.

October 27, 1663—Official Notations for Privy Council Meeting on This Day to Be Entered into the Log-book

Notations taken by Secretary of State Henry Bennet, Earl of Arlington

This day's business was cancelled as His Royal Majesty is much distressed by the queen's health. We pray for Her Royal Majesty, Queen Catherine. May God have mercy upon her soul.

Nothing further to report.
Secretary of State Henry Bennet, Earl of Arlington

November 1 — Drury Lane

The queen will recover! Apparently her physician, Sir Francis Prujean, saved her with his miracle cordial. "Bet it is just wintergreen, feverfew, and betony, mixed with something sweet—and now he will make a fortune," Teddy said, reading the account in the *Gazette*.

Teddy was right. Already Dr. Prujean's magical cordial is sold everywhere at half a crown. It smells like wintergreen.

November 15 — Theatre Royal (a grey day)

Today, being the queen's birthday, Peg says the guns from the Tower will all go off. She also says wigs will become the fashion, what with the king and his greying curls and the queen and her shorn hair. I hope not, as I look terrible in wigs.

December 21, 1663
Coal Yard Alley, Drury Lane
Dearest sister,

I am so sorry to hear that you will not be joining us for our Christmas festivities. I understand your concern over Ellen's association with the theatre but must beg to disagree with you. Margaret, dear, you must know that she could not reduce our station further. We must rejoice in the life that she has found. Rose no longer resides with us here, and we rarely see Nora, so Ellen is my daily comfort. I wish you health and joy this Christmastide.

Your loving brother,
Edward

Somerset House, London
To our daughter, Princesse Henriette-Anne, Duchesse d'Orléans, the
   Madame of France
From Her Majesty Queen Henrietta Maria
December 23, 1663

Joyeux Noelle, ma fille!

The queen's recovery is miraculous, yet I cannot but worry that we may now have a queen who is too delicate to fulfil her duty. She just looks so very small and pale and, at the moment, bald. It is simply not becoming in a lady. I do hope that she confounds my fears and bears healthy children, for if she does not, sweet as she is, what use is she? We certainly know the problem does not lie with Charles—at least he has shown himself capable of this much.

I was greatly relieved when I was able to give your father the heirs he required—and so many heirs at that! Best to have several, I feel. A queen without children is like a beautiful dish that tastes terrible—pretty but pointless.

All love,
Maman
Queen Henrietta Maria

When Rose Is in Trouble

December 26, 1663 — Theatre Royal (rain and hail!)

Rose is in gaol! I heard it from Meg tonight. I was delivering trinkets from Lord Sedley (an orange for Kitty, a lemon for Becka, and a posy for Lizzie—naughty man) when Meg found me backstage. Breathless, she suggested I sit on a nearby bench, and then she delivered the news directly: Rose is accused of stealing from her customer at Madame Ross's and has been taken away by the bailiffs. Bailiffs! Impossible—Rose wouldn't—there is a great deal she would do, but not this. We do not know where she is held. I must go to Lewkenor Lane right away. It is sleeting, and Moll has insisted I take a hackney—on Mr. Killigrew's account, she reassured me. Bobby, the theatre's errand boy, has run to Covent Garden to fetch one. If only he would hurry!

How can Rose work for such a filthy-tempered person? Madame Ross was awful. A young, *very* young girl in a low-cut white taffeta gown opened the door and showed me to a small parlour. Her curls were stiff with pomade, and her bodice was clearly stuffed. From another room I could hear men's voices and the high-tinkling crystal sounds of women and wine-glasses. Despite the situation, I was fascinated. The rooms were dimly lit, and the walls were hung with evocative paintings—this I had expected. The furniture was covered in crimson damask—this, too, was no surprise. But everywhere women wandered about in *underclothes*, French underclothes! The most elaborate underclothes I have ever seen—trimmed with pale ribbons and lace and made from expensive French silk. Some wore a tight bodice and full petticoat but no gown or chemise, and others wore French *drawers!* I've heard of women wearing drawers but had never seen it. These fanciful creatures looked at my street clothes with something akin to contempt.

Just then, the girthsome Madam Ross, fully dressed in heavy black brocade, barrelled into the room. "Out, out!" She shooed the girls like pigeons. "You're Rose's sister? The orange girl?"

I nodded.

"Nothing to talk about. Either she pays back the money or goes with the bailiffs. Get out."

I must have looked startled for she leaned close to me and laughed a horrid, grinding laugh. "Now you come and see me, do you? You were too good to speak to me before, and you think I will help you now? Get *out*."

I was confused. "Before?"

"Ha! Ask your sister." She snorted.

"But—"

"Open you ears, girl! *Get out!*" she shrieked.

"But my sister—"

"Yes, your sister. He says one thing, and she says another. He's a bit of a rascal, and she is Nora's daughter—lay even odds, but he's the customer, so . . . ? I need my money." She shrugged, as if this sentence was conclusive.

"But Rose . . . ?"

But she had already barrelled out again.

The girl with the stuffed bodice returned to show me out. Walking swiftly down the long hallway, she hissed out of the side of her painted mouth, "She didn't do it. He drank too much and couldn't pay his bill and tried to pin it on her. Eight guineas."

"Eight?" Rose could never raise such a sum. "Where . . ."

"No idea where they took her. They wouldn't say."

"Thank you," I said as the door shut firmly behind me.

I am pacing in the wings: ten steps from the curtain to the door. Ten steps there and ten steps back. I am waiting for the performance to end so I can speak to Hart. He will know what is to be done. His loamy voice drifts from the stage and winds around and around me like a net: catching and calming.

Later—eight o'clock

As soon as he took his final curtain call, I came forward, my words tumbling out in a heap.

"Ellen, *Ellen*, slow down, let me understand, your sister Rose is *where?*"

"Oh, Hart, I don't *know* where! I have asked at Lewkenor Lane, and no one knows. She has been accused of stealing money—a lot of money—by a man at Madame Ross's, where she . . . works." Defiant, I kept my eyes upon him.

"I see, and her. . . . *client* has accused her of theft? And the bailiffs have removed her. Is that right?" asked Hart unflinchingly.

"Yes," I breathed, eased by his forthrightness. "But it isn't true. She wouldn't do that," I quickly added.

"No, of course she wouldn't. All right, Tom is out of London until Twelfth Night. *I* can approach the king, or even Lacy could—" Hart considered aloud.

"No, Harry Killigrew! It should be Harry!" I interrupted impulsively. "Harry goes to Madame Ross's, and they are . . . friends," I finished awkwardly.

"Harry," Hart said, turning over the thought. "Yes, *Harry*, he is now a Groom of the Bedchamber, is he not? *Close to the king.* And he is fond of your sister, you say, and the boy has a good heart." Grabbing quill and ink, he bent over the props table and scratched out a brief note. He shoved it into my hand. "Go, Ellen. Here is the address," he said. Fishing into his pockets, he pulled out some coins. "And here is fare for a hackney. Fetch Harry here. I will write the letter for him to take to the king. *Go!*" Snatching the coins, I hurried out the stage door.

Even later—ten o'clock (back at the theatre)

"No! No! Hart, we *must* accede that she is a prostitute. The king *likes* prostitutes. It is no dishonour," Harry argued.

"But it will imply guilt. A prostitute is more likely to steal than an ordinary girl," Hart countered.

"Please, it is getting late. Rose is in gaol. We must get this to the king *tonight*," I urged them.

"Ellen, if we are honest in this letter, your sister will be branded a whore to the king. Can you live with that?" Hart asked bluntly.

"Oh." I shrugged. "My sister *is* a whore. What does it matter how it looks? May as well tell the truth."

"All right, Harry, sign it. Let us all to Whitehall," Hart conceded.

"Together?" I asked disbelievingly.

"Of course together, you mouse," Hart chided affectionately. "You don't think I'd leave you now, do you?"

Later, two a.m. (Whitehall Palace— The Matted Gallery)

My head is heavy on Hart's shoulder. Harry has been gone for hours. How long have we been sitting on this bench? If I just close my eyes for a few minutes—

Four o'clock in the morning— The Matted Gallery

"Hart, what have we here, sleeping *Ariadne*?" an amused voice asked.

"Your Majesty," Hart stuttered, leaping to his feet and executing a perfect bow. Sleepy and bewildered, I remained on my bench, squinting up at the exceedingly tall figure in front of me. He was slimly built but had a coiled restiveness about him, like a spring waiting to stretch. A mixed crowd of grim-faced councillors, foppishly dressed young men, and women in carnival-coloured gowns stood about him, and a great puddle of spaniels nosed about his feet. He was the fixed centre of the mêlée—the substance anchoring the chaos. Nothing about him was quite right: his face was too long, his eyes too deeply set, his lids too heavy, his moustache too lank and his mouth too wide, yet he fit together perfectly. And he was the king: a king waiting to speak to me.

"Majesty? Majesty! Are you . . . are you him?" I asked sleepily, shaking myself awake.

The king threw back his head and laughed. "Yes, I am he, and it is customary to curtsey when you meet me," he teased.

"I, oh . . . oh, pardon me," I said, flummoxed, leaping up to copy Hart's bow exactly.

The king whooped with laughter. "Is that how ladies curtsey these days?"

Indignant and impatient, I forgot myself. "My sister is in prison this night. I do not worry about a proper curtsey!" I heard Hart's sharp intake of breath beside me. The ladies stopped nattering, and the fops stood aghast. "I, oh, Your Majesty, forgive me!"

The king's eyes crinkled merrily as he composed his mobile face into a serious countenance. "No, no, you are quite right. There are prostitutes in prison this night. This is no time to stand upon ceremony. Mistress . . . Gwyn, is it?"

"Ellen," I said miserably. "Please, please, don't hold my rudeness against my sister." This was a disaster. One of the spaniels promptly sat upon my foot, rooting me to the spot.

"Ellen, do you suppose I am the sort of king who would?" he asked, gently lifting my chin with his long, cool fingers until I looked up into his intelligent face.

"No . . . no, I do not think you would. Please, help her," I said softly.

"I have already sent Harry and John Browne to secure her release from Newgate, but now that I have met *you*, I will also send the royal berline to fetch her home. All charges against her will be dropped." He waved his hand, sending servants flying to follow his commands.

"Thank you, Your Majesty," I whispered, and sank into a deep and correct curtsey.

He chuckled, and bent low to whisper into my ear, "I preferred your first attempt. God give you good night, little Ellen."

"And to you as well, Your Majesty."

I watched him as he moved down the stone-vaulted gallery. The air felt so quiet once he had gone.

When I Enjoy Modest Success

Sunday, January 3, 1664

Morning service at St. Martin in the Fields with Grandfather and then home. Music sounds so beautiful ringing through that lovely old building. Rose is too anxious after her recent *trouble* to risk church. She is justified— everyone knows what happened. Madame Ross kept her on, but appearances mean everything to Rose. A thieving whore is worse than an ordinary whore. Mother spoke truly when she pointed out that she could hardly be more thoroughly pardoned than by the king himself, yet the whole event greatly pains Rose. This morning I saw Jane Smedley, who commented on Rose's recent *royal favour,* as she phrased it with a smirk. I do wish Mother wouldn't tell people. Rose won't speak of it to anyone—including me.

I have told no one of my conversation with the king. The conversation I hear over and over as I fall asleep.

Later—in our room

"Rose," I began awkwardly as she dried her hair with a bath sheet. "Madam Ross said something strange that night."

"Mmm?" Rose shook out her heavy hair and, sitting on her bed, began to pull her white comb through the tendrils in long strokes.

"She said I had refused to speak to her *before*? Rose? *Rose?*"

Rose didn't seem to hear me.

Wednesday, January 6, 1664 — Twelfth Day (The Usurper)

Lacy brought me a tightly wound winter posy, and Hart brought me a new green silk hair ribbon.

"Ah! Our protégée! Just to stretch your theatre wings, mind you," Lacy cautioned cheerily, holding the ribbon up to my skin. "Perfect for your complexion, my dear."

"No reason to be nervous; save that for your *real* debut!" Hart said, gently tugging on my long curls.

"One for luck!" said Nick, firmly smacking my bottom.

"You'll wrinkle me before I ever get out there," I grumbled, smoothing my new skirts.

All this fuss just for me to stand at the back in the ballroom scene and deliver one line—it seemed excessive, but left me fizzing with excitement.

The flickering candles blur the faces of the audience. A wink from Teddy, who squeezes my hand behind my back. I swish my hips and say clearly, "My lady, there is a gentleman to see you without!"

And it is over.

"Brava!" said Teddy.

"Well done!" said Nick.

"Magnifique!" said Lacy.

"My clever mouse," said Hart, dropping a quick kiss on my nose.

MEMORANDUM
JANUARY 7, 1664

To: Mr. Thomas Killigrew

From: Mr. Charles Hart

Concerning Mistress Ellen Gwyn's Progress as an Actress

Dear Tom,

She stands out. No question. Small and bold and neat as you like. With her fiery hair and pert little figure, she will make a brilliant foil to the current rash of dark, sloe-eyed favourites. She is fearless and quick, and she will thrive in this realm. We mustn't waste her on nonsense roles. She must star, but it must be the right part. Best to keep her under my tutelage whilst we consider. Lacy agrees with me in this.

All best wishes,
Hart

January 8, 1664
Theatre Royal, Drury Lane
Hart,

Yes, I saw the performance as well. I left soon after Ellen's scene. I agree that she deserves a proper debut. I will advise you as to my thoughts on her career at a later date. At present I am content for her to remain under your guidance, but really, Hart, she is quite young and, I find, quite singular. I do expect you to behave with some discretion and great care.

Yours, etc. . . .
Tom

Sunday January 10, 1664 — Lord's Day

Last night Hart took me to see *Henry VIII* at the Opera. (The play that *everyone* has been talking about.) All the talk is true, Betterton *was* ferociously regal as the king, and the procession with all the faces pressed against the windows and on the balconies *was* magnificent. During the interval a startlingly attractive man introduced to me as Johnny joined us in our box (I found out later from Teddy that this is the *infamous* Lord Johnny Wilmot, second Earl of Rochester). What I noticed most was his absolute equanimity of countenance. Whether dealing out his obviously scathing wit or delivering the most splendid compliment, his features remain uninvolved, as if he really cannot be bothered to muster expression.

"Watch out, he has made lechery his profession," Teddy said seriously. "Well, lechery and drink, I suppose." I could tell from his tone that he both liked and admired him.

I found Johnny serious and cynical by turns. His biting humour unsettles Hart but amuses me. He reminds me of a bored, restless dog who may bite, just for the fun of it.

Afterwards, we piled into carriages and went on to supper at Chatelin's in Covent Garden with the actors of that house. Hart was much engaged with the serious Sir Will Davenant (who wears an inky black kerchief to cover the hole where his nose should be—gruesome). I try my best not to stare but find it difficult. Everyone was talking about the rising price of lace, tea (the curious new courtly drink), Davenant's new *Tempest* (written in collaboration with Dryden), and war with Holland.

"The *Dutch*? Aren't they our ally?" I quickly whispered to Hart, and was silenced by a small downturn of his mouth. Wasn't Princess Mary of Orange the king's sister? Now that she is dead they are our enemy? How disloyal, I thought silently. I was too afraid of looking ill informed to question further, and the conversation just moved on around me.

"Their pride is insufferable!" Hart proclaimed with feeling, banging his wine-glass down on the table.

Seeing my evident confusion, Johnny Rochester leaned in to explain. "They are perceived to be a threat to us," he whispered under his breath, rolling his eyes to let me know that he considered them nothing of the sort.

"A threat to us how? By prospering away in Holland, planting tulips and . . ."

"Making cheese? Yes. Really by being smart and rich and unencumbered by self-doubt," Johnny said quietly, taking a long swallow of a smelly something I could not identify. "They do not need a war to assert their place in Europe."

"Do we?"

"If the king would throw out his mousy, pandering, pompous, self-serving Council, then no, we wouldn't. But he is too afraid of going the way of his father to refuse them this absurd war. Oh, excuse me, Mrs. Gwyn, but I really must . . ." He pushed his chair back from the table and deftly slipped off into the crowd.

"Jane," said Henry Harris, the tall, lightly built actor from the Duke's (permanently condemned to second leads but quite good, I understand), as Johnny left. "He has just seen Jane, who has been . . . away."

"Jane? Jane Russell, the tavern maid?"

"Ha! Tavern maid—very genteel. Yes, Jane Russell, although bar-keeping is not her primary profession, but I would never expect someone so deliciously protected as you to know that."

I looked at him in dumb wonder, my mouth hanging open like a broken door. *Protected?* Is that how I appear now that I enter the room on Hart's arm? I was not about to apprise him of my intimate understanding of that profession and so laughed at his obvious and not particularly clever remark.

I was sleepy and a bit tipsy (Johnny Rochester had given me rum) and thoroughly ready to take off my pretty but pinching shoes. Hart walked me home and, at the end of our lane, kissed me sweetly. I allowed him to do so, and it was not, in truth, *unpleasant*.

Tuesday

Hart told me tonight that Jane Russell has been taking the mercury cure for the French pox—a whore's curse. Mercury baths are said to be hideously painful and are often not successful. I worry for Rose! I shared my fears with Hart tonight, and he listened carefully and questioned me thoughtfully. It made me like him very much.

Getting somewhat used to kissing and have taken to stuffing a handkerchief up my sleeve to discreetly wipe my mouth when he is through. I have found that there is no point in wearing the berry lip paint that Peg gave me, as it just winds up all over both of us—messy. I cannot in truth say that I *like* the kissing, but I do enjoy the affection and protectiveness that come over him afterwards. What do *I* feel? Not great *passion,* certainly, but not dispassion, either—curious.

Early, six a.m.

I heard Rose come in just as it was getting light. Instead of readying for bed, she came and sat in the window-seat.

"Rose?"

"She asked me. Madame Ross. She kept asking me . . ." Her voice trailed off. This is how she has been lately, faraway and incomplete.

"Asking you *what?*" I prompted.

"About you. She wanted you. Sisters are very popular, you see."

Oh. Oh, I did see. "And you said?"

"No. I just said no."

Later

Hart has offered to give the commissions for the new costumes to Rose! She must sew two sets of green livery and one blue satin gown for Ophelia. Her designs are breathtaking, and her stitching is exquisite; he will not be disappointed.

When I Spend Time with Mr. Hart

Wednesday, January 13 (unseasonably warm)

Hart directed his coachman, Hugh, to take us to the river. We walked through the infamous riverside pleasure gardens at Foxhall, where illicit lovers are known to make use of the many private nooks and concealing hedges. Everywhere we looked were couples walking hand-clasped, or embracing under the wintry trees. I looked away, my cheeks flaming with embarrassment. Hart seemed unperturbed and loudly called out to acquaintances. He did *not*, however, get so close as to require an introduction, I noticed. He slipped my mittened hand in the crook of his arm as we ambled through the criss-crossed covered pathways, where you can find glass-houses; festive hawker's stalls selling roasted nuts, cider, pastries, meats, and fruit; and pretty views of the river at each turning. I was surprised at how comfortable I felt in his company. We laughed easily (his: a great rolling baritone; mine: I fear, a sort of wild goat noise) and gossiped about the company: Becka's efforts to ensnare an unenthusiastic young viscount; Michael's troublesome gout, worse this winter; Lizzie Knep's complicated ménage with her invalid, gambling husband, her ever visiting cousins, and her philandering lover; Sam Pepys, who is *always* in the tiring rooms. "He wears his *spectacles* so he can get a better look!" I laughed. We spoke of everything except us—and the company is currently rife with gossip about *us*.

Under a leafless mulberry tree, we sat on a turfed bench sharing a mug of steaming chocolate with snow cream. Abruptly jumping up and entering a glass-house, Hart returned with a white winter rose for me. I tucked it into the boned bodice of my new cloud-grey gown.

Without discussion, Hugh drove us to Hart's enormous house in Maiden Lane. Once there, Hart looked at me apprehensively. "Only if it would please you, Ellen."

"Would it please *you* very much, Hart?" I asked, teasingly.

"Very much," he said gravely.

At that I burst into fits of giggles. "Oh Hart, you are so very good, aren't you?"

"Only to you, my mouse," he said, laughing, and with a light heart he bore me up to his bedroom.

Later—at home

Not terrible, but much more *vigorous* than I had imagined. He was tender and attentive. He declared himself "my truest heart." He asked me to call him Charles, but I find it impossible and have settled on just "Hart." With his proud broad chest he does resemble a hart, although much less rustic.

Sweetly, he cleaned me up afterwards with warm soapy water and carefully tucked me into the carriage with plenty of cushions and coverlets, instructing Hugh to go *slowly*, anxiously clutching my hand.

The berline was far too broad for our little alley. I alighted at the end of the lane and gingerly walked home. Gently lifting our sticky latch, I let myself in. Grandfather had waited up for me. The fire had nearly died out. Jeffrey lifted his head and licked my hand before resuming his snooze.

Without preamble, Grandfather asked, "Do you care for him?" I felt he had long been rehearsing this question. He continued, "Despite your great-aunt's misgivings, I *can* believe that there is much good in this life you have found . . . as long as you are not . . . *distressed* by this man's attentions."

I busied myself hanging my cloak and scarf upon the peg. At last, turning back to face him, I replied, "Mr. Hart is a good man, Grandfather. He cares for me sincerely and I will be . . . *safe* in his care." I sounded more confident than I felt, and I did not quite answer his question. In truth, I was not sure of the answer myself, but I wanted to reassure him of my present contentment. I think I knew where his deepest concerns lay. "Are you . . . concerned that I will follow in Rose's . . . *profession*?" I hedged.

Outside, I heard the night watchman calling the hour and declaring the king's peace. Eleven o'clock.

Grandfather sighed, "Ellen, let us call a spade a spade. Your sister, whom I love sincerely, is a common whore, and I could not wish such a life for you. You have not the temperament, and I have not the heart."

I shifted uncomfortably, "I have no plans to become—"

"I'm sure Rose did not intend to become . . . no, no." He shook his head, interrupting his own train of thought. "I know that you could not give your body without your affection. You are too much your father's daughter for that."

At that, I looked up, surprised, for Grandfather so rarely mentions his lost son. "Am I really like him? I know so little of my father," I said cautiously, the name sounding unfamiliar on my tongue, not wanting to press, knowing his loss still pained Grandfather.

"Oh, my girl. You have his neat bright looks, his quick wit, and his passionate nature. People are drawn to you, the way that they were drawn to him. All his life he was very much loved, and now he is still very much missed. Your mother can hardly breathe for want of him, and I . . . I think of him every day." Then, recovering himself, he said gruffly, "Now, no more questions, that is all much in the past. My concern is that you are cared for, and happy—and you are. That was all I needed to know."

Now in my own bed, I hug my secret close. Not like Rose, I tell myself. Not like Rose. I will be treasured. I will be cherished. I will be faithful to just *one* man, and I will love and appreciate him as best as I can. I do *like* him very much. That is something. That is a great deal. That is surely different from a common whore, isn't it?

January 25, 1664 — Theatre Royal (The Indian Queene, first performance)

Not such a secret, it seems. This morning, after rehearsal, Becka cornered me in the tiring rooms. "That gown is lovely," she said in honeyed tones. (*Another* new gown from Hart, this one cut low after the French fashion, in pear-green taffeta, edged in cream Venice *pointe,* and beneath it is a *beautiful* fluffy petticoat.) "Is it new?" she asked, with false innocence.

"No," I lied. "It was my sister's before me."

"Oh, Ellen," she chided. "We all *know* it is new, and we all *know* who gave it to you."

How do they all know, and why do they all care? Gossip is much less fun when I am the topic. No idea how to stop these rumours. So exasperating.

Later—in the tiring rooms

"I swear I didn't tell." Teddy held up his right hand in a mock oath. "Anyway, why are you so bloody concerned? It is just bloody Becka, after all." Teddy dislikes the Marshall sisters.

"Yes, but if it is Becka, then it is Nan, too. I just don't like people *knowing. Knowing* that I go to his house. That we—"

"What you mean is that you don't like people talking. Talking about you going to his rooms, and what you do once you get there," said Teddy, going straight to the heart as usual. "In any case, I don't see how it could stay a secret for long, not with the way he moons around after you."

"Shh!" There were others in the tiring room.

"I think it's sweet, and your gown *is* pretty," chimed Peg from her dressing table.

"Oh! Is there anyone who doesn't know?" I wailed, quickly unhitching my skirts, concealing my beautiful petticoat.

"Know what?" asked Theo, entering the tiring room. "Teddy, have you seen my boot buckles? Anne shined them, and I thought I put them on the vanity, but somehow already I seem to have—"

"Here," Teddy rooted around and produced the missing buckles. "They were under Rob's wig." Theo is always losing *everything.* "Know about Ellen and *you know who,*" he finished in a noisy stage whisper.

"Teddy!" I protested.

"I didn't actually say it!" Teddy countered amiably.

"Oh, yes, Anne told me," Theo said absently. "You two seem to get on so well. I think it is lovely, my dear."

"Anne!" I screeched, "How did *Anne* know?"

"Oh, sweetheart"—Peg shot me a pitying glance—"*everyone* knows. It is not such a bad thing, after all," said Peg, checking her pale blond wig in the mirror (she is on this afternoon). "He seems gone on you, and he is a major shareholder and really is the *star* of the theatre. It *could* be Teddy here, who is just a lowly—" She ducked as Teddy sent a powder puff flying in her direction.

"Oh really, Teddy!" exclaimed Theo, who suffered a direct hit. I giggled in spite of myself.

Note—Hart has insisted I give up working for Meg. "Why should you tire yourself out peddling fruit when I can easily provide for you?" he asked genially, erasing the structure of my life. He is giving me a generous weekly allowance that will support Mother and Grandfather and Rose as well as afford me any luxury I could wish.

"But surely I will be earning a salary as an actress soon?" I hinted leadenly. He did not respond.

WHITEHALL, LONDON
To our sister, Princesse Henriette-Anne, Duchesse d'Orléans
From His Majesty King Charles II
January 25, 1664

There you see! A boy! A healthy boy! You did it, my darling. As a princess, as a duchess, as the Madame—it is your greatest duty, and you have fulfilled it. Philippe Charles, an auspicious name; I am deeply touched. Of course I will stand as godfather. I am forever your,

Charles

Note—*My poor queen wept upon hearing the news. She is most pleased for you but too overcome to write at present. Dr. Fronard prescribed a restive tonic of juniper and feverfew to help her sleep. Our own lack of such happy news is breaking her heart.*

Another—*Thank you for the snuff, it was very well received here. Could you also send some gold sealing wax—the kind that you use on your letters? There is none to be got in this town.*

January 25 — Drury Lane (late)

My family is impossible! Mother has already spent *all* of my week's allowance on drink (I had to confess my penury to Hart—very embarrassing), and Rose still insists on staying on with Madame Ross. I had hoped she would turn her hand to full-time sewing, but she has refused. "The work's not steady enough, Ellen." She shrugged. "Besides, Lewkenor Lane is what I know." Hopeless.

When We Endure a Great Loss

Tuesday January 26 — Will's Coffee-house (rain and fog)

The morning began like any other:

"We must have another one *soon,* Dryden!" said Hart, waving his toast for emphasis.

"Not too soon," cautioned Tom, stroking Kitt's folded ears.

"Well, that is good to hear, as I have not yet started on another play. I only finished *Queene* last week!" said John Dryden, dramatically putting his hand to his brow. He is a slight, round-faced, mannered man, given to theatrical gestures.

"Ugh, *quel désastre!*" said Teddy dramatically. "*Three weeks* of script changes!" I looked at Dryden, who did not seem the least apologetic for the turmoil he has caused in the last month. He was wearing the most astonishing canary-yellow hat, complete with ostrich plumes *and* small feathers *and* velvet ribbons *and* gold buttons *plus* an enormous blond periwig with ringlets almost reaching his waist. He looked like a frosted lemon wedding cake. He is not a tall man, and I feared he might crumple under the weight of this complicated confection. He was holding his coffee cup in the most curiously affected way, with his smallest finger arched awkwardly in the air. Did he think it elegant? His new play, written with his esteemed brother-in-law, Mr. Robert Howard (whom he never seems to mention), is a raging hit, and I know that Hart wants him to write him a significant heroic role in the next one, but is tactfully waiting for Dryden to suggest it first.

"Is it true they are queuing up already?" Teddy reached for a second slice of pie. "Mmm, this is delicious. Theo, you must have some."

"No, no, I am all right," said Theo quietly, sitting beside me, closest to the fire.

"Darling, you have hardly been eating and are withering away. Isn't Anne feeding you?" Teddy clucked automatically. As Teddy lives with the Bird family, he well knows that Anne keeps a hearty table, easily feeding him as well as Theo, young Theo, Eliza, Michael, and their new baby. Teddy married two years ago, but his young wife, whom we never see, seems to be forever visiting her parents in the country.

"Yes," said Tom, with contained pride. "They have been outside the theatre since nine, and the chief constable called just before I left to discuss the troublesome traffic congestion we are causing."

Dryden took another dainty sip, crooked finger still hanging in the air. Yes, I decided, he must think it is elegant. His heavy curls bobbed as he spoke. "Ah . . . I have been thinking about this problem—"

I sat back in my great chair, warmed by the fire, and let my thoughts drift away. This conversation did not require my attention, as it seemed as if my stage ambitions were to end in Hart's bed. Since I became his mistress, all talk of my famed debut has vanished. Ah well, so long as I am warm and dry, what matter if it happens sooner or later?

"Theo, Theo!" I suddenly heard Teddy cry anxiously, leaping from his chair.

Alarmed, I came back to the room with a jolt. "Theo?" I asked, kneeling beside him, ignoring the commotion around me. I gently took his hand in mine. His head had pitched forward oddly, and he looked down at me with strange, clouded eyes.

"Anne," he said simply.

"No, it is Ellen. Dearest, we will find Anne and get you home." I felt Hart's solid bulk behind me. His hands were firm on my shoulders.

He said in a low and steady voice, "Tom has already gone to fetch his personal physician, and Dryden's gone to bring his carriage from the theatre. Teddy and I will stay here with him. Quickly, go now and find Anne."

"Yes," I said, gathering my skirts and throwing on my cloak. I squeezed Theo's hand once more and firmly kissed his cheek.

"You know where it is?" called Hart. "Katherine Street!" But I was already out the door.

I knew just where it was. The snug and happy yellow house with the blue door. I ran through the grey streets until I found it.

Wednesday, January 27, 1664—one in the morning

Hart has finally brought me home to Maiden Lane to sleep for a few hours. Although I doubt if I can sleep. Dr. Bangs says Theo has had an apoplexy, and he will not survive it. How calm and accepting I sound, and most likely that is how I appear to others, but it is so untrue. I hurry and prepare remedies of egg whites, orange water, and liquorice and soothing poultices of relaxing herbs in the hope of relieving the horrible constriction in Theo's limbs. Anne applies them with diligence, but we both know they are of no use. I just need to *do* something, as does she. In truth, we are just waiting.

Anne—the only word Theo has spoken since this nightmare began.

Will Cartwright stood in for Teddy tonight, even though he is far too old for the role and does not know the lines. He carried the script onto the stage with him. Teddy would not be persuaded to leave Katherine Street. He hovers outside the door to the sickroom. He is also waiting.

Anne sits beside the bed and murmurs into her husband's ear. He senses her there and rests easy with her beside him. Eliza keeps busy, bringing victuals, endless cups of coffee, canary wine, and small beer to the many friends crowding into the little sitting room. Michael watches over her anxiously. Everyone returned after the performance. Young Theo plays with baby Elisabeth, who at nearly a year old is beginning to talk.

Wednesday—midday

"*Anne,*" Theo said clearly, opening his eyes and looking at his wife.

"Yes."

"*Anne,*" he said again, with a lifetime of tenderness.

"Yes," she answered, gently smoothing his hair from his brow.

He closed his eyes again, and slept.

Wednesday, January 28, 1664 — quarter past nine in the evening

At last Anne came out of their bedroom and shut the door behind her. It was the first time she had left that room since Tom and Teddy first laid Theo on their bed. Teddy, white-faced with pain, needed only to look at her to know. Theo died tonight, in the happy yellow house, privately and quietly beside his Anne.

4.

Actress Ellen

When I Protect My Secret Joy

November 11, 1664— Maiden Lane

It has been some time since I took up my quill, but in truth the year has flown by. I have become somewhat mistress of this house and have taken to it with an ease that surprises me. I sleep here most nights but return to Drury Lane for Sunday church and supper with Grandfather and Rose—Mother is often out. *Out.* Out and drunk—God knows where. Their household rumbles steadily along, and with the added benefit of my allowance they do well. Hart is calling for me as we are to dine at Tom and Cecilia Killigrew's home today, although the prospect of eating is nearly unbearable. Mustn't forget . . .

Later

. . . My green hat. Cecilia wanted to try it on and have Madame Sophie make up a similar design. She wears her hair all bundled on top of her head, and so the design must take this encumbrance into account. I find many women want to imitate my clothes and dress of late. It pleases Hart endlessly to have me admired by other women so. Men's admiration—far more troublesome.

Cook has made sugared wafers to tempt me, but I find all they do is make me ill. I left the tray untouched in my closet and have come to my small sitting room to write. I will encourage Hart to eat them after his bath, as I do not want Cook's feelings hurt, although perhaps he shouldn't. His already fleshy face seems to be getting fleshier lately. And he is wearing his neckcloths higher on his neck to conceal his jowliness, but I have pretended not to notice.

I just had to leap up to shut the door to the cooking smells wafting up the stairs from the kitchens. I find the strong smells of spiced food, meats, ale, goats, or horses make me retch. I have begun wearing a lemon-nutmeg-scented sachet tucked into my bodice. I missed my course again this month but have told no one but Hart and Rose my news, yet this whole household seems to know. Betsey cautions me to go slowly up the stairs, and Hugh is driving less recklessly (and more soberly) of late. Cook has suggested I avoid herrings. Hart is pleased. Rose scolded me for not taking more care. I had no idea there were so many different ways to take care. Whores' tricks, said Rose flippantly, tossing her head to avoid meeting my eyes.

Lady's Household Companion
A Complete Guide to an Englishwoman's Home

Scented Small Linen Bags:

Mix dried lemon peel, angelica root, and finely beaten
nutmeg into a smooth dry powder.

Fill a soft linen bag with this powder, adding a sprig of
dried rosemary if desired.

Wear the linen bag about the body to detract from
unpleasant odors.

WHITEHALL, LONDON
TO THE PRINCESSE HENRIETTE-ANNE, THE MADAME OF FRANCE
FROM HIS ROYAL MAJESTY KING CHARLES II
NOVEMBER 2, 1664

My dear sister,

I am puzzled as to the naked aggression of my countrymen towards the Dutch. The Dutchmen do not seem particularly interested in war with us, and have no great need to provoke this nation, but each and every Englishman seems passionately committed to war with them. It is motivated by our jealousy—of their wealthy navy and prolific trade. I am being urged towards war on all sides, but I am resolved to allow them to strike first, and thereby avoid the appearance of provocation.

Could you not persuade King Louis to join with me, or, at least, could he stop supporting them? The last thing that I desire is conflict with France.

I remain forever your,
Charles

Note—*We are guilty of at least one act of aggression as we have captured their colonial city of New Amsterdam, on the coast of America, but I do not feel that is such a substantial crime as to constitute a need for war here at home. We have renamed the town New York.*

November 21— Theatre Royal

Coffee-house rumours:

Tom Killigrew is finally going to put on his great epic, *The Wanderer*—a dramatic, true-to-life, two-parter telling the story of the beleaguered brave Cavaliers in exile, *tra la la.* He has been sitting on it for ten years. "Now is the time!" he proclaims with gusto.

Lacy predicts that Hart will play the king, pompously—although he does do royalty well (they say that kings could take lessons from *him*). Nick says that I would be perfect for the courtesan Paulina. Bright, kept, and full of mischief—but it will not come to pass.

"My *protégée*," brags Hart in company.

Your *protégée* who will never be permitted to perform, I think.

A courtesan. True enough to life.

At this rate I will never be cast.

Somerset House, the Strand, London

To our daughter, Princesse Henriette-Anne

From Her Majesty Queen Henrietta Maria

November 30, 1664

Ma fille,

Terrible rumours are circulating here: that your brother has advocated war only then to declare peace and use the voted funds for himself. I have told everyone that Charles is absolutely in favour of war and will use the funds to bring England to victory over the Dutch (who, in my opinion, richly deserve what they get). Charles, on the other hand, keeps harping on about the cost and refuses to increase the hearth tax as I have suggested. Instead, he is accepting loans at eight to ten percent interest—ridiculous. He really ought to show more backbone.

Please stop any such similar rumours in France.

With affection,

Maman

P.S.: *As you are now in a* delicate *condition you must forgo the green salad vegetables you are so fond of. A woman in your condition cannot risk such impure foods—meat and plenty of red wine will ensure a healthy male child. Do* not *loosen your stays like some sort of baker's wife.*

December 1, 1664 — Drury Lane

I am no longer *enraged* but am worn out by my anger and am strangely empty of feeling. I understand his jealousy—or at least I pretend to—but tonight he went too far!

I have left Maiden Lane for Drury Lane, vowing never to return. Hart arrived back after the theatre tonight (in cups and in temper) and was upset to find me not at home. Tonight, Peg and I went to the Duke's House to see Davenant's *The Rivalls*. Betterton was excellent as Philander, and his wife Mary was passable as Heraclia, although she is getting quite stout for that role. Henry Harris, who played Theocles this time around—in September he played Polycines with greater success—treated us to a late supper at the Bear, and we were well received and joined by the jolly members of that house. I know they are meant to be our competitors, but in fact I enjoy their company, and to see a play acted on a different stage makes for such a glorious change. As well the Duke's are so much more lavish with their staging than we. Their stage machinery is more varied and complex (and less noisy) than ours. It is exciting to watch, for no matter what they enact, we are sure to see a spectacle.

We were seated at the cosy long table by the fire, enjoying canary wine and pots of sweet custard, when Hart barrelled through the door. Brushing aside the greetings of his fellow actors, he jerked me to my feet. "Ellen, I am taking you home now," he growled for all to hear.

Mortified but composed, I shook off his hands and answered back sweetly, "Why, Hart, we were just enjoying lemon custard, your favourite. Perhaps you would care to sit and join us, instead of exhibiting such rudeness in front of our friends." That elicited twitters from Henry and John Downes, the company prompter, serving only to further enrage Hart. Tightening his grip on my arm, he marched me from my chair and into the waiting barouche, leaving behind a tavern full of gawking witnesses. *Heigh-ho.* He would not look or speak to me once inside and did not loosen his hold upon my arm, even when we were well away from that company.

"Hart," I tried to coax, "what is so amiss? It is not so very unusual for me to visit that house."

"At the invitation of Henry Harris?" he replied with a bite. As if I were to know what that meant.

"Henry has asked us to dine often enough and is a friend of—"

"Don't be naïve, Ellen." Hart interrupted. "You know Henry would like nothing better than to steal you away from me." He looked at me with sorrowful eyes. "*Promise* me that you will never leave me. Promise. Say it now."

"Oh, Hart," I said putting my head on his shoulder as we pulled up to the house. "I am here. I wouldn't leave you for—"

"Proof! You are a *whore*! You cannot even promise me so little when I offer you so much!" he burst out suddenly. "And you *would* leave me for the highest bidder, like the slut you are!"

Humiliated and angry, I jerked my arm away from him and shouted for Hugh to stop the coach. I opened the door with a bang and hopped down before Hugh could help me. "Do *not* follow me," I hissed over my shoulder. "I do not *want* you!" I said vengefully, uttering his worst fears aloud. Poor, shocked Hugh tried to pretend that he hadn't heard our exchange and closed the door behind me. As I had alighted on Chancery Lane, it took me an hour to walk home, and my new blue satin mules are ruined.

Later—Drury Lane (in my own bed)

Whore. It is not an unfitting word. I am an actress, but not an actress. With child, but not a wife. I live in a grey no man's land. Is this where whores live?

Wednesday—Drury Lane

My anger has melted into fear. I understand his jealousy stems from his great love for me but do not feel I can take back my fierce words. I think of the life rooting inside me and know I have made a mistake.

Friday, December 9—still in Drury Lane

"What do you plan to do, my dear?" Grandfather asked, gingerly sitting on the edge of my trundle bed, where I have taken up residence this week.

"About what?" I answered evasively, tugging at the coverlet. My troubles were numerous at this point.

"Well," he said, shifting to look at me directly, "it seems you may be abandoned, penniless, and, according to Rose, pregnant." His face held no judgement, only concern and love.

"Oh, Grandfather!" I sobbed, diving into his arms like a child. "What do I do? I dare not go back to the theatre: I no longer work for Meg, since becoming Hart's mistress, and I never went onto the stage. I have no money of my own. I am not fit for anything," I babbled. Grandfather brushed his hand through my unkempt hair.

"I suspect that it will all come right, if you truly want it to," he said evenly. "Do you want it to?"

"Do you mean do I want Hart?"

"I mean do you truly care for Mr. Hart? That is what he wants from you," Grandfather said, handing me his clean handkerchief. "That is what he is waiting for."

"I do care for him," I said, blowing my nose loudly. "He has grown overly suspicious of me, but he is kind and good and looks after me—and that is something."

"It is a great deal," said Grandfather generously. "But I suspect he needs more."

"I have tried to love him—but in fact I cannot imagine how to begin. I know he is a good man, and I know that he is sincerely attached to me, but somehow that does not add up to the passionate love he feels for me. It is as if I do my figures wrong every time and come out with friendship and gratitude. And he looks at me with such a . . . wanting." I breathed deeply, relieved to confess my unloving secret. "I feel as if I owe him everything and I do miss him . . . but I said such terrible things and I can never go back." Grandfather just kept stroking my hair until I fell asleep.

Sunday, December 11

I am resolved. I must find him and make it right. What other choice do I have?

Later— Maiden Lane

All is forgiven. I braided my untruths with half-truths and said enough to give him peace. It was not difficult. He has been as miserable as I. I ought not to have left it so long. We are united by the baby I am carrying. Determined to get out of this particular pickle, I have convinced Hart that I will be more settled, occupied, and happy if I am permitted to go on the stage. A truth of sorts. He will not allow it once I am showing my condition, but for this brief window I am permitted. I cannot sleep for excitement! I am to be cast early in the new year. I will *never* allow myself to be so dependent again.

When I Experience a Terrible Loss

January 3, 1665 — Will's Coffee-house

Nearly skated here as we have had such a hard frost. No matter—I have been given my part and shall be on the stage in less than two weeks' time! I am a tiny bit bigger each day and have asked Rose three times now to let out my gowns. I take great care not to rest my hands upon my belly or to stretch my back as expecting mothers do. Surely people will begin to notice soon?

Hart, Teddy, and Lacy coach me every morning. I must *astonish*, they say. Not sure how I will do that, but their faith in me is touching. "*Astonish*, but *not* move about so much," Hart complains. He is ever watchful as I have a tendency to "romp," as he puts it. The script is strong, James Shirley's *The Traitor*, and I have learned it off by heart—and been deemed an eccentric for my care. At the most, actors learn their own words—to remember the whole script is unheard of, but I will be far too nervous to make up my lines on the spot like the others. Elizabeth has an extraordinary memory for words and always keeps to the script and reassures me it is no bad thing. Becka and Nan think me gauche and green, but then they just play to the audience and hardly bother to learn their words anymore. Now, Dryden refuses to write for them.

Note—In the morning rehearsal, Hart, good to his word, has pronounced me *ready*. Not necessarily *astonishing*, but ready. And would I *please* sit down and rest now?

Sunday, January 8 — Maiden Lane

An accident—terrible pain.

A great tearing away.

Forgive me.

Undated

I ask for my diary, quill, and ink.

No, you must rest.

I want . . . I want . . .

What do you want?

Who is here with me?

Sleep.

Undated

Voices:

She will recover, but only if she *rests.*

Infection is the great danger.

Her womb is still open.

January 13 — Maiden Lane

They tell me it was a carriage accident. The horse slipped on the ice. The carriage overturned. Hugh was lucky to jump free. He pulled me out, but I have been in a fever for days. My womb is empty. I am alone. *Sleep.*

January 20 — Maiden Lane (now)

Teddy visits every day. Sometimes I am asleep, but I know he has been here with me. He says *The Traitor* is a success, but Kitty is not half as good as I would have been. My gold-and-silver gown has been remade to fit her. She tends towards affectation, Teddy says. Lots of flailing about and waving hankies. I try to muster jealousy, but it will not come. Such a long time ago. Did I *ever* want to go on the stage?

February 11 — Maiden Lane

Dr. Bangs has proclaimed me healed. How can I be healed when I feel so unwhole? I am in such small pieces I cannot imagine how to fit them together again. The doctor tells me, as long as I maintain a light diet (now I can eat all the herrings I wish) and get plenty of rest, I can get up, move about, and return to the theatre, if I choose. *If* I choose? I choose to hide away in my little blue study in this great grey house.

When I Receive a Gift

St. Valentine's Day

"You are my only Valentine," Hart woke me, kissing me gently. I suppose he is mine as well, as he is the first man I saw today. I will try. I will look at him and talk to him and even send Betsey out to the New Exchange to find him a Valentine's gift. I will pretend and pretend and pretend.

Note—I opened my door and caught Betsey kneeling on the floor, quickly bundling something into brown paper. I asked to see it, and she was reluctant, but I insisted. A small posy of handpicked yellow roses wrapped in a crude string. "From whom?" I asked. Wordlessly, she led me to a small, unused bedroom on the third storey. Inside were dozens of similar bouquets—all placed in small jars, mugs, vases, and even tankards. "For me?" I asked, touched.

Three p.m.— Maiden Lane (hard, bright day)

Betsey came to my closet this afternoon. I was surprised to hear her knock, as Hart is at the theatre and everyone knows to leave me be at this hour. Poking her head round the door she told me that my mother was here to see me. Wrapping myself tighter in my blanket (I have been constantly cold since . . .) I bid her tell my mother I was sleeping and not receiving visitors.

"But, Mrs. Ellen," she faltered, and with that, Mother pushed past her and into the small room.

"Not receiving," said Mother, her voice throaty with contempt. "Coffee, Betsey," she said, throwing open the heavy window draperies, flooding my dim room with dazzling winter sunlight. "You could suffocate in a room like this," she muttered, settling into the cushioned armchair opposite. "And Betsey, bring cakes, if you have them, and *brandy,*" she called after my retreating maid. "You look like you could use some plumping up."

I winced. It is true. I have grown quite gaunt of late; it does not suit me, and I do not care. What does it matter now? The one I was to grow plump for is gone.

"Stop it," snapped Mother, as if reading my thoughts. "You are young, there will be others. Dr. Bangs says that your womb is intact. You *can* have others."

"Dr. Bangs? You spoke to Dr. Bangs? You were *here?*" I asked, shaking my head and struggling to recall, struggling to shake out the cloudiness.

"Yes, I was here. Teddy came to fetch me. He is a good boy and thought you might want your mother with you."

She pulled off a small green hat I have never seen before. I looked at her more closely: her thick brown hair was neatly combed and pinned and her dress carefully pressed. Her fingernails were clean, and her face had a raw, fresh look, as if it had been recently scrubbed. I was moved by her effort.

"Of course," she continued, "Teddy wasn't to know that you don't care a jot if your mother is with you or not. Grandfather and Rose were here, too, by the by. Rose was quite shaken, but Grandfather was sanguine as always—plenty for him to write home to Margaret about. She's never approved of me anyway."

This wasn't about her, but I did not say so, as Betsey returned with the tray. Mother poured out two cups of coffee and laced only mine with brandy.

"Surprised?" she scoffed, catching my expression. "I do not *have* to drink. I simply *choose* to drink," she said, handing me my cup and saucer.

I was surprised to see how easy she seemed in these surroundings—unfazed by the rich oak furniture and silk curtains. But then she was the daughter of a clergyman and the wife of a captain, I thought to myself—she was not born to poverty but has brought poverty upon herself.

"Here, eat this. You look terrible," Mother said, cutting a generous slab of cake.

"Oh no, I can't," I said, repelled by the food.

"Oh yes, you can," she said, laying the dish on the side table. "Pretty soon you are going to do such damage you won't come back. I know about sadness that eats you up from the inside. It will kill you. Long before it kills your body, it will kill *you*. You won't be able to find your way back."

I looked at her quizzically. Everything—my mother's sadness, her happy life with my father, the destruction of that life, her sadness for something that could not be changed—does she look for a way back or just plunge ahead into greater darkness? I picked up my fork.

"There you go," she said approvingly. "That's the way. Keep living or it will catch you up."

"Mother . . ." I faltered, tears in my voice. I wanted to tell her so much: my dread of the awful pain that lies beyond my fogginess; my inability to share it with Hart; the coldness in my fingers; my sleeping heart, waiting to break.

"No," she said firmly. "We won't speak of any of it. What would be the point?"

So we sat in silence by the fire, my mother and I, and ate cake.

Note—Betsey is now leaving the posies on my vanity—pinks, yellows, and clear white, such cheery colours. I wonder . . . Hart?

February 22, 1665
Theatre Royal, Bridges Street
Dear Ellen,

Lacy and Hart tell me that you are improving, and I am heartily glad to hear it. There is a part waiting for you, whenever you feel up to returning to our theatre. Please call upon me for anything you might require.

Your etc. . . .
Tom Killigrew

Note—*As I know you missed your birthday celebrations during your convalescence, I have been so bold as to include a small gift.*

February 22, 1665
Maiden Lane
Dear Mr. Killigrew,

Thank you for your kind invitation to return to the theatre. I believe I shall be able and ready quite soon and am looking forward to seeing you all again.

Thank you truly, sir, for your gift! She popped out of her travelling basket, made herself at home, and licked my cheek directly. I have not felt such joy in the last months. She is curled asleep beside me as I write this. I have decided to call her Ruby, for her ruby red tongue that poked out and licked me when I first held her. It was a most welcome kiss. What a surprise for Hart when he returns from rehearsal! Again, I thank you,

With all my heart,
Ellen

Tuesday, February 28—home at last

Exhausted!

I had forgotten how much life there is out there. Talk, talk, talk. Everyone talking about: the Dutch, the king and Castlemaine, the increasing price of lace and sugar and meat. Rehearsal this morning: singing with Hart, deportment and dancing with Lacy. Teddy partnered me, and we acquitted ourselves well, considering we have not practiced in months. Lacy thoughtfully asked us for a French *branle*, with a tempered choreography without *caprioles* or *jetés*. Becka and Michael lumbered through a *courante* without half our panache, consulting Playford's *Dancing Master* constantly as they went. It takes Becka forever to learn the steps.

"More kick!" Lacy kept shouting at them.

What does that *mean*? They never seemed to figure it out, and Lacy threw up his hands in exasperation.

Then we all headed off to Will's before the afternoon performance. I was hesitant, but Teddy was insistent. "Now that I have pulled the mole from her hole, I am going to get the most out of her," he said, firmly steering me in the direction of the coffee-house. He tactfully avoided the corner of Drury and St. Martin's lanes, where my carriage overturned.

At least I am not cast for another week. I still get so tired. Ruby slept peacefully in her travel basket throughout the ruckus. She is a pug—pale brown with a velvety black snout, quite the most fashionable dog. I feel very *au courant*.

Note—A comet. Everyone is also talking about ill omens. Teddy (who believes all this guffle passionately) says that a coffin appeared in the sky above Vienna last week, causing much fear among the people, and in Warsaw, a hen laid an egg marked with a flaming cross, a rod, and a drawn bow. Seems a lot for one egg.

WHITEHALL PALACE, LONDON

TO OUR BELOVED SISTER, PRINCESSE HENRIETTE-ANNE, DUCHESSE D'ORLÉANS,
 THE MADAME OF FRANCE

FROM HIS MAJESTY KING CHARLES II

MARCH 1, 1665

My dear sister,

I fear I have at last exhausted my good queen's patience, and Monmouth has at last exhausted mine. All this conjecture as to his legitimacy has put dangerous ideas into his head (spurred on by Buckingham, no doubt), naturally upset the queen, and ruffled our brother James (this amuses rather than bothers me). The rumpus began when Monmouth ordered a coat of arms without the baton sinister. Such a public claim of legitimacy embarrasses me as well as him and must be dealt with. Rumours are one thing, public acknowledgement is quite another. I will send him to you for a visit in the spring if I may? If only to get him out of here.

While James's animosity towards my son is no secret, the queen has gone out of her way to befriend him. Such a snub and pointed reference to her infertility is uncalled for. That she can produce an heir is a fiction we all must uphold. Must go as we are supping on the river tonight. And, speaking of aquatics—have you received my gift?

I will always be your,
Charles

Saturday— Theatre Royal

Rehearsal, dinner, rest: capriole, jeté, pas de bourée, sing, dance, laugh. Slowly, slowly, I come back to life.

Note—Blushing cream roses today in the same rough twine.

LONDON GAZETTE

Sunday, February 26, 1665

Most Deservedly Called London's Best and Brilliant Broadsheet

The Social Notebook

Volume 167

Ambrose Pink's social observations du jour

Darlings,

It is all topsy turvy at the palace, my pets. The ladies of court have run quite mad. This week, Mrs. Sarah Jennings, of the Duchess of York's household, got herself all dressed up as an orange wench and began pitching her wares throughout the corridors of Whitehall. It is now the epitome of fashion to dress as if one is off to market day—the boots, the bonnet and the *très décolleté* bodice—well, if one is to attract a customer . . .

And if that were not enough news for one week, *la famille* Castlemaine is airing their royally dirty laundry in public again. Lord Roger Castlemaine is returning from France, apparently intending to make amends with his famous wife. Ignoring her impending nuptial visit, Lady Castlemaine has been heard to proclaim this week that her royal daughter, the lovely little Lady

Charlotte Fitzroy, at two years old, will be the first of the king's daughters to marry—and it will be a wedding fit for a princess. *Quelle effronterie!* Who will give her away, do you suppose? *Dommage*, my darlings—families can be so difficult, don't you think?

À bientôt, dearests,
Ever your eyes and ears,
Ambrose Pink, Esq.

Sunday— Will's Coffee-house (light snow)

"Ohh! You have to listen to this!" squealed Teddy over coffee this morning.

"They say she actually sold some of the oranges! What will be next? Castlemaine peddling fish?"

"I'll bet she couldn't outsell our Ellen," Lacy said fondly.

"I'll bet Mrs. Jennings could afford to give them a better price," I countered, cutting a slice of apple cake for Hart.

"Yes, but I'll bet she gave 'em less for their money," giggled Becka. It was a crude joke, and I looked at Hart with unease. Thankfully, he had not been paying her any attention. He does not like our relationship to be discussed publicly.

Hart grunted from behind his news sheet. "Lacy, do you think our navy is up to this?"

He disapproves of my gossiping, refuses to listen to the tattle, and only wants to discuss the impending war with the Dutch.

"We'll have to be, if it comes to it," responded Lacy with equanimity—he is given to politics and gossip in equal measure.

The conversation moved on to state matters, and I was able to concentrate upon feeding Ruby wedges of buttered toast.

Note—Hart told me after supper this evening that it was officially read out in the Exchange—we are at war with Holland. What does this mean?

Tuesday, March 7, 1665

Sad news:

The *London*, one of our great ships, sank today. Twenty-four men and women were saved, but three hundred drowned in the lost ship. *Three hundred.* All the bells toll out a sad, steady beat. May God have mercy upon their souls.

Tuesday, March 14, 1665— Maiden Lane

It is today. All the staff of Maiden Lane wished me luck as I left for the theatre. Strange, after so much fuss and to do, I feel quite calm. I am sure the butterflies will come once the make-up is on and the house fills up. My costume, finished by the seamstress at three o'clock this morning (Hart spent a fortune), is perfect: green and gold, with just a touch of Aztec mystery. Rose suggested the design, and her creations always have a certain dramatic flair.

Hart just poked his head into the tiring room to check on me. He has been anxious about me since the accident. Peg has just arrived to help with my toilette. I can hear her in the hall outside . . .

As I was waiting in the wings for my entrance, I caught Hart looking at me sadly, as if I were a great treasure he was giving away. I put my arms about his neck and kissed him more than usual.

March 15, 1665— Will's Coffee-house

"A triumph!" Teddy squealed theatrically, pulling me out of my chair and twirling me about.

"Yes, I must say you did look well in that green," Lacy said, watching us *pirouette* about the room.

"Ooh! Mind Ruby!" Nick warned.

My patient puppy darted out of the path of our wild *courante*. Teddy loves the French dances. My green hat came off and rolled under a chair. Hart picked up Ruby and held her on his lap, watching us spin round and round, but did not join us. Another performance this evening—Mother, Rose, and Grandfather are coming. It all happens so *fast*.

Later

The audience goes mad for us, and I am awed by their affection. It is not a thought-out organised thing to perform a play but a wild irregular roar, impossible to tame. My blood thrums and my heart bumps noisily in my own ears, but I am happy. In the midst of the terror and chaos, I am vibrant with happiness.

March 17— Theatre Royal

Listen: Can you hear them?

They call me *Nell*.

They gave me a new name.

They call for *me* to come and take an extra bow when the curtain comes down.

They send me flowers and trinkets and letters and cards.

They write as if they know me.

They want to know where I buy my shoes, my gowns, my creams, my soaps.

They like my small feet and forgive my red hair.

They wait outside the theatre.

They call me *Nell*.

But I am Ellen, I think.

When I Solve the Mystery

Monday, March 23 — Maiden Lane

Hart no longer likes to dine out after the show:
  "We are never alone," he complains.
  "We can always be alone," I answer, pulling on my coat.

March 24, 1665
Farm Cottage, Oxford
Dear Ellen,

While I thank you for your courteous invitation, I find myself unable to attend such a performance in such an establishment. It is also far too cold to visit London at this time of year, and I am sure that Nora does not keep the house heated properly. I wish you well in this unusual and, if I may point out, unsuitable endeavour of yours, but I do hope that reason will prevail and you will give it up and make a proper match. I assume that Rose has also followed this path? Your grandfather is in great remiss and does not inform me of her doings.

Take care of your grandfather. His cough is often troublesome in early spring. Make sure he wears the thick red muffler I knitted for him myself—it is much warmer than that threadbare blue one he insists on wearing.

Great-Aunt Margaret

Note—I assume you know how to make a paste against consumption, should his cough worsen? Your mother will know, and if she doesn't she ought to.

Thursday, March 26, 1665 — Maiden Lane

We are going away! Tomorrow evening, after the performance, Hart and I will depart for his country home and stay away for four whole days. As tomorrow is Good Friday and Saturday is Lady Day (end of Lent, thank goodness—I have been breaking rules with abandon) and Sunday is Easter, Hart decided to take me to his newly purchased country house as a treat. Tom Killigrew is furious, as the last performance of *Emperor* is on Lady Day, but Kitty (she will have to let out my costume) will fill in for me, and Nick will fill in for Hart. I must admit, I am sad to be missing it and have grown self-important enough to think the audience might miss me just the tiniest bit.

Saturday, Lady's Day — Gill House, Surrey

The country is plushly green and heavy with quiet, and the blue air feels crisp and pure—it is difficult to adjust to such peace.

Hart began teaching me to ride yesterday. He gave me long, soft riding boots and a black velvet riding suit. I looked quite smart until I actually sat *on* the horse. My horse is called Danny, and she is gentle and patient with my ineptitude—to a point, and then she turns and, despite my instructions, heads for home. "Use your legs! Heels down!" Hart calls out to my retreating back, but it is hopeless.

Hart, a natural horseman, showed off doing high *caprioles* in the air. His horse Sampson, an enormous grey, looked nonplussed at all this effort, only to hop up and then go nowhere. I feel far from the bustle and spark of London, and I must own that I miss the vitality of the city. Hart is happy here. His great bear's body makes more sense out of doors, as if his natural expansiveness is confined by the smallness of the city. The sun bronzes his pink cheeks, and his damp sullenness gives way to an easier affection. Regardless of his happiness, he looks at me all the time with an expression of wanting. Wanting me to take to the quiet. Wanting me to be content. *Wanting* me only to *want* him. I am anxious for more company but do my best not to let it show.

But then in company, he is only interested in the news of the Dutch war, so at least I am spared that. I am heartily sick of the Dutch war. I seem to be alone in my lack of patriotism, but *heigh-ho.*

Early, five a.m— Hill House

I solved the mystery!

This morning Ruby woke me earlier than usual, anxiously licking my face and whining to be let out. I obliged, throwing on a warm dressing gown and slippers. When I opened our bedroom door, I found Hugh, the coachman, sitting on the landing tying a familiar twine around some bushy white hydrangeas. "It's you!" I said happily. "I'm so glad!"

"Shh, Mrs. Ellen," he said hastily. "I wouldn't want Mr. Hart to hear."

"Oh, he wouldn't mind. In fact, we must tell him at once. Your posies have been making me so happy," I bubbled, smelling the flowers.

"Oh no! I wish you wouldn't. He might not understand. I know he is a jealous . . . as he should be . . . as any man—"

"But Hugh," I said with sincerity, "they have brightened my day and cheered my world at a time when I've needed it."

"Well, that's the thing." He began to shift his weight from foot to foot in his discomfort. "When I pulled you out of that carriage, you just seemed so small and so alone, and I knew, we all knew, right then that you'd lose the babe—"

My face must have registered my shock, for he quickly changed tack.

"I don't mean to bring it up . . . I just thought you could use some cheering . . . Mrs. Ellen, are you all right?"

"Yes, thank you, Hugh, I'm fine. It's just that no one has spoken of it. Not really, not directly. The baby, I mean. This is the first time"—I took a deep, steadying breath—"the first time I mentioned . . . *her.*"

"Ah," he said, as if he understood. "A little girl, was it? Cook thought as much, said you were carrying high. Did you give her a name?"

I shook my head.

"No, you wouldn't have been able to, would you, being unconscious and all. Well, I'm sure Mr. Hart gave her one for you. Can't have an unnamed baby baptised, and we saw the priest come . . ."

I regarded him with wonder. "A *priest*?" I repeated like a parakeet. "A priest was *here*?" I straightened, recovering myself. "Thank you, Hugh."

"Best to get it out in the open, I say," Hugh said, clearing his throat nervously but looking me straight in the eye with absolute complicity.

"Yes. Well again, thank you, Hugh," I repeated formally. "Thank you for saving me and for the flowers and for, for remembering—" I stopped, unable to go on.

"It isn't just me. Cook, she picks 'em mostly, but I sometimes do, if I'm out and about and see something pretty. I always wrap 'em, though," he said with a touch of pride. "Keep my string 'ere in my pocket. I'm glad they helped. Would you like me to take Ruby for you? She looks like she's itchin' to go, and it's cold out there."

"Yes, thank you again, Hugh." I grimaced at my repetition and handed over the wiggling Ruby. I opened my bedroom door and heard him move down the stairs. "You are quite right, you know," I said, turning back to him. "Flowers always do help."

"Yes, they do," he said, and continued on his way.

WINDSOR CASTLE, ENGLAND
TO OUR PRINCESSE HENRIETTE-ANNE, DUCHESSE D'ORLÉANS AT VERSAILLES
FROM HIS MAJESTY KING CHARLES II OF ENGLAND
EASTER SUNDAY, 1665

My dear sister,

Sam Cooper has finished his portrait of me, and I am well pleased. He finally agreed to paint me in semi-profile. I am sending him to you, whom he can paint from any angle and you will look like the angelic beauty you are, although perhaps I should wait until late summer before I send him—after the event?

De Grammont tells me how you love your new English barge. I am delighted! And thank you for sending him with the French sealing wax I have been longing for—the English excel at a great many things but the production of golden wax is not among them.

With dearest love I remain your,
Charles

Easter Sunday — Chill House (raining)

A house party! Dryden and his wife, Lady Elizabeth (Beth) Howard—she is a tall bony sort of woman with a surprisingly wry wit and is the eldest daughter of the Earl of Berkshire and sister to the four playwriting Howard boys: Robert, Edward, James, and Henry—arrived in this morning and will return to London with us tomorrow. After attending church in the village we enjoyed a lively afternoon of dancing and music—Cook was shocked—dancing on Easter Sunday. Beth played exquisitely and taught me the latest French *gigue,* much more complicated, with a very quick *capriole* in the first pass. For such a tall woman, her timing is excellent. After supper Dryden and Hart were much taken up with plans for a new heroic tragedy. I keep telling them that I long to play a character who possesses a *gaieté du coeur*—and does not *die* at the end. I feel so terribly awkward, dying onstage, and each time I worry that my gown will fly up and I'll just have to lie there with unseemly bits of underclothing hanging out. A corpse can hardly adjust her skirts.

Note—I have made so bold as to ban all talk of the war and insist on frivolous light conversation. Hart looked askance at me but complied. He was shocked I would make such a firm request.

Monday, March 27 — London (at last!)

What a trip! It never ceased raining, one of the horses threw a shoe, the baggage cart got stuck in the mud, and Hart got a cold. I cheered our party by doing imitations while we waited at the inn (the blacksmith took forever). Dryden and Beth were falling about laughing but Hart was out of sorts and disinclined to be amused. Now perversely he refuses to talk about the war—what a bore.

Note—Pink peonies with a note: For our Mrs. Ellen, Love from H & C.

Later (three a.m.)

"Hart." I nudged him. "Hart, are you awake?"

"Mmm."

"Hart, may I ask you something about the accident?"

"What is it, my dear?" he asked tenderly, instantly roused.

"The . . . baby. Hugh said a priest was here—did you have her baptised?" I held my breath. I did not put much faith in religion, but I did not want my baby to wander forever as a lost soul.

"Of course I did, my dear, while she was still—just before, just before—" He broke off, unable to go on.

"Before I lost her?" I finished for him.

"Yes," he said, his voice a whisper. "Before we lost her."

"Her name?" All baptised babies are named—it was a comfort, a recognition. I gently took his hand.

"Elizabeth, for my mother."

"Elizabeth?" I tried the unfamiliar name on my tongue. I looked at him, puzzled. Hart knew well if it was a girl, I had wanted to call her Rose, for my sister.

"But . . . why?"

"You were unconscious, and I had to make a decision. I felt it was the right thing. In any case, it did not matter terribly to you—did it?"

"No. Not terribly," I lied.

The unshed tears burned my eyes, and I turned away from him and went to sleep.

When I See the Merry King

An extraordinary evening:

Went to the Duke's House to see Roger Boyle in Lord Orrerey's *Mustapha*. Betterton dazzled as Solyman, and Mary played Roxelana (Hester Davenport's famous role). Henry Harris played Mustapha, and while I would love to be able to tell him that he was wonderful, I avoided him for Hart's sake. Teddy was meant to join me, but at the last minute he had to fill in for Nick, who has caught Hart's cold and could not make it. Becka came along in his place—not my favourite. Outside the theatre, we were recognised by an audience member who offered us a bottle of canary wine in return for a kiss. I allowed Becka to do the honours, as it was surely her kiss he was after, but I drank my share of the wine. We got rowdy and giggly (she is much improved by drink) and made somewhat of a spectacle of ourselves before the show even began, but no one seemed to mind.

It was only once we were quite tipsy that we realised that the king and Castlemaine had slipped into their box. Ignoring the play, we watched them, fascinated, but then we suddenly lost sight of the king. Castlemaine apparently did, too, as she craned her neck about to see where he might have got to. Wondrously, he turned up in *our* box! The audience all turned to gape, and even Mrs. Betterton on the stage took note. Becka instantly tugged her already low-cut bodice lower.

"Ladies, it would seem that you have some available wine. Perhaps you would care to share?" he asked, casually dropping into a gilt chair beside Becka, folding his long legs neatly under the seat. I was struck by a surprising sense of familiarity: his great height, the drape of his soft am-ethyst coat cut in the latest French style, and his large-featured grace—all so right, like a bolt sliding into place. I shook my head in an attempt to rejoin my scattered thoughts. Did we get up and curtsey? Had the moment passed?

"Yes, Your Majesty," Becka said coquettishly, leaning forward to afford him the best view and handing him the bottle. There was lip paint on the rim, and I wished she had wiped the spittle off first.

I sat strangely dumb, watching the rich lace of his cuffs as he lifted the bottle to his lips. He took a long swallow and returned the bottle to Becka, his lived-in face relaxed in easy comfort. This is the *king,* the *king,* I kept telling myself, and yet he has a way of putting one at ease. As in our first meeting, a curious feeling of giddy warmth came over me. Why, he is just a *man,* I discovered, surprised. *How funny and how right.*

"Mistress Gwyn, you are staring. Is something wrong?" he directed at me.

I opened my mouth as if to speak, but only a flock of giggles came out. "Forgive me, Your Majesty," I gasped, horrified. "I must be nervous."

"She has had a bit of wine, Your Majesty," Becka interrupted, shooting me a warning look.

"You were not so nervous the last time we met," the king teased. "If I remember rightly, you reprimanded me for not taking your sister's trouble more seriously. How does she, by the by?"

Becka's eyes narrowed suspiciously. "You have met before?" she asked in an accusatory tone.

"You remembered?" I breathed in surprise, ignoring Becka's question. "You were so kind that night. We were in such trouble and you just . . . solved it. I wanted so to thank you—you were so generous and helpful and graceful and good—but I was not sure how to thank you or find you." Oh dear, I was running on and on, but I could not seem to stop. "And then I just assumed too much time had passed and you would have forgotten all about it, but it meant so much to us, Rose and my family and me—it is just the four of us, Rose and myself and my mother and Grandfather—and we are all so grateful . . . so I am happy for the opportunity to thank you now, so . . . *thank you.*" Breathless, I finished. Will I ever learn to curb my tongue? And this to the *king.* I felt Becka staring at me, shocked by my wordy, informal *faux pas*. "My sister is well, thank you," I added awkwardly, finally answering his question.

"Ha!" The king laughed, amused at my discomfiture. "Ellen, isn't it? You see, I would never forget one who scolded me so charmingly."

"Yes, Ellen, but . . ."

"But?" coaxed the black-eyed king.

"But they are calling me Nell out there."

"And so you will be Nell out there. Here," he said, leaning over to touch my forehead lightly with his long tapered fingers, "you will stay Ellen."

"But *they*—"

"They, they, they . . . *they* will not know Ellen." His expression suddenly shifted, and something dropped away. There was a fierceness about him, an anger even. "She will be secret, she will be safe. She *must* be. A person *must* have a secret if he is to be constantly on the stage." And then, like the passing of a summer storm, he was back to being the king but not the king. Once again, he resumed his easy, flexible, royal self. As if the darkly fervent man had never been. With that, he thanked us for the wine and, gracefully rising, bade us good night.

"Good thing, too," Becka hissed. "Look, Castlemaine is watching." Sure enough, we looked over, and the famous lady, swathed in cherry-red ruffles, was unabashedly staring at us; that is, until her royal lover returned to her side, and then she did not give us another glance the whole evening.

"On the stage," I mused later.

"What?" asked Becka, arranging her skirts in the carriage, leaving little room for me.

"On the stage." I wonder if he meant him or me.

"What a silly thing to think about," chided Becka.

And we were silent the rest of the way home.

Note—Beth told me that Lady Castlemaine is ill again in the mornings. Poor Queen Catherine. Perhaps it will be a girl, and then she might not feel as bad.

April 5, 1665 — Maiden Lane (raining)

Today is proclaimed, at the king's command, a fast day in support of the Dutch war. We have been terribly good and kept to it most solemnly. Rose was here going over dress designs. Her ideas are bold but expensive. "Simplicity is always expensive," Hart said approvingly, looking over her shoulder at the drawings, asking how much each would cost.

Note—All the talk in the theatre has been of our encounter with the king, although if Becka is to be believed, he did not speak to me at all. Teddy is in *anguish* (his word) that he missed it. Hart has just popped his head in to tell me that our performance at Whitehall has been cancelled. Could that be because . . . ? How silly I am, and how self-important.

Sunday, April 16, 1665

We heard in church this morning that we engaged with the Dutch. We captured three of their ships and lost none of our own. Happy with our success but still not sure *why* we are doing this.

When I Become a Comedienne

Monday, April 17 — Maiden Lane

Went with Teddy to see *The Ghosts* at the Duke's. It was simply done, but the acting was excellent. "Gravitas," Teddy proclaimed. "Betterton always manages to exude gravitas. I think I am too thin for gravitas," he complained, looking in the mirror.

"Yes, but you look far better in yellow," I consoled him. Betterton's costume had been a ghastly banana hue.

Afterwards a quiet supper at the Bear with Hart, Lacy, and Teddy. There is talk of my being cast in a comedy—*at last*! I have become tiresome with my constant pestering.

Thursday, May 15 — Theatre Royal (rainy)

Not a comedy but a dull, dull tragedy. *Love's Mistress,* by Tom Heywood. I do not shine in such parts. Dryden is writing again; he has been sporting his floppy black cap, his favoured headgear when visited by "the Muses." I fear it is another heroic tragedy. The Muses seem keen on heroic tragedy lately. Johnny Rochester is merciless in his persecution of Dryden's pompous heroic style. Johnny does a wonderfully overblown hero's death—a Dryden death, he calls it—lots of writhing in agony on the floor while spouting selfless sentiment in perfect diction.

May 17— Will's Coffee-house

The endless discussion:

"But she is *funny,* Hart!" pressed Dryden, dressed today entirely in lavender frills (minus the black hat: no Muses today). He has joined my cause and is fighting for me to play comedies. "Surely you must see that humour suits her light touch?"

"It is true, Hart. No one wants to see this bright little poppet *die* onstage. They want to see her *laugh,*" Lacy added, pinning his colours to the mast.

"I will not have her laughed at," Hart responded adamantly, disappearing behind his news sheet.

"Not laughed *at,* dearest," I said softly, taking his big hand in mine. "I wish to make others laugh. It is so very sad for me to play sad roles all the time. I would much rather be merry."

"Humph," grumbled Hart non-committally, tugging at his great periwig—new and too mousy for his rosy colouring and ill fitting to boot. "If you want her to play comedies, then you had better write comedies," Hart said pointedly to Dryden.

"Yes, yes," Dryden said airily, waving his frilly hand as if it were nothing to create such things, entirely forgetting the tortuous creating process. "*L'enfer,* darling, *l'enfer,*" he always calls it.

"We will talk to Tom and Robert," Hart finally conceded.

"There, you see," whispered Dryden in a conspiratorial tone, reaching for more toast. "Tom and Robert will agree. It is as good as done."

Undated

Tom and Robert *did* agree. I am to laugh and laugh!

"Ugh." Dryden held his head, realising what he has brought upon himself. "Comedy is the *worst;* sad endings are far easier. There is always so much to *say* when one is dying."

I hid my smile behind my hand.

May 20, 1665 — Maiden Lane

Hart has agreed, on the condition that he play opposite me. I worry, as he is not known for comedy. His touch is certainly not *light*. I know I should not, but I resent his intrusion. Can I not stand alone as an actress, unclaimed and unsupervised?

Note—Two plague deaths reported in St. Giles in the Fields, just north of Covent Garden.

May 29, 1665 — Will's Coffee-house (hot!)

"Johnny Rochester has become a kidnapper!" Teddy announced over breakfast, waving his news sheet about excitedly. He read out: " 'This known *bon viveur,* Wit, rakehell, and royal intimate, has abducted Mistress Elizabeth Malet, the great heiress of the North, who is only sixteen years old!' Mmm, what good taste he has—she is scrumptious: swan neck, musical laugh, lovely hats."

"Teddy, much as you love them, you can no longer *wear* women's hats," I said briskly.

"Who is she? I didn't know he liked *anyone,*" Peg said, trying to read over Teddy's shoulder.

"She is lovely," I filled her in quietly. "Beautiful and sensible and entirely too good for him. He has always fancied her—since she was absurdly young—but there was never any chance of a match. Her grandfather would not hear of it. When the king spoke to him about Johnny, he apparently swore that he would not unhand such a sweet lady to one who would so surely make her unhappy."

"Well, now her family will certainly raise a fuss," Teddy said, scanning the news sheets for any mention of our wild compatriot. Relocating the article, he paraphrased, "She had just dined with *la belle Stuart,* who *still* refuses the king"—Teddy grimaced—"and then was leaving for home with her grandfather, Lord Haley, when she was snatched from under his very nose, stuffed into a coach and six, and whisked away."

"How romantic," swooned Peg.

"Hardly," I snorted. "I would think she was terrified. How could Johnny resort to that?"

"Well, it does have a certain highwayman glamour, but these days Johnny plays entirely too rough for my taste," Teddy said, not looking up from his paper.

Peg shot me a look. We had always wondered about Teddy and Johnny Rochester—Johnny who openly admits to sleeping with men, out of sheer boredom, he swears. What rot.

"Has she been recovered?" I asked, turning back to our subject. "And more importantly, *where* is he?"

"Ooh, listen to this: 'Rochester, for whom the king has often spoken to the lady but without success, has been placed in the Tower, and the lady has disappeared!'"

"The Tower." I shuddered.

"Oh, not to worry," Teddy said without looking up. "Johnny loves the Tower. It is the only place he gets enough peace and quiet to write."

"Is that that dreadful Ambrose Pink?" Peg asked, snatching the paper from Teddy. "He writes the most horrible drivel."

"Accurate though," Teddy said, pouring more coffee. "And quick—he always has it before anyone else. But he has been known to call me 'Ned,' and I really can't bear that. Sounds like my name said through a stuffed nose. Remember when he linked me to Buckingham? We only spent one evening together. How he got hold of it, I'll never know."

Peg shot me another look. *That,* we didn't know.

"I thought for ages it was Harry Killigrew, Tom's son, but his writing is just not that good," Teddy said mildly. "I hate bad writing."

"It would make sense though—the court, the theatre—but the Duke's as well. How would Harry manage that?" Peg puzzled, fanning herself with her news sheet.

"Harry has plenty of friends at the Duke's, but he has been in Paris lately . . ." I shrugged. "Could be. But then it could be anyone. Why pick on Harry?"

Peg sighed, "I hate secrets."

Note—nine plague deaths in the city itself this week, and eight in the nearby countryside. I touch wood to ward off sickness. Rose and I are making up extra batches of plague water.

Lady's Household Companion
A Complete Guide to an Englishwoman's Home

Plague Water

Fill a large pot with white wine.

Put into the pot: a pound of rue, rosemary, sorrel,
    sage, celandine, mugwort, red brambles,
      pimpernel, wild snapdragons, agrimony, balm, and
      angelica.

Let it stand four days.

June 1— Maiden Lane (hot!)

Great reports of plague in the city. Now everyone is worried. Rehearsals are cancelled. Frightened, we are staying home.

5.

Annus Mirabilis

When We Flee

June 5, 1665 — Maiden Lane

The theatres shut down today. The Lord Chamberlain has closed all public entertainments, including the Southwark and Bartholomew fairs as well as both playhouses, until the plague abates. As men in the Lord Chamberlain's livery went round the theatre posting notices, the company gathered on the street in small clutches to discuss what to do. Tom passed around packets of tobacco—everyone is chewing tobacco against the pestilence. Dreadful taste—I must buy extra tooth tonic.

"I'm for the country," Lacy declared with assurance. "If we are called to entertain the court, then you know where to find me."

"But I have no relations in the country!" squealed Kitty in alarm. "Where am I to go?" Teddy and I exchanged glances.

"I shall stay in London," Lizzie announced. Lizzie's long-time *benefactor*, Sam Pepys, administrator in the Royal Navy (and a notorious philanderer), is also staying in London, I gather.

"Any members of the company who are without acquaintance out of town should feel free to come to me," offered Tom Killigrew with gentle reassurance. "My wife, Cecilia, and I would be glad to accommodate you." Privately, I thought Cecilia might not be glad of the whole company descending upon them *en masse* but chose not to say so. On the other hand, Harry would very much enjoy a bevy of actresses coming to stay. "In any case, I am sure it shan't be for long. We must make good use of the time," Tom went on in a convivial tone that was not quite convincing. "I for one shall order some renovations to be done on the theatre. What do you think,

Lacy, Nick? Don't you agree it is time to fix that awful muffling in the musicians' gallery?" The men peeled off to discuss the much-needed refurbishments, and Kitty, the Marshall sisters, and Lizzie moved away to discuss their various options. Teddy and I stood alone on the street.

"You will go to your wife, I suppose?"

"Yes, I think I shall have to." Teddy frowned. "I must remember to pack my peach India chintz, as she is always after me to borrow it," he said, chagrined. "Although I must put my foot down at my pink wrapper."

I giggled. Teddy and his wife's constant tousling over dresses was a steady source of amusement to the company. He claimed that lovely feminine clothes were often wasted on the unlovely feminine sex.

"And you'll go with Hart?" he asked, confirming the obvious.

"Yes, and I suppose my family shall have to come, too."

Teddy made a face, with good cause. He has suffered two brief but memorable encounters with my inebriated mother and endured a lengthy lecture from Grandfather on the evils of cross-dressing.

"I shall miss you," he said, planting a kiss in my hair. "Please, please, take care. Take very, *very* good care." I reached up and hugged him. We stood like that for a long time.

June 16— Maiden Lane

The numbers are growing. Hart forbids me to leave the house now. He himself goes about with a long beaked mask packed with protective herbs. "He looks a bit like an avenging stork in that thing," Rose said, giggling this afternoon. I wish she would not make light of it, for in truth, I am very afraid. Afraid but not alone. Grandfather, Mother, and Rose have come to live here until transport can be arranged to take them to Great-Aunt Margaret in Oxford—the wheel of our coach is finally beyond mending, and Hart is negotiating to buy another. Prices are extraordinary as suddenly everyone has need of an extra coach.

Despite the crisis, my family will not stop bickering over who gets the best guest room, the best linen, the best cake, and on and on. Mother sent back her bath-water twice last night, complaining that it was not hot enough. I finally intervened, insisting that she bathe in what she is given. She *must* bathe—the smell of spirits is overpowering. I have locked all liquor in the sea chest in the pantry. She is now not speaking to me. Cook rolled her eyes: As if it matters? her look said.

Bill of Mortality
for the City of London
For the week ending on June 27, 1665:

Apoplexy	2
Childbirth	4
Consumption	2
Convulsions	1
Gout	1
Plague	267
Unknown	2

July 2, 1665— Maiden Lane

The king, queen, Prince Rupert, and the Duke and Duchess of York, together with all of their households, have decamped to the clean country air of Hampton Court to escape the plague. London is fast emptying. There are already red crosses in Drury Lane. Hart wants us to go to Hill House, as Surrey is still untouched. Everything feels as if it is coming apart. Ruby does not understand why we no longer go outside.

Note—The plague numbers rose to above five hundred this week—we are leaving in the morning, *if* we can. The congestion has been so great that it has taken some more than a day just to escape London. Already six houses on this street are empty.

July 3, 1665— London (late—we leave at dawn)

Once we decided that we must leave, the entire household was thrown into a tizzy. Chests opened, clothes everywhere, valuables strewn about waiting to be packed. What to bring: Hart's family portrait, the silver candlesticks that belonged to his mother, his wigs, my gowns, my seeds for the flower bed I am planning, and on and on. All foodstuffs are being left behind in case they are contaminated, except the eggs. I must ask Cook to hard cook eggs for the journey.

Hart will send my family on to Oxford the day after tomorrow (we could not hire another coach as *everyone* is running away).

Note—I can hear the cart moving past the house even though I try my best to block it out. The awful wooden burial cart and the tinny-sounding bell. It has stopped—on this street—this street! We have to get out of here.

Note—Cook just told me: the cart stopped at the Griffin house, four doors down. So close! Both children were taken. Two little girls: Clemence, eight, and Polly, eleven. The parents are quarantined for a further thirty-six days and cannot attend the funeral. God help them. God help us all.

Gill House, Surrey

It was terrible. So many of the doors we passed bore red crosses and had guards posted outside—to keep the victims *in*, I thought, shuddering. The streets were crowded with carts and carriages and people on foot, carrying whatever was too precious to leave behind. It took us eleven hours to crawl the mile and a half out of the city gates. Grandfather sweetly held Ruby on his lap the whole way. In Lincoln's Inn Fields there was a frantic knocking on the little door. When I went to look, Hart sharply asked me to close the coach curtains instead.

"But we could fit—"

"No, we couldn't," he said firmly. "We do not know who carries the disease."

Mother and Rose were silent for once. They did as they were bid and did not look out the windows. They were sure, as I was, that without Hart, we would be out there with them.

Later—Bill House

Once free of London we threw open the windows and breathed in huge gulps of country air. As soon as we arrived, Cook took all our travelling clothes off to be burned, and we each took turns scouring our skin clean in the big copper bath. Ruby went last and was most unhappy. Hugh must be exhausted but is not stopping to sleep before he returns for the rest of the household staff. He is so brave to go back. I could not face London again. I do not know when we will return.

Note—Despite the fact that they are here for only one night, as I write this I can hear Mother and Rose out in the hallway arguing over rooms. Mother's room overlooks the stables, and she would prefer Rose's room, which has a view of the park. Good grief. If they were to sleep in the scullery, it would still be far nicer than Drury Lane.

July 4 — Bill House

Hugh has safely returned with the rest of the household. He says he passed door after red-crossed door with "Lord have mercy on us" writ below and saw the burial carts stacked high with bodies—they are working during the day now as so many have died. Betsey says she covered her eyes and could not bear to look. "It feels safe here," Cook said with a sigh.

July 20, 1665 — Bill House

A proclamation was read out in the village this morning, giving thanks for our recent sea victory over the Dutch at Lowestoft. Our flagship, the *Royal*

Charles, sank their flagship with the Dutch commander still aboard. It still feels like boys playing at soldiers and sailors, and that all the dead will return to shake hands at the end of the game—to do otherwise would be unsportsmanlike. Johnny has gone out to fight and has apparently distinguished himself, currying messages between commanders through dangerous waters, messages no one else was reckless enough to deliver. Funny to think of him out there. His belief in God must be absolute for him to take such risks.

Note—Unpatriotic thoughts: Could this pestilence be a punishment for an unjust war? I put them from me, as they do not help present matters.

SAINT GERMAIN
22 JUIN 1665

Dearest Charles,

We cannot delay any longer, Monsieur and I, to send you this gentleman to congratulate you on your victory. I hope this success will enable you to bring the war to an end in an honourable way. I assure you that this is the opinion of all your friends here, of which you have many. You have now shown not only how great your power is but also how dangerous it is to have you for an enemy. Is that not enough?

Thank you for sending Mam to me, as I have great need of her this summer. When she arrives, we will stop at Saint Germain and then continue on to Colombes before visiting the baths at Bourbon. Monsieur will stay behind in Saint Germain. I will always, always be your,

Minette

HAM HOUSE, OXFORDSHIRE
TO OUR SISTER, PRINCESSE HENRIETTE-ANNE, DUCHESSE D'ORLÉANS
FROM HIS MAJESTY KING CHARLES II
JULY 20, 1665

What a brood you have, my dearest. Congratulations! Another beautiful princesse *for the House of Stuart. How brave you are! She will be a comfort to your ailing mother-in-law, Queen Anne. Please tell the Monsieur and King Louis we pray for our beloved aunt. Take care, my sweetheart. Please, for my sake, take care.*

I am always your loving,
Charles

Note—Has the comet been seen in Paris? I have not yet seen it with the tail, although I stay up most nights watching the sky.

July 28, 1665
Hampton Court
Dear Ellen,

Thank you for your sweet note. We gratefully accept your invitation to Hill House, but first I had to journey to town to check on the theatre, and thence on to Hampton Court to see my brother Henry, the king's chaplain. I am still with the court now, and we move on to Salisbury tomorrow. Is the middle of the next month convenient? Yes of course I will endeavour to bring my son, but Harry is ever with the court. I understand that Dryden and the Howards will also be returning to Surrey in August.

The theatre is safe, but in truth London is in a sad state. Every street has boarded-up, marked houses, and the city is hot and still. Everyone breathes through beaked masks and chews tobacco to ward off the sickness. The numbers rose to above seventeen hundred this week, but I hear rumours through town that physicians are not even reporting the true numbers, in order to save families from the required forty-day quarantine within a plague house. Also, the poor are difficult to count, as are the Quakers, who will not have bells rung for their souls.

It is pleasant and diverting here, but strange to enjoy such entertainments after the horrors I have just seen. I am called to billiards. I will be happily anticipating your reply.

Yours,
Tom Killigrew

August 15 — Bill House (still warm)

Ring a ring a rosy
Pocket full of posy
A tishoo, a tishoo
We all fall down.

Children in the village are singing this gruesome song. Do they know what it means, I wonder? It has become custom to bless someone if he sneezes. Suspicion rules. We are all afraid.

Note—The Bill shows the London numbers rose above six thousand this week, but Hart says the true reports are closer to *ten* thousand.

September 1, 1665 — Bill House (late afternoon)

"Darling, the court has moved to Oxford," Hart said when he returned from his morning ride. Oxford—which is still mercifully uninfected. Please God, let it stay that way.

"Will we join them?" I asked, helping Hart out of his riding coat.

"Ah, but here, we can be alone," he said, hugging me close.

Note—Scandalous news from Oxford: Teddy writes that while *la belle Stuart* still refuses the king, she does not refuse Lady Castlemaine. The two of them had a pretend marriage and then climbed into a marriage bed, for all to see. At the last moment, the king hopped in, replacing Castlemaine. *La belle Stuart* claimed indecency and fled, better late than never. I am amazed at what lengths Castlemaine will travel to manipulate the king. All this while the country is ravaged by plague.

September 2

Terrible news. Rose writes that Mother is unable to live with Great-Aunt Margaret any longer and is returning to London. London! Unable to live— what she means is unable to *drink*. I despatched Hugh with an urgent note begging her to stay in Oxford or at the least to come here. Fretting. Fretting. Fretting.

COLOMBES, FRANCE
TO MY BROTHER, KING CHARLES II OF ENGLAND
FROM PRINCESS HENRIETTE-ANNE, THE MADAME OF FRANCE
10 SEPTEMBRE 1665

My dear,

The reports we receive are frightening. France has embargoed all ships bound for England, so I have little hope of this letter reaching you, and yet for my own peace of mind I must write it. I know that your nature, so opposite from its reputation, tends towards action rather than patience, but I beg you to take care. There is little that you can do but send out monies and medical supplies, and I am sure you are already doing both. Protect yourself, my dear. For all our sakes.

Mam arrived safely and is busy overseeing her renovations here at Colombes. Louis has agreed to the figure you suggested, but already I am quite sure she has spent twice that amount. I send my love to all your children and your dear queen. Tell them that I pray for their safety, as I pray for yours.

All love,
Minette

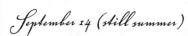 *September 14 (still summer)*

She's done it! Rose writes that Mother has left for town.

Later—six p.m.

"I must go and fetch her!" I repeated for the tenth time. "She is my mother, I cannot just let her return to London! Everyone is dying in London!"

"Be reasonable," Hart said in his most patronising voice. "It is far too dangerous. I could never allow it." Sitting heavily in his armchair, he picked up his news sheet, signalling an end to the discussion.

Breathing deeply to collect my calm, I began to explain it to him again.

Even later—eight p.m. (a cool country rain beats on the roof)

I slammed the door. Utterly childish, but when one is treated as a child, what options are there? Many options, I know, but I chose not to take them.

Everyone knows that the death toll is at least double what is reported in the Bills. Some say twenty thousand a week are dying of plague. No one can bear to turn in those they love, condemning them to die alone. Unable to stop myself, I imagine Mother bricked up in Drury Lane for forty days, waiting. And on the forty-first day?

They say the stench of the dead is overpowering. Farmers cannot coerce their cattle to enter the city; the poor creatures would rather be whipped to death than venture into such a place.

And Mother is there. Somehow I must get to town.

Midnight

Hart knocked gently on my closet door.

"I would like a truce," he said, his large hands held out to me in supplication.

I remained where I was.

"I understand: she must be fetched. Regardless of how foolish she may be, she is your mother, and she is in danger."

"That is what I was telling—"

He held up his hands to cut me off: a commanding gesture that he uses to quiet the audience when he is about to make a great speech on the stage. I find it irritating. "I do not argue with that. I argue with *your* going. We will send someone to collect her, and you will stay here."

"When?" I challenged, pressing my advantage.

"Tomorrow. I have already asked Hugh to find someone."

One a.m. — my closet

I left Hart's sleeping bulk and have come here to think. I know I should feel gratitude, relief, and even tenderness towards him, but I feel curiously bereft, almost robbed of a fight I wanted to have. Why? Why should I wish for discord? It is unlike me. Not discord, I think: freedom.

September 16 — early morning

Daniel, one of the grooms, has gone to fetch her. I made him repeat the directions to Drury Lane twice before I let him leave. He will take Hart's beaky mask and collect Mother as well as his cousin near Charing Cross. He is strangely undaunted and seems ready for adventure. How foolish.

September 17 (sunny)

Not back yet. I am waiting.

September 18

I was amazed and appalled when Daniel returned with his cousin Maybeth and her husband, George, but without my mother.

"Where is she?" I shrieked as Henry handed Maybeth down. Maybeth obviously enjoyed her excursion in a fine carriage very much and seemed utterly unbothered by the plague—it must run in their family.

"Oxford," Henry said, bewildered. "Farm Cottage, River Meadows, Oxford," he recited proudly. "See, I remembered."

"Ellen," Hart said warningly from behind me. I had not heard him come onto the drive. "Come inside."

"You sent her to Oxford!" I screeched, wheeling on him. "She ran away from Oxford!" I stormed past him into the house.

"Never in front of the servants, Ellen! How many times must I tell you?" Hart began without preamble. His huge frame looked even bigger in the pale green morning room (it is exquisite; the decorators have just finished it), his body overwhelming the delicate furnishings. I remained in the cushioned window-seat next to Ruby, who had been startled from her afternoon nap.

"You have lied to me for three days, and you want *me* to hold my tongue in front of the servants?" I asked, struggling to keep my voice level.

"Not lied!" he thundered, slamming his hand onto the writing desk and sending scripts flying and a glass candlestick shattering to the ground.

One of a set. I will never be able to match it, I thought irrelevantly, looking at the mess.

"I never said she was to come here!" Hart said, stepping over the broken glass and loose papers. "You simply assumed."

"Ha," I snorted. "Not lying is not the same as telling the truth."

"She won't run again. I have seen to it." His meaty pink face took on an air of self-satisfied complacency. I wanted to reach through the thicket of his smug reserve and shake the puffy pride from his fat features.

"Meaning you gave her enough money so that she can drink herself silly and have no need to run away?" I threw the words at him like sharpened icicles. They hit their mark, and he crumpled into petulance. This was a dangerous course for me to take. Hart could not bear any slight to his pride, but this was the health of my family he was risking. I threw my rage onto the table and waited for his response.

"I did not have to do anything for her," he said brutally. "Or for you. You are not my wife. Be grateful I did as much as I did."

I did not respond, as there was nothing to say.

Later

Supper in my closet tonight. It is true. I am not his wife. But then, do I wish to be? I know what I do not wish—to be out there, where death walks hungrily through the town.

Sunday, September 25, 1665

Church was awkward. He pretends nothing was said, and I pretend . . . what do I pretend? I feel unravelled and adrift.

Wednesday (raining)

"Ellen, would you please ask Cook for lemon cake instead of cinnamon?" Hart asked when he met me on the stairs. It was the "please" that caught my attention. "I think it might be the cinnamon that has been upsetting my stomach."

"Your stomach? Do you not feel well?" I asked, surprised out of my reserve, as Hart rarely admits to frailty of any kind.

"I have felt sincerely unwell of late," he said, taking my hands and bringing them to his lips. "Sickened from missing you."

I have relented. Peace: if not passion, then peace.

September 30 — Bill House

A lovely day. Tom Killigrew sent a box of new scripts (not that we will get to perform any of them soon), and we spent the day reading the parts aloud. Hart particularly enjoyed my Julius Caesar, complete with a tablecloth toga and a walking stick sword. We are both trying.

When I Meet the Court

October 1, 1665 (still warm)

I have become a passionate gardener—well, student of the garden, anyway. It is lovely to spend afternoons in the quiet green. Hart takes my industry for contentment and is happier than ever.

Foley, Hart's man of all work, has been taking me after luncheon, and slowly, slowly, I am learning to tell the plants from one another—medicinal, flowering, fruiting, perennial, coniferous. Ruby is not impressed. She does not care for dirt. I work with Cook each morning, choosing the menus—although we often have surprise guests, so they tend to change. Still, it is something to do, something to ward off the devouring boredom of this house. Hart is all my safety, I keep reminding myself—trying to rein in my wandering heart.

Note—Our neighbour in Drury Lane, Mrs. Gresham, writes from Warwickshire that her husband has died, leaving her alone with the three children. He died when he went back to town to find work. He never returned to the country but suffered his quarantine and sad end alone. She does not know where he is buried, as the city has stopped keeping records. I send up a quick prayer of thanks for the safety of my own family.

Undated

Rose writes that Mother has been drunk for three weeks. *Heigh-ho*. Drunk but alive.

After supper—nine p.m.

Hart is called to Oxford to entertain the king! We leave tomorrow. What luck! Frantically packing.

Can't find: my violet embroidered dancing slippers, riding gloves, new dandelion-yellow hat with the grosgrain ribbon, veiled hat with the striped ribbon that needs replacing, my silver hairbrush, or my copy of Fitzherbert's *Guide to Husbandry*. Hart can't find his gold-tipped walking stick for town, *his* silver hairbrush, his good riding boots, or Dryden's new manuscript—disaster: Dryden is travelling with us and will be so cross if it is left behind. Hart has asked Dryden particularly *not* to employ his new chicken-dung remedy for baldness during the journey.

Later—after midnight

Betsey had taken our brushes for polishing, my book was in the garden shed, and Dryden's script was under the armchair. Must remember to . . .

November 15, 1665 — Oxford

No idea what I was trying to remember. Life has *finally* settled down here. Betsey no longer gets lost on her way to the market. Hugh has found a man able to mend the coach wheel—the *new* coach wheel. Cook has ordered replacement pots from London, as these are not up to her standard, and Ruby has piddled on every tree in our garden—something Hart feels I should not allow: even his dog must show decorum. Some things can be taken to excess.

Hart has yet to do much entertaining as the king is mostly entertained by Lady Castlemaine, but is regardless away all day with the court. I find it lovely to be in the city of my birth. Hart has rented a large house on Longwall Street, very near Magdalen College, with its even quadrangle of golden stone. The house is light and airy and has an enormous, gracefully weeping willow tree in the garden.

Grandfather remains in Farm Cottage by the river with Great-Aunt Margaret, who is bossy but good-hearted, but Rose and Mother have come to live with us here. I am quite strict and will not permit their ridiculous quarreling. Mother is difficult to manage, and I have taken to locking the pantry closets against her drinking, but I would rather her here than with Great-Aunt Margaret, who heartily and loudly disapproves of her. At least I know she will not try to return to London again. When she arrived in town, she passed Jane Smedley's house and could hear her inside beating upon the red-crossed door, begging to be let out. Mother hurried past, unable to help. When next she passed the house, it was silent, the door hung with black ribbon.

The news:

Dr. Hodges, who bravely has stayed in London ministering to the sick, has introduced a new Virginian snake-root cure and is having some success! Hart has ordered some of the good doctor's anise-and-angelica-root lozenges from town, also said to be effective against plague.

I saw him. The king. He was standing at the edge of the duck pond, throwing crumbs: half for the ducks and half for the dogs. I did not notice him at first (he was wearing a great black curly wig), but then that swimmy, giddy feeling came over me when I recognised the long line of his back and the supple tilt of his head. Failing the courage to approach him, I stood in the shade and watched.

November 20, 1665 — Oxford

Teddy is called to the king and has arrived full of news. He tells of a drunken bagpiper who, mistaken for a dead plague victim, was placed on the burial cart. When he awoke and began to play his pipes, everyone began to scream, taking him for the devil himself! Teddy says that grass grows on Whitehall, there is so little traffic in the streets. I, on the other hand, have no news, as I spend all of my time with my family or cooped up in this house—safe but crushingly dull.

* * *

"I am far too low-born and unimportant to be presented at court," I told Teddy when he stopped by for lunch—luncheon at the court is too rowdy for his taste. The court seems all the more debauched in contrast to the sick and fearful citizenry.

"But you are a great actress now!" he argued, wiping the honey water from his lips. "Anyway, what else is there to do here?"

Not a lot.

Later

Hart, on the other hand, has *not* encouraged me to join the court. I try not to be resentful but find myself complaining to Teddy. Why should he want to keep me here?

"Well away from the eyes of the king and his cronies," says Teddy.

"Piffle," I say. The king is too wrapped up in Castlemaine, who is nearing her time, and *la belle Stuart* to take any notice of me, *great actress* or not.

Teddy will brook no refusal and is taking me with him to court tomorrow!

November 21, 1665—Oxford

A glorious day!

After Hart departed this morning, Teddy arrived with his box of paints and his magical trunk of shoes—shoes in all styles and sizes, of which he is a passionate collector. "Shoes are everything, Ellen," he gravely instructs. "They ground and centre your ensemble. Now, we shall begin with the silver lace mules, although they might be a bit big. Perhaps the embroidered black? I bought them off Peg after her *divine* Desdemona two years ago. Pity Desdemona spends so much of that play in her nightie," he clucked, unpacking his goodies.

We settled on an apple-green gown with a wide pink sash, slim black slippers ("to cut the sweetness," he says), and velvet ribbons woven through my curls instead of a hat. Teddy could not find a hat that suited.

"Ribbons give you a fresh look, in any case," he said thoughtfully. "Everyone will be wearing hats, and you will stand out." He stood back to appraise his work. "Perfect!" he declared, twirling me about, sending my dress out in swirls of frothy green.

"Make-up?" I asked, breathless, sitting down at my vanity table.

"No," he said, studying my reflection in the glass. "You look perfect as you are, with all that pinkness whipped into your cheeks."

Later— Longwall Street (late)

They have such fun: games and entertainments and amusement all the day. The king (elegant in a soft grey surcoat) is relaxed and encourages an informal court. He also seems to wink at the lewd behaviour rampaging around him. He laughs at the bawdy jokes but, I noticed, does not make them himself and encourages outrageous flirting but does not join in. His manners are beautiful and his easy demeanour appears effortless, but I suspect is too consistent to be natural; I do not think anything is natural in this world. Castlemaine appeared tonight with a midnight-blue patch on her cheek depicting a galloping coach and four. Is there any part of her vast person she does not wish to decorate?

Blind man's bluff is *la belle Stuart*'s favourite game and thus their most frequent entertainment. When it is announced, she claps her hands, widens her eyes in childish wonder, and exhales a soft breath of contentment. The men stand enraptured, the king among them. It is silly game, and as far as I can tell only a pretext for courtiers to grab one another in places they shouldn't—still, it is the favourite's favourite, and so they all pretend to be enchanted.

I kept to the edge of the lawn under a leafy horse-chestnut tree. All went well until Hart discovered me in the crowd, and his eyes bulged in anger.

"Ellen! How could you! When I told you . . . And yet you still . . ." He was unable to finish his thoughts in his fury.

I tried to speak soothingly to quiet him, but it was useless. He would not stop. Instead, he rounded on Teddy.

"And you! You pansy! You brought her here! You knew I did not want it, and still you insisted. Just so you could play at dress-up!"

Teddy just shrugged. "She was bored. Why should you have all the fun?"

Hart's face flushed with fresh rage, and he let out a steady stream of invectives. I was getting nervous. Hart was entirely capable of a public scene—he would never tolerate someone else creating one but was easily able to excuse his own. Teddy just wrinkled his nose at him as if he had smelled something distasteful but did not stoop to argue with him. Hart's voice grew loud, louder than he intended, and others were noticing, but he persisted, deaf to my warnings. Hearing the ruckus, the king ambled over, startling Hart.

"Ellen!" he said warmly, as I dropped him a pretty curtsey. "Hart, how can you keep such a treasure at home?" he went on, raising me up. Hart looked uncomfortable but forced a horribly mechanical laugh.

The king extended his arm and whirled me away for lawn games. I felt surprisingly comfortable and made the king laugh with my imitation of Henry Bennet's laboured, breathy voice that he uses when he visits the tiring rooms. Henry Bennet gets very excited in the tiring rooms. "A jewel!" the king declared, and I am commanded to return tomorrow. I shot Hart a triumphant look, but there was no pleasure in my victory as he only looked like a wounded bear.

Later

He became a sulky bear the moment we arrived home. He ordered his supper to be brought to his closet and has refused to come out. In truth, I did not really mind. Teddy joined me for a cold chicken supper in the kitchen instead. *A jewel. A jewel.*

December 1 — Oxford (raining)

Tonight:

Billiards with Elizabeth and Teddy. I won two games but got red chalk on my new ivory gown. Rose will be furious. I secretly watch the well-born ladies of the court: how they sit and speak and move and eat. Teddy caught me watching.

"I will never acquire such grace," I confided, missing my shot.

"Do you really want to?" he asked, sinking two. "You are unpredictable. You sparkle and others take notice. It is a different kind of grace. It is all your own."

It is certainly my own, whatever it is, but is it grace? Do other women worry incessantly over making mistakes, as I do? I am sure not. The washed-out, dainty women of the court flap and flutter and follow a set of unseen rules: who takes precedence over whom, when to sit, when to stand, how low to curtsey—endless. I try to keep to the background, but my noisy laugh has already drawn much attention, and although men and women alike profess to love it, I cannot help but feel like a wild girl who has stumbled into an unfamiliar land.

December 10 — Oxford

A wild girl, perhaps, but one who is having a wonderful time! Life has become a whirlwind of theatricals, games, suppers, treasure hunts, and parties. I am boisterous and no longer mindful of my rougher ways. I can make others laugh, and it sets me apart from the great sheep herd of squeaky, moonfaced, giggling women.

Castlemaine, too, stands out—speaking her mind loudly and loosely, uncaring of decorum. The queen is distinguished by her gracious demeanour. Although it is said that she passionately loves her husband and despises Castlemaine, her placid expression and regal bearing never betray her. She is at the heart of this court and yet keeps much to herself.

Hart vacillates between extraordinary pride in my popularity and a fierce possessiveness that results in petulance—very trying.

I still cannot get used to the sight of the king, and my soul dissolves into a million bumble-bees at his approach. I sometimes wonder if he can hear me buzzing.

I am called to dance!

Later

This company seems to exist without sleep! We stay up until three, and then some rise again with the king at six for his customary exercise—walking and swimming and tennis—and then he spends hours in his laboratory, preparing experiments for his beloved Royal Society. I do not have such stamina and, after a late night, sleep through most of the morning. People are kind—kinder than I would expect to one such as me. Only yesterday, the Duke of Buckingham came to find *me*.

"Ah, there you are," he said. "We are about to begin the dancing, and you *must* allow me to partner you for the *sarabande*. It is *imperative*."

This is how they speak—*dramatically*. I have become known for my light dancing and my small feet, and courtiers often make such requests of me. Tonight, Buckingham asked again, and off we went. Hart, who was partnering Beth Howard, looked unhappy when he saw us take our places at the top of the figure, as did Buckingham's dumpy little duchess, Mary Fairfax. I caught Hart's eye and smiled at him down the line of dancers, but he turned his head away.

I never see Rose, as she is not part of these exalted circles, but I understand from Harry Killigrew, recently back from Paris, that she enjoys *friendships* with several young men of the court. Friendships conducted well away from this glittering golden world. Friendships that keep her away from home for days at a time.

Note—Reports from London indicate the plague is in retreat. God be thanked. Finally, there is mercy for our city. Rose sewed a pale blue ribbon on my ivory gown to cover the chalk marks. An improvment, I think.

Undated

Rose flirts with the young men and, what with the new ensembles Hart has bought for her (hats, slippers, and cloth: three shades of taffeta and one of *moiré* for new gowns), has risen somewhat above her station and more or less left her profession for the moment. Nevertheless, her reputation still clings to her. As I fear it will always cling. Hart is being an angel and endures my wayward family with grace. It is all for love of me. I am finding affection again, and surprised by how much it pleases me.

Note—Castlemaine actually tried to lead off the dancing tonight instead of the queen! The queen just gently nodded to the musicians, signalling them to stop playing! Happy to oblige her, they stopped at once, and Castlemaine was left to dance without music. The queen did not stay to gloat but led the court off to the gaming tables. I admire her enormous pluck.

December 28, 1665 — Oxford

Castlemaine gave birth to a son today, at her lodgings in Merton College. The whole court circles around her in her joy, and she revels gaudily in the attention. If only she wouldn't gloat so. The childless queen must be so lonely tonight.

LONDON GAZETTE

𝔖unday, 𝔉ebruary 4, 1666

Most Deservedly Called London's Best and Brilliant Broadsheet

The Social Notebook
Volume 216
Ambrose Pink's social observations du jour

Londoners,

The king is returned to Whitehall, and the dreaded sickness is in full flight. Our poor bedraggled city will revive, my dears. The list of whom we lost is too long to count, but they shall be remembered, by each and every one of us. Most solemnly. God has at last shown mercy to our fair city, and we are most humbly grateful to receive his blessing. Amen.

À bientôt, brave friends,
Ambrose Pink, Esq.

Whitehall, London
To our sister, the Madame of France
From His Majesty King Charles II
February 1, 1666

I left Hampton Court this morning and arrived at Whitehall in time for luncheon (late). Already the plague is, in effect, nothing, although our women are still terrified. Catherine and Castlemaine both stayed behind in Oxford (an uncomfortable pairing, I know, but what to do in time of crisis?). Castlemaine's new son is well made and sucking strongly. Perhaps this time Catherine can . . . Pray for us.

Affectionately and forever your,
Charles

Note—Have you heard the rumour that the plague is God's judgement upon my unruly court? If God wanted to punish me, why would he inflict sickness upon the lowest among us? Not logical.

And another—Exciting developments in the Royal Society. The artery of a small mastiff was joined by a quill to the vein of a spaniel (not one of mine), and then another of the spaniel's veins was opened to allow the equivalent amount of blood. The mastiff sadly bled to death, but a week later the spaniel is still thriving. In time, perhaps such practices can be used to revitalise people instead of the abhorrent practice of bleeding an already weakened patient. A report is being prepared to send to King Louis, as I know he shares my passion for the anatomical sciences.

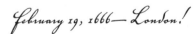

February 19, 1666— London!

We are returned! Mother elected to stay in Oxford for another month, as the house is leased through March, and Grandfather has chosen to stay on to look after Great-Aunt Margaret, who has been poorly this winter, but Hart and I are back! The court has slowly been filtering in this week, and the queen (whom I have never spoken to but who seems so dignified and sweet) returned to Whitehall yesterday.

London is a sad shade of itself. Many of the houses and shops are boarded up, and grass *does* grow in the streets. A young family is living in Jane Smedley's house. We no longer know our neighbours; so many have moved away or . . . There are only two options these days: moved away or . . . They say officially that one in five Londoners died, although I have heard the figure was closer to one in three. Everyone knows someone . . . lost someone. Lizzie lost her father-in-law; Elizabeth lost her sister and aunt. From the theatre, we lost: Daniel, our doorkeeper; two stagehands; one of the dray horses (not from plague, of course); Mary, the wig mistress; and Sue, our charwoman. I think the Duke's only lost Paul, their lamplighter. The plague pits, just beyond the city, are shallow and full. *Oh London, what have you been through?*

Tom is recalling everyone, as the Lord Chamberlain is thought to be re-opening the theatres this week. Nick should arrive tonight. Teddy travelled down with us. We are, all of us, ready to laugh.

Note—The queen miscarried—again. And at Merton College to boot—the very place Castlemaine had her last healthy baby. I understand her pain and pray for her.

When We Are a Mad Couple

Tuesday, April 17, 1666— Theatre Royal

A success! At last I am a comedienne!

James (the middle of the Howard boys), together with Dryden, wrote *me* a comedy! Well, in truth, they just wrote a comedy, but they kept *me* in mind for a part as they wrote it. I am honoured! The play is *The English Monsieur*, and I play Lady Wealthy, costumed in a beautiful striped silk gown donated by Castlemaine herself (Rose had to take it in by half, as she is of a more rounded figure), and Hart plays Wellbred, my lover whom I much abuse but then reform and marry—and very well he does it, too! His timing is much improved. We tease and joust with barbed words but then call a truce and commit to loving each other. It is a brilliant new formula, and the audience thoroughly enjoyed us. We shall play it again tonight!

Note—Hart told me this evening that the queen's mother died last month in Portugal, but they have not told our little queen, as she is in a course of physic and they dare not upset her delicate emotional balance. How horrible to be lied to.

Later

I am a success, but Rose has returned to being a whore—terrible, not to be spoken aloud, but true—sadly and, I fear, permanently true.

April 22 — Maiden Lane

They have finally told the queen. All the court is now in deep mourning (finally). The queen is so small and looks even smaller in black.

April 30, 1666 — Maiden Lane

Our new styled comedy is a sensation, and I have become something of a known figure in town. They are calling it "mad couple comedy." Last night we were dining out, and an elderly husband and wife approached me. Hart tried his best to shield me from the attention (it discomfits him to have me looked at), but I did not mind their affection. I found it true and touching. They told me I am in person just as I am on the stage. "It must be a mark of my poor acting," I responded gaily. Hart rolled his eyes.

Note—There is *finally* talk of peace with the Dutch. I am ashamed to admit that often I forget we are even at war.

HAMPTON COURT, ENGLAND
TO OUR SISTER, THE MADAME OF FRANCE
FROM HIS MAJESTY KING CHARLES II
MAY 30, 1666

My dear sister,

I am tired of war. We have nothing to gain by pursuing this course. I have no longer the stomach, nor the funds (actually I never had much of either) to go on. I can only now wish for peace and leave the rest to God.

With love,
Charles

Hampton Court, England
To our sister, the Madame of France
From His Majesty King Charles II
June 5, 1666

It is being called the Four Days' Battle, and the outcome was terrifying. Only now are we understanding the full extent of our losses—eight ships and six thousand men; many burnt to death in their flaming vessels, a horrible death. The Dutch lost two thousand— together, eight thousand men—and for what? The wounded are pouring in, and we have not the physicians to treat them all. I have appointed Thomas Clifford as Commissioner for the Sick and Wounded Seamen and set the ladies of the court to cutting linen for bandages.

And still this country wants more. In my own council chamber, Arlington told Carlingford (making sure I was within earshot), "Our fleet is almost ready, and the Dutch are expecting us." As if we are to call upon them for an afternoon of tennis.

The vanity of this war sickens me. Holland was good to me during my exile. I still owe the House of Orange a substantial part of Mary's dowry—and this is how I have repaid them? This was a mistake.

Sick at heart but always your,
Charles

July 4, 1666— Gill House

The season is over, and we are away to the country. I am glad for the rest. Here is peace: away from the tumultuous stage and the bustling city. Here I can take the time to truly care for Hart, as I know he has been feeling neglected. Here we will take time together. I will try harder to quiet my mind and enliven my heart. Yet I can't help thinking, if it were true love, would it require all this effort?

Note—I invited Rose to come, but she declined. She seems fixed on her course.

When We Are Struck by the Fire

Sunday, September 2, 1666— London, Maiden Lane

Hart woke me in the night with the news that there is a great fire east of here. He had already sent Hugh to fetch Rose. Luckily, Mother and Grandfather are with Great-Aunt Margaret. "How did it happen?" I asked, rubbing my eyes.

"My love, this city is made of wood. Each house has hearths, candles, ovens, torches . . . It is easy enough."

We are as ready as we can be: our valuables are packed (we had not yet unpacked from our last trip to Hill House) and waiting in the hall; Ruby is on her lead next to me as I can't have her running off should we need to go quickly; and we have put wet sheets under the doors and water buckets beside every window. In the end we ran out of buckets and used pots and vases and even the footbath. Is there anything else? Oh the . . .

Chickens. Rose, Hugh, Cook, and I rounded up all the chickens and locked them in their coop. Hugh can put it in the wagon when we go. *If* we go.

Tom, wigless and hatless, arrived after breakfast to say that he has hired men to remove all the costumes and paintings in the theatre to a safer location and to stand by with water buckets in case the fire reaches Bridges Street. Hart left with him to secure the theatre, promising to be back in two hours. We are not to leave the house.

If it is not out soon he is sending me to the country. "Won't you come with me?" I asked, surprised by how very much I wanted him to come.

"I think my duty is here," he responded heavily.

Sunday, September 3, 1666 — Maiden Lane

Hart is just home for an hour's rest and food. He is exhausted, his hair singed and his face blackened. The fire seems to have begun in Thomas Farriner's bakery in Pudding Lane, just behind the Star Inn on Fish Street—we bought sugared buns there last Christmas. Farriner swears he properly banked his ovens, but nevertheless the fire broke out. Mayor Bludworth arrived quickly but refused to pull down the neighbouring houses to create a firebreak (disastrous!)—so it spread down to the warehouses of Thames Street and on and on. It is a monster. It raged through the lovely old church of St. Margaret's and St. Magnus the Martyr (a church that has stood in that spot since the conquest!), and then it reached the wharves: timber, pitch, hemp—a fire's favourites. There is a strong south-easterly wind, which is making matters worse.

Eventually the king and his brother the duke overrode the mayor and took control of the fire-fighting (so bold—they are at the forefront of the fire-fighters!), but it burns out of control. Hart has been at the king's side aiding in the organisation of the fire engines—the water supply is not consistent, and the streets are too narrow for these great machines to get close, and so really, all we have are bucket brigades to the river and hooks to pull down houses as fast as we can. I fear for our home in Drury Lane, but Hart says he cannot imagine that it would reach that far west, but then yesterday he would never have imagined it would reach St. Botolph's. This crisis has brought out his best self—efficient, patient, brave, and reasonable. There is nothing of the spoilt, sulky man he can be when threatened by things far less tangible.

Nine a.m.

Hart and Tom shared a hurried breakfast of sausage, buns, and pottage before setting out. Cook packed them a basket of hard-cooked eggs, dried meat, cheese, and bread, as well as flasks of goat's milk (cider and ale are far too flammable). They are both exhausted but still determined. Tom's left shoulder was burned yesterday when a street lamp collapsed on him. Rose rebandaged it this morning, but Hart forbade me to go to the apothecary for a cooling salve, even though it is just over in Chancery Lane. They want us to stay home and have promised to send word if the fire gets close. I am afraid of the blaze but anxious to be doing something useful.

Later

We went out. It was a silly thing to do, but I needed to see for myself that the house was safe, and Rose wanted to get some things from Lewkenor Lane. The air was white with ash. My face felt papery and hot in the obscured morning sun. I reached for Rose's hand and pulled her close beside me. We walked arm in arm as we had as little girls as we made our way through hazy streets. Everywhere were signs of hasty departure. On Longacre, packed cases stood outside an abandoned coach, its wheel cracked and left unmended; on St. Martin's Lane, chickens ran about the street, a goat rummaged though a rubbish heap, and the smell of rotting meat clouded about the deserted butcher shop. And then, in the hot, smoky air of Bow Street, we found a friend.

"Oh no!" Duncan said when he saw us. "Back home to Maiden Lane for both of you."

Startled, we both stood open-mouthed in the road, unsure of what to say. What *is* the etiquette when one runs into an old friend after a long and painfully awkward separation in the midst of a national crisis?

"But Duncan, we are just—" Rose began.

"Just being foolish as ever. Turn around," he interrupted, roughly took our hands, and pulled us in the opposite direction.

"Duncan, we are going to check on the house!" I tried to reason with him.

"The house is fine. I checked this morning."

Rose and I looked at him, surprised. *"This morning?"* Rose and I spoke in unison.

"Girls! Move!" he said, herding us back toward Maiden Lane.

It was only after he had safely escorted us back to the house that I stopped to wonder how he knew I lived there.

Rose spoke to Duncan in the music room for several minutes while I went to organise hot water for a bath. We were all covered in the fine ash that was drifting over the warm streets like a snow in summer. It seems Duncan has followed our lives from a careful distance, in case we had need of him. He looked in on Drury Lane during the plague until he finally left town. He checked on Drury Lane this morning. He has seen me sing upon the stage. He has seen Rose stand in Madame Ross's window, has seen Rose at the market, at the dress-maker, at the cheesemonger, at the mercer. He has watched over both of us, but it is Rose—summer, winter, autumn Rose—whom he waits for. He has never stopped waiting for Rose.

September 3, 1666—Official Notations for Privy Council Meeting on This Day to Be Entered into the Log-book

Notations taken by Secretary of State Henry Bennet, Earl of Arlington

Emergency session, three p.m.

The king and duke were both absent as they insist on fighting the fire personally. His Majesty and the duke sailed downriver to Queenhithe and, dispensing with Mayor Bludworth, who has proven inept at managing this disaster, called for Alderman Sir Richard Browne, a former mayor and hero of the Civil War. His Majesty ordered the Coldstream Guards into the city, organised by Sir Richard Browne. The king and the duke hope to halt the fire at St. Botolph's wharf, and there they remain. It has been documented throughout the city that the presence of the monarch and the heir to the throne do give the townspeople the heart to combat this disaster and the courage to keep order in the chaos. There is much trouble in obtaining the owner's permission to destroy a house—as a house destroyed by fire will be compensated by the government but one wilfully destroyed will not. The king has chosen to dispense with the owner's permission and create firebreaks where he sees fit—he carries with him a heavy purse of gold and distributes compensation where he can.

There is already talk of Catholics setting this fire purposefully. May God have mercy on London.

Nothing further to report.
Secretary of State Henry Bennet, Earl of Arlington

September 3, 1666—Official Notations for Privy Council Meeting on This Day to Be Entered into the Log-book

Notations taken by Secretary of State Henry Bennet, Earl of Arlington

Emergency evening session, nine p.m.

The king and the duke, together with the fire-fighters and citizenry, are making a stand at Three Cranes Stairs, but the wind has shifted to the north and the flames are moving back towards the city. If this continues, they will have to reassess their strategy.

In the twenty hours since the outbreak twenty-two wharves have been destroyed, six Livery Company Halls (including the Watermen, Vintners, and Fishmongers) and nine churches have been destroyed. So far the great Drapers Hall has been lucky.

The townspeople are evacuating on foot, carrying their belongings. Unharmed churches have become makeshift warehouses for the displaced to store their goods.

Nothing further to report.
Secretary of State Henry Bennet, Earl of Arlington

Later— Maiden Lane

We can now see the sky burning orange from the house. The streets are awake with eerie half-lit shadows. The church bells are ringing, calling all civic-minded citizens to help fight the flames. Many from the theatre have gone to help, soaking their clothes and hair in water before they went. In the morning Rose, Ruby, and I are leaving—*again*.

Later, four a.m.— Bill House (exhausted)

We carried six people safely away from the city: a mother, her four children, and an elderly man who had become separated from his family. The coach is only meant to hold four. Hart would be furious, but Hugh has promised not to tell. How glorious to be able to smell ordinary things again—cinnamon, apples, fresh laundry, peppermint—instead of a burning city.

September 4, 1666—Official Notations for Privy Council Meeting on This Day to Be Entered into the Log-book

Notations taken by Secretary of State Henry Bennet, Earl of Arlington

Emergency morning session, four a.m.

Reports that this fire may not have been accidental. Discussion this morning as to whether or not it could have been begun by foreigners (Dutch?) or Catholics. I have written to the forts at Gravesend, preventing any shipping from exiting the country, and have instructed that no persons or vessels may leave the Cinque Ports.

We have arrested Cornelius Reitvelt, a Dutchman and a baker, with a bakeshop in Westminster. He is being questioned in his involvement in the fire's outbreak and progress.

Nothing further to report.
Secretary of State Henry Bennet, Earl of Arlington

September 4, 1666—Official Notations for Privy Council Meeting on This Day to Be Entered into the Log-book

Notations taken by Secretary of State Henry Bennet, Earl of Arlington

Emergency morning session, six a.m.

Grave concerns of rioting in the City. A mob assaulted a member of the Portuguese ambassador's household, believing that they had seen him intentionally fire a house. Four Life Guards intervened when a Frenchman was assaulted by a mob believing that he, too, had intentionally fired a house. Both were placed in Bridewell Prison.

 Reports of looting throughout the City. The townspeople seem to have lost the will to fight this disaster and are looking to save what they can.

Nothing further to report.
Secretary of State Henry Bennet, Earl of Arlington

September 5, 1666
Maiden Lane
My dearest Mouse,

 I rode with the king and the Duke of York all this day. The king was magnificent. He rode to the very edge of the flames, his face blackened, his clothes soaked. I was awed and humbled by his courage and his very force of person. He ordered his victualler to send bread to the poor at Moorfields and proclaimed a day of fasting next month, whereby appointed men will go about to collect money for those suffering. He is verily a good king with a true care for the weal of his subjects. He is also a man, and is distraught and exhausted by the state of his beloved city. Beside him all the day were his valiant brother, the Duke of York, and his young son, James, the Duke of Monmouth (who manned the King's Guard).

The Royal Exchange burnt this day, as did Bridewell Prison. I can only pray that the poor souls held within were freed. I feel hopeful that the fire has almost run its course. Heaven knows what we will find when this is over.

I think of you in the green fields of Hill House. You are my comfort as I face this catastrophe. I understand your mother is to join you in the country? Your grandfather wrote to warn me. Courage!

Be well, my sweet,

Ever your,

Hart

Note—*Miraculously, there have not been above a half-dozen deaths reported. Unthinkably good luck.*

Thursday, September 6, 1666
Maiden Lane
My dearest Mouse,

It is over. London smoulders. The fire cut a mile-and-a-half swath through our city, stopping just short of our theatre. The king made a splendid speech this day at Moorfields. He insisted that it was an act of God and not man—there was no plot. No man was responsible. He promised to take Londoners under his special protection and vowed that together they would rebuild a greater London. He painted a picture of a new, modern city, built of brick and stone. He spoke of "this, our native city," reminding all who heard that he, too, was born in our glorious capital. Those hearing his words were filled with hope, and for myself, I must say that I am deeply enlivened at the thought of a new London. We have been struck down by plague and fire, and our spirits are yet encouraged to hope.

I will send for you soon, my love. You will return to a different city. The markets are all moved, and the Exchange is held in Gresham College (as well as the Royal Society). All churches are opened to house the poor. The city is still unpredictable as there are so many displaced persons, and the talk is rife with plots and arson. The Catholics and foreigners are naturally suspected. I feel easier knowing you are safe and away. I sent Hugh every day to check on the house in Drury Lane. It is safe. You are constantly in my thoughts.

Ever yours,

Hart

WHITEHALL, LONDON
SEPTEMBER 6, 1666

Minette,

It is over. We are safe. The city is in ruins. We must rebuild.

Charles

When We Begin to Rebuild

Tuesday, September 11, 1666—Official Notations For Privy Council Meeting on This Day to Be Entered into the Log-book

Notations taken by Secretary of State Henry Bennet, Earl of Arlington

Eight p.m.

The Privy Council met to consider Mr. Wren's plans for the rebuilding. They are detailed and exquisitely drawn but so quickly despatched after the fire as to cause some surprise among the members. The Royal Society was perturbed not to have approved these plans first, as Wren is one of their charter members, but we are glad to begin the reconstruction with all due haste.

Our reports show that many Londoners are erecting temporary shelters and living on the sites of their destroyed homes. Those Londoners who have cellars have roofed them over and are living within. The disentangling of property rights in the city will be left to the magistrates to decide, but it is a matter that must be dealt with fairly and promptly. It is unfortunate but necessary for some to forfeit their property to the Crown, as the streets must be widened to prevent any future calamity of this kind. If said home-owners feel they have been dealt with unfairly, they may petition the Crown.

His Majesty took Mr. Wren's plans to his own apartments to give them further consideration.

Nothing further to report,
Secretary of State Henry Bennet, Earl of Arlington

Gill House, Surrey

Teddy has arrived to keep us company!

"The smoke *ruined* my new striped silk chaise longue—that was really the final straw, my petals. A man can only take so much," he said, primly removing his pale leather gloves. "Filthy beastly thing, fire—very destructive."

"And so you walked?" Rose asked, tearing a piece off her sugar bun.

We were seated in the garden under the shade of a horse-chestnut tree on what felt like a summer afternoon. The dapper pink gladioli I planted last spring near the boxwood hedge had finally bloomed, the blush-pink peonies—unfashionable but one of my favourites—were out after I had given up on them, and the air smelled of fresh earth and honeysuckle. So clean and clear and far from soot-choked London.

"You walked to *where*?" I asked, puzzled. Teddy lived in Milk Street.

"Out." He said vaguely, reaching for a warm bun. "Well, out to my wretched cousin Henry's house—I always disliked that he lived in provincial little Clapham, but that day it suited me very well. Me and the ten or so who tagged along in the hope of finding food and a bath. Cousin Henry was not happy I had invited company—terrible curmudgeonly man."

"Clapham!" Teddy is not known for physical exertion, and the village of Clapham was miles away. "How awful," I said, imagining a smoke-stained Teddy trudging through the fiery streets.

"Once I fully accepted that my shoes were ruined, it was all right—the lilac velvet pair with the black heels—*dommage*. I am going to see if that lovely little man in Honey Lane next to All Hallows Church can repair them, but then he might not be there now," Teddy mused.

"Honey Lane might not be there now," Rose said, reaching for another bun. "I think I heard the church and churchyard burnt along with the houses in North Cheapside." Rose furrowed her forehead, trying to recall.

"That lovely old church! Wasn't it there from the Crusades?" I asked.

"Mmm, before, I think," Teddy said. "As long as my lovely St. Mary Magdalen is still standing."

I smiled. Teddy often attends morning service at that beautiful church and is surprisingly devout (although he swears it is the cherubic choristers he goes to see).

"How long did you walk?" asked Rose, tipping back her bonnet and tilting her face to the warm afternoon sun.

"Hours," Teddy sighed. "We were quite a jolly bunch once we got clear of that fiasco of a fire brigade. I understand the king came and sorted out that silly mayor. They say Bonnie Charlie actually rode so close his coat caught fire. *Quel courage.*"

"Yes, Hart wrote to me and said he has inspired the city with his bravery and care."

"Yes, but will he *care* enough to rebuild it?" Rose asked shrewdly, licking the sticky sugar from her fingers.

Later

Mother is proving unruly and difficult. Each day Cook hides all the spirits, and Mother spends all day searching for them. Yesterday she ransacked the winter store-rooms and upended a rack of dried hops. Tiresome.

HAMPTON COURT, ENGLAND
TO OUR DAUGHTER, THE MADAME OF FRANCE AT ST. CLOUD
FROM HER MAJESTY QUEEN HENRIETTA MARIA
SEPTEMBER 12, 1666

Ma fille,

What an ordeal! The footmen quite lost their heads in all the commotion. I insisted that they desist their panicking and think properly. I ordered all the birds in the aviary set free as the groundskeeper could not manage to have their travelling cages prepared in time. Unfortunately, the birds flew only as far as the roof, and from there they watched the frenzy below. It will be impossible to round them all up again.

All was in order and then at the last moment I remembered the christening robe. Imagine if we had left it! Luckily, the palace remained untouched (including the chapel), although I shall have to go over the household inventory most carefully, as this is just the sort of opportune moment when a servant could make off with something priceless. Crisis can often bring out the very worst in people.

With love,
Maman

Note—*The servants actually wanted to waste precious time packing their own things. Can you imagine? What could they have had worth saving?*

ST. GERMAIN, FRANCE
TO HER MAJESTY QUEEN HENRIETTA MARIA
FROM PRINCESSE HENRIETTE-ANNE, DUCHESSE D'ORLÉANS
SEPTEMBER 16, 1666

Maman,

There are awful pamphlets circulating in France (printed by the Dutch, no doubt). They claim that the recent tragedy in London was the will of God, visiting his vengeance on the English for burning the Dutch ships.

Please, please, do your very best to ensure that neither James nor Charles sees this terrible libel. James, because he would rush headlong into a brave but foolhardy course of action, punishing printers hither and yon, and Charles, because he would believe it is true.

With love,
Minette

To be delivered by hand to Mrs. Ellen Gwyn, Hill House, Surrey
September 20, 1666
London
My dear,

It was announced today that the king has employed a young architect of genius, Mr. Christopher Wren, to help guide our city to its rebirth. Unfortunately, his city-wide plan would require too many of our citizenry to forfeit their homes, as the restructuring would be quite comprehensive, but His Majesty has given him

the rebuilding of the churches of London, St. Paul's, of course, being the primary
concern. (They say the churches were the gems in Wren's plans anyway.)

The London horses are already growing accustomed to the sounds of rebuilding,
but I am afraid our Ruby is in for a dreadful noisy shock. She hates the sounds of
carpentry!

I long to see you,
Hart

September 21, 1666— Gill House (late)

"Mmm, I hear Wren draws scrumptious things," Teddy said, stretching his
toes out towards the fire. Avoiding his wife and his overbearing in-laws, he
has been staying here with us.

"Isn't he the one from Oxford?" I asked sleepily. I remembered hearing
about him during the plague.

"Yes, the short don we saw striding around the Bodleian—genius comes
in such amusing packages, don't you think?"

Note—We heard this afternoon that both All Hallows and St. Mary Magdalen were destroyed by the fire. "Mr. Wren will build us some new ones," I
said, trying to comfort.

September 21, 1666—Official Notations for Privy Council Meeting on This Day to Be Entered into the Log-book

Notations taken by Secretary of State Henry Bennet, Earl of Arlington

Ten a.m.

Seven petitions today for royal debts in arrears:

Mr. John Wink: Jeweller—1,400 pounds (ruby earrings for Lady Castlemaine)

Mr. Jacob Worthing: Jeweller—2,800 pounds (diamond ring for Lady Castlemaine and a gold timepiece for the queen)

Mr. Francis Hardecastle: Jeweller—600 pounds (jewelled ring for Mrs. Moll Davis)

Mr. Eliot Flat: Milliner—500 pounds (three ensembles for Lady Castlemaine, gloves not included)

Mr. Samuel Parish: Tailor—1,200 pounds (six ensembles for Lady Castlemaine, gloves and corsetry included)

Mr. Christopher Hatley: Clockmaker—1,450 pounds (ten small gold clocks for His Majesty)

Mr. Richard Wincomb: Member of His Majesty's wind orchestra—2 guineas (back pay)

It was suggested among the council that the Crown find the funds to meet these debts privately, rather than apply to the Parliament.

In addition: In order to become less reliant on foreign imports, now that much of our own industry is destroyed, the king has banned French fashions for the foreseeable future. No plans on how to enforce such a law.

Nothing further to report,
Secretary of State Henry Bennet, Earl of Arlington

When We Return Home

September 27, 1666 — London! (wind blowing ash everywhere)

Ruby is perplexed by all our backing and forthing. I am happy to be back in the capital and am relieved to have escaped my family. Their ability to turn even the most public disaster into a personal calamity astounds me. Rose was distraught as she was unable to rescue her gowns from Madame Ross's before our departure, and she is sure that Mathilde, a rival French whore, has made off with them in the chaos. She talked of little else all the way to town—exasperating.

Mother got drunk and fell down the kitchen stairs, spraining her ankle and squashing a bag of ripe tomatoes—messy. We left her to recuperate at Hill House, attended by Perry, Hart's new valet, and Kate, the scullery maid—heaven help them.

I have only today ventured out into the wreckage of London, and I was shocked by what I found. The city is in ruins—that I expected—but daily life continues, *miraculously*. Shopkeepers whose shops burnt to the ground have set up in tented, temporary structures and are carrying on. Blacksmiths are blacksmithing in the street; cheesemongers are cheesemongering out of makeshift barrows; mothers feeding their children in the rubble where their kitchens stood. *Hooray for Londoners!*

Note—Hart just poked his head in to tell me that although the theatres will remain closed for some time, we have been invited to play at Whitehall. To *revive* the spirits, says the king.

WHITEHALL, LONDON
SEPTEMBER 29, 1666

Minette,

You may think me wicked, but I am filled with hope that we may create a new and efficient city. This palace is something I should dearly like to tear down and begin again. It is a mess. If only we can find the funds!

Charles

September 30, 1666— London

I went by hackney to the new market today on Tower Hill. All the talk was of conspiracy. Who started the fire? Everyone is suspected—the Quakers, the French, the Dutch, certainly any foreigners, but Catholics most of all. It is fear that fuels these suspicions. Why would Catholics deliberately burn London? It is not logical. That they are obsessively seeking out a *who* rather than a *what* is irritating. Everyone is always so keen to find a who. A better fire brigade system and designated firebreaks sound to me like a better place to spend energy. There is also more quiet, more secret talk of the government's involvement. That in order to create a new and glorious London we had to burn the old. I do not believe such things of people.

Later

Rose returned from the Exchange (the New Exchange in a new spot—everything is new now) this morning and told me a ghastly rumour. They (the ever chattering *they*) are saying that the king might have started the fire himself! They say with the new building plans he stands to gain three hundred thousand pounds! "No," I told her vehemently. "He loves his city . . . he was the one riding around putting *out* the fire. It is ridiculous." Rose agreed that it was a nonsense rumour, but a sticky one. She's heard it three times already this morning.

When I Give My Royal Performance

What an evening!

We did it. Hart and I and the company played George Buckingham's *The Chances,* for the king and queen and all the court. The queen wore a simply but elegantly cut amethyst gown, and the king wore a dazzling white silk coat with black-worked cuffs—only this king could pull that off. Buckingham stood off to the side and chewed on the end of his thick blond wig in anxiety until the play was over. Rose sewed me a stunning silver gown of layered silk. The light layers gave a floating effect, and I felt like I soared through the dancing without touching the ground. As soon as we left the palace I shamelessly hitched up my beautiful new gown to keep it out of the London mud. The messy rebuilding plus the recent rain has made the city a river of mud.

Rose has been working with Madame Leonine, the famous French dress-maker who has recently moved to London. She has set up a small atelier in Broad Street. She was lucky to get a space, as the reshuffling after the fire left so few vacant, and is already catering to the highest ladies in the land. It is an unlikely pairing, but she and Rose work well together. Both realists, they deliver exactly what they promise.

Later— Maiden Lane

The performance was witty and sharp and energetic—my muscles throb, and my face aches from smiling as I tumble into bed. Still, it is a successful formula—smile, sally, jab, forgive, laugh. Everyone enjoys the fast repartee—except perhaps Hart, who can sometimes look wounded as I hurl these barbed lines at him (all in the script, and all in fun). I always take time to reassure him afterwards, although why he should need reassurance when he can plainly see that they are not my words is beyond me. It is exhausting, and my declarations of love grow more adamant.

"You must become a more convincing liar, darling," Teddy scolded tonight, pulling the last pins from my tightly upswept hair.

"I wish I did not have to lie," I responded with my customary candour, raking my fingers through my heavy curls, scratching my itchy scalp.

His eyes met mine in the mirror. "But if this is the life you wish to live, you pays your money, you takes your choice."

Note—Castlemaine was not in attendance, as I hear she is very much visibly carrying the king's fifth child, but she has requested a repeat performance for select friends tomorrow night!

October 28— Whitehall

It has become custom for us to do double performances with a costume change in between: the first for the king and queen and court, the second for the king and Castlemaine and court. Strangely, everyone pretends that this is not the case. The audience pretends that they have not just seen the play, and we pretend that we have not just performed the play. Bizarre. Tom frets over the expense of extra costumes.

I watch the king, in the centre of it all. He is courteous and even affectionate to his little barren queen, and seems comfortable but not overly enraptured with Castlemaine. It is *la belle Stuart* who holds his interest. She moves easily (if vapidly) between both worlds, and the king's eyes never leave her shapely backside.

Castlemaine has taken to addressing me after the performances. She seeks my advice about gowns and shoes and dancing and toilette.

"I must get some of that lovely appley scent you use," Castlemaine said tonight, cornering me in the Matted Gallery. "It would be charming for the country."

I looked at her uncertainly. Her own scent was an oppressive musk. "I'll ask my apothecary to send some to you," I said with brittle gaiety.

"Oh, do!" Castlemaine said, squeezing my arm conspiratorially. Just then a shy thin girl of about five years emerged from behind Castlemaine's skirts. "My daughter Charlotte," she said, pushing the little girl towards me. "Charlotte is here at the request of His Majesty, her father," Castlemaine said pointedly, just in case I had mistaken her parentage. "She is interested in music and the arts. Mrs. Gwyn is an *actress,* Charlotte," she said in that sing-song voice adults often use with children.

"On the stage?" the little girl asked solemnly, her eyes growing large.

"Yes," I said, amused.

"Do you dance and sing?"

"Yes."

"Tonight?"

"Yes."

She sucked in her breath sharply, considering this important information. "I love to dance and sing. May I be an actress?" she asked, turning to her mother.

Her mother laughed a throaty, rich laugh. "No, precious, daughters of kings do not go on the stage."

Hearing his daughter's voice, the king broke away from his conversation with Lord Arlington and joined our unlikely trio.

"What's this?" he asked his daughter. "Up so late?"

"I thought Your Majesty would enjoy our daughter's company on such a lovely evening." Castlemaine said sweetly, with a sly hint of warning.

The king frowned. "I think it is time for bed, sweetheart," he said, leaning down to Charlotte.

She bobbed him a miniature curtsey good night, and her nurse stepped forward to whisk her off to bed.

"One a.m., madam?" the king said quietly.

Just then I heard *la belle Stuart*'s peal of laughter, and the king's head swivelled round like a dog hearing his master's call.

Without waiting for Castlemaine's response, the king moved off into the crowd to find her. I looked at Castlemaine, who had forgotten my presence. Single-minded absorption played across her face. For a moment she dropped the careful masque of the unruffled first mistress and looked like an irritated fishwife.

Later in the big bed at Maiden Lane I considered the evening. I am flattered by Castlemaine's attention, but find it unsettling, too. I cannot think what has possessed her to take me up. It might be because I am a particular friend of her cousin, George Buckingham. It might be because very rarely the king smiles and winks at me (twice in the last month!), although Hart makes sure never to leave us alone together. Hard to fathom Castlemaine's motives—all I truly know is that they are not without calculation.

Note—Mr. Williamson, who publishes the *London Gazette*, wrote a scathing article defending the king. He said His Majesty would never consider profiting from the disaster, and shame on anyone who would think he would. Bravo!

November 17, 1666— Theatre Royal!

The theatres are reopened! Yet Hart does not seem pleased. How the audience has missed us. It is delicious to play for them again, and they are frantic in their adoration. They howl with delight and thunder their applause. It can be frightening.

Note—Women are *still* wearing the fashionable long trains of last season; Mrs. Kendall's was petal pink, for God's sake. It seems lunacy in this city of dust and dirt and reconstruction. They are trailing London mud all over the carpets—the new carpets Tom bought for the refurbishment. Tom hopes this horrid fashion will go away soon.

December 8, 1666— Maiden Lane (rainy and muddy)

A whole week off—heaven. We have on Beaumont and Fletcher's *The Maid's Tragedy* (dull and long) at the moment. Becka is playing Evadne, and I must say, she does do it well. Poor Teddy is mourning the loss of that part. Evadne was his favourite. "It was my best," he said wistfully this morning over coffee and toast. "Better than my Epicoene, better than my Juliet . . . Ahem, Ellen!"

"What?" I said, surprised, looking up from my script—I am Becka's understudy, and I am nowhere with my lines.

"Better than my *Juliet?*" he repeated, waving his toast for emphasis. "And then you say . . . ?"

"I didn't see it. I was too young."

"Ellen!" he shrieked.

"No, Teddy, nothing has ever been better than your Juliet," I placated, hiding my smile behind my coffee cup.

"Thank you," he said graciously. "Becka, that thundering trollop, has no business in my roles—or my gowns. My yellow silk, she wore last night— the gossamer sleeves were perfection," he moaned. "I'm sure she has ruined them with her beefy appendages."

I laughed. Even if Becka turned in a flawless performance, Teddy would find fault. Thank heaven I am spared such critique. I do not want that part—even with yellow gossamer sleeves—and I could not bear to play another lamentable death scene. I happily leave it to the Marshall sisters.

Nick is cast opposite, so Teddy has the week off as well. We have been running about like truant children, gaming and dancing and dicing. Hart disapproves, naturally. I try my best to keep it from him, but he hears about it anyway; it is not the servants but the gossip sheets that give me away. Damn Ambrose Pink, whoever he may be. The theatre is a hotbed of gossip. Hart's temper is growing, and I fear I shall never make him happy. If I am honest, I will admit that I have less and less of a heart to try.

6.

Independent Ellen

When My Heart Is Troubled

Tuesday, December 18, 1666 — Theatre Royal (snow!)

Back in the harness. We are doing *The English Monsieur* again—and are receiving a wonderful response. London is so ready to laugh after all she has been through this twelvemonth. Parties every night and dancing to dawn, followed by a light cooked breakfast in the morning.

"You cannot keep up this pace, Ellen," Johnny Rochester told me this morning, yawning. We had not yet been to bed. "Eventually, you will have to go home."

I want to dance and dance and never go back to Maiden Lane, I thought ungratefully.

Note—Castlemaine spoke to me at Lady Jemimah's this evening—strangely, I keep finding myself on the most extraordinary guest lists. "You brighten a room," Teddy says. "Having you there pulls an evening together." Odd, as I feel as though I stand out terribly in such company. Anyway, Castlemaine was determined to ensnare me in yet another of her inane conversations about toilette. I find her rapid shifts in tone and volume baffling—shrill and sing-songy when she speaks to women, and then throaty and husky when she speaks to men. I suppose she thinks the throatiness is alluring, but it just sounds like she needs to take a cough mixture. Shifting uncomfortably from foot to foot, I looked to Teddy for rescue, but he was too busy admiring her shoes. Teddy loathes men's shoes, not that his delicate, beribboned high-heeled confections look much like men's shoes.

For lack of imagination, I found myself answering truthfully and pointing out that, *yes*, she wears too much lip paint and, *yes*, it does age her. She looked startled, not expecting that response, but if she does not want the answer, then she should learn not to ask the question. At least it ended the gruesome interview.

Wednesday, December 19 — Theatre Royal (still The English Monsieur)

I am furious!

We were in the middle of the reconciliation scene when Hart (playing Wellbred) left the script entirely. I am quite accustomed to small adjustments everywhere, but when the time came for Hart to ask me to be his wife, he skipped the line completely. Thinking it an honest omission, I covered and proposed to him (most untraditionally—but then these are untraditional characters), and he *declined*! Dumbfounded, I responded tartly, "Well, that suits me, because as you well know I make a most suitable mistress." The audience roared, roundly enjoying the inside joke, but Hart flushed angry red and was most discomfited by my bold reply. How dare he! I will not be shamed by him!

Note—Tom was in the house and thought the script change was brilliant. Now we must perform it like this every night. Torture! I told him if that were the case he must raise my salary by twenty shillings, and he agreed!

WHITEHALL, LONDON
TO OUR SISTER, THE MADAME OF FRANCE
FROM HIS MAJESTY KING CHARLES II
DECEMBER 23, 1666

Happy Christmas, my dear sister,

Spending the Christmas season at Whitehall, again. I had hoped to be at Windsor or Greenwich (the new palace is coming along splendidly!), but it was not to be. I am overseeing the rebuilding, and alas, that means I must be near the rebuilding, and what noisy rebuilding it is. With all the talk of who might have started the fire—the Dutch, the Catholics, the Quakers—I have finally unmasked the culprit: the stonemasons. It must be! For they are profiting from this disaster like none other.

I have finally come to understand the impossibility of implementing the modern city of my dreams. My Londoners are hell-bent on re-creating the cramped, overcrowded city of the past. It would require too much organisation, and certainly too much compensation to build the wide-avenued stone city I desire. Instead of neat, pleasantly laid-out squares, with communal gardens for all to enjoy, they want to fence in their hard-won little patch of earth. I do understand it. Time was when I, too, wanted only a small patch of earth all my own. Do you often think of those lean, desperate years? They seem so very far away now. The only benefit was seeing you often, my dear. Kiss your children for me.

I am ever your,
Charles

December 25 — Christmas (frost)

Hart and I live like strangers. His anger grows apace with my success. I hardly recognise us—he is so tightly strung, and at this point I am uncaring of his discomfort. It is cruel, but I do feel as though I have tried every remedy to jolly him into mirth without success, so now I do my best to ignore it, which is a coarse solution and naturally only makes it worse. Tonight, we are going to the Duke's House to see *Macbeth* (bad luck to say, turn around three times and spit), our own house being closed for Christmas. I ordered a new lilac *moiré* suit and a grey velvet coat especially, perfect with my new silver lace slippers. As I paid for it myself, Hart could not complain about the expense. Rose patterned the gown and Madame Leonine designed the coat, and I was pleased with all the results. Rose's skill is growing, and I am often directing ladies to her for similar designs. I am pleased, as dressmaking is a skill that improves with age, while her other profession . . .

It (I'm not saying it again) is a ferociously menacing play and hardly in the spirit of Christmas joy, but I held my tongue as I did not want Hart to change his mind and decide we should stay here. We almost never go out together anymore, and he refuses to entertain at home. I should be happy for us to spend time alone, but instead I find it wearing and miserable. In company Hart is attentive and solicitous of my well-being. As soon as we are alone, I am invisible and he is foul-tempered. Betsey has made up the white bedroom for me.

December 29— Midnight

"Ellen, are you awake?" Ruby poked her head out from under the covers at the sound of Hart's voice. He considers it ruinous to allow a dog to sleep in the bed, but I love her small sturdy warmth. I opened my eyes just enough to see him standing in the doorway holding a candle aloft, peering into my new room. It is smaller and quite cheery and looks over the garden. "I only thought if you are awake"—he continued awkwardly— "perhaps you two would like to come back to our room. Ellen, *are* you awake?"

I did not stir nor respond. I dread returning to his bedroom, with his heavy masculine furniture and oppressive presence. Ruby settled back down beside me, and eventually Hart closed the door. I listened to his retreating footsteps. How can I refuse him? But then, how can I consent? Comfortable or no, I must leave this house. If the baby had lived . . . but she didn't.

ST. GERMAIN, FRANCE
TO KING CHARLES II
FROM LE ROI LOUIS XIV

The common loss we have had over the death of your sister's son, our nephew, the Duc de Valois, touches us both so closely that the only difference in our mutual grief is that mine began a few days sooner than yours.

Louis

OXFORD, ENGLAND
JANUARY 1, 1667

My Minette,

Oh, my dear. I have just this minute had word—your son. I cannot bear to think of the pain this must cause your heart. I had to write to you, to tell you that I am thinking of you. There is nothing to say but that I will be praying for his soul and for yours.

Charles

When I Run Away

January 15, 1667—Drury Lane

I have done it. Hart and I can no longer live under the same roof. I am returned to Drury Lane. The house feels small and shabby, but here I am, beholden to no one. I miss Betsey, Hugh, Cook, and the ease of Maiden Lane, but I could not endure the constant suspicion and jealousy. In the last weeks, Hart had taken to interrogating Hugh as to my whereabouts and searching my dressing room for imagined love notes—I have had to carry this journal with me always—insufferable. Hart sends sad letters now, begging for my return, but I can never go back. I could not breathe in that pretty prison, and in my heart I know that his suspicions were grounded in fact. I do want truer love than what we shared. All my protestations (ever more fervent) were dishonest. I care deeply for his happiness, but I care for him as my friend and guardian, not as a lover. I grew up in his bed and can thank him for all my present success and security, but I cannot offer him my heart in return. I wish that I could, but I have tried and I have failed.

We have told no one of our separation and painfully maintain our relationship in public. "The public is not *prepared* for our dissolution," Hart says plaintively, asking for more time. "Please come back to me."

I do not care two figs for the public's concern over my private life, but these matters of appearance affect him deeply. It is the least I can do for him. Ruby misses Hart terribly and is confused in our new home.

Note—Johnny is trying to win his abducted heiress again. Let us hope he does not wind up in the Tower. I hope someone ends up finding a true love.

January 29, 1667
London
To Mistress Elizabeth Malet,

  She yields, she yields—pale Envy said "Amen!"
  The first of women to the last of men.
  Marry me.

Ever yours,
John Rochester

February 2, 1667—Theatre Royal (my seventeenth birthday)

Whispers:

Everyone knows now, but no one speaks openly of our separation. Hart threw me a magnificent birthday party tonight. There was music and dancing and heaps of beautifully wrapped presents.

"I cannot accept them," I told him sadly.

"You must," he told me firmly.

"I won't." Ruby and I went home to Drury Lane.

February 7, 1667—Drury Lane (early)

This morning, early, before rehearsals, Teddy hurtled in with a copy of the *Gazette* tucked under his arm. He was wearing his new ladybird-red waistcoat, and it suits him well, although his normally coiffed hair was disordered and his delicate cheeks splotched with colour.

"You *must*," he puffed . . . He had been running, and he is not accustomed to running. "You *must* . . . read this," he panted, thrusting the news sheet at me.

I scanned the page. "What?"

"Here! Here!" He jabbed the paper. "Look, it is *Becka*!" And there was a brief but astonishing article: "Mrs. Rebecca Marshall, having been attacked with a turd outside the Theatre Royal last night, is suing for 'protection and justice for the future.'"

"Becka . . . ?" Disbelieving, for Becka was generally quite popular, I quickly scanned down the page. "In the *face*?" Good God.

"And the *hair*!" Teddy gasped. "It is *fantastic*! It is *genius*!" gasped Teddy, who has never liked the Marshall sisters.

Later— Theatre Royal

Teddy has not stopped giggling all day. I have caught cold and cannot stop sneezing.

Note—Two Dutch ships sunk, and one of ours fired. Absurd waste! After all we have lost recently, why do we risk more? As a country we should be united, peaceful, and constructive—not unheeding of our mistakes and bent on a course that has never suited us.

Later—Drury Lane

My cold has gotten worse. Mother consulted Grandfather's volume of Culpeper's *English Physician*, now worn with use.

"Wintergreen or willow tree juice, for fever," she said, turning the pages. "And lungwort for your cough. You could line your boots with tansy leaves, but we haven't got any. I'm sure Mr. Hart has—"

"No, Mother. I'll stop at the apothecary tomorrow."

"But Mr. Hart could—"

"No."

February 14 — St. Valentine's Day

We opened *Flora's Vagaries* today. I play the jade Flora. She is strong-willed and fickle and constant only in her own self-interest. Yet she is loveable and full of mischief as well. She is parts of myself, I admit.

The audience have made me their own. They seem to love my rougher edges and wilder ways. Is that really me? The edges of my self are getting fuzzy. They call out the name they have given me and cheer for me as the curtain comes down. It is an intoxicating thing to feel their love. It keeps me strong. It keeps me safe. No man can take this from me. Hart watches me from the wings. His expression unreadable.

Note—My cold has improved. Mother suggested blood-letting, but I believe it weakens rather than strengthens me—a lunatic opinion, as far as Mother is concerned.

When I Enjoy My Merry Mob

February 23 — Theatre Royal (Flora's Vagaries)

Johnny Rochester, Henry Savile, a hearty raw-boned sort of man whom Rochester obviously adores, and Lord Sedley came to the tiring rooms after the performance this evening:

I was changing out of my Flora costume and into my new taffy-pink gown with the soft belled sleeves, ruinously expensive but so pretty, when they sauntered through the door, taking no notice of the other players in varying states of undress.

"Your dirty secret is out, my darling," Rochester teased, sitting down at my slim-legged dressing table. "You are a free woman, and all of London is waiting with bated breath to see *who* you will choose."

Sedley drew in a huge breath and held it to make his point. I ignored him. In the mirror I saw Kitty surreptitiously tug down her bodice to catch their attention.

"Well, it cannot be you, you randy reprobate," I threw back at Rochester, hurrying to finish my laces.

"No, alas, I have entered that glorious temple of matrimonial bliss, never to emerge again," he said in saintly tones, eyes pointed heavenward. Johnny *finally* married Elizabeth Malet, his captive heiress—much to their mutual delight, it is said.

I looked at my friend, and in truth he was glowing beneath his unruffled façade.

"Give him a month and he'll be on the prowl again," predicted Sedley, blowing out his cheeks and picking up various cosmetic pots, scattering powder hither and yon.

Ruby, snuggled in her basket on the floor, promptly sneezed.

"Do stop touching things you do not understand." I took the pot away from him. "I am so pleased for you, Johnny. It is like a fairy-tale," I said, tying the last of my laces and checking my face in the mirror—my cheeks were flushed pink, not enough powder, but *heigh-ho*.

"Ah, fairy stories," said Savile. "Keep in mind that they are peopled with witches and dragons and trolls and mean big-footed stepsisters and evil queens—"

"And kings for that matter," added Sedley absently. "Actually, the kings are more often careless, rather than evil, come to think of it," he went on to no one in particular.

"In short, beware of romance and royalty," summed up Johnny, pinching my cheek and giving me a meaningful look—why? "We must eat," he continued lightly. "I am ravenous and I've heard reported that I tend to go into a killing rage when vexed by hunger." The rumours about Johnny are always astounding.

We left by the side door and headed for the Bear Tavern. They serve the best pidgeon pie in London. I choose to believe in fairy-tales, I thought, walking alongside the three greatest cynics of our age. Funny, I'll bet Johnny does, too.

April 1667 — Will's Coffee-house (warm)

Shocking gossip:

La belle Stuart has run away from court and eloped with the Duke of Richmond! He is said to be handsome but somewhat simple (sounds an ideal match for her), has been widowed twice, and has an excellent income. The Earl of Clarendon supposedly helped her to arrange it. When the king confronted her, she challenged him that the duke could offer her the honourable state of matrimony—could he offer her such a thing? How could he deride her choice? The king is said to be in a terrible temper, and Castlemaine openly gloating. I hope it is a true romance. A fairy-tale, indeed!

May 24 — Theatre Royal

Dryden has written me a brilliant part. Florimel (not a name I care for, but *heigh-ho*) is a mad, mad girl. She is tricked with sparkle and wit and a carnival heart. It is a huge role, and I am *never* off the stage. Daunting, but I refuse to be daunted. Unfortunately, it is only one of three plays we are putting on in the next fortnight. I have taken to memorizing scripts during meals, while I walk, and in the bath. *Quel* glamour, as Teddy would say. Hart plays Celadon (a name I do quite care for), and together we are sparring lovers who (bless Dryden's tact) choose *not* to marry but instead remain mistress and gallant. It is getting easier to play opposite Hart, but I do not think I could bear to marry him *again* onstage.

I spend part of the play disguised as a boy and in breeches. *Quel* glamour, indeed. What freedom! What fun! I can dance and dance, loose-legged and free. I become a naughty forest elf in breeches, neither man nor woman, just a small wild spirit. No idea what comes over me.

Note—Johnny Rochester came to the tiring rooms this evening with Charles Sackville, Lord Buckhurst. He cut a carelessly elegant figure with his thickly waved blond hair (his own—very handsome); his silver-trimmed, sage-green coat, and the rows and rows of expensive lace at his wrists (expensive but dusty—he is not careful with his cuffs like other men, but then I suppose he can always afford new ones). Unlike most men who come back to the tiring rooms, he did not fixate on the women undressing, nor drown me in empty compliments. Everything he says is sharp and pointy and aimed to provoke—a wicked tongue (forked, no doubt—must remember to check).

TUNBRIDGE WELLS, ENGLAND

TO OUR SISTER, THE DUCHESSE D'ORLÉANS, THE MADAME OF FRANCE

FROM HIS MAJESTY KING CHARLES II

Minette,

You may think me ill-natured, but if you consider how hard it is to swallow an injury done by a person for whom I have such tenderness, you may begin to understand my distress. The resentment I bear towards her matches the depth of my affection. If you were as acquainted with the fantastical little gentleman called Cupid as I am, you would neither wonder nor take ill at any change in affairs in his keeping.

It is true that the idea of divorce has been much on my mind. Only Catherine's inevitable wretchedness at such a separation, and the satisfaction this course of action will bring to her detractors, has thus far stopped me. And yet I tell you, Frances may have been worth it. Her unassailable virtue and her simple sweetness have driven me mad with wanting. I am sorry to be so blunt, but who else can I tell? If only she were to become ugly and undesirable and I could possess her without rivalry. The business has made me miserable.

All love as I am your,
Charles

May 30 — Will's Coffee-house

"Oh, my dear, astonishing news," Teddy announced over our usual coffee and toast. "He's done it." Teddy's breath was coming in brief, noisy bursts.

"Done what?" I asked absently. I was trying to read yesterday's smudged news sheet describing the queen happily frolicking at Tunbridge Wells in boy's clothes—she seems to also undergo a magical woodland transformation in breeches. How chic. Despite all the rumours, there seems to be no hint of divorce for the royal couple, although it is said he would have thrown over the queen and married Frances Stuart. Well, if he *would* have done it, why *didn't* he? People are so confident of what they would have done once they no longer have the chance. I think he had a lucky escape, frankly. The queen's famed gentleness will only refine in time, whereas Frances's shrill sweetness will rot the teeth. She is such a pedantically predictable woman; his passion is mystifying. I returned from my reverie to see Teddy nervously fidgeting with his breakfast.

"Yes, Teddy?" I prompted. "What has Hart done now?" Hart's behaviour had been so erratic of late and his temper increasingly short since I broke with him.

"Hart, your Hart, has been . . ." He crumbled his toast, unsure how to proceed.

"He is not *my* Hart." I gritted my teeth against the inevitable pun.

"Your erstwhile Hart? Well, he has been frequenting Castlemaine's bed, and now the newshounds have it." Teddy finally got in out all in one breath and then slumped in relief.

"Castlemaine?"

"Yes."

"*The* Castlemaine?"

"Yes."

"You're sure?"

"Yes. Do you mind, dearest?" Teddy delicately wiped his fingers on a napkin and took my hand with concern.

"Since when?"

Teddy shrugged as if to say, Does it matter when? Obviously, he has known for some time—therefore, their affair has been going on for some time. When . . . ?

"No, no," I said automatically, collecting my thoughts. "But she—"

"Yes I know, just out of childbed. Tacky, really. Goodness, she has energy."

"I am pleased for him," I heard myself say, offering empty words, as if from a distance. Hart and Castlemaine? My Hart? His Castlemaine? Did I mind?

Later—Drury Lane

I am startled, surely. But do I mind? I probe the thought like a bruise, searching for the answering pain. No, I do not believe I do. I feel free.

June 5— Theatre Royal

I feel Hart's eyes upon me. Do I know? Have I heard? Do I care? The theatre is full of whispers. I am made stronger by his shame.

Later— Theatre Royal (after the show)

Humming in the hallways, I keep encountering Hart. Tonight, I laughed aloud for no reason. Everyone turned to look.

> *June 5, 1667*
> *Farm Cottage, Oxford*
> *Dearest Ellen,*
>
> *Great-Aunt Margaret is still weak but improving. Her foot stubbornly refuses to heal, but she is quite adept at manoeuvring on her crutch, and of course an absolute master at ordering people about, so I think she can manage without me for a few days. Your vague and infrequent letters have me worried. If they do not improve in volume and content, you shall have to suffer a visit from your old grandfather, who misses his granddaughter terribly.*
>
>

All my dearest love,
Grandfather
>

June 7— Will's Coffee-house

All the talk is of Mistress Mary "Moll" Davis, my rival at the Duke's House. She sings her pathetic song "My Lodging, It Is on the Cold, Cold Ground" and then, to prove her point, curls into a weary little ball and sleeps on the stage. Somehow, at the end of the play she is revived sufficiently to dance a *gigue* in her breeches, *à la* myself. Everyone is comparing us: she has a superior voice, but I am the better dancer; she is all lush curves, and I am wand thin; she is a buttery blonde, while I am a pert, intelligent redhead; she looks well in yellow, while I . . . enough!

Note—Although I would love a visit from Grandfather, I fear now is not the time. He will sense the distance between Hart and myself and only grow more anxious for my happiness. As well, life in Drury Lane is wretched. Mother lives only on the money I provide and no longer goes out, except to buy drink.

Later—the Duke's House (The Rivals, how fitting)

It being our night off, Teddy and I sneaked off to watch this famous Mistress Davis. We were careful to go in disguise and had a roaring good time dressing up. Teddy went as a woman, naturally. He got to wear his lovely yellow silk gown—the one he wore as Juliet (he fretted over the tear in the sleeve and blames Becka, naturally). *He* looks lovely in yellow. I chose a starlight blue gown and matching wide-brimmed hat. The dark veil utterly concealed my face. Thus transformed, we hired a hackney and set out in the rain.

Slipping in after the first act, we took seats in the middle gallery, close enough to see but not to *be* seen. Teddy was grumpy as he prefers either the pit or a good box—money spent on anything else is nonsense. She entered, lonely and forlorn, and sang her sad little song. It is affecting and she sings well enough, but with such sticky sweetness that I found her irritating. Her breeched dancing was pleasant, but she is quite plump and did not convey a sense of delicacy. I think it takes rather a lot to heave her considerable bulk off the ground. Goodness, how mean I am. Teddy enjoyed the dressing up much more than the play. I think he was disappointed that no one recognised us.

ST. CLOUD, FRANCE
TO HIS MAJESTY KING CHARLES II
FROM PRINCESSE HENRIETTE-ANNE, DUCHESSE D'ORLÉANS
JUNE 10, 1667

My dear,

It is only the not having that has driven you mad—and not the object of desire herself. While she is undoubtedly a beautiful girl, and unusual in her determined virtue, she is not singular in her qualities. It is her refusal that sets her apart—and her refusal that inflames your desire. Understand your own character with greater nuance and perception, and you can free yourself from this unhappy tangle.

Do not be angry with her, dearest. Even if you had divorced Catherine and married her, she still would only have been one among many in your affections; your heart is a well-populated country. As one man's wife, she has a chance to be loved alone. It is what every woman wants, and you are incapable of giving it. It is a strange truth.

With love, your,
Minette

When I Take a Great Risk

June 30 — Theatre Royal (Flora's Vagaries, again)

The last performance! Done for the season! To celebrate, Teddy, Lacy, Nick, Peg, and I went to Chatelin's for a lovely roast supper. We were met by Rochester, Etheredge, Buckhurst, and Sedley—Buckingham could not join us, Johnny explained, as he was only recently out of hiding and currently enjoying a short stay in the Tower. They say that on his way to the Tower, he stopped for luncheon at the Sun Tavern in Bishopsgate and dined with Buckhurst and Lord Carbery.

"Yes, he stopped for lunch, but no, I was not with him," Buckhurst corrected. "Carbery might have been—I've no idea."

"Damned persistent story, that," added Sedley, helping himself to more of the stewed pheasant and smacking his lips in anticipation. "I've heard it several places."

"Seems silly of him to stop at a mean pub on his way to the Tower," Rochester observed, "'specially when he has Louis, his own French cook, lodged with him."

"Mmm," said Peg, "Louis has wonderful hands—very light pastry."

"He took a *staff*?" I asked, incredulously. "To prison?"

"Naturally," said Rochester. "Can't manage there without a staff. Every time I go, I have to pack up the whole bloody house. Pots, pans, pets, coverlets, servants . . . It's a bloody nightmare."

The "merry mob," Lacy calls them. Buckhurst watched me all evening, not bothering to conceal his interest. He has a tendency to keep remarkably quiet and then say the most shocking things. I admit, I find him fascinating, but frightening, too, like looking over the edge of a high precipice. These rowdy boys have taken a house together in the country and have tried to recruit me to join their party.

"Come away to Epsom! Let us leave foul London behind!" crowed Rochester, waving about his dripping cup and sending wine all over his new blond wig (he switched over this week from dark—doesn't quite work). Peg quickly moved her skirts out of the way, but her pink silk slippers got splashed. Teddy's forehead crumpled in mild distaste; he dislikes messy eaters.

"The fresh country air, the spa, the music, the parties, the dancing!" Sedley sang, his eyes closed, his head lolling about—he was already quite drunk.

"Not to mention the bathing!" Etheredge chimed in. "The bathing is wonderful." Etheredge is a notorious fanatic for cleanliness and is always catching cold on account of his wet, clean hair.

"Let's be drunk for the summer!" Rochester said, shaking the droplets of wine from his curls. As if he would be sober in London?

"Yes! Let us away tonight!" crowed Sedley, pouring another glass of wine (his fourth).

"I will give you one hundred pounds a year to be my mistress," said Buckhurst evenly, never taking his eyes from my face, his expression never changing, folding his hands calmly in his lap. Did anyone else hear that? I turned to look, but no, they were all chatting away as usual.

One hundred pounds? A fortune. *Could he be serious?*

July 5, 1667
My dearest Mrs. Gwyn,

Please have your things packed and ready by eleven a.m. tomorrow, at the very latest. My coachman Harris will be prompt and convey you to me with all speed.

It is fate. I have decided. You are to be mine.

Buckhurst

July 5, 1667—Drury Lane

How do I respond to such a letter? I find myself packing my trunk. But I know nothing of this man! Ruby is puzzled and looks at me expectantly from her travelling basket. Are we going away? her puggy eyes ask.

LONDON GAZETTE

Sunday July 13, 1667

Most Deservedly Called London's Best and Brilliant Broadsheet

The Social Notebook

Volume 265

Ambrose Pink's social observations du jour

Darlings!

What news, my pets! From orange girl to actress to Epsom? The loveliest little songbird of the Theatre Royal has flown the coop. To Epsom, of all places. What will dear Tommy Killigrew do? Will she come back? A very reliable source whispered to me that she has returned all her parts for next season and plans to give up the stage for good. Can it be true? *Dommage! Dommage!* Never fear, she will be kept well amused. The most dashing of the court wits have flown away with her: The Earl of Rochester, the Duke of Buckingham, and Charles Sedley—not to mention her current amour Charles Sackville, Lord Buckhurst, perhaps the rakiest rake of them all. *Au revoir*, dearest Nelly. Fly home to us soon!

À bientôt, dearests,
Ever your eyes and ears,
Ambrose Pink, Esq.

July 16, 1667
Maiden Lane, London
Ellen,

   I am at a loss to see how you could possibly justify your actions. To leave London in the company of such men is beneath you, Ellen. They are wits to be sure, but they are not men of strong character. Beyond issues of decorum, how could you depart this city and not inform me? Do you not know how deeply I care for your well-being? I am astounded at your effrontery and wounded by your wont of care.

Hart

July 18, 1667
Maiden Lane, London
Dearest Ellen,

   I am lost without you. Please return to me.

Your,
Hart

July 19, 1667
Theatre Royal, Covent Garden, London
Dear Ellen,

   I know you have heard the rumours of Hart and Lady Castlemaine and can only imagine that they sowed the seeds of your departure. I must tell you, as your friend, that yes, they are true, but Hart would welcome you back without hesitation if that were what you chose, although I fear it is not your desire.

   For myself, I miss your merry presence and harbour a hope that you will return to us for the coming season. The audience loves you, as does the company, as do I. Teddy is quite forlorn. Please advise me of your intentions as the autumn season has been built around you. I am coming to Epsom and will take this opportunity to call upon you. I hope you are well, my dear. Cecilia sends her best. You are in our thoughts.

Yours, etc. . . .
Tom

P.S.: Please forgive my brevity and my forthrightness. I look upon you as my daughter and take a profound interest in your happiness and welfare.

July 25, 1667—Epsom

I look around me and cannot quite believe what I have done. I am writing this in a room strewn with wine bottles, dirty clothes, coffee cups, overturned books, and slumbering men. No one managed to make it up to their bedrooms last night, and everyone seemed to have slept where they fell. Ruby picks her way among the debris, unimpressed with my choice of habitat. She has a point. What have I done?

We live in a rented house next to the King's Head, and Buckhurst, Sedley, Rochester and I stay up all the night dicing, talking, and (they) drinking. I have not the head for such strong spirits. It is merry company but strange. Buckhurst treats me as a sister. He is playful and affectionate but only seldom comes to my bed. I do not feel I am getting to know him at all. We do not draw closer, despite my efforts—efforts that humiliate me in their desperation.

I felt so worldly when I flounced out of Hart's bed and now realise I know nothing of the world and have misjudged my place in it. I had assumed Buckhurst would offer the same singular devotion and protection I received from Hart—how naïve! I had hoped he would open my heart and I would feel that sense of belonging, of which I know myself to be capable, but there is only empty formality and, occasionally, lewdness. What have I done?

July 21, 1667
Farm Cottage, Oxford
Dearest Ellen,

I heard the most extraordinary rumour today at the college. Is it possible that you have abandoned the stage for Epsom and a man named Buckworth? As you know, I trust you to make your wisest decisions in every moment, my dearest, but this change does seem rash. What of this man? Is he the love you have been seeking? I can only pray that he is.

Margaret still fares well and, although she would never admit it, is impressed by your exalted orbit. She cares for you truly, as of course do I. I miss you, my sweet elfin child.

> *All the love,*
> *Grandfather*

Note—*I enclose a copy of Milton's controversial* Paradise Lost. *It is frightening and awesome in its scope. Keep up your reading!*

July 27, 1667—Epsom

Tom came to visit today. We went to the New Inn—to get away from the mad house in which I live. He swears that he is here purely for his wife to take the waters, but I know he is also here to see for himself that I am well. I am touched by his concern and amused by his pretext.

"But these *Wits*," he said. "I know their ways." Indeed, his son is counted among them, as he himself was years ago. "They will drop you when they have tired of you, and then where will you be?" he asked, settling into a winged chair by the fire.

Where am I now? I thought but did not say. "Will I always be welcome at the King's?" I asked hopefully, smiling my most charming smile and pouring him more chocolate.

"London audiences are fickle, my dear. They may forget you. If you mean to return, do not tarry."

July 31, 1667
Milk Street, London
My dearest dear,

You have made Epsom ever so chic. I have heard stories all over town of your madcap antics. Could they be true? Did Sedley truly swear loudly and continuously at Durdan House and then run about au naturel *as God intended, shocking Lady Robartes? Did you dance upon the table at the King's Head in your breeches and, when told to stop by a prudish innkeeper, invite everyone in the alehouse next door to your lodgings to continue the dancing? Did you really ask Bucky Buck for payment up front? Five hundred pounds, they say! (Preposterous—you have always been loath to ask for money.) Does little Catherine Sedley wear your clothes and carouse with you all late into the night?*

Goodness, my dear—to have run away with the most dangerously charming men in England. How clever you are.

London is dismal. The rebuilding is slow and messy, and people seem to be leaving the city, rather than suffer to live here. Dirt, stone, and building crews everywhere you look. The City still looks blackened and charred and frankly depressing—but it is better than my wife's family in Suffolk.

I miss your gay heart and loving company. Do not stay away forever. I couldn't bear it.

> *All the loveliest love I have,*
> *Teddy*

Note—Have you heard? Henry Jermyn has been sent away from court for fornicating (what a brilliant farmyard word) with Castlemaine—or aspiring to! She denies it, naturellement. Hart disappears directly after the show each night. It is said, to be with her. I thought you would wish to know.

August 15, 1667—Epsom

I read and re-read Teddy's letter, my heart eased by familiarity. It is loneliness, I realised. I am lonely. But I do not know him yet, my heart reasons. Perhaps when I do he will . . . he will . . . he will what? He doesn't even seem to like me!

August 19, 1667—Epsom (four a.m.)

Four nights alone! I hear them come into the house. The whole street can probably hear them, as these boys make no effort to be quiet. Some sleep where they land (Buckingham never seems to make it upstairs, and I always find him tangled up in the cushions on the floor), but Buckhurst is always careful to retire to his bedroom. He opens my door and wishes me a formal good night, never suggesting I follow him. When I try to suggest it, he pretends he has not heard me. A blandness has come over him, obscuring all the sharpened intensity that came before. In truth, my heart is not engaged either—only my pride and my hope.

Later—six a.m. (still up)

I know I have made a terrible mistake. But I dare not correct it. I feel painted into this unhappy corner. Why is admitting I am wrong so terrifying? Not that I am wrong, I think: that I am unloved—that is where humiliation lives. This is not the love I have sought, and I have travelled too far down this wrong road. I must make my way back. I feel small in my foolish disappointment.

August 20—Epsom

Late:

The boys went out carousing, Buckhurst, it seems, would rather common whores to me, and I was enjoying an evening of blessed quiet, cosy in my nightgown and socks, with Ruby asleep in her basket and Catherine, Sedley's ten-year-old daughter, asleep upstairs, when Johnny Rochester returned early.

"Still up, my Ellen chickie?" he asked, lightly kissing my brow. He smelled strongly of drink. He pulled off his curled wig and scratched his short, dark hair. "Ah, you have tidied up! I was hoping you would. I thought if we left it long enough—"

"Why doesn't he want me?" I burst out unexpectedly. I had not planned to confide my woes to anyone, but they could not be contained any longer.

"Because he got what he wanted, naturally," he said easily, dropping onto the settle opposite. Even drunk, Johnny retains his grace.

I looked at him, uncomprehending.

"Ugh," he said, impatient with my slow absorption. "He wanted to see if he could get you here. And he did. So?"

"But we—"

"Bedded?" he asked crassly, sounding bored and kicking off his shoes. I winced. "Well, yes, of course you did, but that was just for form's sake, really."

Form?

He yawned and looked at me. "Bucky is only interested in what he *cannot* have. Once he *can* have it, there is no joy. That is the trouble with people who *have* everything. Terribly dull way to live, really." He yawned again, but beneath the veneer of dispassion, I sensed an earnest care. "See, for myself, I seem to enjoy nothing. Neither what I *can* have, nor what I *can't* have—which is even duller."

"He does not want me?"

"No. Best thing you could do is run away. *Go.* Leave tonight. Then he will *always* want you. *Vite, chérie! Vite!*"

Later—two a.m.

Vite. Vite. I am packing.

7.

Returned Ellen

When I Am Re-engaged

August 21, 1667 — Theatre Royal, London!

Hart's burning passion has turned to impenetrable coldness. I am not sure I mind. It is easier to navigate his anger than his unfinished love. He opposes my return to the theatre. Dryden and Tom are interceding, but as a star and shareholder Hart carries much weight. I am desperate but try not to show it. We certainly cannot play *mad couple* parts at the moment.

I have engaged a cleaning woman for Drury Lane with the little money I have left from Buckhurst. Ridiculous for so dilapidated a house, but I cannot live in such a mess. I do not think Mother has washed the sheets since I left. Jill, a sweet girl from up the lane, starts tomorrow and will come twice a week. Four shillings. I feel weary with change.

GREENWICH, ENGLAND
AUGUST 22, 1667

Minette,

Finally. The terms of the peace agreement have at last been worked out. We concede our holdings in West Africa, the island of Pulo Run and Surinam, but we keep the former Dutch possessions of New York, New Jersey, and New Delaware—the Peace of Breda. Such as it is. At least it is over.

Charles

Note—The vultures have turned on Clarendon. The Privy Council now hold him responsible not only for arranging my barren marriage to Catherine but also for this unsatisfactory peace—forgetting entirely that Clarendon opposed this war from the beginning. They mostly supported the marriage, too, in fact. Unsurprisingly, Buckingham and Castlemaine are at the root of it. They truly believe that I am ignorant of their compulsive intriguing. I remain neutral and speak guardedly in his defence, but in truth I blame Clarendon for helping the Duchess of Richmond to elope. Petty, I know, but there it is.

Tuesday, August 25 — Theatre Royal

Compromise—*at last*. I am to perform, but in Dryden's *Indian Emperor* (Cydaria *again* to Hart's Cortez), and then Samira in Dryden's *The Surprisal*—not comedies. *Heigh-ho.*

"This way he can exude *gravitas*," reasoned Dryden.

"Not sure Cortez had gravitas," countered Teddy.

"Well, he certainly killed a lot of people," said Tom, "which Hart is *certainly* up for at the moment."

Oh dear. Will he hold a grudge *forever?*

"A wounded pride strikes more deeply than a wounded heart—but then you rather smashed both, so I don't know," Tom offered. "But both mend in time."

Any idea how much time?

Thursday, August 27 — Theatre Royal (Emperor)

We get through it. Hart manages to convince the audience that he is in love with me, despite never looking me in the eyes and flinching when I touch him. I manage to appear an adoring mistress, though I am a tightly wound ball of contempt. Until the epilogue. Hart claimed the prologue, but the epilogue is my moment. The audience—ever up on current gossip—watch us closely for outward signs of our turmoil. Dryden has tactfully written out the kiss at the end. Thank God.

Note—I feel as if the audience has cooled towards me. I am perceived as a wayward harlot. Johnny confirmed it this evening. I am the talk of the town. I am thought to be a fickle, money-grubbing orange girl, raised above her station. My switch from orange girl to actress used to enchant them. I mind much more than I expected.

Note—Teddy was right. Hart does disappear just after the show.

> *August 30, 1667*
> *New Dorset House*
> *My dearest Mrs. Gwyn,*
> *Epsom was desolate without you. I have returned seeking only your company. Will you do me the honour of dining with me tomorrow evening? My soul wastes without you.*
>
>   *I wait upon your reply,*
>   *Lord Charles Buckhurst*

Undated

His *soul*—what rot. His soul did not notice I was there, so I think it will do nicely without me. Mother is already ordering poor Jill about, and so I have raised her wage to four and a half shillings. At this rate I must get back to playing leads soon.

When I Tire of These Games

August 31 — Will's Coffee-house (breakfast)

"You see. *Now* he is on the run," Rochester said, pouring brandy into his coffee (it was only ten in the morning).

"Goodness, you people get up damnably early," Etheredge said, trying to shake himself awake.

"*We* would rather be in our beds, but duty calls," said Teddy, addressing Ruby in a sing-song voice, dunking his toast wedge into his coffee. I had requested an emergency family conference at the coffee-house and insisted they rise before noon. Buckhurst's notes were arriving in droves, and I needed help.

"But I do not *want* a man who only *wants* me if I run away," I said, to no one in particular.

"Then you do not *want* this man at all," said Rochester.

"Keep running," said Teddy.

Later

Johnny is right: I do *not* want this man at all. I wanted to be free of Hart, to be swept away by an ardent lover, to be reckless, and, most of all, to be loved. I have returned in defeat, and I have no interest in trying again.

Note—After several unanswered notes, I finally stopped by Madame Ross's (still terrifying) in search of Rose. I was astonished to learn that she no longer works there. Then where is she? Worrying.

Even later—two a.m. (can't sleep)

Wrapped in my counterpane, I am curled in the window-seat. The glass is cool against my forehead as I look out to the sleeping street below. A mother cat and her new litter are nestled into a pile of loose sacking against the next house, the lamplighters are working to repair the lamp across the street, and the baker and his wife are having a row in their house on the corner. It is a poor neighbourhood, one I had hoped to leave by now.

The money from Buckhurst is dwindling, and I have already had to dismiss Jill, although I recommended her to Peg, and so she is assured a far better position. I am unable to support Mother any longer. I hope that she will return to the tavern, but I fear that she will resort to her other profession and seek out a group of girls to sell—will I ever cease to be shocked by her selfishness? At least Grandfather has found work once more in Oxford and is happily occupied in the library at Christ Church.

Once I have won back the audience, I will be able to command a higher wage, but at the moment, with Hart (a major shareholder) against me, I remain poorly paid. If I become a crowd favourite, then Hart's enmity will count for nothing. If I could only play comic roles, I know I could earn their love. If, if, if: there is a great deal of "if" in my life at the moment.

Rose's absence worries me. I try to imagine her eloping with a wealthy lover—being whisked away in a coach and four—but I know how unlikely that is for one so thoroughly tainted. So where is she?

September 1—Theatre Royal

Buckhurst has been officially banned from the theatre. The doormen, stagehands, and hawkers have all been given instructions to pitch him out should he appear. And he definitely has been appearing. He has been making a nuisance of himself (yesterday he recited love poetry loudly outside the theatre) as the audience leave—insisting to all and sundry that he *must* see me. Everyone certainly saw him: an elegant, golden youth crowned in silver-blond curls, dressed in flamboyant pastels, shrieking sonnets in the street. He was definitely conspicuous . . . pity. So far he hasn't disrupted a performance, but I have no doubt he soon will. Grandfather, up from Oxford for a few days, came to the second show yesterday and was disconcerted to see this young man, restrained by two doormen, drunkenly yelling for me to come out. I feel a bit like a princess in a fairy-tale, with her knight climbing the tower walls.

"But if the knight gets inside, he will *dump* the princess," reminds Teddy. "Keep away from him—that'll fix his wagon." Teddy's talk is rife with endearing old-lady expressions.

How silly this all is. And how sad.

Later—Drury Lane (eleven p.m.)

Rose arrived home!

"Where have you been?" I yelped, leaping out of bed when I saw her. Fumbling in the dark, I struggled to light the lamp.

"Where? Where do you think? Madame Ross's," she said, careful to turn away from me as she spoke—Rose flushes when she lies. She began undressing for bed as though it was entirely normal that we two were returned to the bedroom of our childhood.

"Rose!"

"Not yet, Ellen," she said with steely conviction. "I will not speak of it yet." She slipped her nightgown over her head.

"But . . . !"

"No."

"Good night, girls," Grandfather said, poking his head round the door. "I do hope, on your first night home together, you have not decided to quarrel?"

I had the decency to look shamefaced. Rose just looked exhausted.

"I thought not." He twinkled. "Good night."

Impasse.

Note—Good news! Rose will officially apprentice with Madame Leonine!

September 2 — Theatre Royal (anniversary of the fire)

Notes, presents, trinkets. Will he ever stop? Johnny says no. As long as I run, he will chase. *This* is what Bucky likes. *This* is what he lives for. I am confused—how can anyone enjoy *this*? I am miserable.

"Because you have a real heart," Rochester said, in a quiet moment of gentleness, giving me a lopsided smile. "It is rare in our glittering world, and we don't know quite what to do with it."

"Everyone has a real heart," I shot back. "They just employ a false one."

"You think too well of people, my unicorn. It is why I love you so."

Note—I had a costume fitting today with Rose for the upcoming Howard play. Now that Hart no longer pays for my clothes, I must economise where I can. It was a difficult two hours. Rose not only refuses to say where she has been, but she refuses to tell me where she goes now! She is often inexplicably out in the evenings and refuses to talk about it—frustrating! At least she seems happy. Whether it is her renewed interest in sewing or her mysterious absences, I do not know, but I am grateful for her happiness. Grateful and making an effort to be gracious. Until she establishes herself as a seamstress, I am left funding this bizarre household. I have decided: no more chocolate and meat only twice a week—depressing but necessary.

> September 3, 1667
> Whitehall
> Dearest Ellen,
>   Please may I see you? Do not torture me this way.
>
>   Buckhurst

September 3 — Drury Lane

I cannot bear to torture anyone. Against all advice, I have agreed to meet him—briefly.

September 4 — Theatre Royal (The Surprisal)

Only a few minutes as I am onstage in an hour and have not yet made up, nor curled my wig.

What happened:

I met him at the Swan Inn—a seedy place and no one knows me there—and *nothing* happened. I was not moved by his pleas or his declarations of love. In fact, I was not moved by him at all and felt I was in the presence of a stranger. Did this man ever share my bed? How *strange* men and women can be.

"But we are *fated*," he insisted loudly (drunk, I suspect), bringing me back to the conversation with a jolt.

"Why then, it would be so," I reasoned quietly. "But here we are, and it is not so. How then can it be fate?"

I offered him my friendship.

He is considering.

FONTAINEBLEAU, FRANCE
TO KING CHARLES II
FROM HENRIETTE-ANNE, THE MADAME OF FRANCE
SEPTEMBER 4, 1667

Dear one,

Don't do it. The men (and women) who urge you to do this are looking to their own interests. Buckingham opposes anyone who carries any weight with you. He is charming but selfish and spoiled and even more calculating than you credit him. Clarendon looked out for your best interests when there was nothing to be gained. He was against his daughter's marriage to James, even though it would likely put his grandson on the throne. This old man has served you well. Clarendon is quite right about the petticoat influence. You go too far to avoid conflict, my dear. Lady Castlemaine runs towards it head-on, and you must meet her there.

Henriette

Note—*Dr. Jean Baptiste Denis, Louis's physician, performed a miraculous surgery in Paris this week. A fifteen-year-old boy, weakened by excessive blood-letting, was infused with half a pint of lamb's blood and was successfully revived and is now enjoying robust health.*

September 5, 1667— Theatre Royal

Friendship, it is. I am at peace.

"You will forever haunt my soul," he declared plaintively.

"But I am not dead yet," I responded. I am weary of this overblown talk.

When I Find My Footing on the Stage

My dear,

I understand your concern, but you must understand that the ill conduct of my Lord Clarendon in my affairs has forced me to permit Parliament to make many enquiries to which otherwise I would never have suffered. It is time. Do not think I would take such a step lightly. Clarendon will be well looked after in France. This course of action suits me, as I would lessen the restraints upon my rule. He is a good man and has fulfilled his office. Now I seek to govern alone.

Be assured that I am entirely your,

CR

Note—Jemmy is considering a visit to Paris in the new year. I hope that such diversion will distract him from his desire to join the army. I also hope that it will induce him to adopt French fashions and disregard the periwig. It is fitting on an old man like me, but I much prefer Jemmy's hair short.

December 28, 1667—Theatre Royal (All Mistaken or The Mad Couple)

I finally feel as if *this* part has won me back the London audience (and with them comes the pay increase I have hoped for! Forty shillings a week, to be raised to fifty by the summer—meat and chocolate every day!). James Howard (another playwriting Howard boy) has written me a *brilliant* role. Mirida was made for me—quite literally, in fact. Rose's costume was a success (Madame Leonine helped her with the difficult neckline), and Lizzie Knep has already ordered two similar dresses. I have advised Rose to charge top prices—her work is of fine quality—and it is only fair. I was surprised when she mentioned that Hart had offered the same advice. I did not realise they still spoke. How kind of him.

At last, Hart and I can be easier in each other's company, onstage at least. I feel as though the Londoners cheer for us unreservedly now. I have missed their love more than I care to admit.

To be fair, Hart has softened offstage as well. He brought lovely Christmas gifts to the little house in Drury Lane: a delicately inlaid music box and a heavy crystal bottle of *Eau du Cassis;* as well as presents for Rose and Mother: French soap for Rose and Venice lace for Mother. Luckily, I had a gift for him as well—a new silver engraved hairbrush. He even brought a Christmas ribbon for Ruby, who gets terribly over-excited when she sees him and needs a nap to generally collect herself afterwards. It was a nostalgic family evening, and I missed him when he left, although I did not want him to stay.

Note—I am still widely thought to be a wanton—ironic, since I have slept alone for this half year.

January 1, 1668—Drury Lane

I have woken up to a new year. Ruby looks at me expectantly. Will this year be different?

When My Sister Finds Joy

January 12, 1668 — Drury Lane

Incredible news!

Rose is to be married! Mr. John Cassels, a member of the Duke of Monmouth's sprawling household, has asked Rose to be his *wife*! I am pleased for her, as I know to be respectably married has always been her truest wish.

"That is where you were?" I confronted her. "Why didn't you tell me?" I pulled my counterpane closer around me

"Have you ever wanted something so much that you were afraid to put even the smallest weight upon it in case it should crumble?"

I looked at my sister; she was shot through with happiness.

"No, Rose," I said, feeling literal and earthbound, "I have never wanted anything that much."

January 17 — Will's Coffee-house

Cards and coffee with Teddy and Rose; we are not on until three p.m.— Flora *again*.

"How did you meet him?" Teddy asked, playing a card.

Rose made a face.

"*Oh*. I see. Nothing wrong with trying out the goods before you buy them," Teddy quipped easily. I smiled. Teddy always knows just what to say to Rose.

January 20—Drury Lane

It was a small but lovely ceremony. Rose, looking radiant, wore a simple blue gown with a pink satin sash and carried a small posy of white winter roses. John wore a new blue waistcoat and looked quite smart. I keep thinking he is taller than he is. Mother wore her best gown of deep clover green trimmed with paler green ribbons *and* remained sober throughout the service—miraculous! Unexpectedly, Hart turned up and stood at the back of the church. I was touched. Next to him was a tall man with a heavy wig and his hat pulled low—Duncan! Good God. He left just before John kissed his bride.

Oh, Rose.

Note—She has decided not to open her own atelier but will continue to assist Madame Leonine and take in sewing herself.

LONDON GAZETTE

Sunday, January, 23 1668

Most Deservedly Called London's Best and Brilliant Broadsheet

The Social Notebook
Volume 291
Ambrose Pink's social observations du jour

My Darlings!

Quel shock! *Quel* shame! A challenge! A duel! Rapiers at dawn! The Earl of Shrewsbury challenged the great Duke of Buckingham to a duel, set for early on the morning of this past January 16. The outraged earl could stomach the duke's public liaison with his countess no longer. Their flagrant disregard for even the barest subterfuge rendered the poor duchess in a sorry state and the earl ready to die for his honour.

Unfortunately, he received his wish and now will not have to bear witness to their passion, as he was wounded and killed after only a brief engagement. Let none say that he was not brave. A warning to wandering husbands and flirtatious wives. It is a dangerous row to hoe, *mes amis!*

À bientôt,
Ever your eyes and ears,
Ambrose Pink, Esq.

January 25 — Drury Lane

The Earl of Shrewsbury was a pompous hypocrite who often came behind the curtain to leer at the actresses but could not bear to see his wife take the same pleasure—but one cannot say such things of one who has passed. I *can* say that his wife flaunted her affair before all of London, taking every opportunity to humiliate her husband. She is a dreadful woman and their marriage could not have been happy, but what a sad end. It is Buckingham I cannot believe. To stand up and kill a man, when you know that it is you who have done wrong, and then to go about your day?

"But it is the perfect solution for the wicked couple," Teddy said, laying down his news sheet and recrossing his slender ankles. "She is now a very rich widow, all the better to help Buckingham out of his current financial embarrassment. My God, can that man spend money—and now they no longer have to concern themselves with her irritating husband. *C'est parfait!* And so simple—one has only to be as ruthless as Buckingham to follow such a course."

"But that is just it. How could he?"

"Oh, my dear, I am sure this incident did not even disrupt his breakfast, let alone his conscience. He is a very good swordsman—remember, he is a war hero—and would have been sure of the outcome. The bumbling, nervous earl was hardly a match for him."

"Poor man," I said, fidgeting with my script but not really reading it.

"Oh, I don't know," Teddy said, unfolding his long limbs and yawning. "Now at least he no longer has to live with that horrid woman. If she were my wife, it is probably what I would choose, too."

After he left, I cleared away the coffee things and thought about marriage. So much risked on such a chancy thing—like poor Mary Fairfax, Buckingham's irrelevant little duchess. She was so useful to him when he needed to ingratiate himself with her Cromwellian general father—and so useless to him now that he is the king's man. She is unwanted and unnecessary and dull to boot. How grim.

Rose and John have moved into a small house in Cockspur Lane near Whitehall. Rose—Mrs. Cassels, now—keeps it shiningly clean and has taken several orders for gowns. She is loath to call herself "Madame Rose," as is customary for dress-makers, as she has had too many madames in her life. She is so happy to stay at home—so happy to have a home—so happy to have left Madam Ross's—so happy to love just one man. I hope her marriage *is* happy, and I am envious of her peace, I admit.

When Others Find Love

March 1, 1668 — Will's Coffee-house (raining)

Gossip:

Prince Rupert of the Rhine has been sending for Peg! I keep catching her daydreaming during rehearsal.

COLOMBES, FRANCE

TO OUR SON, KING CHARLES OF ENGLAND

FROM HER MAJESTY QUEEN HENRIETTA MARIA

MARCH 1, 1668

Charles,

I had hardly set foot in France before I heard all manner of rumour that George Buckingham was truly governing England and that Parliament won't vote you any money. For heaven's sake, Charles, stop frolicking through the countryside like a milkmaid and get a tighter rein on your government. Lord St. Albans brought up your penury at a fête at Versailles last week, and it was very embarrassing. And how can you be writing to King Louis for money? Where is your own money? Taxes, Charles, taxes create revenue. This should not be difficult for you to grasp. You are king—rule, for God's sake!

Maman

Tuesday, March 17, 1668— Will's Coffee-house

"Well, is it true?" demanded Teddy, before Peg could even sit down (she did not have much time as she is on this afternoon in *The Storme*).

"Yes, it's true. Ohh, is that lemon-seed cake?" Peg shrugged off her winter wool cloak.

"That is *all?*" Teddy shrilled. "You are *visiting*," he said, vigorously wiggling his eyebrows, "the dashing Prince Rupert, and all you say is 'yes, it's true'?" I giggled at Teddy's impatience. Peg smiled a smile full of mischief and would not say any more.

Later— Theatre Royal

Finely wrapped boxes arrive each evening before the second performance. The Marshall sisters are choked by envy, marking carefully Peg's accumulating treasures: a spotted yellow *moiré* gown, a soft pink quilted petticoat, a striped green travelling suit, a white rabbit muff and matching mittens, boxes of creamy underclothes trimmed with lace, sapphire ear-drops, a small gold timepiece. Peg and I open the parcels with glee, furiously ripping through the tissue wrappings. I, too, am filled with envy, but it is her *happiness* I crave. She is alight with happiness. The beautiful blue *calèche* arrives promptly at curtain fall to whisk Peg away. Dashing Prince Rupert (thicker around the middle and slightly balding, but light-footed and beautifully turned out, nonetheless) opens the door for her himself. Nightly, we watch from the stairwell windows. We see him sweep her a courtly bow. We sigh.

Later

The king (yesterday in a wine-red velvet coat—beautiful!) has been attending the theatre with Prince Rupert lately. He (always surrounded by his circus of courtiers) wanders through the tiring rooms, easy in our company, stopping to chat here and there, and sometimes even helping an actress to unlace her gown. Castlemaine, who often accompanies him and stays very close, works hard to seem unbothered by these brief intimacies. Although when no one is watching her, she occasionally slips and her face takes on the pointy, pinched dimensions of a sniffing fox. I stand back as the raucous royal parade winds through our house. So far the king has never stopped to speak to me. I cannot think what I would say if he did. So why do I find myself hoping and holding my breath until I hear his carriage pull away? What am I hoping for?

WHITEHALL, LONDON
TO OUR MOTHER, QUEEN HENRIETTA MARIA
FROM KING CHARLES II
MARCH 25, 1668

Maman,

I assure you that the Duke of Buckingham does not govern affairs here. I have no doubt that you have heard such rumours from Lord Clarendon's supporters in France. I will say no more on the subject.

Parliament has promised to vote me three hundred thousand pounds to fit out the navy as soon as they find the means to raise it. This is England, Maman, *not France. The people no longer believe in the divinity of kings, as Father so abruptly found out. You should remember how strong the will of the English can be.*

I will send James down to escort you to London as soon as you arrive in Portsmouth. Please give my most special love to Minette.

I am always your,
CR

LONDON GAZETTE

Sunday March 27, 1668

Most Deservedly Called London's Best and Brilliant Broadsheet

The Social Notebook

Volume 300

Ambrose Pink's theatrical observations du jour

Darlings!

Our lovely Mrs. Margaret Hughes (Peg, to those in the know) has been carried off! Her royal *amour,* the dashing Prince Rupert, wants her all to himself. She is to give up the stage for good, my pets. To the theatre, my dears! *Vite! Vite!* See her while you can, for she is leaving us for the rarefied royal air of Whitehall.

À bientôt,
Ever your eyes and ears,
Ambrose Pink, Esq.

LONDON GAZETTE

Sunday, April 2, 1668

Most Deservedly Called London's Best and Brilliant Broadsheet

The Social Notebook
Volume 301
Ambrose Pink's theatrical observations du jour

Darlings!

Actresses are all the rage at Whitehall these days. *Quel* glamour! Joining the witty Mrs. Hughes in the ranks of royal mistresses is the amply formed Mrs. Mary (Moll) Davis—like a ripe, rich butter cow soaring among the larks, my dears! We can only assume that the king's bed is infinitely preferable to the cold, cold ground.

À bientôt, dearests!
Ever your eyes and ears,
Ambrose Pink, Esq.

When I Meet Mrs. Behn

April 4, 1668— Theatre Royal

Tom brought an old friend to the tiring rooms after the show this evening. He introduced her as "Mrs. Aphra Behn, a woman of travels and letters." What an extraordinary way to introduce a woman. We are all off to supper. Must finish changing, as I am late!

Later

Goodness. She has had a gloriously exciting life. Mrs. Behn was raised in Surinam and was friendly with the exotic princes in that country. One in particular, Prince Oroonoko (no idea how to spell it), is to be the subject of the great heroic tragedy she is planning to write—he was a prince then a slave then a prince again. She plans to write—for *money*, in her *own* name. *Quel* glamour, as Teddy would say.

Beyond her wild childhood, she has already been a *spy* for the government, of all things, and has been *spying* in Holland, of all places—during a *war*. Agent 160. How official. How frightening. Upon making her return voyage, she was shipwrecked off the south coast of England and was only saved by a passing fishing boat. She looks nothing like how I would imagine: far too frail for a dashing spy and far too sturdy for a shipwrecked maiden.

Unfortunately, she incurred such expenses in her espionage (expenses not met by the government) that she went to Newgate Prison for debt. Her husband, Mr. John Behn, died of the great sickness in '65, and she has had to make her own way ever since. She has returned to London to pursue a writing career—professionally—unheard of for a woman.

"I was not pretty enough to be on the stage, you see," she confessed over supper. "Tom would only have cast me as a witch or an old crone or some-one's aunt." I privately agreed but did not say. Tom likewise smiled but did not deny it. It was true she was not pretty; her eyes bulged, and her features were overlarge for her oval face, but there was something arresting about the look of her. Her open face invites confidences, and her easy manner encourages laughter, but something else . . .

"It is her candour," Tom whispered, watching me try to puzzle it out. "In the way she looks at you and talks to you. There is a forthrightness. Don't worry," he said, seeing me colour, embarrassed to have been caught staring, "it fascinates everyone."

I tried to change the subject. "And you were really a *spy*?"

"My code name was Astraea, and I reported to the spymaster, Mr. Henry Bennet himself, now Earl of Arlington, God rot him."

"He never paid her, nor helped her to get back to England. She had to find her own way home," Tom said, by way of explanation.

"Home to Newgate for debt. I think he hoped I wouldn't survive. That way I wouldn't pester him about paying me." Aphra laughed.

I looked back and forth between the two of them. Were they serious? I felt quite ill with a sense of adventure in a wide-open world.

April 5, 1668— Tiring rooms

"She warned them about the Medway, you know," Tom said, stopping by my room. "Aphra. She knew the Dutch were planning to burn our ships, and she wrote to warn the Council."

"And what did they—"

"They ignored her. Arlington will never forgive her for that."

April 30, 1668

"What we need is to *feel* the feminine more," Sedley said a bit too loudly (drunk, again).

Aphra and I had accompanied the Wits to see Etheredge's *Love in a Tub,* on at the Duke's, and we were having a heated discussion afterwards.

"Yes, women really are the trickiest to write," added Savile gravely. I could sense Aphra beside me, rolling her eyes.

"The authentic female nature is nearly *impossible* to capture," Etheredge complained, sneezing into his handkerchief. He has caught cold, again.

"I don't expect Aphra shall have that problem with her heroines," I said, catching them off guard.

Note—The king attended but left before the third act. He spoke to Sedley and Savile and even Aphra, but not to me. The earlier intimacy of our first meeting feels forgotten—the unlikely company that calamity creates—well, my calamity, I suppose. His are woven on a larger loom, I think. His face is drawn in leaner lines. He seems grimmer now, less carried along by an effortless light step.

May 1, 1668— Theatre Royal (The Surprisal, again)

A rainy, rainy May Day. The blue-glazed cupola is leaking again, and the crowd is getting wet. *Please put a penny in the old man's hat.* The king and Castlemaine attended the early performance but left on account of the rain. I don't blame them; half the cast could not be understood for their chattering teeth. Now everyone will catch cold.

As I am not cast, Johnny, Aphra, and I took in Tom Shadwell's *The Sullen Lovers (or the Impertinents)* at the Duke's. Henry Harris, whom I am now free to chat to, played Sir Positive At-All. Poor Rob Howard! Johnny told me that this fop's part is meant as a caricature of him. If that is true, it is both ruthless and incorrect. Rob is a good, kind, sweet, and talented man, not this vain, be-frippered pastry puff depicted onstage. Now back to the theatre to rehearse Sedley's new play *The Mulberry Garden,* on next week. The dialogue is a bit stilted, but no one has the courage to tell him.

Note—Johnny is returned from the country, bringing with him an extraordinary manservant called Alcock. Trust Johnny to find a valet with a name such as that. Lady Rochester did not accompany him, and he seems to miss her truly, although I suspect it does not keep him faithful.

May 3 (Lord's Day)

Damn! (Oh dear, I seem to have picked up swearing from Aphra—Grandfather will be disappointed.) We went on the wrong day! Becka Marshall took great pains to tell me how she and her sister Nan saw both the king and his brother, James, Duke of York, at the Duke's last night. But in consolation Downes, the stage manager, said that the king looked bored throughout the performance, and Castlemaine, too, looked to be in an evil temper. Downes could not be sure if the king's boredom stemmed from the dismal play or his ever-demanding lady.

Note—Rumours that Peg has been *accompanying* Lord Sedley as well as Prince Rupert—what rubbish.

May 5, 1668— Theatre Royal (The Virgin Martyr)

Prologues and epilogues have become my specialty—and then a *gigue* in my breeches, *naturellement.* Even if the play is a boring tragedy, Tom ensures me a witty prologue, spoken as myself. It breaks up the monotony, but there is something frightening about going out onstage without a character to hide you. It is like going out before a crowd and realising that you are only wearing your undergarments. I am playing Nell, I tell myself—my never-ending part. The audiences seem to love it. They cheer and call to me familiarly. Do they think I am truly this confident, mischief-ridden sprite? I am always pretending.

Note—Aphra has become a regular in our circle and joins us most evenings after the show. She is informal and easily amused, but her mind is fast as lightning. Johnny and Sedley have both felt the business end of her wit. I just sit by and laugh.

When I Am Sent For

May 6, 1668— Theatre Royal (still The Virgin Martyr)

Aphra told me that the king, who has been frequenting our theatre of late, accompanied by Castlemaine (she seems larger—she couldn't be . . . not *again*?) or Mrs. Davis (still irritating), has noticed *me*.

"But he never speaks to me!" I told her, after the show. It was true. He just seems to sweep in, surrounded by a swarm of women and Wits, watch the play, flirt, collect more women and more Wits, and sweep out.

"Yes, but he *watches* you," observed Teddy, helping me out of my gauzy Angel wings (I love this role).

"You will be sent for, my dear," Aphra predicted with authority. "Careful how you play it."

Later

Play it? I have ever been tongue-tied with the king, and I have never been able to *play* anything. This must be a mistake. Dear God, I hope Hart hears nothing of this. I'll be back to playing tragedy within the week.

May 7, 1668— Theatre Royal (A King and No King—fitting)

She was right. Peg arrived at the theatre tonight with a note. I have been sent for—to *entertain* the king—tonight. I feel ill. Teddy sent me to the company seamstress immediately to wash and change. He said I must wash *everything*, with a great wiggling of the eyebrows. I am wearing Ophelia's new nunnery-scene dress: a kingfisher-blue taffeta. Becka will be furious— it is her favourite, and she paid for it. Peg donated her own lovely white underclothes for the occasion, and I am ashamed to say that she is wearing home my less than white underthings. Both Becka and Peg are taller than me, so I feel a bit hodge-podge. I must not be sick, I tell myself. It will all be over soon.

Lacy insisted on a brief tutorial with my theatre family to bring me up to date with current court news, as I am woefully undereducated in this department.

Things to Remember:

Item: he is in a monetary struggle with his Parliament right now over a bill for three hundred thousand pounds (an unimaginable sum) to pay his navy—avoid the subject of money.

Item: his brother is most likely a Catholic, as are his mother, sister, chief mistress (she keeps a *prie-Dieu* in her bedroom now), and wife, *and* he is arguing with Parliament over the nonconformists (he is for toleration, bravo!)—avoid the subject of religion.

Item: he is very fond of his children (although none of them legitimate)—delicately enquire after them but avoid the question of the succession.

Note—Peg told me that several days ago the queen miscarried; they eased her pain with mugwort and foxglove, and she is now recovering. "But we must not grieve!" she assured me. Rather it is to be celebrated that she can conceive at all—that is the attitude the courtiers mean to take. I pray for the little queen. For her, I am quite sure that it is a cause for profound grief.

Seven p.m.— Theatre Royal

Last-minute advice:

"*Don't* say too much," advised Tom. "A king wants to feel as though you are hanging upon his every utterance."

"*Don't* move about too much," advised Lacy. "You want him to feel he has your full attention. Remember, hands together, feet together, and just the *barest* sliver of delicate slipper poking out from under your gown. Was that your tummy rumbling? It mustn't rumble, Ellen. But don't drink anything, either. You do not want to need the water closet—disaster."

"*Don't* look about you too much," advised Elizabeth. "A king wants to feel that you are interested in him as a *man*, rather than a monarch. He won't if you are busy gawking at the silver."

"*Don't* eat too much," advised Teddy. "A king wants to see his women as delicate creatures, able to subsist on his company alone, and who have no need of food—and besides, belching at Whitehall would finish you."

Don'ts: don't speak, don't look, don't move, and don't eat. Got it. So just sit?

Note—Hart, attuned to my moods, noticed my edgy temper this evening. Breathing evenly, I managed a careless smile. This is a nightmare.

Half past nine p.m.

I was taken through a side door by a Mr. Chiffinch and told to wait on a slim bench in a long hallway. Restless, I kept getting up to pace, but quickly sat if I heard the least noise. My stomach began to growl, and I wished I had eaten some bread before I left.

"Mrs. Gwyn?" A gentleman usher approached from a door at the end of the hall.

I rose to follow him, quickly running my tongue over my teeth to check for any bits of food—I was regretting the peppered capon from this morning. Without another word, he swung open one of the double doors, and I entered the empty fire-lit room. A large meal was spread over the oak table: roasted chicken, stewed meats, figs, apricots in honey, and several soft cheeses on a platter. I was too nervous to contemplate eating anything.

A wooden door in the far corner of the room opened, and the king— dressed as I have never seen him, in a richly embroidered, deeply cuffed robe over a loosely tied lace cravat, creamy shirt, and silk breeches— walked quietly across the thick carpet. He wore no wig, and I saw for the first time that his hair, shorn close to his head, was strewn with silver. His laughing boyishness was gone, and a calm sincerity had taken its place. I smiled to see his herd of spaniels about him; they alone anchored me to familiarity.

I dropped to a deep curtsey, and, as I knew he would, he raised me up with his long, sturdy hands. We moved through the choreographed steps of greeting and flirtation. He lightly took my hand and led me to the table.

"You must be hungry," he said, gesturing to the food. "Peg assured me that these are your favourite dishes."

I looked at the unfamiliar food: had I ever eaten apricots in honey?

"Oh, yes," I lied. Stilted into silence by my long list of "don'ts," I opened my mouth and then closed it again. I had nothing to say. My palms felt sweaty, and I began to get the panicked feeling of every actor's nightmare— onstage and unable to remember any lines.

"Did you perform tonight?" the king asked, leaning down to feed some chicken to his dogs.

"Mmm. *A King and No King.*" Speak, Ellen! Sparkle! Shine! Nothing.

"You seem changed, Mrs. Gwyn. I seem to remember a rather surprising young imp, and I find a formal, serious girl in her place." The king smiled mischievously, as though he meant to tempt me into indiscretion.

"You have more dogs," I said randomly. Why?

He laughed. "Very observant. Yes, two of my bitches had litters. I find I cannot part with them and so keep them all. Not very practical, I am afraid." He laughed a different, private laugh; a musical laugh played on only the loosest strings. It was wondrous. I felt spun into a golden web.

"Well, your children must like them," I said, finally easing into myself, comforted by the growing sense of familiarity. "I know I longed for a dog as a child but was not permitted one."

"Would you like one now?" he asked in all sincerity. I felt like, if I asked, this extraordinary man would rise from this table and help me to choose a dog immediately.

"I have a lovely pug called Ruby," I reassured him. "I adore her. She is waiting with my friend Tom."

"Tom Killigrew? Careful, his Kitt is a beast who would probably devour your Ruby like a macaroon."

His face softened into a gentle smile, and he patted my hand.

At his touch I felt tilted: tipped out of myself into someone new.

"Terrible that you did not grow up with one. All children should have dogs," the king pronounced merrily, aware of his affect on me and clearly amused by my disorientation. "How else are they to learn what it is to be responsible for another creature? My children each have at least one. My eldest, Jemmy, has six."

"Well, if there is only so much food to go round, I suppose children can learn that lesson another way," I said in a light attempt to regain my footing. I had intended to tease, but it fell flatly like a criticism. Grasping about wildly for a topic, I asked how his family fared. "Your mother, Queen Henrietta, and your sister?"

"Both well," he said, pleased by the question. "Henriette is the Queen of France socially, the most admired and accomplished young woman." He smiled warmly when speaking of his sister. I understood. It is good to see a sister made happy.

"And your wife is recovering well from her . . . disappointment?" I had meant the question kindly, but I read the absolute impropriety of my words in his shocked face.

"You must excuse me, Mrs. Gwyn," he said smoothly. "It grows late, and I must go to Newmarket tonight."

And then he left me alone in the beautiful room with the food I did not want.

Half past twelve—Henrietta Street (Tom's house)

I directed the royal coach to return me to Tom's house, where my loyal friends (all but Johnny—he has accompanied the king to Newmarket) waited up for me anxiously.

"Well?" demanded Teddy.

"Disaster," I said flatly, shedding my dove-grey mules (they pinch). "It is over. It was short. It was gruesome. I did nothing."

"Did you—" began Lacy.

"No," I said. "I didn't. I didn't *do* anything. Except—"

"Maybe that is good?" interrupted Tom. "A blank canvas—"

"No, it was dull. I was dull. I was not myself. I was no one, in fact. I was not memorable." I will never have a second chance. "Except—"

"Except?" queried Teddy, his eyes narrowing, like a fox-hound on the scent.

"Except . . . I did . . ." Should I tell them? "I did ask how his wife . . . fared," I ventured timidly.

"You *what*!" Tom exploded.

"Well, she miscarried, and I know how badly he needs a child, and . . ." I cast about the room hopefully, looking for supporters. There were none.

"So you thought *you* would bring it up?" choked Teddy, aghast. "You thought he would want to discuss the queen's, his *wife's*, fertility over a private supper with an *actress*?"

"What did he say, my dear?" Lacy asked gently.

"He . . . he called for the footman to escort me to my carriage." I flushed, remembering the abrupt, awkward moment. "And he told me he had to leave for Newmarket," I finished lamely.

"In the middle of the night?" asked Lacy. "Oh my."

"Marvellous," said Teddy, heavily dropping into a chair.

Yes, I thought. He *was* marvellous.

May 8, 1668

Finished up *Virgin Martyr* (*again*, although I never tire of this role), very late as there was a ruckus during the performance and we had to stop. A drunken member of the audience climbed onto the stage and tried to embrace Becka. I was impressed; she kept herself in check and managed to stay in character (St. Dorothea) while the man was removed. She came back and did her death scene beautifully. The king, not back from Newmarket, did not attend the performance tonight.

May 9 — Theatre Royal

"Anything?" Teddy asked, coming offstage.

"Nothing." I was stumbling my way through a terrible performance, and smiled at Teddy, grateful for his patient forbearance.

"Mmm, difficult." He was whispering. Everyone whispers, trying to be discreet. As if whispering bad news somehow improves it.

"Nothing." I repeated. "Not even a note." I was not expecting anything. But I hoped. Against reason and logic, I still hope.

Later — Theatre Royal

Hart brought me a mug of raspberry sack this evening after the performance, his face creased with worry.

"Ellen, are you . . . all right?" He eyed me anxiously.

"Yes, of course," I said quickly, surprised and touched by his concern. I cannot remember a time in the last few months when he has been anything but vexed with me.

"Yes, of course," Hart repeated awkwardly, as if I had refused him, and then hurried away, presumably for his nightly appointment.

May 10— Theatre Royal

Tom came to find me in the tiring room after rehearsal today.

"Ellen, I have spoken to Hart," he said abruptly.

I waited for him to continue. Hart no longer criticised me openly but was perpetually going to Tom with his complaints: my posture, my singing, my untidy hair.

"I had to assure him that you were not . . . unwell." Tom said, pulling me from my reverie.

"Unwell!" I said, startled. "Why would I be unwell?" I quickly touched the wood of my painted dressing table. I had mercifully escaped the most recent bout of company cold and fever.

"Perhaps not unwell," Tom hedged. "More pregnant . . ."

"Pregnant! By who?"

"By 'whom,'" Tom corrected. "Well, no one, naturally, and I told him as much, but he knows something is afoot and is worried for you."

"Nothing is afoot," I said flatly. "Nothing at all."

Later—tiring rooms

Before the performance tonight I heard Hart's unmistakeable growl in the hallway outside.

"This oil is dripping all over the wall! Did you not see it?" he bellowed at Laurie, our lamplighter. "Clean it up, now!"

I slipped outside, pulling my silk wrapper closely around me. I had been waiting all day to catch Hart alone. I had to reassure him, to thank him.

"Hart . . . I—"

He rounded on me, swiftly redirecting all his irritation at me. "You what?" He scowled, his voice loaded with sarcasm and latent mistrust, all yesterday's tenderness absent.

I slipped back into the tiring room without a word. A difficult man, I thought sadly, and one I no longer understand.

When Men Fall in Love with Their Wives

May 12 — Theatre Royal (The Maiden Queen)

Dryden, Aphra, and Buckhurst were in the house tonight. Dryden was checking on *Queen*—he is perpetually tweaking his scripts and driving the actors mad. Buckhurst did not come back to the tiring rooms, as his presence still infuriates Hart. Then again, *my* presence still infuriates Hart. Everything seems to infuriate Hart. We discreetly joined them in the foyer, where Buckhurst was lurking with Dryden behind a large potted plant.

"We hear you were sent for, my dear," said Dryden, adjusting his complicated hat in the long mirror (ostrich feathers *and* ruffled velvet bows). He is slightly built but insists on following the fashion of long wigs and hats, giving him a top-heavy look.

"Yes, but only once—is that true?" asked Buckhurst, elegant in a pale grey ensemble, with a touch of malice. Aphra shot him a dirty look.

So be it. "Yes, it is true. You may as well know, I was terribly dull and will never be sent for again." There, I've said it.

"*Dull?* You?" squeaked Dryden, surprised. His genuine reaction heartened me, and I gratefully squeezed his arm.

"Yes, dull," Well, dull with one small incidence of fireworks, I thought privately.

"Oh my," said Aphra thoughtfully. "How to recover from dull?"

Exactly.

Note—Buckhurst just returned from Newmarket, brought us all the court news, and, after my anxious enquiries, told me that Johnny is sober but subdued. Alcock, on the other hand, is perpetually drunk, and Johnny encourages him. I did not ask about *him*.

Friday, May 15 — Theatre Royal (The Sea Voyage)

Outrageous news: Buckingham brought his mistress, the Countess of Shrewsbury, a dreadful bullish sort of woman, home with him.

"When his wife objected that the two women could hardly share a roof," Teddy recounted, aghast, "Buckingham told her he entirely understood and therefore had already ordered her a coach to take her to her father's."

"Booted out of her *own* home?" asked Nick, agog.

"The house her father paid for, no less," said Teddy.

"Dangerous world for women," I said softly, to no one.

May 18, 1668 — Theatre Royal

Lovely talk with Johnny this evening; he is back to dark wigs, thank goodness. He returned with the king this morning. Everyone is in town for the debut of Sedley's *The Mulberry Garden*—still too wordy and stiff. He showed me the draft of a letter he is writing to his wife, who is tucked away at his country home of Adderbury. He takes refuge in the overdone style of the time, but his true sentiment shows through. He does love her, but will not change to content her. He says he is *"endeavouring to get away from this place I am so weary of . . . ,"* but he is not endeavouring terribly hard, I must say.

May 21 — Theatre Royal

I am supposed to be making up for this afternoon and I find I cannot sit still. Nothing is wrong, exactly, but things feel just out of place, out of reach, and too loosely knit for me to feel true peace. I am enjoying the stage, but when I let myself look too far ahead, I feel a snaking unease. How will all this end? And who, if anyone, will it end with? I feel I am painting the scenery when I do not know the play. What does the puzzle look like? When will I feel the click of my life piecing together?

May (hot!)

"Everyone is falling in love with their wives, it is quite *à la mode* at the moment," Johnny said, lazily fanning himself with my peacock-blue hat (new—I *love* it). We were lying in the grass in the Foxhall Gardens after a splendid picnic of olives, bread, cold meats, grapes, and cheese spread out over a pink-checked cloth.

"Everyone?" I asked cagily.

"Well, not *everyone*. Buckingham has wreaked havoc in his domestic affairs, and I never seem to see mine, although I am fond, but the king is certainly spending time with the queen," he said, watching me out of the corner of his eye. Trying to gauge my reaction, no doubt.

Later

I will not be so small as to feel jealousy. He is her husband, and it is her right. I hear of the joy his attention brings her and know her love to be profound and unselfish—that is what people say, anyway. I am glad for the unassuming queen—or so I keep telling myself. I have met this man less than a dozen times, and, king or no king, he should not loom so large in my irresponsible heart. *No king*—in fact, I do wish he were no king but an ordinary man, who might notice an ordinary girl.

May — Theatre Royal

"And when the little butterball came out to dance, the queen just up and left," Teddy clucked. "Brava Caterina Regina!"

We had just finished our rehearsal and were lying on the stage, exhausted. Lacy had drilled us for hours, learning the steps for his new dance for the end of Act II. We were discussing the queen's daring snub.

"The Great Snub of '68. That is what they will call it in years to come. And I was *there*, petals!" Teddy said with self-important glee. "Brilliant! Ah, to be a part of history."

"Bold move," Lizzie said, approving. "And how unlike her. She normally seems such a mouse."

"Poor woman," I said, propping myself up on my elbow. "It can't be easy to applaud your husband's mistress."

"Moll Davis is hardly a *mistress*," Nick interjected. "She is more of a hobby, like tennis. You know, something you pick up, and then when you get the knack of it, you drop. She will not be around long enough to be called a mistress."

Can an actress be more than a hobby to a great man? To a *king*?

May 30— Theatre Royal (still hot)

Philaster with Hart—a Beaumont and Fletcher play we both love, although the heavy costumes were stifling in this heat. At least on that we can agree. I play Bellario, a part with wit and verve. The audience were wild for us, and the takings were huge; so little was needed—set, costumes, props, even playbills—as we have done it so many times before. I have finally asked Tom Killigrew to be my banker—unconventional, but I trust him, and I honestly do not know how to handle financial matters. He has explained various trusts he has established in order to keep my money safe—and even increasing. When I told Rose, she shook her head in disapproval.

"How can you trust them—men?"

"He is good to me and is my friend, and I do trust him. Surely you trust John?"

"It is he who must trust me," she said severely, surprising me. "He gives over his wages, and *I* make the financial decisions. As you know," she continued briskly, "I have managed my finances since I was quite young."

"Oh, Rose."

Note—Tom raised my wage to the promised fifty shillings per week!

June 1, 1668— Will's Coffee-house

All the talk was of Dryden's new poem.

"It really is *smashing*, Dryden," said Teddy, bandying about his new *mot du jour*.

"'*Annus Mirabilis*—Year of Wonders' . . . well, it certainly was that, what with the plague and fire and all," said Buckhurst, leaning his neat blond head back and closing his eyes. He was a bit hung over and prone to stating the obvious.

"I thought it was exciting. You found just the right note," I encouraged. Dryden looked at me, clearly pleased. I know how much sincere praise means to him—well, any praise, I suppose.

"And now Tom has taken you on for three plays a year—*smashing*," exclaimed Teddy.

"Yes," said Dryden, covered in daffodil-yellow ruffles and lapping up the compliments like a milk-fed cat. "I am leaving for the country almost immediately to finish my latest, *Evening Love*." He looked at me fondly and quickly added, "I intend for Nelly to star, naturally."

"His success will go well for you, Nell," Buckhurst said with sincerity.

Yes, I thought. It *is* good for me. *Everything* is good for me. Why, then, am I not more *happy*?

8.

Summer Ellen

When I Become Enmeshed in the Bedroom Plot

June 15, 1668
Whitehall
Nelly,

Please come and see me at once—today. The court is moving, and I am departing London on Thursday. Come directly to my rooms at Whitehall near the Holbein Gate. You will be expected. Wait for me there.

George Villiers, Duke of Buckingham

Tuesday, June 15

After receiving Buckingham's brief note, I went directly to Whitehall, taking the time only to change into my new pale green visiting gown (perfect with sky-grey slippers and a slim grey hat). I had never been to his rooms and had some difficulty finding them in that rambling labyrinth of a palace. I finally found them, surprisingly tucked behind the new tennis court, but they were as luxurious as I would expect for the king's closest childhood companion. I was quickly ushered into an inner chamber and told to wait. And *wait*. And *wait*.

Eventually, Buckingham returned, clearly fresh off the tennis court. Without preamble, he addressed me. "So he sent for you, did he?" Then beckoned for his man, Geoffrey, to come and help him out of his tennis ensemble.

Startled, I tried to gather my thoughts. "I . . . uh . . . yes." Geoffrey brought a laver and basin of soapy water and, pulling off Buckingham's soiled shirt, began to sponge him off. My status as an actress exempts me from the common decencies accorded other women—it has its advantages and, at that moment, disadvantages. I rolled my eyes as a soap bubble landed on my hat.

Buckingham, unperturbed, continued, "And you bungled it—is that fair to say?" Geoffrey produced a clean shirt, and I waited for Buckingham's head to pop through before I replied.

"Yes, I bungled it," I repeated flatly. "I was nervous and tongue-tied and dull. And then when I did speak, I said exactly the wrong thing. It was awful."

Buckingham was concentrating on dressing and did not seem particularly moved by my disaster. I sat on the chaise longue of striped silk—blue and silver, very pretty—and waited for my old friend to finish.

Buckingham closed his eyes as Geoffrey sprayed a great cloud of scent—*Eau de Cassis?* Too much, I thought as I began to cough. Thus perfumed and dressed in a fresh shirt, long cornflower-blue waistcoat, white hose, and matching blue ruffled breeches with satin pink bows, Buckingham turned to face me. "Yes, I heard about that. You asked about the wife. A mistake. He *was* disappointed with you. But it is not irredeemable, I think." He paused for a moment to look over the heavily curled wigs Geoffrey had laid out before him. "Which one? The honey or the copper?"

"The blond," I said, still struggling for breath through the fog of scent. "The copper would look utterly ridiculous on a man of your colouring." The blond one looked absurd as well, given that George is naturally dark, but I did not say as much. I think he goes to great lengths to distinguish himself from the famously dark-locked king. Buckingham made a face at my disparaging remark but, nevertheless, reached for the blond wig.

"And so—what do you plan to do about it?" he asked, securing the wig on his head. He has quite a large head, and the voluminously long curly wig only served to accentuate it, but I did not say so.

"*Do* about it?" I asked, confused. I understood the situation to be at a dead end.

"Yes, *do* about it," he replied with a touch of impatience. "You want to wind up in his bed, don't you? It is certainly a rung up from Buckhurst—who, I gather, was disappointing." I coloured. Was there *anything* he did not know?

"I may have spent most of that summer drunk on the music room floor, Nelly, but I am not entirely without deductive faculties. Anyway, you are better off. You never really liked Bucky all that much, did you?"

"I do like the *king* very much," I ventured, in an effort to turn the conversation.

"Like him? What's that got to do with it? He's the king. You don't have to like him." George turned back to his reflection in the long glass.

Side-stepping his last remark with what grace I could muster, I returned to his original question. "There is nothing to *do* about it. He did not care for me. I was home by one a.m., and know for a fact that he spent the night in Castlemaine's bed."

"And how do you know that?" asked Buckingham, sitting on the bed. He had moved on to footwear and was perusing the selection laid out before him.

"She *told* me," I said, painfully reliving that awful moment at the theatre.

"*She* told you?" He looked up from his shoes. "Castlemaine? And you believed her, didn't you, my gullible goat?"

"Of course—why shouldn't I?" I said, cringing at my schoolgirlish question.

"He has not shared her bed in months—just ask your gallant Mr. Hart."

I flushed. Even now, Hart's affair with Castlemaine was difficult for me to fathom.

Seeing my reaction, Buckingham chuckled aloud. "Nell, you must learn not to exhibit *everything* upon your pretty face."

"Why would she say that if it were untrue?" I countered, sounding naïve, even to my own ears.

"Well"—he reached for a shiny pair of powder-blue court shoes with low heels—"it chases you away, which is—to be fair—not difficult to do, and reminds you of her position as *maîtresse en titre*, which you seem only too eager to recognise. No, I think the pink laced court shoes—don't you?"

"No, I don't," I said, removing the pink pair. "Too much going on. Keep to the blue. *Restraint*—you should try it. Why shouldn't I recognise her as such? That is what she is, what she has always been."

"Yes, but things are changing now for my darling wicked cousin. Her bright, whorish light is going out. The end of an era," he intoned in a mock funereal voice. "Basically, the king is losing interest; she is getting older, and her graspyness is showing through—bound to happen eventually. I'm just surprised it didn't happen sooner. She has always had enormous nerve. She is demanding a new title now. Anyway, the game is afoot."

I thought Buckingham looked entirely too pleased at the thought of his cousin's fall from favour. "Game?" I asked, handing him his jacket of embroidered silver-blue velvet with deep-gold-buttoned cuffs.

"Game," he said, pulling on his hat. "And I choose you."

"Me?"

"You are perfect," he continued. "Froth and fun and smarts and heart—the perfect antidote to Castlemaine's domineering reign. And," he said, holding up his hand to forestall my protests, "you will not always be dull. Just *think* about it. It is all I require." With that astonishingly frank remark and one last glance in the mirror, he left the room.

I am thinking.

Wednesday, June 16—Drury Lane

And thinking. And thinking.

> *June 16, 1668*
> *Whitehall*
> *Nelly,*
>
> *I received your note and will be waiting for you in my rooms at eleven this evening. Give your name as the Widow Elizabeth Hibbert. Avoid being recognised.*
> *Buckingham*

June 16, 1668—Drury Lane

Wearing a dark wine *moiré* gown, leather mask, and matching dark veil (hot!), I set out by coach for Whitehall. I was quickly admitted with my false name and shown once again to Buckingham's rooms—only this time I was led up a back staircase I had not previously noticed. He was waiting for me in his small salon. "Well, have you decided?" he asked abruptly.

"Why am I disguised?" I asked, throwing off the itchy veil and removing the leather mask.

"Well, it wouldn't do for you to be seen in my rooms, and *then* to become the king's mistress. It would look as if I put you up to it."

"You *are* putting me up to it," I said, already fed up with intriguing.

"Yes, but it can't *look* that way. It is all in how a thing looks," Buckingham explained pedantically. "Anyway, *have* you decided?"

"I must know *exactly* what it is that you intend." I had prepared my speech thoroughly and sounded more confident than I felt.

"What I intend is to have you installed as the king's mistress, supplanting my darling, devious cousin, and if that doesn't take, I'd quite fancy having a go myself," he said easily, dropping into a chair by the fireplace.

I shot him what I hoped was a withering look and ignored his last remark. Sitting in the chair opposite and carefully removing my skin-tight gloves, I asked, "Castlemaine is your *cousin*. Why would you seek her replacement?"

"Well, having her where she is hasn't done me any good of late. And she is frankly impossible at this point. Her influence over him is monstrous; even the country is noticing now. And she has been disinclined to advance me in any way over the last few years, and in fact has been doing just the opposite—so? She must go, one way or the other. It is time, and I want to keep my hand in. The question is, do *you* want to replace her?"

"Only if he truly wants me," I answered candidly. As much as I truly want him, I thought to myself.

"He wants anyone who is in front of him," Buckingham replied, carelessly kicking off his high-heeled shoes.

No. That is not so. I thought of the black intelligent eyes and the careful mask of informality. This king knows *exactly* what he wants.

Later—Drury Lane

It is decided—although it all feels much like a chess game we have all endeavoured to play and not like a real decision at all. I am the pawn

Buckingham has decided to move across the board in order to trap the unprotected king. But what a chance, what a king. I have no hope of winning, but I am helpless against such an opportunity—not to capture a king, but to spend time near the *man*.

I will travel to Hampton Court on Friday. I wish Peg was going to be there, but she has been dividing her time between Rupert's London townhouse in Spring Gardens and Windsor Castle, where Rupert has been made governor and constable. They are currently renovating both establishments, and it is all Peg talks about.

I cannot shake the unreality from my mind. I feel fogged up with fairytales of love and dancing and castles, and a tall, lithe man who walks too quickly for me to ever keep up.

Later—midnight

Just as I was settling down to bed, a man in Buckingham's livery rapped on the door. He handed me a note and a heavy bag of coins. George has given me a budget for new gowns and a list of what I will need for a summer at court! I am to buy what I like and just return the receipts to him. Anything beyond the budget allowed I am to put on his account. I keep re-reading his note. We are really going through with this? Teddy, Rose, Rochester, and I will shop tomorrow!

Wednesday— Will's Coffee-house

Five hats, eight pairs of gloves (three white, one green, two brown, two black), deep green velvet and ruby velvet (for coats), black *moiré* (for evening, Teddy insisted), creamy lutestring, minty-green brushed satin, soft white linen, rosy-pink taffeta (I worry, with my hair, but Rochester insisted), reams of pale Venice lace, silk hose, four pairs of high-heeled shoes (two buckled and two laced), and a new Chinese fan (I insisted).

"This will do for a start," Buckingham and Rochester agreed. A *start*? I am going to wind up as a greedy spendthrift if I start thinking like them.

"What's so wrong with that?" Teddy asked nonchalantly. "If anyone could make greed *très charmant,* it would be you, my dear."

Rose has taken everything to Madame Leonine—so expensive, I dread to think. She promised that everything could be delivered to Hampton Court next week.

"Until then, stay out of sight," advised Teddy.

"Stay home," says Rose. This new world frightens her, I know. I sympathise—it frightens me, too.

June 18, 1668—Drury Lane

I will not be alone. Johnny Rochester is coming with me! Relief.

Wednesday—Theatre Royal

Evening Love flopped. The audience, the critics, the actors all hated it. Secretly, I am glad: a flop will end the run, and I am anxious to be off. Dryden is not crushed as he himself proclaimed it a second-rate effort—beating them to it, I thought.

"That will mean Hart will be going soon, too," Teddy warned this evening.

"Going?" I repeated. "To the palace?"

"Wherever Castlemaine goes . . ." he said in his sing-song voice.

June 23—Coach and Horses, near Hampton Court

This palace looks lovely from this cosy half-timbered inn where I am lodged but have yet to leave. The red-brick palace is enormous, laid on a grand and elegant scale—a palace fit for a king and stolen by one, apparently: the great Cardinal Wolsey's masterpiece, filched by King Henry VIII. I think of the ghosts that roam here—Henry, his ill-fated queens, and the more recently departed King Charles I. How strange to live in a house with a history of such unhappiness. Does the king think of it, I wonder?

I receive daily instruction in court etiquette from Buckingham and Rochester, who both have good rooms in the palace. We practice the latest dancing—the French *gigues* and *courantes* are all the rage—and then walking and talking and sitting and eating. This morning we spent a whole hour on entrances and curtseys. Buckingham does a lovely curtsey. They encourage me not to lose my Oxfordshire lilt, country accents being so fashionable now, but I am not sure I could if I tried, so *heigh-ho*. We have also been practicing the newest card games (ombre, hazard, and whist) and have been gambling huge sums of imaginary money. I am nervous about what lies beyond these doors.

June 25 — Coach and Horses

Teddy brought my new clothes himself! I am so happy to see him. Tom has spared him through the summer. Now we are a foursome—laughing and dancing and dicing and gambling. Tomorrow is my debut! *"Courage, chérie, you will be fantastique!"* Teddy cheers in a phoney French accent and an unconvincing leer. His enthusiasm heartens me, although I cannot believe I am doing this.

June 26 — Coach and Horses

Bit of a failed debut, as I did not even see the king; although my entrance was lovely, Rochester insisted. Buckingham says I need to practice sitting still. I have a tendency to fidget when I'm nervous, and I will be far more nervous when the king actually shows up. Tonight His Majesty had a private dinner with Castlemaine and did not return. For all I hear of her fading light, they do spend an awful lot of time together.

Still, I was introduced to a number of genial people. I particularly liked Lady Jemimah Sandwich and her husband—she sings wonderfully, and he plays a ferocious game of basset. I also liked a very young gentleman introduced to me as Jemmy—only later did I find out that this is James, Duke of Monmouth, the king's eldest bastard son. I should have guessed: he looks like a softer-featured version of the king. Despite his youth, he is a deter-mined and experienced flirt. Buckingham interceded, steering me away and onto safe ground. Despite my many *faux pas*—using the wrong fork for the roast dishes and forgetting to throw my napkins behind my chair: I kept mine for the whole of the dinner, awful—I enjoyed myself tremendously.

Sedley joined the court tonight, arriving just after the grand and ter-rifying supper, making for a merry time. Jemmy Monmouth and I both beat him in ombre, and then he sang his newest songs, some surprisingly poignant. Afterwards, Rochester, drunk but elegant as usual, encouraged me to do impressions—dicey stuff in this company, but (after several glasses of wine and lots of encouragement) I did a few, keeping only to well-known theatre folk—safer that way. Couldn't resist a waddling imitation of Moll Davis. The Howard boys had collaborated to write a terrible little rhyme, and I performed it while mimicking her lumpy little dance. They roared with laughter. So cruel of me.

June 27 — Hampton Court

Buckhurst has joined us. I am actually quite pleased to see him. He is attentive—but not in his obsessive way—and sweet, and I have the feel-ing that like all the Merry Gang he is keeping an eye on me. Nearly all the Wits are here now. Georgie Etheredge, the playwright, and John Sheffield, the young and thorny Earl of Mulgrave, arrive tomorrow to make our merry party merrier still. Still no sign of the king.

Note—I learned tonight that Hart is here. I caught sight of Hugh outside the inn tonight. How long has Hart been here? And does he know that I am here?

June 30, 1668 — Hampton Court

Terrible news from London:

Will Davenant, manager of the Duke's House, died today. The king wore black ribbons in his hair in memoriam, so Buckingham tells me. Rochester—a great friend of Will's—has been drunk all day. It has already been announced that Tom Betterton and Henry Harris are to co-manage in his stead. "Filthy dogs," Rochester snorted, despising their haste. Relief: Hart has apparently returned to London.

July 18, 1668— Newmarket, the White Hart Coaching Inn (hot!)

Spent the morning happily browsing the brisk tidy market and came home with armfuls of fresh flowers, a volume of poetry, and new bread. Buckingham was waiting in my rooms when I returned—not downstairs but *in* my rooms. *Heigh-ho,* there seems to be no formality in my life. Buckingham paced up and down the noisy floorboards while I put away my purchases. He clearly had something to say and wanted my full attention. Perversely, I took my time and would not give it—very childish of me.

"Ellen, sit!" he finally exploded, commanding me like one of his spaniels. I sat, daintily spreading out my skirts on the rough chair. I knew what was upsetting him—my disheartening lack of progress with the king. I was finding the whole endeavour awkward and trying. All I could do was be myself—a better-mannered, better-dressed, better-educated version of myself, but at the root the same—but this king looks at the roots. Not that the king has looked at me at *all.*

I took a deep breath. "You want me to be bolder? Wittier? Prettier? Sexier?"

"I would settle for visible. He doesn't even know you are here!" he railed. "Do *something!*"

Accustomed to the excited, impassioned critique of the rehearsal room, I was unfazed by Buckingham's words. He is right. I am treating this as a game of make believe that need never come true. In my deepest heart I think the entire enterprise is absurd and *could* never come true. Last year I was an orange girl . . . how could I ever hope to interest the king? But my friends seem to believe it is possible. Do I do this for them? No. I do this for myself. It is a daydream that will not fade. My fascination with this man has a thrumming pulse of its own, and in truth, I cannot pass up this chance, however slim, however unlikely—my glass-slipper heart will not allow it. And so, I am resolved. I will make him notice me. For better or worse I will play one hand.

LONDON GAZETTE

Sunday, July 26, 1668

Most Deservedly Called London's Best and Brilliant Broadsheet

The Social Notebook
Volume 317

Ambrose Pink's social observations du jour

Darlings!

The country has become a savage place, my petals. Eat or be eaten is the rule of the forest! The ladies of the court stalk their prey with shrewd skill and painted prowess. They attack in the ballrooms, at the archery butts, on the bowling greens, and in the gilded salons of louche power. Their weapons are devastatingly pretty silks and satins, corsets and curls, fans and frills, patches and pearls. Beware! These creatures play to win! Their talons are sharp, and their hearts are ruthless. And the prey? He deftly eludes their well-laid traps, enjoying their efforts but denying them the prize. He is, indeed, the King of the Forest!

À bientôt,
Ever your eyes and ears,
Ambrose Pink, Esq.

August 5 — The Unicorn Inn, Tunbridge Wells

The man is surrounded! Besieged! If it isn't Castlemaine, it is Moll, the most irritatingly vapid girl I have ever heard, who seems to want to do nothing but take the waters (good for fertility) and play silly flirtatious lawn games such as hot cockle, and then make play houses out of cards! She sets my teeth on edge with her lack of substance. "Soap bubbles," I told Teddy tonight as I unpinned my hair. "She reminds me, exactly, of a big shiny empty soap bubble."

"Yes, but bubbles are so fragile and elusive," he said, pulling the brush through my hair in long, soothing strokes. "That is their magic. When you try to grab one, they vanish. Smart trick," he said ruefully.

"Moll is a bit heftier than a bubble," I said cruelly.

If it isn't Moll, it would be one of a dozen other ladies here for exactly the same purpose. I understand the inclination—he is like a heat, a strength, a safety we all want to be near. He is dazzling.

Later (back to change again)

The boys all have strong opinions about my clothes and toilette, and my rooms have become an entirely inefficient democracy. They cannot agree on anything, from shoes to hats, and so I spend a great deal of time wandering about in my lovely new underclothes whilst they bicker; as I am accustomed to the crowded tiring rooms, this lack of privacy does not faze me. Buckingham always goes for whichever gown is the most *décolleté* (obviously), and Buckhurst will reliably choose the most expensive. Teddy and Rochester (bless them) are interested in whichever makes me *feel* most comfortable. To create the effect of *ease,* and grace, Rochester explains dramatically. It is sweet to see these brilliant boys, all famous for their scathing wit, playing amongst the silks and lace. It makes them seem so young and free. This morning (after lengthy debate) I wore my new white muslin gown (Rochester's choice) with the cream *pointe,* blue sash, and my delicate little silver mules—lovely! (Teddy's choice). But nothing! No response. The king does not seem to notice me at all. Grumble.

Note—They *all* favour hair *à la négligence*—heavens, it is difficult to make hair look artfully undone. *What* a lot of work.

Later, ten p.m.

This evening after a glorious supper served out of doors under the yew trees—roasted meats, stewed meats, fresh vegetables from the garden (unfashionable, but the queen favours them, as do I), fresh bread, country cheese, artful little cakes glazed in frosted marzipan, and then coffee at long last (goodness, these people do eat)—I noticed the little queen had taken herself off to the gardens alone. She is often alone, a reserved dove amidst the bright noisy larks of the court, all of them angling for her husband's affections. I felt ashamed. I, too, was trying to bed this good, pious woman's husband. And she knew it. Overcome by remorse, I followed her outside the bright circle of torches into the silent, box-hedged garden. I hesitated. How does one approach the queen? She is rigorous about conduct. I lurked by a stone cupid under a flowering peach tree.

"Do you wish to speak to me?" she asked with surprising frankness. Her voice was low and rich and her accent gently rolling.

I dropped like a stone into my best curtsey and stayed bowed low. "Yes, madam." What now? "I often see you alone and . . . and . . ." I stopped.

"And?" she kindly encouraged, raising me up. We were of a similar height, both tiny in this world of giants.

"And I would be your friend, if I could. If you wished it." I heard the absurdity of my request. I am Ellen Gwyn, of Coal Yard Alley, an actress and orange girl currently trying to seduce her husband. She was the Portuguese Infanta and is now the Queen of England—a princess twice over. Why would she choose *me* as a companion? By all the rules of royal etiquette, she should not even speak to me. *Heigh-ho*, in it now. I am becoming accustomed to looking the fool in these circles. And besides, the truth is I *do* want to be her friend. I respect this courageous little woman who remains in a foreign, unfriendly, scrutinising court because she passionately loves her husband.

"Ah, but wouldn't you rather be my husband's friend?" she asked quietly.

I snapped out of my reverie, sheepish and apologetic. She lifted my chin and looked me in the eyes. She has an unexpected directness, a kind of gravity about her. I found her disarming. I could not lie to her.

"Yes," I confessed. "That is just what I was brought here to do." I had no excuse. What excuse could there be?

"By Buckingham?" I nodded. She sighed, unsurprised. After six years in England she was accustomed to such bedroom intrigue—and always in her husband's bedroom. "Lady Castlemaine is no longer helpful to him, I gather, and so he is in the market for a more malleable royal mistress?" Her clear assessment of the situation startled me.

"Do you not mind?" I asked boldly, too boldly. She was every inch a queen and would not allow such intimacies.

Skirting the question, she responded lightly, "And how are you finding the lion's den?"

"More like hyenas," I replied sharply, thinking of *la belle Stuart*'s grating giggle.

She laughed a ripe, throaty laugh, understanding my reference. "Mrs. Gwyn, is it?"

"Ellen," I offered instinctively—*why do I do that?* "Just Ellen."

"Ellen," she mused. "Good night, Mrs. Ellen."

The conversation was over. "God give you good night, madam," I wished her with feeling. She turned to go indoors. I swept her a low curtsey. At the blossoming hedgerow she turned back and said quietly, "I accept. We shall be friends. God keep you, Mrs. Ellen." I did not look up but remained there until she was out of sight. I like this woman.

August 6— Back to the Coach and Horses

The talk ripples across the court: the king left last night for a quick trip to London—to survey the new building works—and coincidentally Moll Davis left for London soon after.

Later, at the gaming tables

"To visit her *mother*," the Venetian ambassador said with a wink.

"Suffolk Street is the *second* new town house he has purchased for that woman," Lady Fitzharding whispered, considering her hand. "The first was not to her liking; she preferred a more *fashionable* street. Of course she wants *more*. She is after all she can get."

"I heard she has ordered crimson silk wall coverings and is planning an entirely *crimson* drawing room," Colonel Wyndham said in a conspiratorial whisper. I saw the eyebrows of his wife, Lady Christabelle, arch in surprise.

"Vulgar," she quipped.

"Common," sniffed the wife of the Venetian ambassador, laying down her cards.

"Worse than common, an *actress*. What did you expect?" Lady Fitzharding sighed. "Actors have a certain charm, I've found, but actresses . . ." She shuddered.

"They are *so* right," I said loudly to Buckingham, well within their hearing. "Actresses can be so greedy, but noble ladies like your cousin Barbara Castlemaine are *always* graciously contented with their lot."

Later, in the gardens

"The rebuilding of his capital city has become my husband's passion," the queen said affectionately, ostensibly oblivious to his other all-too-notable passion. Her ladies twittered in agreement.

August 7 — Tunbridge Wells

I spent a pleasant afternoon with the queen and her companions on the archery course. She is quite accomplished; I was surprised by her athleticism, although I do not know why I should be. Her humour is understated and quite dry. She has been an avid student of this court and understands its intricacies well. I watch her watch her own ladies-in-waiting. She is bright and gay, and leads them in the merriment, but is ever on her guard. With good reason. This flirtatious flock would rejoice in her removal. I would not. She is a good, kind queen, a better woman than I by far. *What am I doing here?*

Later, three p.m. — The Unicorn Inn, Tunbridge Wells

Just back to change my gown. Changing my ensemble must take up half my day. It doesn't do to wear the same gown for morning *and* afternoon lawn games. And evening gowns are a different beast entirely. I complain, but truly it feels so good to be clean and freshly changed so often—and into such beautiful clothes! The tavern-keeper's wife has left the wooden bath-tub in my rooms all week, as I have use of it so often.

"I must say," said Buckingham, entering unannounced and dropping lazily onto the tufted window-seat, "befriending the wife is not a strategy I have seen before."

"Not everything is strategy, George," I snapped, looking for my gloves. It was the cream pair with the enamel buttons that I was particularly fond of. I had chosen to wear my new green gown with the custard-cream under-skirt, and they matched perfectly. "I have befriended her because I like her."

"*Like* her." Buckingham snorted. "What is there to like? She looks like a bat, dresses like a dormouse, and behaves like a frightened cat—three animals I do not find compelling." Lifting up a pile of scripts, he found my gloves beneath. Handing them to me, he said sharply, "Do not get close to her, Ellen. Your tender little heart will go out to her, and *then* how will you bed her husband?"

I pulled on the gloves and shot him what I hoped was a condescending look. "I must get back. She is expecting me for cribbage."

Buckingham laughed. "Christ on the cross! Cribbage and the queen— you do surprise, Ellen."

"Always," I shot back mischievously. I closed the door behind me and left him laughing inside.

August 8— Tunbridge Wells (warm)

We were all lying under the trees in the privy garden, the Wits and I looking over Etheredge's revisions of his *She Would If She Could* (not bad, but still too long) when the talk fell to me.

"The secret is out, Nell," Etheredge said, popping grapes into his mouth like an ancient Roman. "Everyone knows why you are here." Discretion has never been Etheredge's strong suit. "Now the question is, *when* will you make your move?"

"I think she has made it," said Buckingham dryly. "She has come here and won over the queen—*brilliant*."

"It *is* brilliant," Sedley chipped in, reaching across Etheredge for the bowl of grapes. "Everyone has taken note of Nell's subtlety and kindness, and she makes all the other sirens look like greedy harpies in comparison—particularly dumpy, demanding Moll. *Brava*, Nelly!"

"Subtlety!" Buckhurst snorted. "Since when has this court placed any value on subtlety?"

"Well, the king certainly won't notice," said young Mulgrave, his mouth full of grapes (he has the unfortunate habit of speaking whilst chewing). "He likes his women bold and brazen."

"What makes you think he hasn't noticed already?" said Rochester quietly. He was sitting apart under a pink and green apple tree, his eyes closed to the bright afternoon sun. "It is *you* who have no eye for subtlety. This king misses very little."

"Just like you," I said affectionately, leaning down to kiss his nose.

Later, ten p.m.

He *has* noticed me.

Tonight after wild dancing in Buckingham's rooms—I wore my striped ruby-red waistcoat and matching velvet knee breeches and danced on the priceless furniture—Rochester escorted me back to my lodging. We were both a bit tipsy, and he insisted. I was surprised—such chivalry is unlike him, as he does not generally like to be put out. We were making our unsteady way through the New Gallery when he stopped and sat on a bench under one of the archways.

"Why've we stopped?" I whispered loudly, too loudly.

"Just hush and wait," Rochester whispered back, blowing out his candle.

"Oh, Johnny," I said, dismayed to be sitting in the dark. "I wish you hadn't done that. What are we waiting for?"

"Me," said a familiar voice in the shadows. A candle sprang to life. *Him.*

"Good night, Your Majesty," said Rochester, rising to leave—suddenly seeming very sober. The king was expected, I realised. They had arranged this.

"Johnny, I—" *Don't leave me.*

"Good night, Ellen," Johnny said, brushing his lips over my forehead. *"Be you,"* he whispered in my ear, and then slipped away down the dark hallway. Did he really say that? *Did I imagine it?* Everything felt unreal all of the sudden.

"Ellen," the king said warmly, "would you care to walk?"

"In the dark?" Why did I say that—*obviously* in the dark.

"Yes"—he chuckled—"in the dark." Taking my hand in his, he led me out into the Great Court. The moon had silvered the even grass. The messy, busy palace lay in quiet, organised silhouette.

I secretly watched the man beside me. His height, his stride, his graceful lines. This man was the *king.* He had asked *me* for a midnight walk. *Me. Me. Me.* He wanted to walk with *me.* But this is a mistake, I wanted to tell him. I am Ellen, from Drury Lane. I sell oranges, and my sister sells her body. My mother sold her daughter. I act upon the stage. I am a common, common girl. I am not the girl you saw dancing in beautiful shoes.

Reaching for conversation, struggling to clear my head, struggling to absorb the reality of the situation, I questioned him about the progress of the building work in London. The queen was right: here lies his passion. He launched into a long discussion of the current building works. He told me of his great dream for a new city, of his genius architect—Mr. Christopher Wren, the astronomer visionary who would rebuild the churches. I was struck by his earnest care for each of his citizens. He is determined to protect them with a city of brick and stone: "A house of brick, should it catch fire, will only fall in upon itself. It will not endanger the other houses. A wooden house will take down a street."

"Who could design such a city?" I asked, as if I were familiar with leading architects.

"I have decided not to favour one man's plan over another's, but to take the best of each," he said evenly. "Wren's and Evelyn's plans are the best— Wren's for beauty and Evelyn's for sanitation—but I must not set them against each other." Conflict clearly did not agree with this man. "I must draw the best from both."

Forgetting my fear, I got caught up in his vision and began to question him in earnest: "But if you change the city plan, what will happen to those people who owned that land? It will not be the same."

"The Londoners must trust me in this. Together, we will make a London so great that all the land will be of greater value and *all* will benefit." As I listened to him, I realised that they were wrong: all those gossiping nay-sayers who believed that this was a debauched, lazy, indulgence-ridden king. Rochester was right: there was nothing careless in this man.

I could not see his face, but I felt his grip tighten around my hand, saw the heavy white lace of his cuff. He stopped at a stone bench under a large pear tree and turned to face me.

"You have befriended my wife." It was a statement rather than a question.

"Yes," I whispered.

"To get to me?"

"No." I looked up and could just make out the serious lines of his countenance in the dimness. "No, at first because I pitied her, and now because I like her."

"I like her, too," the king said quietly. How strange, I thought. To be standing in the moonlight talking to a man of his wife. It could be any man. Any wife. But they are not. He continued, "I worry for her in this court. And I believe now that she will never bear children. But I cannot abandon her."

"Because you love her?"

"Because she is my wife and it would be . . ." His voice trailed away. "Impossible," he finished quietly. With that, he closed up like a tulip in the evening. I knew better than to push.

I tiptoed back to my rooms in the misty half-light and prepared for bed as the town began to stir. I feel as if I don't need food or sleep or daylight. I can exist on this nourishing wonder. Alone in my rooms, I slip into my nightgown and, curling my arms around my knees, I think: Did this night happen?

When I Walk with the King

August 12, 1668—Hampton Court

We meet each night now, in the Great Court, in the moonlight. The weather has become terribly important to me. I pray for clear skies and fret when rain clouds threaten. I wait for him on the stone bench under the pear tree—our pear tree. We walk and talk and are often silent. I live for this time. I am Ellen and not Ellen. He makes me more. He is the king and not the king all at once. I am fascinated by the *man*. I feel helpless, enchanted by a spell I did not cast.

He does not kiss me. I tell no one.

August 15, 1668—Groundskeeper's Lodge, Ham House

"Well?" Buckingham questioned me this morning, pulling back the bed curtains to allow the sunlight in. The king had arranged a set of rooms for me here in the keeper's lodge, set far away from the rest of the court (although I gave out that they were arranged by Peg). I was surprised Buckingham had found me. "Ten gowns, eight hats, twelve pairs of slippers, and lots of precious time later—what have you accomplished?"

I quickly glanced over at the new striped apricot gown the king had given me, carelessly slung over a chair.

"What time is it?" I asked sleepily, sitting up. I had not returned until after five in the morning.

"Late, nearly luncheon. What are you doing sleeping? You went to bed early last night." His eyes suddenly narrowed. "Unless you were not sleeping? Not alone? I will not pay for—"

"I was alone," I cut him off. "I just did not sleep well," I lied.

"He is swimming this morning. Do you swim? No, thought not. Well, get out there and cheer then. He is racing Mulgrave this morning—wiry little thing, swims like a fish, irritating." He roughly handed me my wrapper. "Get up!"

He stomped out, leaving me to dress, but then banged back through the door. "Nell," he said loudly, wagging a finger at me, "if you fail with him, then you're for me, you know. I've *paid* for it."

I cringed. "I am not for sale," I told him pertly.

He turned to go, fed up with this conversation. "Ha! All women are for sale," he said crassly, banging the door shut behind him.

Why didn't I just tell him? We *did* make a plan. I have a different plan now. I *am* succeeding. I do not want to be a bought woman, and when I am with the king I am not, no matter who paid for my shoes.

August 20— Oxford, the Bear Inn, Bear Lane

The court has returned to Oxford for the end of the summer. The king—Charles, *my Charlemagne*—regards this city as his second home; he was delighted to discover it is the city of my birth. I am pleased, too, for it begins to feel like my home as well. With rooms of my own in this ancient snug inn, away from damp Farm Cottage and the empty echoing house in Longwall Street, I am beholden to none. No one understands my refusal to stay with the court, but I know I would be lessened there. And I cannot bring myself to lodge beneath the same roof as the woman I am so egregiously betraying—well, not betraying yet, but certainly hoping to. It would be a step too far.

After the court goes to sleep, we walk through the hushed city. Each night we visit a different college, sneaking about the quadrangles like runaways. He matches his long strides (he is so tall!) to my small ones without any appearance of effort. He is passionate about architecture and explains the different features of each building: pointing out the mediaeval elements of Merton, the Italianate renaissance details of University. Each college is like a jewel box that we open together. My mind is hungry for all he knows. Each night we walk a little farther.

He tells me of his life: his twelve-year exile and his hopeless cause. Wandering through Europe, a pauper king with no country or crown. He understands the humiliation of charity. He knows what it is to beg, to want, to need, to fear—it is something we share. I look at his plush velvet coat and his deep cuffs frothing with lace—such luxury; it is hard to believe he was not always like this. And then I look at his face—the fleeting, hunted looks that flash across like an interval in a play—and I can believe this man has been through anything. His mind is agile, and his laughter has a freeness I would not expect after hearing his stories.

He tells me of his small, warlike mother. The notorious Queen Henrietta Maria who drove this country away from the House of Stuart with her Catholicism and her inflexibility—her constant determination to rule her husband and her children, and her ruthless inability to forgive.

He tells me of his brother Henry's terrible Protestant consumptive end, and his mother's cruel refusal to see him unless he converted to the true faith. The stalemate lasted until death. Yet, he says, she is not a woman without feeling. He describes his parents' marriage as passionate and devoted. He understands, I thought. That is the root of his magnetism. He sees people clearly and accepts their failings. It is a great strength.

He does not tell me of his father. He does not speak of that January day that must haunt him still, when they led his father out one of the great windows of his own dining room—the beautiful banqueting hall where his son still sits—and cut off his head. I know the stories. I was raised on them. How, at the final hour, they moved the place of execution. How he waited patiently, listening to them hammering together his own scaffold. How he wore two shirts against the bitter cold, lest the people mistook his shivering for fear. How he handed his ring to his confessor, Bishop Juxon, in his last moments, and bid him tell his children to "remember." How the crowds watched. How he was fearless unto death—calm and resigned. Of these things, we do not speak.

He tells me of his beloved youngest sister: Henriette-Anne—Minette, the Madame of France, married to the loathsome Phillipe, Duc d'Orléans, the Monsieur. She holds his whole heart. His happiest memories always include her.

He tells me of his children: his first-born, James, Duke of Monmouth, born of his love affair with the wild beauty Lucy Walter, now nine years dead. His children by Barbara Castlemaine: Anne, Charles, Henry, Charlotte (his secret favourite), and George.

He tells me of his wife: his tender regard for her childlike ways, his acceptance of her devotion to him, his acceptance of her religion, his sincere desire to see her happy.

He tells me of his troublesome mistress. He cannot bear to see a woman distressed, and Castlemaine exploits this to her best advantage. With tantrums and rage—with excess. I have promised him that I will always speak the truth to him, and when he asks I am openly critical of her domineering habits. He listens to me, but what can my opinion matter to him? Yet he continues to seek it.

I tell him of my small life. He is full of questions. My family: Grandfather, Mother, Great-Aunt Margaret, and Rose. My home: cramped and poor but full of music and spirit. I am honest. He has known poverty. I tell him of Mother, of the nights of putting her to bed. He already knows Rose's secret. He understands frailty and necessity and does not make me feel ashamed. I have become proud to have been raised in such love. We whisper our stories late into the night, and then suddenly I am returned to my bed—where I dream and dream of him.

Note—He has not kissed me.

And so I wait.

Undated

Buckingham knows. He bribed the king's footman for the information and is furious at me for the added expense. "You could have just told me!" he thundered, looking gloomy. "Twelve and two! Footmen are the *most* expensive!" I had been summoned to his rooms like a child to answer for my offences.

"I couldn't—there is nothing as yet to tell," I said with absolute conviction. "And if anyone hears of it, I promise you whatever there is will come to nothing!"

"That makes no sense." Buckingham giggled. "There is nothing, but this nothing will get destroyed if anyone knows something?"

"Yes!" I said, delighted he understood.

When I Take a Stand

August 22 — Oxford, the Bear Inn, Bear Lane (beautiful, clear blue day)

"Darling," Teddy began hesitantly, "I do not mean to be rude, but you look dreadful."

Rochester opened one eye to look at me, watchful of my response.

"Is it because *he* has returned to the court?"

"He?" I puzzled.

We were lying on the grassy bank of the Isis, enjoying a quiet afternoon picnic under the high elms. I spread out a faded blanket, and we laid out our little feast: bread, cheese, apples, and wine.

"He. Your he. Well, your old he." Teddy sighed in laboured exasperation. "Hart."

"Hart? Oh no," I said airily, closing my eyes against the sun. Hart had returned several days ago and was athletically engaged once more in his relationship with the wicked Castlemaine. "Why would that disturb me?" I asked dreamily. These days nothing could disturb me.

Teddy eyed me warily. "Ellen, what on earth . . ."

"I have not been sleeping," I hedged.

"Not sleeping?" Teddy asked archly. "Because at night you have been . . . what? And, more importantly, with *who*?"

"With *whom*." Rochester corrected, leaning back onto the tree trunk. Being out of doors always makes him sleepy.

"Not what you think." I would trust Teddy with any secret, but it was as if to speak of it would break an enchantment. Would I turn back into a pumpkin, as in the fairy story? The bells chime at midnight and the magic ends. I did not want to risk it. I turned my attention to feeding Ruby crusted bread.

"I am sure it will pass," I said lightly. "Not to worry, old mother hen." Teddy makes a habit of worrying over those he loves. It is one of his best qualities. I felt disloyal and selfish in my deception. Teddy gave me a rueful look, as if I had disappointed him.

Note—Rochester has postponed his visit to his wife *again*, poor woman. He speaks of her with great tenderness. "She is all that is selfless and good," he said reverently last night. When I asked why he does not make more effort to see her, he went strangely quiet. Selfishly, I am relieved, as I do not know what I would do without him.

Later, ten p.m.

I am a fool! I have been ensorcelled, bewitched, wrapped up in a fairy love that only *I* feel. The king—*my Charlemagne,* gave his *other* mistress, Moll Davis (who arrived in Oxford today quite visibly pregnant) a diamond ring worth six hundred pounds. A *fortune.*

"It has no bearing upon his feelings for you!" Buckingham rants.

I do not believe him. I see my rank in the pecking order and am wary. Moll does not overtake Castlemaine, and is scorned for her position as an actress, but she is acknowledged. Where am I? Nelly: an amusing, sprightly, courteous stranger in public. And then I am Ellen, secreted away in the moonlight. I promised myself long ago: just one man. Not like Rose. But if he cannot love just one woman? I ought to know better.

Two a.m.

He is waiting for me. I will not appear. I feel shamed by his secrecy, yet I have not asked him for acknowledgement. I feel betrayed, yet he has promised me nothing. I feel lied to, although he has never lied. Oh, my unruly heart. Was *this* the ungovernable feeling I wished for? This wild tide of emotion?

Even later

A page (out of royal livery) arrives with a note:

> *Ellen,*
>
> *Will you not meet me? How have I offended?*
> *Send Jerome back with your reply.*
>
> C

"You are Jerome?" I asked the page.

"Yes, madam." He could not have been older than thirteen.

"Why do you not wear the king's colours?"

"His Majesty ordered that I remove it," he said, clearly flummoxed by my question. So as not to be recognised, I thought. More secrets.

"Please tell His Majesty that I have no reply."

Later still—four a.m.

Jerome knocked lightly on my door—in royal livery (it made him look even younger). He handed me another note.

Ellen,

> *It is not as you think. Please come with Jerome now.*
> *I must speak to you.*

C

Early—seven a.m.

I am back. What happened:

"How did he seem when he gave you this?" I asked the waiting Jerome.

"Seem, madam?"

"Did he seem distressed at all?"

"Yes, madam. He will not allow his gentlemen to ready him for bed. He is waiting upon you." Jerome shifted from foot to foot, uncomfortable in his role as go between. I quickly made a decision.

"I will be ready presently." I threw a shawl (peach, warm and pretty in candlelight) around my lawn nightgown and followed him into the street, careless of what people would think. When Jerome turned right at the gates, I turned to him. "Are we not going to the Great Court?" Our meeting place.

"He awaits you in his rooms, madam," he said, holding his flambeau aloft, lighting the way.

His rooms.

Heart and courage, Ellen.

I stood in the shadows as Jerome knocked upon the great door. The Royal Apartments. His rooms—his bedchamber. The door swung inward. True, the bed was hung with richest velvet, and the carpet was thick and soft. Still just a room, I told myself. Nothing to fear. But a *king's* room. A deep breath. I stepped forward.

He stood just inside, as if he had been waiting. "Ellen." He opened his arms, folding me into his protective embrace.

And then there were no more words.

Later, lying together in the great bed, I asked him my question. "Are you ashamed of me?"

"Ellen—"

"I know I am only an orange girl, an actress. Even Moll is better born— base born, it's true, but at least her father is—"

He quieted me with a kiss.

"And still she is reviled—"

"Hush now. I am not ashamed of you." He tilted my face up to his. "With your pure spirit, how could I ever be? It does not matter who your father was. You have a nobility all your own. Unpolluted, untainted, and marvellously whole. I am so happy when I am with you."

"Then why—"

"To be my love is a public role. It will change *you* forever. It will change everything for *you*. You will be exposed to scrutiny, criticism, intrigue, malice, and unhappiness. Men wanting power will court you. Women wanting to reach me will despise you. You will be plagued with insincerity, unable to trust anyone's motives. My wife considers you her friend, and she will distance herself from you. People will watch you, guessing, is she in favour, out of favour? Your life will no longer belong only to you. How could I have done that? To you, who are so free."

"And now?" I asked, holding my breath.

"And now you *are* my love. It is for you to choose."

Relieved, I nestled my head back onto his chest and slept soundly. Jerome arrived to take me back to my room at six—early, before the court rose.

"Hurry back before the gossips awake. I do not want to share you yet, if I can prevent it. Is that all right?" he asked tenderly. I nodded happily and reached up to kiss him. How had that seemed so impossible, unbridgeable, only a few hours ago? He neatly tucked my shawl around my shoulders and sweetly kissed me good-bye. I tiptoed away in my nightgown and slippers.

In the grey-pink light the whole world had changed. I felt flooded with fragile magic. Entering my room, I was surprised to find that everything was just as I had left it. The poppy-red gown I had worn to the picnic was still carelessly heaped on a chair, my velvet slippers still shunted beneath. A cup of cold chocolate was left on the windowsill, and a plate of toast lay on the desk. It felt like the room of a different girl.

This is happiness, I thought, watching the town come to sleepy life, through the sash window. I must remember this feeling.

August 23, 1668— Oxford—the Bear Inn, Bear Lane

I keep vigil over our secret. If his name is mentioned, I quickly leave the room, terrified my powerful reaction might show upon my face. Now that it is *our* secret, I want only to guard it. They carelessly bandy his name about, sending delicious ripples of feeling through me. How can others not see it? I am so lightly tethered to this earth; my joy is so great.

Later—the Bear Inn

She did not notice any change in me, I tell myself. I was just the same.

Tonight:

As we were sitting down to a game of basset after dessert, the queen unexpectedly rejoined the court. She had retired early with a headache but, after taking a tonic from her physician, decided to return to the gaming room. Changed into an ocean-blue satin gown with a simple but elegant neckline of seed pearls, she looked lovely in the candlelight. She pleasantly moved around the room, lightly resting her hand on her husband's shoulder, standing behind his chair as he played his cards. They seemed easy in each other's company, enjoying the familiar, genuine affection of a well-matched couple.

I quickly dropped her my deepest curtsey as she approached my chair, and she raised me up with a small sincere smile. "I see you have been lucky tonight," she laughed musically, gesturing to my pile of winnings.

"So far." I grimaced. "I will likely lose it all by the end."

"Ah, more likely you will lend it to your friends, and *they* will lose it," she said kindly, her ripe accent rolling through her words like a tide.

"True." I laughed. I did have a tendency to lend away all my money rather than lose it myself.

"Be sure to save something for yourself, sweet Ellen," she said, gently patting my cheek and moving off to rejoin her husband.

Now alone, I wonder how I can do this to such a very, very good woman?

September— London

Back in the theatre. I cannot concentrate on my scripts. I cannot stop daydreaming. I float through my rehearsals—dancing rehearsals, singing rehearsals, script rehearsals—

"Ellen!" shouts Lacy. "Catch up!" They had moved on to one of the French dances—I was still moving through my exercise figures.

The season is all for me. I will star. I will shine. But I am not here. I am away. I am with him. Waiting. Waiting for it to be dark. Waiting for the carriage to come—softly, quietly pulling up at the far end of Bridges Street. Waiting for Jerome to meet me at the gate. Waiting for Mr. Chiffinch (the infamous, procuring Mr. Chiffinch—who is quite sweet, really, despite his infamy) to lead me up the small staircase through the doors to the King's Suite. And then he is there, and I come alive.

Note—Alive in both joy and shame. There can be no excuse for what I am doing. My only atonement is to remember that.

When My Heart Is Divided

LONDON GAZETTE

Sunday, September 13, 1668

Most Deservedly Called London's Best and Brilliant Broadsheet

The Social Notebook

Volume 324

Ambrose Pink's social observations du jour

Darlings,

What daring! What pluck! It seems (from a very reliable source) that during their recent royal hunting excursion to Bagshot, the Duke of Buckingham attempted to place himself above Prince Rupert of the Rhine (Prince Rupert of royal blood, mind you). While stopping at an inn, on their way back to London, the duke discovered his own horses to be stored in a less-desirable location than Prince Rupert's. Without hesitation or consultation, the bold duke turned out the prince's horses and installed his own. Who knew such high drama could happen in a stable, my pets?

When dashing Prince Rupert complained to the king, His Majesty overruled in favour of the dastardly duke. It seems that Buckingham rules all. Be warned, my petals.

À bientôt,
Ever your eyes and ears,
Ambrose Pink, Esq.

September 16, 1668— Theatre Royal

A strange day:

We performed the new Dryden, *Ladies à la Mode*, this afternoon to a half-empty house. It was terrible. Dryden had in truth done little but translate the play from the French, and the language felt patchy at best (his new post of Poet Laureate—he took over when Will Davenant died—has made him neglectful of his playhouse duties). We were ill rehearsed, for which I must take my share of blame as I have not been working as I should. After the show, Tom strode onto the stage and delivered a scalding reproof, which was deserved but thoroughly unpleasant. The play shall be pulled and replaced with Rob Howard's *The Duke of Lerma*. Good—he is in need of a boost since his Sir Positive-At-All fiasco. I shall play Maria, a part I quite well remember and hardly need to study again—thankfully—because I have finally been invited to a late supper with Charles (it has been over a week since our last meeting), and I did not want our plans to be interrupted by an emergency rehearsal. Lacy took us through the great dance only once and then released us (to be back at eight in the morning—but no matter, freedom today!).

Spoke to Peg for a few minutes after rehearsal. She is angry at the high-handed behaviour of Buckingham (no surprise there) towards Rupert. Something to do with horses; I am afraid I wasn't really listening.

At the stage door Jerome was waiting (not in livery) with a note:

> *My little love,*
> *I am not yet returned to town and must see to a friend*
> *who is unwell. My thoughts are ever with you.*
>
> C.

Teddy, seeing my crestfallen face, gently steered me out the door into the street. "Ellen," he said, trying to gain my attention. My attention, still fixed upon Jerome—Jerome, who had not waited for my reply. He must have had instructions to return directly.

"Ellen," Teddy said again, this time taking me firmly by the shoulders. "I *know*. I have known throughout that you were entirely successful in Buckingham's royal bedroom adventure. You have been snuffled out, my sweet fox." (Teddy loves animal metaphors.) "I know, too, that you wish to keep it secret, and to that end"—he looked at me squarely—"you *must* change your habits." I looked up into his face, ashamed at my duplicity.

"Oh, Teddy," I whispered. "How did you know?"

"Ellen, you really are the most diabolical liar. *Everyone* will soon know. It shows upon your pretty face when anyone mentions the king. What a silly girl you are, my sweet."

I bristled under his criticism, however kindly meant. "Yes, I am his mistress. What of it? I am happy!"

"Happy, but in a dreadfully precarious position," Teddy said quietly. "That note, I would wager that it tells you that he is indisposed this evening and cannot meet you. Am I correct?"

"Yes, but—"

"Yes, because the Duchess of Richmond, Frances Stuart, *la belle Stuart* herself, is ill. She has the small pox."

"Oh," I recoiled at the mention of the dreaded, disfiguring disease.

"It has not altered her appearance and her case was light, it is said, but the king has been ever attentive, even at the risk of his own health."

"He has *seen* her?" He had told me that he has business in Oxford with the architect Christopher Wren this past week. He had told me that since her elopement they have been estranged.

"He has not left her side since she fell ill, and even now, when she is out of danger, he clings to her."

Later

Now away and alone, I think on what Teddy has said. I am the invisible mistress, the secret mistress, the whore. It is for my well-being, I can hear Charles argue—my well-being or his convenience? I did not believe he would forgo all others—not really, not forever—but I did think there would be an honesty between us, an accountability of sorts. That is not true. I had hoped that for now, now when we are so happy . . . Well, I suppose it was only I who was so happy.

The truth: his heart still belongs to another. The clocks have chimed at midnight.

Friday, September 18, 1668 (grey and drizzly)

Teddy and I went to Bartholomew's Fair this afternoon. We are rehearsing *The Silent Woman,* a comedy, in the mornings, but neither of us is cast in *Rollo,* which we have on at the moment. The fair was lively, and the puppets and children and music and sweets were all diverting, but I find myself unable to fully enter my surroundings. I feel as though I am set apart by my thoughts and cannot engage with the world. Teddy understands and is patient with my ongoing strangeness. I am making a decision, I realised. Can I do this? Do I want to do this? It will mean giving my heart to a man who will not protect it. It is a dangerous game to play, for I will love. I will love with all of myself, and I will not gain entrance to all of his heart in return. My stubborn hope still flickers. Perhaps, perhaps.

"You will never be on equal footing," Teddy says in answer to my unspoken thoughts. "It is only your heart that will break."

"But, Frances—"

"Frances never capitulated. She just conceded the field. You cannot compete with that."

I do not want to compete. I want to love and be loved in return. But love requires honesty, and that is not where this path seems to lead.

Still thinking.

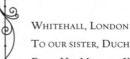

WHITEHALL, LONDON
TO OUR SISTER, DUCHESSE D'ORLÉANS, THE MADAME OF FRANCE
FROM HIS MAJESTY KING CHARLES II
SEPTEMBER 18, 1668

My dear sister,

Frances has contracted small-pox. I think with horror upon my selfish wish for her beauty to fade—and now this, my God. I have been too harsh on her in the past. She wanted a simple life and was true to that simplicity. I cannot help but wish her well now. Guilt spurs me to her bedside. Do not fear, I take precautions not to touch her and am careful to breathe through a cloth mask. Pray for her, my dear one. Will you send one of Louis's famed physicians—Dr. Denis, if at all possible? I would feel better knowing that I had done all I can.

Keep safe,
Charles

Postscript: *Thank you for the gloves, my dearest. They are as soft and lovely as they could possibly be. I will take them with me to Newmarket this month.*

When I Walk with Peg

Friday September 18, 1668—Official Notations for Privy Council Meeting on This Day to Be Entered into the Log-book

Notations taken by Secretary of State Henry Bennet, Earl of Arlington

A successful motion this morning to reduce staff meals in His Majesty's residences today. Senior members of the household will be given two meals per day, and lesser servants shall be given none. This should reduce the court expenditures significantly.

Nothing further to report.
Secretary of State Henry Bennet, Earl of Arlington

Saturday, September 19, 1668— Theatre Royal (The Silent Woman)

A great success. Finally!

We played to a full house—this being the second night of the run and word having got out that this is a worthy comedy. The pit laughed hard.

Lizzie Knep was superb as Epicoene, the title role. My part was smaller but well written, and my breeched dancing much anticipated and well clapped. Even Ruby seemed excited after the show and leapt out of her backstage basket to lick me. I am returned. I am awake to my life. I am still undecided. The court is in Newmarket and then off to Audley End this month. I can think more clearly when I know he is not close by. I will do nothing. The answer will come—now off to supper with Aphra, Teddy, and Johnny.

Note—A brief message today from the king, congratulating me on my success. Inviting me to the races at Newmarket. I have not replied.

Sunday, September 20, 1668— Will's Coffee-house

Such a lot of nonsense. I am losing patience with grown men everywhere. Today in the coffee-house:

Dryden; his brother-in-law, Rob Howard; his wife, Beth; Aphra; and I were enjoying a leisurely Sunday repast after church. The discussion fell to Dryden's *A Defence of an Essay* (his answer to Rob's *Essay of Poesy*). I have made it a point to read neither, as they both seem quite silly and seem to inevitably lead to shouting and disagreements. The argument became heated, as Aphra tried to gently mediate. I finally caught the gist of the thing and was shocked.

"*Rhyme?* You are arguing like this over *rhyme?*"

"Rhyme in *drama,* my dear. Quite another thing," Dryden said pompously. "It truly elevates the form."

"No, it *muddies* it," countered Rob. "A true dramatist can keep it *pure.*"

I looked at Aphra, who rolled her eyes as if to say, *Men.* She is now trying to get her first play produced and is not remotely concerned about *elevation* or *purity,* only revenue. Just then Johnny Rochester came in, fresh from Newmarket, and, depositing a kiss upon my head, dropped into the nearest armchair. Ruby excitedly began to scale his legs and climbed into his lap.

"John," began Dryden officiously, "you will be able to arbitrate this matter."

"I doubt it," said Johnny, affectionately rubbing Ruby's soft, crumply ears.

"Well, regardless," Dryden plodded on, his heavy curls bobbing, "how do you feel about *rhyme* in drama? Don't you believe it to be an essential *tool*? An *art,* an *asset*?" Dryden was warming to his theme. I looked towards Aphra with apprehension. Dryden can be tiresome in this mood. And Johnny never brings out the best in him, as Dryden is so eager, so desperate to impress him that he rapidly becomes unbearable.

"I think that it is *second*-rate writers who worry about tools and arts and assets," Johnny said levelly, not looking up from Ruby. "First-rate writers write *originally* in their own forms and are guided by *God*." I recognised this reckless, dangerous mood of Johnny's and was anxious to steer poor Dryden away.

"But my dear Lord Rochester . . . look at Shakespeare, his use of—"

"That is right. *Look* at Shakespeare. He copied no one." I prudently held my tongue—in other moods I have heard Johnny refer to Shakespeare as an outright thief, unable to originate a plotline. "Unlike your pale, imitative dribblings. It is pathetic to think that we go to such trouble to enact them—or to watch them, for that matter. How truly bored must we be in our gilded, debauched age."

Dryden's round face flushed.

"Johnny," I said, placing my hand lightly on his arm, desperate to change the subject and knowing that Dryden would be mortally wounded by this lacerating criticism—he fairly worships Johnny. "Have you eaten, my dear? May I order you some seed cake? It is particularly lemony today."

"Well," Dryden said pompously, his blond curls bouncing again in righteous indignation, rising and putting on his ridiculous hat (*another* one), "I certainly don't see God's hand guiding you."

"Ah, God." Johnny said thoughtfully. He looked up at Dryden for the first time. "God and I parted ways long ago."

Later

How sad. Sometimes I truly feel that Johnny believes that. It is at the root of his wild ways: the unbridled freedom of an already condemned man. How lonely and afraid it must make him.

Note—I still have not replied.

Monday, September 28— Theatre Royal

Ladies' Day today at the playhouses. All the profits go to us! Teddy made a guest appearance in his sugar-pink frock (didn't get paid but had great fun) and was cheered mightily. Lady Jemimah Sandwich blew him a kiss, and Lady Fenworth's powder-puff dog yipped. All the Wits turned out in support. Buckhurst cheered me particularly loudly and tossed a heavy bag of coins at my feet during my curtsey. Johnny brought me yellow roses tied in a black ribbon after the performance.

Note—I had half hoped, despite my injunction, the king would come. If I wish for something, I should learn to ask for it. But then, I wish to be whole and unharmed, singularly cherished and unhurt—a tricky thing with this man.

Tuesday, September 29, 1668— Michaelmas Day

(warm and sunny)

Peg stopped into the theatre after rehearsal (I am not on the rest of this week) and whisked me away for some afternoon shopping in Paternoster Row. "But I have lines to learn!" I wailed. *And* a new prologue *and* new steps for Lacy's dance . . .

And, and, and. I keep my thoughts perpetually occupied with *and. And* is my armour against the devouring unhappiness of wanting something I cannot have. Better to break my own heart now than to have it broken for me later, I tell myself again and again.

"Get your hat. We're leaving." She would brook no refusal.

Shopping with Peg nowadays is a joyous experience, as she is on Rupert's seemingly unlimited budget. We strolled arm in arm and talked of this and that: the renovations for their sumptuous apartments at Windsor (they have moved into a suite of rooms in the Round Tower, and Rupert has proposed several ingenious alterations), her favourite spaniel's new litter (half-pug and half-spaniel—not what she expected and ugly as can be, but she adores them), plans for her new flower garden at Windsor. Walking past the great Westminster Abbey, I recognised this gnawing at my heart: envy.

In the dress-maker's shop:

"How does the queen fare?" I asked, talking around my subject.

"Well enough, what with the circus she must contend with. Three ambassadors—Venetian, Spanish, and French—all not speaking to one another, all feeling slighted. Ugh." She blew out her cheeks in an exasperated sigh, then held up a particularly lovely length of crimson silk. "What do you think?"

"Not for your colouring, Madame Hughes," clucked Madame Leonine. "Try the deeper blue, in the softer fabric. What do you think, Madame Gwyn?"

I think it would cost me a week's wages. I think I cannot afford such luxury.

"Beautiful," I said.

In the candle-maker's shop:

"Why slighted?" I could not care less about these spoilt foreign ambassadors and was only hungry for news of *him* but, even with Peg, was determined not to ask.

"Oh, such silliness. The Venetian did not greet the Spaniard at the door, and now they will not speak," said Peg impatiently, handing her man a fat bundle of long white wax tapers—an unimaginable expense.

"And the French?"

"He's *French*," she said, throwing up her hands as if this explained everything. "Heaven knows why he has taken umbrage. It is all a mess and has landed in the queen's lap, as the king is unwilling to deal with these brawling diplomats."

In the milliner's shop:

"The queen will find a way to soothe everyone," I said, thinking of her tranquil air.

"She's working on soothing Monmouth. The king promoted him to Lord Gerard's post as the head of the Royal Life Guards last week—after years of Jemmy's pestering. Jemmy is sweet but frightfully stubborn. Now he is strutting about in rich clothes, expecting to be named heir to the throne any day, but the king told him absolutely not. He didn't take it well and is being difficult about it. In any case, Monmouth makes the queen uncomfortable, as he openly assumes she will never . . ." She glanced quickly at the milliner Madame Sophie.

I shook my head slightly. "No." Best to be discreet; Madame Sophie is a notorious gossip.

"I had no idea Gerard was retiring," I said, changing the subject and picking up a wide-brimmed pink hat—all wrong for my hair.

"He wasn't going to retire. The king bought the post for Monmouth for *fifteen thousand* pounds, plus the cost of the swearing-in ceremony. Gets expensive, especially for this king and his currently . . . restricted budget. Ooh, what about this one?" Peg reached for a small green hat with ostrich feathers. She turned this way and that in the glass. It did not suit.

"So the *queen* is having to manage Monmouth's growing expectations? That won't be easy," I said, putting my own hat back on.

"Perhaps the cream voile, Madame Hughes?" offered Madame Sophie, holding out a light, puffed creation.

"Frankly, I do not think she is up to it," Peg said, trying the hat. "Confrontation of any kind is quite beyond her, and he is quite volatile." She turned, examining herself in the glass. "Oh yes!" she exclaimed, turning to me. I nodded my approval; it set off her high pale forehead beautifully. "I'll take two," she said.

In the apothecary's shop:

"Well, are you going to ask me?" questioned Peg, sniffing a pot of rose-scented face cream.

"I was trying not to," I confessed, fidgeting with a vial of verbena scent. "Is it so very obvious?"

"He does care for you truly, Ellen. He knows you are distressed. He sent me—"

"He *sent* you?" I shrilled, louder than I had intended.

"Yes, I was supposed to make it look natural, but I could not lie to you. He sent me to find out if you would care to . . . that is, if you want to continue—"

"Continue," I said, roughly picking up the glass pots and banging them down again on the marble counter. The apothecary looked at me warily. "Continue what? What is it that he wants of me?"

"To be your friend . . . and more, if you will permit," Peg said simply.

"Is that you talking or *him*?" My voice sounded roughened and coarse.

"It is me, but the question came from him to Rupert to me."

"Have you nothing to say in your own words?" I asked meanly, and then instantly regretted it. Peg has always been my friend and does not deserve such treatment.

"He wants you back, Ellen . . . if in fact you have deserted him."

"All in secret though. Not like Castlemaine, constantly pregnant, like a ship in full sail. And not like dull, doughy Moll, also pregnant and quite obviously his mistress, although also quite obviously second tier." I sat down on the bench with a hard, indelicate thump.

"No, not like them, like *you*," Peg said gently, taking a seat beside me.

"And what is that, like me?" I asked warily, thinking of Rose.

"Ah, that is for you to determine." Peg distractedly pulled at the lace of her cuff. I regretted my harsh words. Peg was clearly in the process of determining her own way as well. "He likes you, much more than he lets on," she continued. "Rupert says he is quite smitten."

"When does he find the time," I asked bitterly. "Between Castlemaine and Moll and Frances Stuart and the queen and his horses and presumably ruling the country—"

"You know you care for him deeply. I can see that you miss him," Peg said quietly.

"But how will it end?" I whispered, my true fear.

"For girls like us, how can we ever know that?" responded Peg.

Slowly, we wandered back to the theatre.

Later

I have sent a note. I will see him and talk—no more than that. I have forbidden him to come to the theatre; that is *my* stronghold, my strength.

Audley End

To be carried by hand to Mrs. Ellen Gwyn, Theatre Royal

Wednesday, September 30, 1668

Dearest,

Rupert tells me that you spoke to Peg. My heart hangs in the balance. Please inform me of your decision.

Your Charlemagne

Audley End

To be carried by hand to Mrs. Ellen Gwyn, Theatre Royal

Thursday, October 1, 1668

My love,

Yes, of course, I will send the carriage for you. It will be waiting for you in the usual place at the end of your performance. I must tell you that I have heard reports of you this week and am tempted to disobey your harsh command and spy on you as you dance upon the stage. Why should those loutish brutes of the pit enjoy your pretty legs and not I?

Your Charlemagne

WHITEHALL

TO BE CARRIED BY HAND TO MRS. ELLEN GWYN, THEATRE ROYAL

THURSDAY, OCTOBER 1, 1668

Ellen,

I am not sure I understand. You wish the carriage to wait in front *of the theatre? I am not sure that is wise, my little love. Perhaps you should come here and we discuss it together.*

Charles Rex

WHITEHALL

TO BE CARRIED BY HAND TO MRS. ELLEN GWYN, THEATRE ROYAL

FRIDAY, OCTOBER 2, 1668

Ellen,

Where were you? The coachman said he pulled up at the usual spot, but you were nowhere to be found. Jerome reports that when he asked after you in the theatre, Tom Killigrew (or so I gather, from his description of the man) told him that you had departed for a late supper with friends. May I know the reason for your careless and cruel behaviour?

Charles

WHITEHALL

TO BE CARRIED BY HAND TO MRS. ELLEN GWYN, THEATRE ROYAL

FRIDAY, OCTOBER 2, 1668

Ellen,

I do not understand your reply. Why should it matter, where *a carriage picks you up? It was not as if it was an inclement evening. I had a lovely supper prepared and was left to eat it alone. Please come tonight. I will send the carriage. It will wait in the usual spot.*

CR

Friday, October 2 — Theatre Royal

I have broken down and confessed all to my theatre family. Tom and Lacy called an immediate family conference. Bless them. Bless their unconditional love.

"Stand your ground," Tom said with uncharacteristic belligerence. "You have made your position known, and now you must stick to it. You will not be kept a secret any longer. You must have status. You must have station . . ."

Teddy and Lacy nodded their vigorous assent.

"Yes, my love. If he sees that you can be so easily outmanoeuvred, he will not hold you in high esteem," Lacy said helpfully. "It is your *wit* that sets you apart from these other court trollops. Do not compromise."

"No. It is her *heart* that sets her apart," said Rochester. He had entered the tiring room unnoticed and was insouciantly lounging against the doorframe. "It is your heart that he is drawn to. Do not bargain and brawl like the others. Love him, and you will receive all that you truly need."

"To do that, I must trust him," I challenged.

"Exactly."

Later — Drury Lane

I returned to the theatre after supper to collect my Florimel costume—it has a tear in the sleeve that Rose has promised to mend for me—when Hart came into my tiring room. I looked up, startled. He usually takes care to avoid me in the theatre. Ruby hurled herself into his arms.

"You are worthy of him, Ellen," he said quietly, without preamble, stroking Ruby's folded ears. "You must decide if he is worthy of you."

"Him?" I hedged, trying to gauge if he knew.

"Him." He said with finality and, setting Ruby down, walked heavily from the room.

Yes. He knew.

9.

Travelling Ellen

When All Becomes Public

October 4, 1668, Windsor Castle
To: Mrs. Gwyn, Theatre Royal, London
My dear,

He is the smallest, the pluckiest, and definitely the ugliest of the bunch, but he has enormous heart, as do you, my dear. I think he should belong to you. Rupert sends his love as well and requests you play a musical role next. He says it has been far too long since we heard your sweet voice at the King's. I agree.

Thinking of you,
Peg

Theatre Royal—my tiring room (Henry IV)

Definitely not a singing role. *Heigh-ho.* A surprise today! I was in my tiring room, gritting my teeth over a meaty script, when the wicker basket arrived. I scooped the mottled brown fluff ball out from his pink blanket. Bleary-eyed from travelling, the tiny puppy fell asleep in my hand, nuzzling his squashed black face into my palm. Ruby came over, wary of this intruder, and I brought him down to her level so she could see. Luckily, she licked the top of his fuzzy head and began sucking on his ear, and he happily gave himself up to her ministrations. It seems she has acquired a brother. Johnny popped his head round the door and came in to see the puppy.

"What *is* he?" Johnny asked, picking up the animal.

"No idea. Peg doesn't say, and I can't quite tell. Somewhere between a spaniel and a pug: so much for pure-bred fashion."

"Fashion is for those without imagination. To be unique and be recognised as being utterly yourself, that is the trick. Peg is right: he really is hideous. Does he always lick his lips like that?" Johnny asked, peering at him.

I shrugged. I'd only known him five minutes longer than Johnny.

"But I suspect he has personality. You have the most scandalous expression I have ever seen on an animal," he said, addressing the puppy. "Oh yes, I see he does lick his lips like that. You will grow up to be quite a reprobate, my scandalous pup—a favourite with the ladies . . . and the gentlemen," he predicted in a sibylline voice. He received a prompt lick in return.

I raised my eyebrow at his racy suggestion. "What makes you think he is *that* sort of dog?" I asked with mock hauteur.

"Ah, that sort of dog . . . you see, all the best dogs are," he said with a lopsided grin.

The name has stuck, and half the theatre is already calling him Scandalous. I hope he does not live up to the name.

Later

A note arrived from Whitehall. I am resolved. Teddy has ordered a coach for me. I am bringing both dogs and am not even stopping to change.

Saturday, October 5—morning (raining)

There were tears. There was frustration. He was tenacious and stubborn but weakened when he saw my true distress.

"But it is to *protect* you," he kept repeating, sitting on the edge of the bed in his lawn nightshirt, clearly dismayed by my weeping.

"But if I do not *want* such protection?" I countered, feeling small among the pillows—and dogs: there were at least ten on the great bed.

"But I want it," ruled the king.

"Then *I* will go." My only card to play.

"Don't go."

We went on like this late into the night and then fell asleep in a warm, tangled heap. But I held my ground. With a weary sigh, he declared himself outflanked.

"You realise that it is not . . . ah . . . a wholly unique title? Being my mistress?" he asked gently.

"From what I gather, it is not even a particularly rare one." I giggled boldly.

He whooped with laughter and had the decency to look sheepish. "Such tender pragmatism you have, my darling," he said, pulling me close. "If it is what you truly want," he said, stroking my hair. "I could not bear to disappoint you, Ellen."

I nestled deeper into his embrace. "There are other things I truly want as well." I smiled, looking up at him archly.

"Ah, full of mischief, are you, my wild girl?"

At dawn we rose, and he wrapped me in his warmest dressing gown. Together we crept out into the damp autumn morning. The weak sun had turned the palace a grey-pink, and the shadowy grass was wet beneath our feet.

"Come see my realm," he whispered, taking my hand in his.

It is decided: I will be public. I will keep my independent life of the theatre. I will be treasured. I will never be abandoned. I will act as if this is all my choice instead of a compulsive love beyond my control.

Sunday, October 11 — Theatre Royal (The Faithful Shepherdess)

Tonight:

We sat in the royal box, he and I. I held my breath as Hart, playing Daphnis, strode onto the stage and swept the king a neat courtly bow. He caught my eye as he rose up and gave me a ghostly smile. A blessing. The audience gaped and craned their necks to watch us. I am sure that Becka upon the stage was disgruntled with the lack of attention paid her. Charles raised my hand to his lips, kissing the inside of my palm—a lover's kiss: a shockingly private gesture. Rochester and Teddy sat with us. Rochester was unusually quiet and left before the curtain fell. Home now, and everything seems different.

October 12, 1668
London
To Mrs. Ellen Gwyn, Theatre Royal, Bridges Street, Covent Garden
My darling,

My goodness! I just heard from Mrs. Watling (you remember, the ferocious orange wig?), who was at the King's last night—and what a night. If she is to be believed, he did not look at the stage once (Becka must have been hideously put out), but only at your pretty face. How wicked of you not to tell me. I must write something befitting your new and elevated status. I am so happy for you, ma petite chère.

With love,
Dryden

Monday — Theatre Royal

"Of course Hart knew," Peg said easily, shaking out her dripping umbrella.

"What do you mean 'of course'? I didn't tell him," I said, moving my pile of scripts so that she could sit down.

"I mean, did you really think the king's messenger could show up here three or four times a week and Hart *wouldn't* know?"

October 19 — Drury Lane (still raining)

Everything is different, indeed. Tonight, Johnny, Aphra, Teddy, and I attended *The Queen of Aragon* at the Duke's, and it was intolerable. I had expected stares, but I had not expected pointing and guffawing and loud laughing. "Well done, Nelly!" one particularly vocal member of the pit cheered.

"Does he mean—?" I turned to Rochester.

"No idea," he said, looking perplexed. Even he was startled by the crowd's reaction to me.

Finally, Teddy came back to our box, gasping and giggling with the truth. "It seems"—he struggled for breath—"it seems that you have been labelled a *poisoner!*"

"What!" Johnny and I cried in unison.

"Teddy, really," cautioned Aphra, looking around to make sure no one had heard him. "Lower your voice. You cannot say such things."

"*They* are saying it," he said, gesturing wildly towards the pit. "*They* are saying that you invited Moll Davis over for tea and fed her sweetmeats laced with jalap weed, provided by"—he swung around to point at Aphra— "*you!* Apparently you brought it back from Surinam," he added helpfully. He was doubled over, with tears of laughter coursing down his pretty face. "She could not leave the privy for . . . for . . . for three days, and thereby missed her assignation with the king."

"They think I would do that?" I asked, too astonished to laugh.

"It does have a measure of wit attached to it," Johnny said, softly chuckling. "I wish we *had* thought of it."

"They are calling it *'l'affaire du jalap,'*" Teddy exploded.

"Priceless," Johnny whispered, looking genuinely amused for the first time in months.

When We Enjoy Our Country Idyll

Friday, October 23, 1668—Little Saxham (late)

What a few days. Honestly, these boys *seem* so harmless, but lately I wonder. I am writing this tucked into a window-seat, wrapped in a coverlet, with the castle finally asleep.

What happened: *Thursday*

We arrived in Little Saxham, close by Bury St. Edmunds, early on Thursday afternoon. Just to get away from London and the fomenting gossip it breeds (*l'affaire du jalap* was the last straw for me) for a few days and to enjoy the crisp, clear autumn air of the country. A small intimate party of close friends: Sedley, Johnny Rochester, Buckhurst, Buckingham (the Countess of Shrewsbury couldn't come—thank goodness; I find her grating), Peg and Rupert, Charles and me. Jemmy Monmouth and his wife (whom he dislikes) were to join us, but her hip is still bothering her after her fall last month. We planned a long afternoon walk over the hills, and tomorrow a visit to the ancient Cathedral of Bury St. Edmunds.

After our walk we returned to our rooms to dress and then enjoyed a huge repast of fresh country bread, roast chicken, stewed carp, pike with quince cream, artichoke pie—a new vegetable from Italy—mallow salad, hard cheese, sack posset, cider, and canary wine. Followed by nursery treats like baked apricots, apple cake, and orange pudding with cream. Sack and cider make my head swim, so I kept to watered wine. After supper, Sedley, Buckingham, and Buckhurst announced that they wanted to experience the nocturnal delights of Bury St. Edmunds. It did not take much encouragement for Rupert and Charles to agree to join them. Johnny curiously chose to stay behind to "entertain the ladies," he said in a martyrish voice.

We three were sitting up by the fire chatting, drinking chocolate, and playing noisy round robin games of backgammon when Charles, Buckingham, and Rupert returned, gay but very drunk.

"Ah, the portrait of domestic bliss!" Rupert crowed, falling to all fours (heavily—he is not as agile as he once was) and burrowing his head into Peg's lap.

"No, no! I'm winning! Johnny's beat me three times. We can't stop now, when I'm winning!" It was true—Johnny never loses at backgammon.

"Hmm." Charles, likewise, buried his face in my neck. "Is it bedtime yet?" he growled.

"Seems to be Buckingham's bedtime," Rochester observed. Buckingham was already snoring in an armchair by the fire, his frilly court shoes kicked to one side. "Where are the others?"

"Naked," came Rupert's muffled reply from Peg's skirts.

"Oh, naturally," said Rochester, as if this had been the answer he was expecting, continuing to methodically pick up the backgammon pieces, black, white, black, white.

"*Naked?*" I asked, attempting to prop up Charles's head. It resiliently returned to nestle into my neck. "Did you just say *naked?*"

"Mm-hm." Rupert was falling asleep. "They thought the high street was just the place to be naked."

Peg rolled her eyes at this absurd response.

"*We* could think of better places to be naked, and so came home," Charles mumbled, his hands beginning to roam.

"But you *left* them? Drunk and naked in the high street? *Alone?*" I asked, concerned, struggling to still the king's relentless hands.

"Should we have left them a trail of bread-crumbs to find their way home?" asked the sleepy king. "How thoughtless of us. Bed," Charles mumbled insistently, pointing vaguely towards the ceiling.

Oh well, as they brew, let them bake—off to bed.

Saturday

I awoke early, to the distant sound of raised voices and banging upon the front door. I looked at the clock (Charles's favourite blue enamel travel clock that he keeps with him always), and it was not yet six. Charles was still soundly asleep beside me, his bed-clothes thrown off as usual. There was a light tap on our bedroom door, and I opened it to the solid bulk of Mrs. Walsh, the housekeeper, waiting without in an agitated state.

"I do not know how to tell you this, madam, indeed I really don't."

"Try, Mrs. Walsh. Try to tell me whatever it is that has you at our door at this hour," I said, struggling for patience.

"They arrested them, last night, for disgraceful behaviour, and kept them all night in the gaol, not that it won't do them good, mind you—"

"Wait, Mrs. Walsh, slowly, they have arrested who?"

"Lord Sedley and Lord Buckhurst, for doing indecent things in town. They say old Dr. Fanning got the shock of his life when they leapt out at him from behind a tree, naked as . . . well, *naked,* and he is a *doctor* and used to seeing, you know . . . *things*—"

"And now they are arrested and in *gaol?*"

"Only place for them, if they insist on acting like that—"

I stopped listening. Mrs. Walsh seemed to have forgotten her timidity and was fully prepared to hold forth on the proper punishment for nudists. "Thank you, Mrs. Walsh," I said abruptly, cutting her off.

"But, what do you want me to tell them?"

"Them?"

"The constables downstairs."

"Ooh! Constables . . . constables are *here*! Thank you, Mrs. Walsh, just please tell them to wait, won't you, and perhaps give them some breakfast," I said, steering her along the passage. "Some of your lovely macaroons and maybe eggs and sausages?" Thinking quickly, I decided that Charles was going to find out regardless, and most likely be furious, but it was better if he stepped in *now* and got them out of gaol and then punished them privately rather than have everyone suffer the embarrassment of the king's companions in prison. Hurrying back into the bedroom, I awoke the sleeping monarch.

"Your Majesty!" Constables Cole and Gunstun jumped up in unison from their cooked breakfasts to bow to the king. Not sure of how to do it, between them, they managed to knock over a chair and drop a butter dish. Charles just smiled and accepted their clumsy obeisance with his customary good humour.

"Now, constables, perhaps you would care to join me for my traditional morning constitutional walk?"

"*Walk?*" they echoed their king, their mouths full of food.

"Yes! Vigorous walking—good for the body and good for the spirit. I go at least five miles every morning, and then perhaps a swim? Nothing beats a swim to get the blood moving." The constables looked at each other in confusion. *This* was the fabled lazy, debauched king? The same pleasure-ridden king who permitted his men to run about wholesome country towns naked? Without waiting for their reply, Charles headed out the garden doors, and the bewildered constables had no choice but to follow.

I retrieved the butter dish and righted the chair. All would be well. He would see to it. I dreaded to think of what he would do to the boys in private, but Charles would not abandon them publicly. Johnny appeared at my side. Early for him—the ruckus must have woken him.

"He will forgive them," he said in answer to my thoughts. "He will forgive us anything. That is the trouble," he said, watching the unlikely trio make their way down the drive, the king striding ahead, boisterously pointing out various trees and plants of interest with his gold-tipped walking stick and the startled constables trailing in his wake.

Johnny was right. How well he knows the king. By the time Buckingham, Rupert, and Peg emerged, Sedley and Buckhurst were returned—Sedley with a black eye and Buckhurst limping—and their royal favour restored. They retold the story of their night in jail over luncheon—a lovely outdoor affair, served on long tables covered in cloud-white cloths with roast carp, fresh salad from the garden, and bowls of strawberries with thick country cream. I so much prefer simplicity to the rich court food.

They told of the Sunne Tavern and then the King's Head and Betsy the serving maid, who challenged them to run the length of the high street naked before she would kiss either of them. This same Betsy who disappeared once they began their drunken, naked serenade outside the tavern. Of the doctor, who shook his cane at them, the tavern keeper, who shooed them away—locking the tavern with their clothes inside—the seamstress, who offered from her window to sew them some clothes, and finally the watch, who chased them and arrested them.

"But they beat you?" I asked, eyeing their injuries.

They looked at each other furtively, as if deciding whether or not to be truthful.

"No," began Sedley awkwardly, "that was from . . ." He let his sentence trail off.

"We ran into some trouble with . . . Betsy," finished Buckhurst.

"Betsy!" whooped Buckingham. "Don't tell me she did that!" he said, pointing at Sedley's black eye.

"The doctor is her uncle," Buckhurst said, rising to her defence. "And she is much stronger than she looks."

"Yes," agreed Sedley solemnly. "Betsy is burly."

Later

I asked Charles, just before he fell asleep, why he was not wroth with them. This was our private time at the end of the public day. Snug and safe, I could let my thoughts uncurl. The moonlight striped our silk coverlets as he held me close.

"They are wild boys," he said indulgently. "They are brilliant and extreme and cannot be held to codes of normal behaviour. And besides," he added thoughtfully, running his long fingers through my sea-horse curls, "I do not care enough to reform them."

That is him all over, I thought. Charles notices everything but will only exert effort if it interests him.

"Johnny, too?" I asked, sensing that Johnny was special.

"No, Johnny is different. I would move heaven and earth to reform Johnny," he answered quietly, looking at the moon.

Sunday, October 25 — Windsor (rainy)

Moved *again*. After our unexpected Suffolk publicity we decided to remove to Windsor Castle for some peace. We arrived in time for chapel and all trooped in, still dressed in our travelling clothes—all except Johnny, who never attends church. Rupert and Peg had sent word ahead, and the castle was all in readiness for us—as ready as it can be in its current state of renovation. After a simple supper together we looked over the modifications to the ancient fortress.

"But it must be better, Rupert!" Charles thundered with excitement, racing about the crumbling building and gesticulating vigorously.

Building projects *energise* him, I remember the queen saying. Charles had returned from his Continental exile inspired by the luxury and efficiency of his cousin King Louis XIV's grand palaces. His designs for a Long Walk here at Windsor look much like the drawings of Louis's gardens at Versailles. I love to watch him whip himself into an architectural frenzy. His artless enthusiasm is infectious.

"We must renovate, redecorate, improve, improve, improve! Things can always be better! More beautiful, more *modern*."

Charles is obsessed with modernising his residences, his cities—his country, for that matter. Rupert shot Peg a look as if to say, *Modernity takes money,* but held his tongue.

Rupert showed Charles his experiments with *mezzotinting,* his newest passion, while Peg and I looked over fabric samples (bright Chinese silk and hand-blocked India chintz), the sketches of the delicate blue-and-white Chinese porcelain bowls (meant for the Yellow Salon), and the drawing of the great golden dinner service he planned to import from France.

"All my residences must have proper place settings," Charles announced, looking over our shoulders at the drawings. "It is barbaric for more than one man to share a plate. And we must have courses after the French fashion; it is absurd to lay out all the food at once. It gets cold."

"Sixty guineas?" I asked, just making out the figures at the bottom of the sketch. "For one plate?" To me, it seemed a small fortune.

"Place setting, my dear," said Rupert kindly. It is very different.

"We must look like a court again," Charles went on, more to himself than to us. "My father's court had all this and more, until . . ."

I held my breath. I saw Peg grip Rupert's hand. Charles so rarely spoke of how his father lost everything—his plates, his country, his crown, his head.

"Sixty guineas?" Charles said, turning to me and reverting to his light jovial tone. "For you, my little lark, I could not have you eat off anything less." He swooped down to kiss me. Only I could feel that he was trembling.

When I Begin to Understand the Court

Sunday, November 1, 1668— London, All Souls' Day

(raining)

Ugh! Back in bickering, wrangling London. I have come to crave country quiet, and my patience for the pettiness of Whitehall and all its slithering, shape-shifting intrigues wears thin. The walls, the chairs, the carpets all listen, and agendas abound. Everyone works for someone. Everyone has a price. Who will rise? Who will tumble down? No one falls without a push. I cannot bear such scrutiny. Buckingham and Castlemaine are mortal enemies, even though they are cousins, and even former lovers, some say—hard to picture. They were certainly childhood playmates, but nevertheless they would go to the death now. They grapple and snarl over the king's affection like wild dogs.

This evening

Tonight Charles offered me a suite of rooms inside the palace (not just a single sleeping chamber but a closet and sitting room as well—a coveted honour), but I do not want them. Charles just laughed at my eccentricity but did not question me as to *why* I do not want them. He did not want to hear the answer and so did not probe further—always the smoothest road, how like him.

Thinking about it now, I do not know how I would have explained it. To take a room in the palace would be to overreach, and this is not a man to understand overreaching. In truth, I do not want to set myself against the good queen. I do not want to cause unnecessary hurt, and for myself, I need to be able to get away and be apart from this artificial place.

Mrs. Barbara Chiffinch, the queen's chief seamstress and wife of the increasingly friendly Mr. William Chiffinch (brisk but kind), always comes and helps me to bathe and dress (in the King's Closet) and then, if the weather is unfit for walking, finds me a hackney—less conspicuous than the royal coach—to take me back to Drury Lane. The king does not understand my reluctance to hang about this viper's nest of a court, but Mrs. Chiffinch does. She bustles me out quickly and efficiently.

"You'll get used to it, dear. They all do. Give it time," she always says.

They all. That is just the trouble: *they all.* Ruby and the puppy, on the other hand, are quite at home in the palace. They settle down on the large cushions by the fire with four or five of Charles's many spaniels and are disgruntled when they get uprooted in the morning.

This morning I hurried through the Stone Gallery and met Rose at the King Street Gate, taking care to stay in the shadows as this gate is too near Castlemaine's apartments for my comfort. I can see her conspicuously white cambric undergarments fluttering away at her window. Why bright white underclothes displayed in public denotes breeding, I'll never understand; it would seem to me to indicate the reverse. On her bloated allowance Castlemaine can afford to order some for wearing and some for hanging, ridiculous woman.

My encounters with Castlemaine are now cutting and brief. She takes great pains to point out any outward signs of my low breeding: my loud laugh, my tendency to run, my love for the guitar (a base instrument), even my Protestantism—she being recently baptised a Catholic (no coincidence that this is the unofficial religion of the half-French royal family). Last week when I dashed into the Banqueting Hall without waiting for Watkins, the footman, to open the door (he is nearly blind and takes an age, but he served the old king and is therefore guaranteed a place for life), she made sure that all and sundry heard of my rough-hewn behaviour. What she did not know was that I had to be at the theatre at two; it was after one, and I could not find Ruby. Damn her refinement. If my dog is lost, I will bloody well go running after her. Castlemaine's own illustrious pedigree does not help her on the road to good manners, I have noticed—nor does her new religion. The king just finds it annoying. He finds most things about her annoying—or so he tells me—except her children. For them, he has endless patience and affection. I can understand it. They exhibit none of their mother's imperious behaviour and seem sweetly tempered. Mighty Castlemaine's power is said to be on the wane, and the court can smell blood. There is much talk of who the father of this child might be, and *King* Charles is not on the list of likely candidates—Charles *Hart* unfortunately *is,* as is, remarkably, Jacob Hall, the rope-dancer; Wycherly, the playwright; and, most likely of all, Henry Jermyn, the Earl of St. Albans.

Rose was waiting for me, and we made our way across Pall Mall to the stationers and then on to St. Olave's in Hart Street. We chatted of this and that: she has begun work in Hatton Garden, at the King's Theatre Nursery for apprentice actors and actresses.

"John does not approve, but it is lovely to spend the day with the children, helping them learn their lines, to stage fight, to make up, to dance—all of it."

Hart kindly arranged this place for Rose, and she is clearly enjoying it. His affection for my family has never wavered.

"John has agreed that I stay on, until, of course, we have some children of our own," Rose chattered on.

This steady life of house and husband and the prospect of children clearly suits her. I squeezed her hand in sisterly affection.

"I am happy you are settled," I said firmly, thinking of my own far-less-ordered life.

"You will be, too," she said gently. "I am sure everything feels strange now, but it will settle, Ellen," she said confidently, guessing my fears.

We arrived at the solid squat building and made our way into the dimness. It was curiously comforting to kneel there, in the small stone church, to hear the familiar words and just feel the ordinariness of it all. I peeked at the people around me: bakers, clerks, grocers, and their wives and children—nobody of particular note. Nobody of interest, of merit, of *quality,* I could hear Castlemaine saying in my head. How untrue, I thought. These people have great merit. They are what are good and real and grounded about this country. They certainly lead better lives than the loose, rambunctious court.

"*Ellen!*" Rose hissed beside me.

Dutifully, I lowered my head and, closing my eyes, enjoyed the ordinariness.

Note—Since our return to London I still have not seen *her*. The queen. At the end of the service, when we were asked to pray for the safety of the royal family, I squeezed my eyes shut and said a fervent prayer for the queen: that she might bear healthy children, that she might find happiness. I am too selfish a woman to pray that her husband might truly be faithful to her. Above all, I prayed that she might forgive me. Perhaps no one has told her? Perhaps she does not yet know of my betrayal. If only it could remain so.

November 4, later— Whitehall

This afternoon the clouds broke briefly, and Charles and I seized the moment to go walking in the Privy Gardens. The great chestnut trees were bathed in weak November sunshine, and the damp air had the fresh feeling of renewal after days of rain. Crunching along the gravel pathways, we came upon Arlington and Buckingham seated on a secluded bench tucked into a corner of the high box hedge. I felt Charles tense beside me, his body tightening like a drawn bow.

"Plotting?" Charles said easily, his expression belying none of his unease. Arlington and Buckingham's obsession with Earl of Clarendon's unlikely return to power irritates Charles—the poor old man has been dishonoured, dismissed, and driven out of the country: What more can Buckingham want?

"Discussing," Buckingham said casually, half rising to offer a sloppy courtly bow. "We were just saying—"

"No, no," Charles said, uncharacteristically interrupting him. "It is not a day to discuss, but a day to enjoy. Good afternoon to you both." He moved off, leaving Buckingham staring after him agape.

"My dear," I began, once we were out of earshot. "Why did you . . . ?"

"I had no wish to hear it," he said gruffly, quickening his pace. I was trotting to keep up. "I do not need to hear again how my brother is not sufficiently vitriolic about his father-in-law for their liking. They are nothing short of ghoulish over that old man, and his daughter Anne, however much she eats, is married to my brother and it is enough."

I giggled. It was true. Anne, a plain plumpish sort of woman, never stops eating. We spoke no more about it and continued wandering in the chilly autumn afternoon.

PALAIS, D'ORLÉANS, PARIS
TO MY BELOVED BROTHER, HIS MAJESTY KING CHARLES II
FROM PRINCESSE HENRIETTE-ANNE, DUCHESSE D'ORLÉANS, THE MADAME OF
    FRANCE
6 NOVEMBRE 1668

Chéri,

A disturbing rumour has reached me. Have you borrowed eight thousand pounds from your banker in order to acquire Berkshire House for Lady Castlemaine? That is a vast sum, and I would imagine it of greater use elsewhere. Has she not several estates already, as well as prominent rooms in each of your residences? I understood your affections to be shifting to Mistress Gwyn of the Theatre Royal, an unsuitable but less-expensive choice. From what I understand Mistress Gwyn's popularity and graceful bearing overcome her insufficient birth. Lady Castlemaine has given you five children and does deserve to live in considerable comfort—but this degree seems excessive, dearest, when your treasury is so depleted and your debts so numerous.

Affectionately and always your,
Minette

Note—*The building at Versailles moves at an astonishing pace. There are plans for a Galerie de Glace—beautiful beyond belief.*

Une autre note—*Does it not strike you as indelicate for Lady Castlemaine to want to live in her former adversary's home? Clarendon served you well, and his estate should not be handed over to his enemies. I have seen him since his arrival to France and know that he mourns the loss of Berkshire House greatly. Must she gloat so? It is unseemly in one so intimately connected with your house.*

For Mrs. Ellen Gwyn, Theatre Royal, London

My dearest Ellen,

Well, the rumours have filtered to us in deepest Oxfordshire. If it is true, and given your undoubted power to charm and your appealing loveliness, I have no doubt that it is, then I hope it brings you joy. It has not been a conventional life for you, my dearest, but then that is too muted for your capacity for living. He is, I believe, despite his terrible reputation, a thoughtful ruler, and I am sure a thoughtful man. I can only hope that he understands what he has found in you.

With fondest love,
Grandfather

Note—*Your great-aunt has bid me to remind you to cross your ankles when you are seated, remember not to swing your arms when you walk, do not bite your fingernails, and to please change your underclothes at least twice a week. I have no doubt that further instructions shall follow.*

When I Learn Not to Play Court Games

LONDON GAZETTE

Sunday, November 8, 1668

Most Deservedly Called London's Best and Brilliant Broadsheet

The Social Notebook

Volume 332

Ambrose Pink's social observations du jour

Darlings!

C'est incroyable! C'est impossible! The royal maw of Whitehall has swallowed up yet another of our lovely songbirds of the stage. None other than our own orange-girl wonder, Nell Gwyn, the delicate, dancing darling of the Theatre Royal. With a light tread and a whisper of satin, she goes into the mist, into the mystery, into the golden realm. Alas, alack. She goes.

But wait, wait! *Quoi?* She does not mean to trade the high-stakes glamour of the stage for the comforts of the royal bed? We are not forsaken, my dears. Like the first footprints in new snow, intrepid Nell leads the way. Trust our girl to find her own path. Ah, balance restored, my pets. We shall not lose her after all.

À bientôt, dearests,
Ever your eyes and ears,
Ambrose Pink, Esq.

Tuesday (sunny and warm)

Delicate darling, my foot. Damn Ambrose Pink. Now she *must* know—not that she reads the gossip pages, but someone in her viper's nest of ladies will make sure to tell her. It would be folly to think otherwise. I can never hope for her favour or goodwill, I can only hope that she knew my regard to be true, even if my friendship proved false. A friend does not do what I have done. I can feel the long fingers of shame curling around my heart.

November 1668

"I need the wig-maker for John and stay-maker for me, and to pick up supplies for the Nursery Theatre (ribbons, paper, and rouge), and if I cannot find Venice lace here, I'd best go over to Madame Leonine's," Rose said, listing her errands as we walked up the Strand.

We were off to the Exchange, to do some shopping on a crisp November morning. The light had shifted to the slanted, amber light of autumn, and the air smelled faintly of snow—of a dozen other less savoury things as well, but also of snow. The shopkeepers were sweeping out their doorways with thickly bound brooms, and the hawkers, out far earlier than the shopkeepers, were already doing brisk business in the morning sun. The cheesemonger was bringing up an armful of waxy wrapped cheeses from his cold storage below, and the flower seller was winding together bushy bundles of creamy pink roses. Rose, still disdainful of her eponymous flower, did not slow her pace, but I dawdled and daydreamed at the pretty gardened window.

"Where do you need . . . Ellen? Ellen?" Rose called impatiently as I hurried to catch up.

"I also need to stop at Madame Leonine's," I said, "and the apothecary, and I would love to pop into the hat shop, but only if there is time." I had rehearsal at one.

"Madame Sophie?" she asked, making a face.

Her hats were exquisite but expensive, and her clientele was very exclusive and not the sort of place where Rose, without me, would otherwise be welcome. I squeezed her hand in reassurance. "It will be fine," I told her confidently.

Rose just tossed her head as if she was untroubled by the opinion of others—a blatant untruth, but no matter. I needed a new hat, something with a veil. Going out has become more complicated lately, as more and more I am recognised on the street. A more concealing hat would help. Perversely, I had hoped for a few more months of anonymity, but it is not to be. Everywhere I go, people look and point as if I am an animal in a menagerie. Charles was right—it is difficult. Even now, two young and elegant men, out for a morning walk, were obviously following us several paces behind.

"You must adjust," Rose whispered beside me. "You are the most famous actress in London and the king's mistress—it is natural that they be curious about you. Anyway, this is what you wanted, isn't it?"

But I could tell that even she was taken aback by the degree of their interest.

In the apothecary's shop an overly made-up woman with frightful red hair approached me. "Nelly," she addressed me informally—everyone seems to do this, to behave as if they know me. "What do you use on your skin? I have red hair as you do, but I am afflicted by freckles. Your skin is just lovely."

I warmed to this sincere clown-faced woman immediately.

"She uses our Adams Cowslip Wash," interjected Mr. Adams, the apothecary, proudly. "She has done for years."

"It's true," I said cheerfully. "I am sure it is the sole reason for my lack of freckles."

Rose rolled her eyes beside me. Even as a child I never suffered from freckles like others of my colouring. But it helps Mr. Adams, and it is a lovely wash, to be fair—much better than the sticky buttermilk or the smelly puppy dog water usually prescribed.

"I'll take six bottles," the woman decided, turning to Mr. Adams.

"I'm afraid I only have four in stock, but we do have the velvety soft Adams Honey Almond Meal Face Cream that Mrs. Gwyn also favours."

The woman looked to me to confirm it, and I nodded.

"I'll take four pots."

Mr. Adams busied himself wrapping up her purchases while Rose and I patiently waited.

"And your scent?" the woman asked, pointedly sniffing me. I involuntarily stepped back.

"Lemon verbena," Rose answered for me (not true—I use vanilla water with a hint of apple).

I started to protest, but Rose made a face as if to say, They do not need to know *everything*. Mr. Adams popped another vial in her bag.

"He had better not charge you after that little performance," Rose hissed in my ear.

"He won't," I said easily. "He hasn't done for years."

"Well, good luck in *all* your endeavours, Ellen," the woman said, meaningfully waggling her eyebrows. "My husband and I do so like to see you upon the stage. When are you next—?"

"We are readying Dryden's new play now," I reassured her. "Do not worry, I'll never leave the theatre!"

"Good thing, too," the woman said pompously. "After all, we are the ones who brought you where you are today."

"Very true, and I shan't forget it."

I felt Rose shaking with suppressed giggles behind me.

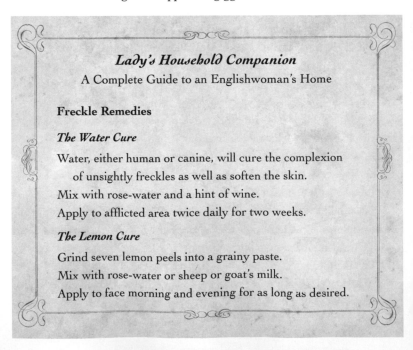

Lady's Household Companion
A Complete Guide to an Englishwoman's Home

Freckle Remedies

The Water Cure

Water, either human or canine, will cure the complexion
   of unsightly freckles as well as soften the skin.
Mix with rose-water and a hint of wine.
Apply to afflicted area twice daily for two weeks.

The Lemon Cure

Grind seven lemon peels into a grainy paste.
Mix with rose-water or sheep or goat's milk.
Apply to face morning and evening for as long as desired.

Undated

Rose tells me that Mr. Adams now has a sign in his window listing all the products favoured by *Mrs. Nelly Gwyn of the King's Theatre and Whitehall.* Good grief.

PALAIS, D'ORLÉANS, PARIS

TO MY BELOVED BROTHER, HIS MAJESTY KING CHARLES II

FROM PRINCESSE HENRIETTE-ANNE, DUCHESSE D'ORLÉANS, THE MADAME OF
   FRANCE

10 NOVEMBER 1668

Chéri,

Sad news. Our Dr. Denis gave a patient three transfusions in an effort to save him after a riding accident. Unfortunately, the poor man died, and now his widow is suing the good doctor. There is talk of passing a law banning his transfusions.

I am ever and ever your,
Minette

November 12, 1668— Theatre Royal

George Buckingham dropped by the tiring room after the performance. I had removed my costume and was wearing just my corset, chemise, and petticoats (Teddy quickly threw me a silk wrapper) and was beginning to remove my heavy stage make-up when George ambled in. With a twitch of his head he dismissed Teddy (the high-handed gall of that man!). Teddy, who was taking down my tightly upswept hair and had a mouth full of pins, made a move to go. I turned around to glare at Buckingham. How dare he appear in *my* tiring room and send *my* Teddy away, my look told him in no uncertain terms.

"Stay," I said in a studiedly casual tone, turning back to the mirror.

"Go," said Buckingham evenly, matching me pitch for pitch.

Teddy just stood there with the pins in his mouth, not sure what to do and clearly disliking the idea of a scene. George Buckingham, as Teddy is forever pointing out, has a ruthless streak—beware.

"George, my love," I said with sugary sweetness into the mirror, "Teddy, as you can see, is taking down my hair just at present; if you want to see me alone, then you can bloody well wait."

That did it. Teddy turned back to my hair and worked quickly, fingers flying, eager to escape.

"Oh, fine then," Buckingham said, conceding defeat and restlessly moving about the room.

"What is the matter with you anyway?" I asked, watching him fidget. "You should be happy."

This past week Buckingham's position as first man of the realm has been truly cemented. It has been all the talk of court. He is set high—even above the Duke of York, his mortal enemy *du jour*. The gruesome vultures are picking over the bodies Buckingham leaves behind. Buckingham had Lord Anglesey removed from his lifetime appointment as Treasurer, and it looks as if he will also have Lord Ormonde (such a sweet man, really a pity) replaced as Governor of Ireland. The Council will soon be made up of entirely his men. The king seems strangely uninterested in this obvious strategising and is disinclined to discuss it.

"I am happy. I just wish—" He shot a look at Teddy. "*She* is still as present as ever, and I find it grating."

She. Castlemaine: the pregnant, meddling, opinionated, rich, and still powerful *maîtresse en titre*. *She*—still angling for a higher income and a grander title, even though she no longer shares the king's bed. *She,* who has wormed her way into the good graces of Bab May, the Keeper of the Privy Purse, and now has seemingly unlimited access to the royal purse. *She,* who wears enough diamonds and rubies to outshine the queen—as if her evident fertility were not triumph enough. Wretched woman.

"If anyone should desire her downfall, it should be me, yet you seem far more put out at her continuing influence," I said lightly.

"Her influence," Buckingham said, through gritted teeth, "is driving me mad."

"Ha! Only because she *could* be doing much to advance you and isn't." I laughed. Buckingham's motives are always far more transparent than he thinks they are.

Note—Tom mentioned as we were leaving that Her Majesty the Queen attended the performance tonight. "But she did not laugh and left before the final act," he said, holding the door for me.

"I suppose there can be no worse thing than watching hundreds of people standing and applauding your husband's mistress," I replied sadly.

"Especially if your husband is the one leading the applause," he said as we wandered home. "You could only keep one, Ellen," he said, watching me carefully. "You could have the love of either the king or queen, but never both."

November 13 — Whitehall

Damn and blast. Grandfather would cringe to hear me using such language, but honestly, the monarch and his Parliament are both behaving like school-yard enemies. Each only wants the other to pay due deference, but no! Pride before all! It is at a standstill. For heaven's sake—say whatever they want to hear to make them feel involved and then get the money to pay the navy! I am starting to sound like Buckingham, who is always banging on about the navy and fairness to the common man.

Charles says he is working on a solution with his sister Henriette-Anne, the Madame of France. She is secretly brokering some sort of deal between France and England—well, between her brother-in-law and her brother, really. God knows what Charles will have to promise to elicit money from the fanatically organised Louis; he was vague about the details. It is really too bad that Louis married Marie Theresa, the Spanish heifer, as Charles called her, instead of the elegant Henriette-Anne, who is said to be the most beautiful, most loveable, and most accomplished woman in France, and married to the most frivolous man in all Europe.

Note—Buckingham has made the situation a great deal worse. Tonight at dinner he loudly and unfavourably compared Charles to his cousin Louis.

Unfortunately, Buckingham described Louis as a king who *understands* how to make his kingdom great, and then went on to liken Cliveden, his new country house (hardly a house yet, as the construction is taking forever), to Louis's great building project at Versailles. Unlike our own king, who is having trouble managing his legislators—unlike our king, who has no such monies to indulge his passion for building. I could wring Buckingham's neck for the unnecessary hurt he causes Charles.

November 26, 1668—late

It happened. And it was as awful as I feared.

Last night we attended an evening of cards in the Duke of York's apartments.

"Everyone is happy you're here. You twinkle. Most people don't twinkle," Buckhurst quietly encouraged, smoothing his beautifully cut velvet coat and taking a seat at the card table. He knows how the king's brother still can make me nervous. I squeezed his arm in gratitude.

"Vino!" Johnny called from his chair by the fire. He had been sitting there for some time, and I was not sure he could stand if he tried. His black curled wig was askew, and his eyes seemed unfocused. A pretty actress from the Duke's was sitting with him, and I caught him shamelessly leering down her bodice.

I frowned at him.

"You've drunk it all," Sedley said, reclining on a golden silk-covered sofa with his eyes closed. It was well after four, and the room had thinned out to only ten people or so. Charles was involved in a heated discussion with his brother and his son Jemmy by the matching fireplace on the far side of the room, and I was quietly dozing off in the armchair opposite Johnny.

"Can't have drunk it *all*," Johnny said, slurring his words so it sounded as if he had a stuffy nose. "Where's our host, the heir to the throne?" (It sounded like *thwone.*) "He should send some flunky out to the yard to squeeze more grapes." (*Gwapth.*) "James, find some young women with good feet and tell them to get out there. Nell, you have lovely feet . . . maybe too small to squeeze grapes . . ."

I ignored him. Charles had invited him to attend his private chapel that morning, and it had left him in a foul mood all day. Johnny and God did not seem to be on good terms at the moment.

"Mmm, yes, more wine . . . tell James," Savile murmured distractedly from the card table, not looking up from his hand. He had bet an unthinkably enormous sum and lost it all in the last hand.

"Bucky, more wine, whad'ya say?" Johnny yelled belligerently.

"Splendid idea—make sure the flunky has clean feet," said Buckhurst, laying down his cards and grinning.

Abruptly, Johnny stood up unsteadily, stepping on the pretty actress. "Well, I'm off to look for some. Nell? You coming?" The actress looked put out that she had been trod on and then not invited. Without waiting for my answer, and without bowing to James, he swished out of the room. Turned out he could walk. But he had left without a word to—

"Nelly, are you there?" Sedley asked. His head was tipped back and his eyes were lightly shut.

"Mmm."

"Did he bow? Or ask for York's leave? Or the king's, for that matter? Did I miss it?"

Cultivating a relaxed tone, I lied, "Yes, he bowed, and asked for their leave, didn't you hear him?" Such a flagrant breach of conduct would be difficult even for Johnny to shrug off, especially in James York's own apartments. James is sensitive to slights and is meticulous about form.

"Hmm, going deaf, I suppose. You should go to bed, Nelly; you must be tired," Savile said sleepily.

Just then Charles appeared at my side and took my arm to lead me off to bed, his face a hard blank shell. James remained on the far side of the room, and Jemmy, tense and white-faced, rigidly bowed good night to his father. They have been arguing lately, and I know how much it pains Jemmy. I gave him a sympathetic smile and dropped my curtsey good night.

Once tucked in the royal bed I felt wide awake again, and together Charles and I stayed up to watch the dawn break, laughing and loving and whispering in the fading dark.

"We shall sleep late tomorrow," Charles said, pulling the bed curtains closed.

I looked at him, surprised. He always awoke at six for his constitutional exercise, regardless of the hour he went to bed. As a result I almost never awoke next to him.

"But . . ." I yawned.

"The queen wanted me to . . . ah . . . visit last night, and I told her I was unwell, so I can't very well go walking in the morning."

I squirmed in discomfort. It was not jealousy, as I truly want the queen to be happy, but rather a profound wish that Charles was not married to such a good woman. I snuggled deeper into the covers, determined not to unravel my contradictory wants.

An hour later, at about six, I heard the doors to the anteroom opening and a woman's voice. It was a woman speaking English with a ripe, rolling accent. Good God! The queen. The queen, here! "Charles"—I shook him awake—"the queen!" I could hear the startled sentry in the outer room, stammering and moving to open the great doors.

Panicked, I hopped out of bed—whatever happened I did not want her to discover me *in* the bed—and hid behind the heavy window curtains.

"Ellen . . . where are you," Charles hissed, poking his head out of the bed hangings. At the sound of the door he disappeared once more into the great bed.

"Good morning, sweetheart, and how are you feeling? Improved?" Queen Catherine asked from the open doors. It was a seductive private voice I had never heard her use.

"Oh, yes, vastly," I heard my lover answer his wife.

"Well, your fever is down, but you do not look as if you slept well. Did you take the posset I made up?"

"Mmm, the lemon and sugar . . ." He trailed off into a dense silence. I heard a rustling of silk like autumn leaves underfoot. "Catherine . . ."

"You had better return this," she said evenly. "I wouldn't want the owner of such a little foot to catch cold." Her shoes clicked across the floor, and I heard the bedroom doors bang shut behind her.

When I emerged from my hiding place, I found Charles seated on the edge of the bed with my shell-pink slipper in his hand.

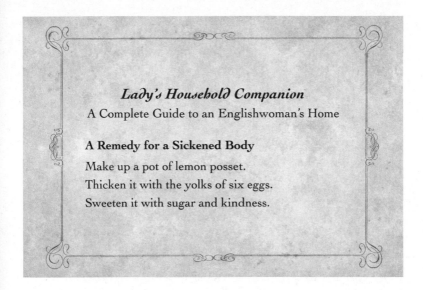

Lady's Household Companion
A Complete Guide to an Englishwoman's Home

A Remedy for a Sickened Body
Make up a pot of lemon posset.
Thicken it with the yolks of six eggs.
Sweeten it with sugar and kindness.

Later

Charles left for his walk, snapping his fingers for his spaniels. "You mustn't mind, Ellen," he said, gently lifting my chin. "She does understand, you know. She understands me very well."

I threw on my clothes without waiting for Mrs. Chiffinch to bring in the bath-tub or to help me dress. I pulled my hair up into a messy twist, crammed my hat on my head, and hurried out the door. It was in the long gallery I saw her coming. She was walking with her household chaplain, surrounded by her swarm of brightly gowned ladies. I dropped swiftly into my deepest curtsey. I felt her standing above me, waiting for me to rise.

"Mistress Gwyn." It was a statement. Not Ellen.

"Yes, Your Majesty." Slick sweat trickled down my back.

"Yes, that fits," she said flatly. She was looking down at my slippers—my shell-pink slippers.

December 1, 1668—Official Notations for Privy Council Meeting on This Day to
Be Entered into the Log-book

Notations taken by Secretary of State Henry Bennet, Earl of Arlington

Discussion in the Council today of His Majesty's growing reputation for licensed
behaviour and the possible repercussions on the country, and the stark contrast
to his sister, the Princesse Henriette-Anne, and King Louis's court at Versailles.
The princess is acting as principal hostess and the first lady of the French court
while Queen Maria Theresa is in her confinement, and her gracious deference to
the absent queen has been much noted throughout Europe. Unfortunately, during
our session we received word that His Majesty's companions Lords Sedley and
Buckhurst were arrested for being drunk and disrobed in a London street on a
Tuesday in the mid-afternoon.

Also further discussion of His Majesty's increasingly difficult financial
embarrassment. Mr. Baptist May presented the household accounts, and there
were several extravagant expenditures that the king was disinclined to discuss.

The Duke of Buckingham became animated over the subject of the unpaid
seamen and the state of His Majesty's Navy. The Lord Admiral, His Grace, the
Duke of York was not available to discuss the matter, as he was meeting with
Lords Brouncker (recently reinstated) and Sandwich over the matter of Tangier.
York's clerk, Matthew Wren, delivered a message to the Council: the returned
formal request to immediately find funds for payments in arrears (for the previous
three years) that the Duke of Buckingham had drawn up and strongly called
for York to endorse. It was returned without York's signature. As the Council is
still waiting for Parliament to pass a bill granting His Majesty three hundred
thousand pounds, we are unable to currently meet such a demand without the
assistance of Parliament.

It was mentioned by the Duke of Buckingham that perhaps Lady Castlemaine
could contribute a portion of her considerable personal income. His Majesty did

*not acknowledge this request but instead alluded to a solution coming from France.
The Council as a whole was not aware of such an arrangement.*

*The duke went on to suggest that perhaps the Lord High Admiral himself,
His Grace of York, could alternatively donate a portion of his personal income.
King Charles and the Duke of Buckingham stepped outside to speak privately
after the Council meeting was adjourned.*

*Nothing further to report.
Secretary of State Henry Bennet, Earl of Arlington*

*December 2, 1668 — Theatre Royal (The Usurper, by
Ned Howard—another playwrighting Howard boy)*

"You've got to talk to him, Nelly!" Buckingham thundered away in my
tiring room—my private tiring room that never seems to be private these
days.

I winced as he banged his fist down upon my delicately carved dressing
table—it was new, a present from Tom.

"He listens to you. You must make him see sense! He must dissolve this
Parliament and call another—one that will grant him proper funds!"

"So tell him that!" I said, exasperated.

He will not listen to me on this matter," Buckingham snarled. "Get on
with it, Nelly! Today!"

Everything is always *today!* with Buckingham. Everything is always
imperative! Urgent! One grows deaf to his impassioned nagging. He has
no sense of subtlety or timing. But then I suppose one who feels utterly
entitled to everything has no need of timing. "I can't speak to him today; he
is Touching for the King's Evil at Greenwich all afternoon." I shuddered.
It was a bizarre and, I am quite sure, ineffectual ritual as the same batch of
afflicted sufferers showed up every week.

"Ha!" Buckingham snorted. "As if that cures anyone. If he would charge for his services, that would be useful at least." I held my tongue. For once I agreed with Buckingham and have lately mentioned to Charles the possibility of establishing a proper modern hospital instead of this weird enchanted nonsense.

I watched Buckingham pace about the small room like a caged panther. I waited. Eventually he would exhaust himself—although he had been going on for some time. I heard a rustle of skirts and looked up to see both Marshall sisters casually loitering by the open door. I stood and firmly shut it.

"Now," I said soothingly, "you know what he is like. There is no talking to him until he is ready. I'm sorry," I said, turning back to my make-up box, hoping that would be the end of it. I was on this afternoon and could not find my new pot of silver eye paint—I suspected the light-fingered Becka Marshall.

"But this is what you are *supposed* to do for me. This is why you are where you are: in his bed instead of mine."

I ignored the crass remark but took his meaning clearly. He had got me into the king's bed, and now I am therefore in his service—otherwise, he assumed I would be in *his* bed and at *his* service: not true, but that was not the quarrel to pick today.

I turned and said carefully, "Your cause is a good one, and as far as I can tell it is relatively free of self-interest—surprising for you." The acclaim he would garner for solving the navy problem would increase his growing popularity with the common people, but I did not mention that.

"Nelly!" he exploded. I held up my hand; I had no time for this today. Buckingham has never been one to see himself clearly, and this afternoon was not the moment to make him do so.

"I care for you a great deal and will help if I can, but I will not push him. You of all people should know that is not wise." He had evidently forgotten his recent stay in the Tower and could not see that he was balanced on a knife's edge with the king at the moment—childhood companion or not. He had traded too long on their history of affection, and their fathers' affection before them, to heed the warning signs. I knew (from Johnny) that he had already dangerously bullied the king's brother James: trying to force him to sign a request for funds he did not want to sign, and then humiliating him in the council chamber.

"Patience," I said, putting a placating hand on his arm. He is not ready yet."

"Well, he should be bloody ready!" he bellowed. "These are the men who are supposed to *die* for him if the need arises. You'd think he'd be able to pull his prick out of my cousin's cunny long enough to notice that!"

With that, he slammed out of the room, scattering the eavesdropping Marshall sisters like geese. I sighed, stung by his crude remark. In anger or frustration George will say anything. It was no good telling him that it was not a matter of not noticing, but of not knowing how to go about obtaining the funds *and* saving face.

Note—Hilarious rumour of Johnny Rochester having his clothes and money stolen while he was with a wench, walking home stark naked, only to return (clothed) to find that is was the wench who had stolen the clothes in the first place (and stuffed them into her feather-bed). She ransomed them back to him for a good sum. All was returned and good humour restored. It is said that it was Savile who put her up to it. It sounds like him. Charles never tires of repeating this story. Johnny laughs along. It is good to see them together. Charles loves him so.

Note—Home in Drury Lane. The rain is leaking though the roof above the window. The paint has almost entirely peeled from the damp walls. It is a strange thing to spend so much time in the royal palaces of this country and then return to my dreary childhood home. As I am hardly here, it hardly matters, I suppose. Mother is rarely home; she has set up a temporary "establishment" at the Cock and Pie tavern. I try my best not to think too much about it and can only hope it never becomes known at court. I have learned to take all her improprieties in stride. A family is a messy, unwieldy thing bounded only by blood and—beneath all the embarrassment—affection.

December 10, 1668, Saturday—Ham House

Rainy day in the country with Charles. He was distressed over a letter from his sister, Minette (well, not Minette to me, but the Princesse

Henriette-Anne, the Duchesse d'Orléans, the Madame of France, married to King Louis's notoriously mean and effeminate brother Philippe, the Duc d'Orléans, the Monsieur of France).

"He bullies her, beastly man. How can anyone bully my sister? She is an angel. She writes to apologise that in her official letters she is no longer permitted to express affection for me, as her husband has deemed it unseemly and disloyal."

"Disloyal to whom?"

"Him, of course. Ridiculous."

Charles was pacing in front of the fire, waving the letter about as he spoke. The letter was brought by one of the special fleet of couriers Charles employs to ferry secret correspondence betwixt them. The pugs and spaniels, recognising this mood and not wanting to be stepped on, had taken refuge under the sofa. I leaned over to check that Ruby and Scandalous were safely among them. Satisfied, I returned to my reading.

"He believes that before Christmas she arranged the dismissal of his wretched lover—what's his name, Chevalier de something or other—and now he seeks his petty revenge upon her."

"De Lorraine, I think. What is he like?" I asked, lowering the script I was hopelessly behind in learning. Rumours about Minette's vicious husband were legion.

"The Monsieur? He is vain, frivolous, spiteful, vindictive, and possibly the worst husband my mother could have found for her," he said, dropping wearily onto the sofa and laying his head in my lap, knocking my script to the ground. *Heigh-ho.* "She ought to have married our cousin King Louis, instead of his dreadful brother, but at the time Louis wasn't interested in her. Like dancing with the bones of holy innocents, I think he said. Very rude."

"But I thought she and Louis—"

"Oh yes. Later, after she was married, Louis was terribly interested in her, declaring his undying *this* and everlasting *that,* praising her slender frame, exquisite taste, and flawless complexion, on and on. Which of course only enraged her jealous little husband more. Fey Philippe is petty by nature and has been encouraged to wear frilly dresses and face paint and be a silly pastry puff of a man since birth—pettiness and vanity, awful combination. He is not even interested in women and has publicly either mistreated or ignored my sister since their wedding. Not to imply that he does not privately hound and torment her. She writes that he has daily reports brought to him recording all her activities and correspondence—to whom she speaks, what she reads, where she goes—and so she must be extra cautious when writing to me. Any loyalty to me angers him greatly. Of course she is loyal to me, her own brother. How absurd!"

"Philippe wears dresses?"

"Mmm, two sons can be very dangerous. The Queen Mother, my aunt Anne of Austria, trained one to be an inconsequential, spangled circus bear. That way, Louis can reign unchallenged. God help us should anything ever happen to Louis."

I did not know what to say to that and so called for Mrs. Chiffinch to bring a collation and the strong coffee Charles favours, hoping to tempt him out of his ill humour.

"Now Minette's lady-in-waiting, the little la Vallière, is Louis's mistress, plain but sweet, an excellent horsewoman, if I remember, and Philippe's dreadful lover—that greasy Chevalier—is returned to court, and Minette is virtually a prisoner at St. Cloud. And I am unable to help."

"Can your mother not do something? She is, after all, there," I asked, reaching over him to move the books and clocks—everywhere he goes, Charles brings clocks—out of the way to make room for the coffee tray.

"My mother? My mother firmly believes that those whom God has joined together, let no man . . . on and on. Totally forgetting that it was not God, but she and my dreadful aunt Anne, who did all the joining together. I doubt God was consulted. Ugh," he groaned, closing his eyes in disgust.

The subject of his family always leads to noises like that.

"Well, I shall send her something," I said brightly.

"My mother?"

"No, your sister. Her wicked husband can hardly object to a gift from a common actress in London, can he? What would be the harm? And it may cheer her to know how deeply you worry for her and fondly you think of her. Yes, I shall look for a gift tomorrow. Toady husband be damned."

Charles threw back his head and laughed. "Ah, Nell, there is truly no one like you."

He sat up and twined his arms around my waist. I giggled archly, wiggling deeper into his embrace. By the time Mrs. Chiffinch brought the lemon cakes she found the door locked.

Note—Together we picked out several lovely gifts for the princess: an inlaid music box, sapphire ear-drops, and several miniatures of Charles's favourite spaniels, done in oil. Charles wrote a touching letter and tucked it inside the music box. I wrote a brief note, introducing myself and humbly wishing her well.

Undated

Missed three rehearsals in a row, as I was literally ordered by the king to stay in bed. How delicious. I am sure I will never be cast again. We've stayed up the past three nights until three or four, either roistering with the Wits or simply curled up, the two of us, on the royal sofa with the royal spaniels, whispering until dawn. Yet each morning Charles rises at six for his customary constitutional: a five-mile walk and a one-hour swim. His poor councillors scramble to keep up with him, reading their reports aloud to him as they trot along, and then must shout their counsel from the side of the lake each time he comes up for air. He ends with feeding the ducks in St. James's Park, by which time his advisors are quite winded and need to sit down.

Note—Charles asked me tonight what sort of hospital I would like. "A hospital for unwed mothers? A surgical hospital? A leper hospital?"

"Ex-servicemen," I answered promptly, surprising him. For my father.

December 17—Drury Lane

It began all right: Charles and I went to the Theatre Royal, where we saw *Catiline's Conspiracy*—thank goodness I was not cast in that. Doom and gloom for three hours, Ben Jonson or no. Hart was good as Catiline but a bit stiff in his right leg. I wonder, has he injured himself? He never will admit a weakness. And Nick was convincing as Cicero, but it is a part I know he loathes. After the performance we went backstage to congratulate the cast. There was a moment of terrifying awkwardness when my former lover (Charles) bowed to my new lover (King Charles), and then Johnny Rochester and Buckhurst (also Charles) turned up and began to giggle at the tableaux.

"Remind me never to introduce you to a man named Charles," the king whispered playfully in my ear, slipping a protective arm around my waist as we left.

In the carriage I broached the subject: "Buckingham stopped by the theatre the other day," I opened.

"Mmm," the king responded mildly, fastening and unfastening the catches on the curtained windows. He must always take everything apart to see how it *works*.

"He told me what has happened—about your brother and the navy." I sensed danger but decided to press ahead. "Maybe you should—"

"He told you what?" he asked in a tight voice. "That he and Arlington have banded against me? That they are trying to discredit my own brother, my *heir*, for not better financing the navy—with what money, I ask you?" He pulled the tassel off the curtain fabric in his agitation. "That when he talks of being off with his women, he is, in fact, secretly meeting almost daily with the republican parliamentary leaders Wildman and Owen? Men who supported *Cromwell*! That he is filling my son Monmouth's head with ideas of legitimacy and kingship? Impossible ideas that will only lead to his ruin. That Buckingham, my oldest and dearest friend, whose father was my father's oldest and dearest friend, is bullying my brother—the heir to the throne—and single-handedly trying to strangle my government? What? What is it that Buckingham told you?"

I sat back, shocked at this outburst. "No, he said—"

"Buckingham *always* has an axe to grind—he only grinds for himself alone—so careful, my dear, when you throw your lot in with him," he said brutally.

"I've thrown in my lot with you!" I protested, catching at his sleeve in my panic.

He turned away and did not respond. When we arrived at the palace he alighted alone, without waiting for a footman, slamming the coach door closed behind him.

Kissing my hand formally, he wished me good night. "See the lady back to her lodgings," he told the coachman, and rapped on the roof before I could argue.

And then I understood. Our time was a refuge. *I* was a refuge. With that benign question I had become one of the many who wanted to manipulate him—to profit from him. Alone in the coach, I wept into my expensively gloved hands.

Later in my little room under the eaves, I realised: he knew and understood everything. He had all along. He was *always* ahead of them. He *wants* his courtiers and advisors to underestimate him—it is how he controls them. If it is not too late, I must never follow suit.

When I Try to Make Amends

December 18
Drury Lane
To be delivered by hand to Whitehall Palace, care of Jerome, the page
My darling,
    I trespassed where I had no right. Please forgive me.

                                  Your Ellen

December 20, 1668 — Theatre Royal

I am not cast, but I hang about the theatre anyway. It is *my* refuge, my family. Teddy, my anxious shadow, tries to cheer me out of my unhappiness. His remedy is food. All day he has brought little cakes and sweetmeats to tempt me. I am too agitated to eat. Tom sees my malaise and does not ask questions but instead engages me in small meaningless tasks and decisions.

"Best not to brood!" he says with determined gaiety. Together, we plan the Christmas festivities and decorate the theatre for the holiday season. Despite myself, I wound up giggling watching Nick, Michael, and Tom argue—in their booming, classically trained voices—how best to hang the ball of mistletoe.

"To the left!" Tom shouted to Nick, who was precariously balanced on a rickety ladder.

"My left?" Nick called down as the ladder wobbled dangerously.

"No! My left! My left!" Michael yelled as he hobbled in a circle at the base of the ladder, gesticulating wildly. His gout is worse this Christmas.

"Your left keeps moving!" Nick grumbled, struggling to hammer the nail into place and eventually dropping the prickly green ball on Tom below.

"I'll do it!" Tom said, fed up. "I know where my own left is."

"You won't once you get up there," Nick said, cheerfully coming down the ladder.

Later— Theatre Royal

Jerome arrived at the stage door of the theatre after the performance, wearing his livery (as he is careful to do whenever he sees me).

"He is not prepared to respond, Mrs. Ellen. He misses you terribly but is not ready," he said sorrowfully.

"Did he send you or—"

"No, I just thought I should come. For you . . . so you would know . . . Please don't tell him."

"No, no, of course. I promise," I said, looking him in the eye. "Is he angry?" I ventured.

"Tired, I think. He has these decisions to make, and the Duke of Buckingham is about all the time, nagging and nagging and never letting him be. The king has pushed everyone away and only wants to spend time with the queen now. And, of course, correspond with his sister."

"*The* queen? Our queen?"

"She does not ask anything of him, and he needs that right now. They assemble his clocks together and have designed a great sundial."

"Yes, that fits." I laughed. He always liked to engage his mind in mechanical puzzles when troubled. Clocks were a favourite. "Thank you, Jerome." I gave him a shilling for his trouble. "You are all right to get back?"

"Oh yes, the boat is waiting for me. Do you want me to deliver any message?"

"Only that I am thinking of him and wishing him a happy Christmastime. He and the queen both."

I watched Jerome until he was out of sight and was surprised to feel a heavy hand on my arm. Without a word, Hart folded me into his broad chest.

"It is not you," he murmured, gently stroking my hair. "He is a complicated king, and beyond that he is a complicated man."

"But I feel like the ground is always moving about beneath me," I said tearfully, stepping back to look up into his worried face.

"That is because it is moving. You inspire a man to be more than he is, Ellen. To reach and grow and thrive. A man cannot do that by standing still. I understand that now. Your love will not root in quiet ground." With that astonishing remark, he dropped his arms from my waist and strode away.

December 21 — Theatre Royal

Becka mentioned today (to Nan but deliberately in my hearing) that she had heard that the king just bought a coach and four for Lady Castlemaine—an early Christmas gift. The horses (dappled greys) are to be stabled at Whitehall, and the coach (japanned black lacquer with lots of gold trim—gaudy) brought round to her special entrance when she has use of it. I held my tongue and did not tell her that the king had the special entrance constructed because the people so hate to see Barbara. I tell myself that the coach is most likely for the benefit of the children, of whom Charles is very fond. Outwardly, I just smiled politely. It would not do to gossip, no matter how much the ground moves.

December 23, 1668
For Mrs. Ellen Gwyn
No. 9 Coal Yard Alley, Drury Lane, London
Dearest Ellen and Rose,

Your great-aunt is failing. I apologise for my bluntness, but there is little time— it is her heart, and she will be taken from us soon. If you could spare the time, my dears, could you (and Nora, of course) come to Oxford? It would make Margaret so happy, and for myself, I have missed you both and would like nothing better than to see you. We understand, of course, if your busy lives do not permit such a journey.

All my love,
Grandfather

December 26, 1668 — Farm Cottage, Oxford (snow)

She did not go quietly, but rather like a general leaving the field of battle, issuing orders to the end: Rose should be pregnant; John should be promoted; I should be married *and* pregnant *and* promoted; Grandfather should stop eating green vegetables (terrible for the constitution) and give up reading after dark; Mother should perk up and give up the drink (obviously); and Jezebel should *not* be allowed to climb on the roof. I am sitting with Ruby (who is now permitted inside the house) in the tiny attic bedroom watching the snowfall, feeling somewhat dazed.

January 1, 1669 — London (cold)

I have returned as I am cast this week in Shirley's *The Sisters*. I will play the amusing Pulcheria opposite Hart's Prince Farnese. It is all wrong for me right now, and I must force an awkward gaiety I do not like. And then it is back to Dryden's *The Maiden Queen*, always a sure hit. It is good to be in the theatre and oddly comforting to play opposite Hart. He is frequently impatient with my lack of focus, and we certainly never mention his bizarre liaison with my lover's mistress, but his proximity is bolstering somehow.

Luckily, the crowded routine of rehearsal, memorisation, and performance does not leave much time for brooding. Ruby and Scandalous are sleeping in their basket, happy to be back in familiar surroundings. I left John, Rose, and Grandfather in Oxford to sort things out—the farm, the books, and the animals. Grandfather will stay on for a bit deciding what to do with Farm Cottage before joining us in town.

Note—Grandfather wants to bring Jezebel to town. No one in Oxford will buy her. No word from the king, but Becka reports that he has kept a merry court this Christmas. Also that he has given Castlemaine another gang of titles. She is now the Duchess of Cleveland, Countess of Southampton, and Baroness Nunsuch. Nunsuch is said to be the most beautiful house in England; no doubt she will ruin it. She cares only for status, nothing for beauty.

Friday, January 15, (still cold)

"It was hilarious, my darlings; you should have seen it, so unflattering," said Teddy, settling Scandalous on his lap.

Scandalous is far more discerning (well, bad-tempered) than Ruby and will only acknowledge certain people. Teddy is his undoubted favourite.

"Hilarious that such ridiculous women take up so much of the king's time? Clarendon was right. He really is under the petticoat influence," Aphra said, pouring the coffee.

We had gathered at Aphra's for an evening of cards and chat and were just waiting for Tom to make up the fourth. Teddy was regaling us with this afternoon's theatre antics. The mature (she must be at least fifty) actress Catherine Corey had stunned London audiences by ruthlessly imitating Lady Hervey, the queen's favourite lady-in-waiting. Lady Hervey, an easy target, has an unfortunate and unmistakeable lisp.

"And you really think Castlemaine put her up to it?" I asked Teddy.

"Well, old Catherine Corey is hardly likely to imitate the great Lady Hervey without encouragement. She hasn't the imagination," he said carelessly.

"Just because Lady Hervey carries influence with the queen?" Aphra asked.

"Everything to do with the queen infuriates Castlemaine," Teddy said mildly, "especially with the way Lady Hervey has been throwing her weight around lately: boasting that she has Secretary of State Arlington in her pocket, and telling all and sundry that to make way she had her own husband posted as ambassador to Turkey. Castlemaine, sorry, Cleveland—still doesn't sound right—wouldn't like that: Arlington is *her* stooge."

"Pocket." Aphra snorted. "Don't you mean bed?"

Just then Tom was shown in, flustered and pink from the cold.

"I'm sorry to be late, it has been bedlam, literally." Tom pulled off his mittens and set them on the hearth rail. "I have been listening to Lady Hervey rant for the last half hour and have been threatened with everything from bankruptcy to the clink, and I'm drenched."

I giggled. Lady Hervey has a tendency to spit as she speaks.

"That woman is awful," Tom said, unwinding his muffler and gratefully accepting a cup of chocolate.

"She can't have Corey . . ." I began uncertainly. Catherine Corey is irritating, but she is gullible rather than malicious, and I would hate to see her fired or, worse, put in gaol.

"No, she can't. And she won't. She knows as well as I do who put old Corey up to it. Silly woman—what a way to boost a fading career."

"Which one? Corey or Castlemaine?"

"Well, both, actually."

January 16— Theatre Royal (The Maiden Queen)

Chiffinch arrived at the theatre this morning. I have never seen him away from the court.

"Patience," he advised gruffly. "He will come round. He cannot face you until he is resolved in his own head about . . . well, about . . . his governmental worries."

I was amazed he revealed that much. Dear Chiffinch is fanatical is his loyalty to the king and famous for his discretion.

"Yes, I understand."

"You made him feel as though he was letting down the country with his indecision," he summarised briefly. "He thinks the world of your opinion, and cannot bear for you to see him in such a tangle. Now that you have spoken it out loud, it can no longer be ignored, and he cannot bear to see you until he acts."

"But I think the world of him. Surely he knows that?" I asked, alarmed. "I would gladly help him with any tangle, not judge him for it." I care nothing for his political face or pride. I just miss the *man*—terribly.

"You really see *him;* that's the trouble. The others, they only see what they want him to do, how he can advance them, except the queen, of course. But then, she is quite close to being a saint, isn't she?" He cleared his throat, disconcerted by his own frankness.

"Yes," I agreed. "She is. Patience, then."

"Watch, you'll see. He'll come round and pretend nothing was ever amiss between you. That's his way. Just go along with it. He can't bear confrontation, and no tears. He cannot manage tears."

I giggled. "How on earth has he managed with Barbara Castlemaine?"

"More and more he is managing without, I am quite pleased to say," Chiffinch said with satisfaction, giving me a wink. "But he does care greatly for the children. They are the real reason he keeps heaping titles on that woman. Now, this will all be cleared up soon, but Mrs. Chiffinch misses you and wonders if we could sneak you in for a quiet supper in the backstairs with us. Roast lamb and fresh salad—your favourites, I believe. The king is off to the Duke's and then to see Mrs. Davis tonight," he said candidly.

Appreciating his honesty, and missing Mrs. Chiffinch as well, I agreed.

"He has a chosen a beautiful site, by the way," he said, pulling on his hat.

"A site?"

"For the Royal Hospital Chelsea, a hospital for ex-servicemen." Oh, Charles.

Later

Lovely dinner. I loitered in the courtyard watching the moon throw velvet shadows on the ramshackle palace. Hoped and hoped but didn't see him.

Note—Not managing *that* well without. Castlemaine was just granted a lifetime pension of forty-seven hundred pounds a year from the Post Office revenues. And he no longer even shares her bed! Good God, what a sum.

January 17 — Theatre Royal

Old Catherine Corey is in the clink! Lady Hervey got the Lord Chamberlain, her cousin, to lock her up. What an absurdly silly woman to allow herself to be used thus. Castlemaine is cruel to use such a pawn to provoke the queen's favourite. Not that I care for Lady Hervey; I cannot bear her insincere, simpering manner when she is with the queen. But she is the queen's chief lady, and that should mark her out for special respect. Corey is just a fool. It is Castlemaine who has shown herself to be a stooping, conniving harpy—but I suppose I knew that. How can Charles not stop this nonsense!

Undated

"She's out," said Teddy, sitting down heavily on the stage. "But that silly woman is going to do it again, all at Castlemaine's goading."

We were rehearsing Lacy's new dance steps before the performance this afternoon. Lacy is hoping to lighten up the leaden feeling of *Horace* with dancing between the acts. Doesn't quite go together, if you ask me.

"*Again?* How can Catherine Corey do it again?"

Teddy just shrugged his slim shoulders. "She is a relentless old goat." Teddy loves animal metaphors.

"That woman is an idiot," I muttered, closing my eyes to rest between run-throughs.

"Once more, everyone! Ellen, Teddy, up you get! Hart, would you please switch partners with Nick? Thank you," Lacy called out, thumping his marker on the stage. "Remember it is a *four*-count rhythm! Not three and a half, Lizzie. Begin! And one, two . . ."

Note—She did it. Castlemaine really is a witch, and Catherine Corey a fool for being taken in. The house was in an uproar. Tom and Hart are pleased; ticket sales are booming. Against everyone's hopes, the king did not come to witness this debacle. Why would he? I am not surprised. Not surprised, but disappointed all the same. I am fractured by fear. What if he never returns to me?

January 23—Rose's House, Cockspur Lane

Breakfast this morning with Rose and Mother. Mother was oddly silent throughout the meal. Rose cleared away the dishes and brought out her new sketches to show me. We were looking over her designs for a new winter coat.

"If I nip the waist in just here," she pointed, "and then flare it out like a bell—"

"They say it is because you asked it of him," Mother said suddenly. Rose and I looked at each other in confusion. It was half-past eight in the morning—had she begun drinking already?

"Is it true? The new hospital for the wounded soldiers. Did he do that for you?" She looked at me through clear, lucid eyes.

"Yes," I said with fierce pride. "Yes, he did that for me."

"Good," my mother said, and smiled a rare, youthful smile.

When I Buy a Home

I've done it! I've found a house!

The adventure:

Tom and Teddy arrived at Drury Lane early yesterday morning (before eight) and demanded that I get dressed and join them. A country outing, they said. A cure for melancholy, they said.

"In January?" I asked, dubious.

"It will invigorate us," Teddy declared with conviction. Invigorate *me*, he meant. He had accused me yesterday of behaving like a soggy duck. "Wet hen," I corrected him.

"But soggy duck is so much more appropriate. You have not acquired the wisdom to be a hen."

"Ugh!" Despite Chiffinch's encouragement, the ongoing silence has left me restless and edgy.

"It is freezing," I grumbled, feeling frumpy.

"Don't worry, we have blankets and warming bricks in the coach," Tom whispered under his breath. He himself was bundled up into a strange woolly, oblong shape.

Reluctantly, I obliged. Dressed in a simple wool gown, thick cape, and my old boots—well, if one is going to the country—with Ruby and Scandalous in tow, we set out.

After stopping at the Cardinal's Cap to pick up a hamper of apples, bread, hard cheese, cold chicken, and small beer, we made our way up White Cross Street and left the city behind for the wintry fields beyond.

Tom's coach, a snug compact vehicle, manoeuvred easily over the rougher roads. We munched our breakfast and chatted of this and that: the upcoming season, the appalling state of the stock costumes, and whether or not the king will donate new ones (he donated a splendid pair of split rhinegraves for me to dance in, but I do not want to wear them until he is in the audience—they fly up and show my legs beautifully), Tom's improvements to the musicians gallery (much better, they no longer sound as if they are at the bottom of a well), the terrible traffic around Covent Garden, and Moll's new baby, Mary Tudor.

"Yes, last week on Suffolk Street. A hard birth, apparently."

"I hadn't heard," I said, staring down at my hands. "Has he . . ."

"Acknowledged her? Yes, I suppose so, although the child's surname is to be Tudor rather than Fitzroy or even Stuart. Strange," Tom mused.

"He visited Moll during her sitting up," Teddy clarified. "And has already arranged for an annuity for her and the baby. That is enough acknowledgment right there. Brought tons of flowers—pink tulips—which apparently caused her to sneeze violently for several minutes. Looked at the baby but did not pick her up. Kissed Moll on the cheek, *not* the lips," he said pointedly to me. "Stayed exactly ten minutes, and then left for a walk through St. James's Park, apparently intending to feed the ducks." Teddy slumped against the seat, exhausted by his laundry list of royal doings.

"You seem very, ah, well informed," said Tom, regarding him with surprise.

"Speak to the dress-makers; they are always well informed." Now *I* looked at him surprised. Poor Teddy—since being forced into male roles, he has had less use for his beloved dress-makers.

Answering my unspoken question, he said defensively, "They still make my nightgowns. Better needle work than a shirt-maker, and cheaper, too."

Tom whooped with laughter, but I held my tongue and looked at my quirky friend fondly.

"Anyway, Winifred Gosnell stood in for Moll in *Tempest*. It was terrible; her voice is too squeaky."

"But then she is *so* much lighter on her feet than Moll," Tom said mischievously. "Moll is *not* light on her feet."

"Where are we headed?" I asked, trying to force thoughts of Moll and her new baby from my head.

"Wherever the day takes us," Teddy sang out, enthusiastically bouncing Scandalous on his knee. Poor Scandalous. He did not look as if he was enjoying it.

"I think we just passed the village of King's Cross." Tom had put on his spectacles and was peering out the window. "And this is the village of Bagnigge Wells. God, what a name." He was struggling to make out the faded signpost. "Oh, I remember, I think there was talk of a spa here—good water apparently, but now that Epsom and Tunbridge have become so popular, I don't know."

It was a pretty town, on the banks of the Fleet River, with a small, neat square and evenly cobbled streets (rare).

"Shall we stop?" I knew Tom's joints suffer after too long in a coach, and I was sure Ruby could use a trip to the great outdoors. "What did you say the name was?"

"Bagnigge Wells. It's a bit pokey."

"Terrible name," Teddy muttered, lifting Ruby down from the coach. We set off to find refreshment and a warm fire.

Later, comfortably seated in a clean if sparsely furnished inn on the north side of Wells Square, and revived by bowls of warm chocolate with foamy cream and a dish of buttery French macaroons, they arrived at their subject.

"We love you, Ellen," Tom opened, squeezing my hands, "and we cannot bear to see you suffer so . . ."

"Publicly?" Teddy offered, reaching for another macaroon (his third).

"Consistently," Tom finished. "This affair with . . . *him*. What can it lead to? Other than material goods, which you do not seem to garner like his previous ladies, although I can't think why not," Tom puzzled, anxiously folding and refolding his serviette.

"I do not ask for them, and when he hints, I do not jump for them." It was impossible to explain, I thought, blowing out my cheeks in exasperation. "I do not want to grab and grasp and squirrel away all I can. It is what everyone expects of me, being—"

"From your particular background," Tom cut in smoothly.

"And you mean to confound them?" Teddy asked. "Ellen, what *exactly* have you turned down?"

"Everything! A house, a coach, a sedan chair, jewels, horses, hats, sculpture, painting, palace rooms, shoes, servants—" The looks on their faces made me stop. "I do allow him to buy me dresses, *lots* of dresses, and I am *seriously* considering shoes," I offered lamely.

"But *why?*" Tom exploded. He was forever worrying about my lack of a husband, lack of a coach, lack of a *house*. Lack of, lack of, lack of.

"It suits me. I do not want what he can give me. I want *him*."

"But a *house* . . ." Tom shook his head.

"And hats! My God, the hats," Teddy mourned. Teddy loves hats.

"And that is why it must end." Tom looked me squarely in the eye. "You will never have him, not all of him."

"I think I can live without all," I said carefully. "I just need . . . *enough*. Enough to feel . . . set apart. Special."

"And do you have that now?" Tom persisted.

"I think I had more than I knew, was more special than I knew, but now . . . Still, whatever mistakes I have made, I know that my intentions were good. If he does not want to hear the truth from me, or from anyone, then we are better off apart." I heard my own voice ring with conviction, sounding true and strong and not betraying the deep lonely regret that lurked beneath.

"Reasonable," said Tom, sitting back and regarding me critically. "As to the rest, then, we shall see."

As we were leaving, we passed a foursquare brick house with a circular drive just at the edge of the village. The tiny house had a large poplar tree in the front and a peeling green front door. There was a notice on the weathered gate, announcing that the property was for sale or long let.

"Stop!" I cried out, louder than I had intended, surprising myself. Dutifully, the coachman brought the horses to a halt.

January 28 — Theatre Royal (Island Princesse)

"But you haven't even seen it!" Tom repeated, pacing the floor and running his fingers through his thinning hair—he removes his itchy wig in his private study. "As your friend, manager, and financial advisor, I can't allow this. Hart, tell her," he went on distractedly, returning to the papers on his desk.

"I have found that it is impossible to tell her anything," Hart said, winking at me and taking himself off to check the stage.

We have *Island Princesse* on at the moment, and the third scene of Act II, when the town burns down, has everyone in a state of constant anxiety. We just burn sulphur and *aqua vitae,* but Tom is convinced we will burn the theatre down as well. The good news is that Peg has returned to play Panura, and Rupert comes to see her every night, boosting ticket sales enormously. Nick is wonderful as Soza but is not enough of a name to draw a crowd.

Just then, Teddy came into the office without knocking; he never knocks, just assumes he is welcome everywhere.

"Talk to her, Teddy," Tom said, standing up to pace some more. "The foundations could be unstable. There could be damp or mould or mice or—"

"Rats!" Teddy shuddered. "Oh, my dear, you can't possibly, not if there are rats."

"And anyway, how could you possibly afford it?" Tom went on. "You would have to borrow a huge sum of money, even though the price *is* remarkably low. If it were a smarter village, it would be double. Oh, this is not the week to be talking about this!"

"Fashionable villages are ruinously expensive. Just look at what happened to Epsom," Teddy said absently, ignoring Tom's agitation.

"But this village is not fashionable. This house is not expensive. It is near enough to town. And it is perfect. I just know it."

"Ellen, I thought you could manage without a house, a coach, all the whatnot that goes with being an established lady? Didn't you just tell us—"

"I told you I did not want it from *him*. Not that I do not want it." That was partly true. Mostly I did not want to be thought of like *her*—Moll, the graspy actress—making the most of it and salting away all she can. "It *is* perfect, Tom. Please, just trust me." Just *how* I know this I am not sure: something to do with the optimistically green front door, or the arbour covered in sweet-brier and holly, or the giant curved poplar in the yard, or maybe even the melancholy name of the road: Grays Inn.

I shook my head and listened again to Tom, who was now holding forth on my financial precariousness—meaning my unusual penniless royal mistress, yet unmarried, state. I was not currently able to follow the well-trodden path from the stage into the marriage bed of a rich man. I was taken and yet not settled, a state my friends found very *un*settling.

Finally, they agreed. It was Teddy who came up with the solution. For some time I have been quietly helping Tom choose plays and design the season (much more so than the useless stage manager, Mr. Booth), and Teddy suggested that I receive a small part of the takings as my reward—unofficially, of course.

"It is only fair, Tom," Teddy reasoned. "She has an unerring gift for suggesting the right play at the right time. And she has been doing it for ages, to all our benefit, I might add. She has no share points, and she is the only one who can get Dryden to actually write instead of just ponce about."

"She is not allowed to have share points; she is a woman!"

"But she is doing a *man's* job."

"Hart would have a fit," Tom pointed out quietly. I held my breath, knowing this was the real sticking point.

"Why tell him? It is only half a percent anyway, not enough to notice. No one will know."

"But it is enough to buy me a house!"

"Well, we will all be broke if the theatre burns down, points or no points," Tom said gloomily.

"Don't say it! Bad luck! Go outside, close your eyes, turn around three times, and spit," Teddy shrieked.

Tom rolled his eyes.

"Oh well, the audience loves a good fire onstage," I said mischievously. "The bang last night when the sulphur went brought the house down."

"That's what I am worried about," grumbled Tom.

Tom signed on as my guarantor, thank goodness. I move in three days.

January 31, Bagnigge House! (Anniversary of the king's murder)

"It's not much when you pile it all together, is it?" Rose said, looking at my meagre stack of belongings.

The stack: my dress-boxes, my hat-boxes, my scripts, Grandfather's books, cooking pots and crockery, a few worn rugs, coverlets, my guitar, an armchair, and Scandalous and Ruby's bed. We had decided to leave our beds behind, as they virtually fell apart when we tried to lift them. I ordered new beds today—terribly expensive but essential. They will hopefully arrive next week.

"The dress-boxes are impressive," Rose's husband, John, offered lamely. "Where is this house again?"

"Grays Inn Road, Bagnigge Wells," trilled Teddy, alighting from what could only be described as a wagon. "I know, terrible name, but soon to be a most fashionable address."

"Teddy! You came!" I was so pleased. "Where did you get—"

"Wouldn't miss it. Tom has the keys and is waiting for us at the house. Thank God, *Princesse* is over and he can relax. You are throwing your first party tonight, my love—a bit impromptu, but we'll put something together."

"What?" I asked, alarmed. A party! I hadn't even been inside yet.

"You'll love it. Nick, Johnny, Aphra, and Dryden will be arriving for supper this evening—must remember to pick up some supper for them. Do you have a cook yet? No? Thought not, never mind. I would think Aphra is quite deft in the kitchen—must be, she can do anything, spying, fencing, writing . . . Buckhurst and Sedley are coming, too, but I would really rather they didn't. The drinking does get out of hand as soon as that pair arrive. Etheredge is down with a fever and cannot make it. We are to pack up and join Tom now. Shouldn't take long, I think"—he giggled, eyeing my small heap—"although we may swoon with the fasting."

I grimaced. It was only half past ten, and I had already broken the fast (toast and coffee). Nothing more until sundown, I resolved, not even the apples I had stuffed into my travelling bag.

"Johnny?" I suddenly realised. "But he was meant to be going down to Adderbury to see his wife. What is she now, six months along?"

"Seven," Teddy said grimly.

"Oh, that's awful, and her first baby, too. He always talks about going; why doesn't he just get on with it?"

"Oh, you know Johnny. He's a puzzle."

We put everything into what turned out to be the theatre's prop wagon in a matter of minutes. I turned to look at the little house of my childhood.

I turned to Rose. "Sure you will be all right with, with—"

"With Mother?" Rose voiced the unspoken.

I had tried to convince Mother to move to Bagnigge House with me, but she staunchly refused to leave town—although she has agreed to give up her *business* (provided I supply an income for her—expensive but essential)—and so has moved in with Rose. Grandfather has chosen to spend the winter in Oxford and then will join me.

"Oh, we'll rub along. There will be no drinking in my house, so she may not stay long," Rose said cheerfully.

"We're off!" said Teddy, handing me into the wagon. I held the squirming dogs on my lap and waved good-bye to Rose, John, and the little house I was leaving behind.

Later

I was right. It is as perfect as I suspected. The rooms are small—except for the disproportionately huge rectangular dining room—and need work, but possess charm: uneven floorboards, crumbly thick moulding, lumpy mullioned windows, and a creaky stairway. It is a perfect jewel box of a house, and it is mine.

Supper was a picnicky sort of affair—blankets and cushions on the floor and a toasty fire. Teddy was right, Aphra *can* cook, and she brought along her young actor friend Tommy Otway, currently studying at Christ Church, Oxford, who makes delicious pastry and can't be more than seventeen. God knows what she is doing with him; Aphra never ceases to surprise. After supper we all trooped over to the Pindar of Wakefield, the ancient pub on the far side of Wells Square, and drank warm fizzy beer out of thick country mugs.

Monday, February 1, 1669

This morning I hired Mr. Lark from the village as coachman (although I have yet to find a good coach to fit my budget and think I will have to buy Mrs. Eustace's unreliable antique), gardener, and carpenter. He is really only a carpenter, but I can only afford one man. I also bought a dining table and chairs from Mrs. Eustace up the road—unfortunate fabric on the seats, but Rose should be able to re-cover them. Picnics are well and good but would get tiresome every night.

Six chickens, two ducks, a cow, and a fuzzy grey gosling named Molly also came with the house. Mr. Lark says we can sell the milk and eggs in the village market, but what one does with a goose, I have no idea. "We could wait until she gets a bit older and then . . ." Mr. Lark hinted.

"Don't even think about it. I refuse to eat geese I know personally." Ruby and Scandalous are suspicious of these ferocious creatures and refuse to leave the kitchen garden.

February 2 — Theatre Royal (my birthday)

Spent the morning glazing sprigs of candied rosemary for the front hall, just one of the heavenly domestic tasks I delight in daily. I find all I want to do is nest in my cosy house. But alas, the wide world awaits, and so Lark drove me in for an afternoon of birthday shopping with Peg—dangerous— I must remember that I am on a restricted budget since I have my beautiful house to pay for.

Now I am at the theatre waiting for Teddy to finish in *The Heiress* so we can go out for supper. Peg has gone off to fetch Rupert and the others: Tom, Dryden, Johnny, Etheredge (now recovered), and Aphra, without her young friend, will all meet us after the performance. The Wits are all in the house tonight, but I cannot have them *all* come to my dinner—it will get out of hand. We seven are hoping to slip away unnoticed. Teddy loosely impersonates Sedley in this performance, all in fun, but the rest of the Wits have turned out in a disapproving force—thank goodness Savile and Buck-hurst are in the country, two fewer to worry about. Teddy is toning it down tonight to appease them.

Later

Johnny could not remember where he told his coachman to meet him (he was too drunk), and so he and Aphra came back to my house to sleep. We all rode home in my new—well, new to me, and very unsound—coach, and will return to town in the morning. Mr. Lark drove—his third time driving in town, but he drives boldly and does not err on the side of caution. Aphra thinks either I must learn to drive myself or both Mr. Lark and I will be dead by the end of the month. Everyone loved the house, but had a few questions.

"But, my love, more furniture? Where do you sit? Or sleep or write or read?" Johnny asked, looking around perplexed. Rose's husband, John, had come to collect the chairs so she can begin working on them.

"Or put your boots?" Aphra asked, muddy boots in hand.

"My dear, I know I'm soused, but is that a *duck*?"

"Certainly not. It is a *goose*, not a duck; the ducks don't come in at night. Johnny, Molly. Molly, Johnny," I introduced them formally.

"But inside?" Johnny sputtered. "Are we inviting the pigs in, too?"

"No. No pigs," I told him firmly. "Just her. She was so cold I asked her in to warm up by the fire, and, well, the dogs eventually got used to her, and so she just stayed. She is very well behaved, and at least now the dogs will go out into the yard. They all go marching out together; it is sweet." They both stared at me in disbelief.

The dogs got up from their bed without disturbing the sleeping goose, came over, and sniffed the intruders. Deeming them friendly, they went back to bed.

"Oh, I see, your farmyard menagerie have beds, and we are to make do with the floor?" Johnny asked.

"Beds are delivered next week, I promise," I said, cheerfully handing out blankets.

Wednesday—St. Joseph's Hospital

Pacing: eleven steps from the window to the bed. Eleven steps there and eleven steps back. Breathe, Ellen.

Eleven a.m.

Teddy was attacked. We don't know by whom. No one saw it, and Teddy is still unconscious. A group of children found him lying in the dirt this morning in St. James's Park, crumpled and bloody but breathing. Thankfully, they fetched a constable, and the constable, being a theatregoer, recognised him and fetched Tom. Tom accompanied the constable and sent Etheredge to fetch us. Nothing was stolen from him, not his money, not his precious worked-gold pocket glass, not even his frilly high-heeled boots. Tom, Rochester, and Aphra are here now. Hart, Nick, and Peg are on their way.

"Teddy, wake up, please," I pray over and over, watching his bruised, sleeping face.

Two p.m.

No change. Everyone is here now.

Six p.m.

A huge ruckus downstairs—shouting and stomping of feet. I stood up to see what was going on, but my legs, cramped from sitting for so long, buckled beneath me.

"Sit, dear," the nurse, named Elspeth, said, coming around the bed. "He knows you are here. It helps, I promise."

Teddy was still not conscious, but his breathing was regular, his ears had ceased to bleed, and his pulse was steady. "All good signs," the nurse keeps telling me.

Just then the double doors swung open and the king marched in, looking ferocious, pushing Lord Sedley roughly before him, with Chiffinch trailing behind. Johnny reached out his hand, alarmed, and then checked and bowed instead.

"Do it," the king said, his voice tight with rage. He seemed to notice no one else in the room. He shook Sedley violently by the neck like a lion. "Do it now."

Sedley cringed. "I—"

"On your knees," commanded the king.

Sedley gasped when he saw Teddy's broken form and knelt on the stone floor at my feet. I could see that his fine amber coat was torn at the collar, and he had an angry purple bruise on his left cheek.

"Nelly, I am so sorry. I . . . I ordered the attack on Kynaston. I was drunk and annoyed by his mockery, and it is no excuse. I know better. Please forgive me. He is my friend, as you are, and I so truly regret it."

I looked at him, stunned. I looked at my lover, whom I had not seen in two months. I looked away. I found I had no thoughts for anyone but the man lying in the bed. I tried to speak, but no sound came. Johnny took my hand in his, and I felt warmed with love and faith.

I looked at Sedley and, surprised by my steady voice, said, "It is not from me you should be asking forgiveness. It is from Teddy, and it is from God." With that, I turned away from him.

"Take him," said the king. Guards I had not noticed before stepped forward and pulled Sedley roughly to his feet.

"The Tower?" he asked with a shadowy smile.

"Newgate," replied the king grimly. "Now."

Sedley, ashen, was led from the room. I looked back at Teddy, lying motionless on the bed.

"Ellen, I—" began the king.

I looked around. Rochester, Nurse Elspeth, and Aphra had quietly gone.

I had not heard them leave. Chiffinch still stood, unobtrusive as always, behind the king.

"I know," I said wearily. It was unimportant, this drama of reconciliation. "It is all right. I understand, and I am glad it is over."

He knelt beside me, pressed me close, and kissed me tenderly: my eyes, my throat, my lips. I remained listless in his embrace, too distracted to respond.

"I have missed you," he said into my hair. "I have missed you so much."

"You knew where I was. You should have come to find me," I heard myself say flatly. I saw Chiffinch blanch. This was not how it was supposed to go, not how I had rehearsed it. "And now, I would like it if you left me alone. I will come to you soon enough, just like everyone else."

"When?"

"Soon."

I turned back to Teddy and heard the king's boots on the floor and then the door softly shut behind him.

"I must say," Teddy spoke from the bed, without opening his eyes, "that was very well done, old girl."

"Yes," said Chiffinch quietly. "Very well done."

When My Friend Is in Trouble

Good God, when will these boys stop punching each other? Last night at the king's private dinner for the Dutch ambassador (excellent manners, very white teeth), Johnny began to tease Tom Killigrew, who usually begs off and does not come to these things, as his wilder days are long over, but the king had asked for him personally. I think he thought Tom's presence would ease my nerves—it did. It was an informal dinner, but I am unaccustomed to dining with foreign dignitaries.

The king himself helped me dress, choosing a square-necked, deep raspberry satin dress (I wasn't sure with my red hair, but he insisted) and slender black slippers. Once I was dressed, coiffed—*à la négligence*—and scented, the king returned and presented me with a beautiful necklace of enormous, evenly matched pearls. I threw my arms around his neck, and Monsieur Bertrand, my hairdresser, cried out in alarm as his delicate work was crushed. Charles was delighted with my reaction and proceeded to spend twenty minutes explaining the mechanics of the newly fashioned spring clasp. We were very nearly late for supper.

In any event, the dinner went smoothly, and we were all enjoying some music—the beautiful and famous Arabella Hunt played the lute and sang in her haunting soprano, and James York played some lovely compositions of his own, I had no idea he was so musical—and fine claret afterwards, when Johnny, drunk and looking for trouble, began to antagonise Tom: asking him why it is that the King's playhouse is so much less imaginative than the Duke's? Was he short of good writers? Obviously, he must be if he employs Dryden, he reasoned in a menacing voice. Does he lack the money to pay good writers—and, if so, would he care for a loan? Does he want for good actors who can enact good plays? And on and on and *on*. Tom sat thunderstruck. Johnny is his friend, and while he is always teasing about the writing, Dryden's writing mostly, and the re-used sets and the patched costumes, it is unlike him to be outright cruel. Tom flushed furious pink and began to counter the assault when the king and the duke (the respective patrons of the two theatres) broke in, good-naturedly calling for an end to the unpleasantness. Just then, while the king was still speaking, Johnny leaned over and boxed Tom's ears. Without another word, Charles stood and, gripping him by the elbow, marched him from the room. They did not return.

Later— King's Apartments, Whitehall

"You forgave him? Already?" I asked Charles, bewildered. Dot and her new litter (six pups!) settled down beside me. "You do not require him to publicly apologise to the ambassador, or to your brother, or just to Tom, at least?" Or me? I thought but did not say.

I was sitting on the edge of the bed, watching Charles take off his periwig and slippers and hand them to Buckingham, who was acting as Groom of the Bedchamber—he really is lazy, not bothering to turn down the bed and leaving the door to the King's Closet ajar, meanwhile drinking most of the wine—but Charles invites such familiarity and chooses not to curb him. Buckingham was weaving about the room, royal slippers in one hand and a wine-glass in the other.

"In the wardrobe," I directed curtly. "Dot will chew them up by morning otherwise."

"Of course he forgave him," Buckingham answered for the king, putting the slippers away. "What is he to do? Punish him for a silly prank? That would make Charles look ridiculous. It was harmless, Nell," Buckingham said easily. "Johnny had a bit to drink and was just roughhousing. Tom knows that."

He banged the wardrobe shut, startling the sleeping spaniels. Privately,

I thought Tom knew nothing of the sort and was shocked and hurt by Johnny's behaviour.

"Roughhousing in front of the Dutch ambassador, the king, and the Duke of York?"

"Why not?" Buckingham shrugged. With that, he swept an elegant bow and swaggered out, without waiting to be dismissed.

"You can't think that? Surely, he must be shaken out of this and not indulged?" I asked Charles once we were alone. He had been strangely quiet. "Johnny has been drunk before, but this was different. He was so angry, and his behaviour, well, it was just not acceptable."

"Yes," Charles said soberly as he climbed into bed. "Yes, he is angry. And I forgave him."

"Angry with *whom*?"

"Everyone: you, me, James, Dryden, the queen . . . everyone who is content in their life, as he can find so little contentment in his own. Ellen, he is . . . ill."

I had heard vague rumours of Johnny's illness. The French pox. "I thought it wasn't confirmed by a physician," I said weakly.

"I have sent for Dr. Denis from Paris—he will make a final diagnosis—but it is not hopeful, sweetheart. And Johnny knows it."

I turned into his chest and closed my eyes to the deranged, disfiguring horror of his words.

"But I know Johnny will remember himself," Charles said softly. "He will regret his behaviour in the morning and apologise, without my asking. He loves me too much not to."

I hope so, I thought. I very much hope so.

February 18 (early)

No apology—instead, disaster. This morning Johnny, still drunk, dismantled Charles's great sundial. Without reason or explanation, he left it in gleaming golden chunks on the lawn. Charles is furious.

Dr. Denis arrives tomorrow. I cannot find it in myself to be angry with Johnny.

February 22

Diagnosis: as predicted. Prognosis: terrible. Dr. Denis prescribed a course of mercury baths and returned to France.

February 27, 1669— Bagnigge House (snow)

I was sitting in my tiny drawing room reading a new comedy for the spring season when I heard a single carriage thunder into the drive. I looked up, hoping it was a furniture wagon bringing the new feather mattresses. The bedsteads have arrived but no mattresses yet—uncomfortable.

"I've decided," the king said, stamping his boots to shake off the snow. "I'm sending him away. This morning was the last straw."

Johnny. I knew from his tone that it must be Johnny, and from the taut lines of Charles's face that it must be serious. I rang the silver bell for Mrs. Lark to bring the coffee and cakes. As Mr. Lark was spending so much time here, I had decided to hire Mrs. Lark to do the cooking and washing and to take care of the animals, the growing number of animals— Grandfather has come to join me and brought his bad-tempered goat Jezebel; sadly, Jeffrey passed soon after Great-Aunt Margaret. The Larks have happily moved into the small apartment above the stables and are quickly whipping this house into shape. Grandfather and Mr. Lark have finished repairing the moulding in the huge rectangular dining room and have moved onto refitting the draughty bedroom windows. Grandfather loves a project. Mrs. Lark has scrubbed down the entire house, top to bottom, unearthing very pretty woodwork buried beneath years of dust and dirt. And this is just my tiny country home. God knows how many people I will need to hire when I move to the new London house that I finally accepted from Charles.

"Away?" I asked, turning back to Charles, who was settling himself onto the rug, spreading cushions by the fire. Even though I now have furniture, very fine furniture that Charles helped me to order (and pay for), he seems to prefer the floor. Molly immediately came waddling over and, shaking out her feathers, settled down beside him, pushing her long beak into his coat pockets. Ruby and Scandalous were busy cavorting with his pack of spaniels under the dining table and did not notice the treats for the taking.

"Away where?"

"France, soon. I'll pack him off with letters for my sister. Let him try this kind of nonsense in Louis's court. I won't have him here." Molly found the crackers meant for her in his left pocket and began to crunch them with gusto.

"What happened this morning?" I asked, fearing the answer.

Mrs. Lark brought in the coffee tray. She always keeps a pot brewing in case the king unexpectedly visits, which he does—*often*.

"He was baiting the Duke of Richmond, Frances's husband, who is not bright but harmless, and it was resolving into a duel. Frances was hysterical and came to fetch me. I broke it up, calmed the dullard duke, and sent Johnny away. He will leave in a few weeks, once the correspondence is arranged. At least he can do something useful. Until then, he is to stay at Adderbury." Charles leaned his head back onto a cushion, his mouth set in a resolute line.

"Will you see him before he goes?"

"No. Not unless he is sober. And I do not think he has been sober for some time."

March 12, 1669 — Newmarket

Johnny sailed this morning, and as promised, Charles did not see him. I sent him a brief note, wishing him a good journey and a peaceful stay. I did not wish him joy. It would have felt false.

Later

Cards tonight with Savile and Charles. Savile told a story I had never heard. When Johnny was in the navy, his ship came under heavy enemy fire. Standing on the deck in great danger, Johnny and two other sailors made a solemn pact. If any of the three were shot and killed, the dead man must appear to the other two and reassure them of the sweetness of God's grace in heaven. Both of the other sailors were killed that day, but neither returned to Johnny.

April 13, 1669

Johnny's wife, Elizabeth, gave birth to a daughter, Anne, at Adderbury yesterday. She is to be called Nan for short. He missed it. Rose and I sent a basket of new baby linens, a wooden rattle, and a soft woollen blanket. Charles sent a gold-and-pearl pendant and his love.

10.

Exit the Actress

When My Greatest Rival Is Removed

May 1669 — Theatre Royal

"It is awful, admit it. His worst yet," Teddy said, banging the script down on the stage. Papers went flying; it was cheaply bound and came apart easily.

"It isn't my favourite, but at least he's turned out *something*," I said, starting to pick up pages.

"*Tyrannick Love, or the Royal Martyr*—what sort of title is that? Dryden ought to know better," Teddy continued, roughly taking off his soft rehearsal shoes and banging them down on the stage, too. It had taken nearly two months for his collarbone to completely heal but he was now back to performing, and was irritated that Dryden had not written him a part. "And Nell keeling over at the end—who wants to see that?"

"What?" I asked, alarmed.

"Honestly, Ellen!" Hart scowled at me. "The man writes the play for you, and you didn't even bother to read it, did you?" Without waiting for my response, Hart stomped off to his tiring room.

He was right. I had not finished reading the script and had no idea how the play ended. I have been behind lately, spending all my time with the king. He is currently occupied with his secret negotiations with the French. Ostensibly, it is an alliance to end the Dutch war—still dragging on, who can believe it? His sister, the Madame, is acting as intermediary as this is a treaty of some delicacy—they are also, I was appalled to discover, considering a future secret contract that will bind Charles to enter the Catholic faith in exchange for Louis's considerable financial aid—a contract that does not specify *when* he must convert to Catholicism but gets the king out his current horrifying debt without resorting to Parliament. Dear God, let no one find out.

"If it solves my money problems, pays my navy, builds my hospitals, and helps me to better safeguard my people . . . won't God understand?" Charles reasoned.

"*God* will, but your *people* won't," I replied quietly.

In any case, with all this going on, I had not had time to concentrate on Dryden's new script. "I have to die, *again*? Onstage? We're back to that?" I wailed.

"Not just die, my dear," Nick said groggily. He had been awoken from his nap by the banging and was now helping me to reorder the script. "You stab yourself, right at the end—a heroic death, very tragic, very Juliet. A real Dryden special—you'll love it."

"Stop!" I said, swatting him with loose papers. "I can't do it. Not again. I can't do it properly. Everyone knows that. I look ridiculous. It is why I *never* play Juliet."

"True," Nick said bluntly.

"Oh, and to do it in front of—"

"Oh yes, what will your royal lover think to see you die pathetically, undone by a blemish on your shining virtue? Good God," Nick said, beginning to giggle.

"Undone by bad writing, more likely," Teddy grumbled. "But the name, the *name* is priceless," he said, brightening. "Valeria—you sound like an ancient Roman pox."

"Brilliant," I said, snapping the pages together.

Saturday, June 1, 1669 — King's Closet (rainy)

I was peacefully revising the list of plays for the shortened summer season when I heard his boots clacking furiously down the parquet floor, accompanied by the lighter tapping of his gang of spaniels.

"That woman! I will not have it!" Charles thundered, noisily throwing open the doors to his dressing room himself, without waiting for his gentleman usher. He is incapable of opening a door gently. He roughly pulled off his wig and hurled it in the general direction of the sofa. I smiled encouragingly at Francis, his frazzled usher, who, after a nod from me, quickly left, pulling the double doors closed behind him.

"Will not have what?" I asked, retrieving his wig; it had fallen quite close to the fire, and it wouldn't have been the first royal wig to go that way. Awful smell.

"She expects me to acknowledge this baby! This child who could not possibly be mine! Even Lucy did not try that, when Mary so clearly wasn't mine. And Lucy genuinely *needed* the money."

"Castlemaine?" I asked cautiously.

I cannot get used to calling her Cleveland, and she is not worth the effort, so I have given up trying. Whatever her name is, she is a touchy subject. Castlemaine recently gave birth to a daughter here in Whitehall—a child she expects the king to recognise as his own. We deliberately de-camped to Newmarket for the event, and the queen and some friends went to Tunbridge Wells to take the waters. No one calls it a fertility treatment anymore; it seems to be understood that it is hopeless.

Lucy and Castlemaine's situations were not terribly similar. Lucy Walter, Monmouth's unfortunate mother, was, unlike Castlemaine, living in a sepa-rate city and had not seen the king in a year when she gave birth to Mary and so had no grounds to claim patrimony, but I did not point this out. Nor did I mention the six-hundred-pound allowance he still gives Mary each year, whether she is his daughter or not.

"Of course Castlemaine. Who else? She knows just when to cause a ruckus; with the new French ambassador arriving next week, this will look awful. Her sense of timing is flawless."

"Could it . . . ?"

"No. Definitely not. This baby is most likely that toad Jermyn's, and he won't 'fess up. Swine."

I looked quickly at Chiffinch, who had just slipped in the private door. He has a way of appearing when the king has need of him.

"Did you . . . ?"

"Confront him? Of course not. I am not about to go trawling for this child's father. Henry Jermyn can look after his own bastard or not as he chooses. Of course it could be Hart's child, or Wycherly's, or that circus performer's, or even my own grandchild! That woman."

He sat down heavily on a pink embroidered chair, gathering his spaniel Dot into his lap.

"Your grand—" I began, but when I saw Chiffinch, behind the king's chair, vigorously shake his head, I stopped.

"Let her speak, William," the king said, without looking up. "We have no secrets between us."

An overstatement at best, but I let it lie.

"Monmouth?" I breathed in disbelief. "She wouldn't. Jemmy wouldn't. It is unthinkable."

"Oh, they would and do, *often* it seems, and I honestly do not care," he said, closing his eyes and pressing his fingertips to his temples. "Barbara Castlemaine is a grasping, greedy whore, and Jemmy has not the sense to see it, nor the character or the respect for me to refrain."

"But are you sure?" I saw Chiffinch shaking his head, warning me to stop, but I persisted. "Perhaps it is just rumour."

"Not a rumour, Ellen: a certainty." He paused, opening his eyes. "We crossed paths."

I bridled at that. I had assumed he no longer visited Castlemaine's rooms, but then I had never asked, and was not so frequently at Whitehall to see for myself. Charles more often visited my small house to escape the suffocating court and was now giving me a new house in town so I could be nearer. I smoothed the skirt of my gown—coffee-coloured silk. It had a mud stain on the hem. I must have Mrs. Lark look at it, I thought randomly.

"While I was visiting the *children*, Nell," he stressed, guessing my thoughts.

He rose from his chair and crossed to me. I saw Chiffinch leave, soundlessly closing the door to the secret stairwell behind him. I did not respond.

"Be reasonable," he coaxed. "Their nurseries are in her apartments, too, if you recall. You cannot expect me not to visit them," he continued, tilting my face up to his. "You must not worry so. What you have, you will always have. I have, of late, been with no other women but you. Nor do I have any plans to."

"I am always reasonable," I countered spikily.

He kissed me gently, and I softened in his arms. It is impossible to stay angry with this man. His labyrinthine selfish logic is too endearing and too genuine. The evening moved on, the incident was forgotten, and we went on to discuss this and that: his daughter Charlotte's aptitude for compass reading, King Louis's affair with la Vallière, the construction of the hospital, Buckingham's scandalous ménage, anything and everything but *her*.

What I have. What is that exactly? The precious property that I have claimed in his heart will always be mine, but the rest is reserved for whatever comes next? Yes, I suppose so.

"The heart is an ever-expanding organ," I could hear Grandfather saying. "Do not underestimate it."

I must believe it.

June 3, 1669 — Whitehall

Good God! Castlemaine has threatened to dash that baby's skull on the stone floor if Charles does not recognise her. Dreadful woman. Charles is in a state and believes she might actually do it.

Note—Awful reviews for *Tyrannick Love*. The news sheets hated it; the audience hated it; Dryden hated it; I hated it. All wrong.

Later

A note arrived from Johnny in Paris asking Charles to stand godfather to Nan. Peace at last.

June 4 — Theatre Royal

"I am sorry, my dear," Dryden said, the ostrich plumes on his enormous hat quivering as he spoke. "I should have known it would not suit you, but

I wanted to write something more *serious,* more *lasting.* But in my self-service, I have done you a disservice," he said forlornly.

"It is lovely play, an *important* play," I said, taking his arm, knowing that was what he needed to hear. "It will be remembered long after my appalling performance is forgotten."

"But what to do now?" he asked, wiping his eyes with his heavily embroidered handkerchief. Did every inch of this man require ornamentation? It was a typical Dryden ensemble: long velvet jacket in a garish yellow, frilly laced cuffs, gold breeches, pink shoes with huge pink satin bows, and a terrible yellow velvet hat with pink ribbons and ostrich feathers: *disaster.*

"Now," I said firmly, tucking his awful hankie back into his awful coat, "you will write me a superb epilogue so that I may rise up as myself and apologise in person to my audience."

"Oh, yes!" He brightened. "That is a wonderful idea! I can add something light and humorous without ruining the play—and *you* can still play Valeria." I cringed at the hideous name.

"Yes. Now get to work. I'll not have another performance like last night. The applause did not last long enough for me even to exit the stage. Very embarrassing."

Note—The epilogue did the trick. After my deplorable death scene—I cannot figure out how to fall gracefully and so make the most God-awful thud—I rose up as Nelly and sparkled anew. I am saved.

By Most Particular Desire

THEATRE ROYAL, COVENT GARDEN

Audiences Brilliant and Overflowing

Are Invited to Attend the Premiere Performance of

TYRANNICK LOVE

Or

THE ROYAL MARTYR

A Heroic Tragedy by Poet Laureate, Mr. John Dryden

Now with a New Prologue and Epilogue

Written for and Performed by Mrs. Nelly Gwyn

This Present Wednesday, June 4, 1669

It will be repeated tomorrow, Thursday, and Friday next

PRESENTED BY THOMAS KILLIGREW,

LEASEE AND ROYAL PATENT HOLDER

To Be Performed by:

THE KING'S COMPANY (ESTABLISHED 1660)

With: Mrs. Nelly Gwyn, Mr. John Lacy, Mr. Michael Mohun,

And: Mr. Nicholas Burt, Mrs. Lizzie Knep,

and Mrs. Anne Marshall

PERFORMANCES BEGIN AT 3 O'CLOCK DAILY

Five a.m., Tuesday—Bagnigge House

"He's not coming back," Charles announced as he strode into my little bedroom under the eaves.

"Careful!"

"Owww!" Charles hit his head, as he always does, on the low doorway. He is just so tall. I loved to see him in the pearly grey light. It is almost like waking up together, I tell myself—almost.

The mattresses *finally* arrived, and Charles had Mrs. Chiffinch sew me some delicious snowy bedclothes. My tiny house is slowly coming together—naturally, as next week I shall have to move.

"Who is not coming back?" I asked sleepily, sitting up in bed. It was early, not yet light. Charles must have already completed his requisite five miles of walking in the dark. It is what he does when he cannot sleep.

I had fallen asleep over my latest script. Tom says I am improvising too much and must be more diligent—improvising instead of acting, not good.

"Johnny, of course." Charles sat on the small coffer at the end of the bed and began to remove his muddy boots.

When he is here, he prefers to dismiss his retinue and dress himself—he is much quicker than one would expect for a prince, but then he was for a long time a stone-broke prince in exile.

"Why?" I asked, now fully awake and moving the pile of pages over to the bedside table.

I had been looking forward to Johnny's return, as I know he had. Johnny still has not seen little Nan, who is now two months old, although I know he has written rhymes and songs for her mother to sing to her—her mother, who must have heard of his numerous infidelities in France. *All* the rumours cannot be true. There are not enough hours in the day.

"He has been brawling again, drunk, and making a public nuisance of himself—this time at the Opera," Charles said in an exasperated voice. "Naturally he selects the most highly trafficked location in Paris as the stage for his spectacle. All of the French court frequents the Opera. I am sure my illustrious cousin Louis has heard all about Johnny's behaviour. Apparently, he has not sobered up yet. I cannot take him back now. I would look foolish."

"Drunk since he left *London?*"

"I think drunk since he left the *navy*, and that was three years ago." Charles rolled his eyes. "In any case, Dr. Denis would like to keep him in Paris a bit longer for some additional treatments. But all will be well, and we need talk no more about that," Charles said, glossing over any unpleasantness as usual. He cannot bear for me or any other woman to be distressed.

Yawning, Charles haphazardly slung his clothes and wig over the damask chair, put his blue enamel travel clock on the marble-topped nightstand, and climbed into bed next to me, nuzzling his face into my neck.

"Have you decided what to do about Castlemaine?" I asked. It is a subject that has lately been preoccupying me—her power to manipulate the king. I try not to let it rankle, but I am not terribly successful.

"Shh, we are not going to allow her into our bed," he said, resuming his nuzzling.

I gave up and snuggled deeper into the thick covers and soon forgot all about her.

Note—The audience numbers have greatly improved for *Tyrannick Love,* but they are coming for the prologue, leaving to dine during the play itself, and then returning for the epilogue. *Heigh-ho.* I am not built for serious theatre.

Later

An unexpected note arrived this afternoon. A letter from Duncan! He asks after the family (Mother and Grandfather, in particular, but no mention of Rose) and begs a favour of me. Could I recommend him to the Coldstream Guards? His letter is a sweet blend of over-formality and childhood familiarity. He always wanted to join the military. I will see what I can do.

LONDON GAZETTE

Sunday, June 5, 1669

Most Deservedly Called London's Best and Brilliant Broadsheet

The Social Notebook

Volume 363

Ambrose Pink's social observations du jour

Darlings,

Can you believe it? The greatest goose in England rousted from her roost! The Duchess of Cleveland (the former Lady Castlemaine) has been invited to vacate her sumptuous apartments at Whitehall. We can be sure that she will not go quietly. *Quel* fireworks! *Mon Dieu*, the rumpus this will cause in the complicated ménage of His Majesty. Yet the steadfast Queen Catherine remains above the fray. *Bien*, as it should be.

But where does that leave our Nell? Can we now call her *maîtresse en titre?* Will she move into the palace and replenish the vacated royal nurseries? Can such a quixotic sprite be happy without her beloved theatre? *J'espère non!*

À bientôt,
Ever your eyes and ears,
Ambrose Pink, Esq.

June 5, 1669 — Theatre Royal (after morning rehearsal)

"My dear, have you heard?" Teddy hissed, as I rushed into rehearsal, late as usual.

"Mrs. Gwyn, that will be five shillings for tardiness," Mr. Booth called out officiously.

"Honestly, Nell, you are going to rack up enough late fees to buy that man a house," Nick whispered.

"Shh, both of you, or I will be fined for talking as well."

"But *have* you heard?" Teddy persisted. "No, I can see by your face that you haven't."

"Heard what?" Nick asked.

"He's asked her to clear out. Of the palace: furniture, dogs, children— well, I suppose the children could stay if they wanted to, but they probably won't—"

"*What* are you talking about?" I hissed as we took our places for Lacy's dancing class.

Hart was glaring at us from across the stage. He hates chatter during rehearsal. We took up our places. Teddy, standing opposite, shook out his long limbs, turned out his pretty feet, and, lifting his chin, assumed his elegant opening stance. Honestly, sometimes his grace makes me feel like a squat little hen.

"*Glad dance:* four count rhythm, *jeté* on the first pass, *capriole* on the second," Lacy called out, banging his counting stick on the floor. "Partners: Lizzie and Nick, Ellen and Teddy, Hart and Kitty, Rob and Nan, Becka and Will. On four, please! One [*bang*], two [*bang*], three [*bang*], and [*bang*] now."

"Quick, tell us!" Nick said, edging Lizzie closer so he could hear.

"Castlemaine, Cleveland, Nunsuch, whatever! Barbara! He is insisting she move out! One and two and—"

"When?" Nick and I asked in unison as we began moving through the figures.

"Today, tomorrow, as soon as possible." Teddy said, completing a perfect *capriole.*

"Long neck, Nell!" Lacy called out. "You are not a tortoise!"

"Why?" Lizzie asked during the third pass.

Teddy caught my eye. I shot him a warning look in return. Lizzie is incapable of keeping any information to herself and would tell anything and everything to her nosey gossipy lover, Sam, within the hour. In strict confidence I had shared Charles's paternity trouble with Teddy. Teddy kept his own counsel and blandly shrugged at Lizzie.

"Shoulders down, Edward!" called out Lacy, "three and [*bang*]."

Later

It's true. I had to see for myself. I needed some black gloves at the New Exchange and told Lark to meet me by York House—the traffic is less congested there. I walked south, having every intention of stopping at the Exchange, but found myself in front of Whitehall instead. In front of Castlemaine's special entrance there stood all manner of carts and wagons being loaded with household goods. A steady stream of royal staff carried beds, toys, rugs, tables, mirrors, and even a silver bath-tub to the overfull vehicles. A small crowd had turned out to watch. I pulled my hat low and stood carefully at the back so as not to be recognised.

"It's that Davis woman, the actress. He is finally throwing her out," a thickly built woman in a feathered hat commented.

"She doesn't live in the palace, never did. No. It's Buckingham's awful woman, the Countess of Sherborne," said a baker, still smelling of pastry.

"*Shrewsbury,* not Sherborne, and she doesn't live in the palace, either," his wife corrected. She, too, was covered in flour.

"Well, it's not Nelly," the feathered hat said loudly. "She'd never be so presumptuous as to take a room at the palace, and quite right, too."

"No, she belongs out here with us," the baker's wife agreed. There were murmurs of approval. I pulled my hat lower and took a half step back under the shade of a horse-chestnut tree.

"Bet it's Cleveland," offered an old woman who was holding an equally old black pug.

"Nah, we'd never be that lucky," the baker countered. "She'll hang on to the end, that woman. An institution, that's what she is."

"An institution of prostitution?" snickered a young errand boy in patched breeches. The feathered hat shot him a disapproving look. "That is an ugly word, young man."

"Did you hear that she actually invited that circus man—what did he do, something with fire? Acrobatics? Anyway, she asked him to dine at the palace. What kind of court is that? The old king would never have borne it," clucked the baker's wife with authority. "My sister-in-law's nephew works in the kitchens and swears it's true."

"The old king had no mistresses. He was a family man," pointed out the black-pug woman. "That's the trouble. This king has lost his family, and he now thinks that he can just do as he likes. No foundation. No principles. Tearing around Europe from the age of twelve. What sort of upbringing is that? Bastards everywhere."

"*That* is another ugly word," said the feathered hat primly.

The boy in patched breeches snickered again.

I could not listen to more and quietly stepped away from this opinionated little bunch. Remarkable that they feel so able to judge him, judge us, all of us. I must never move into the palace, I resolved, and moved on to meet Lark.

Note—I asked Jemmy Monmouth, as he is in charge of the Coldstream Guards, and he readily agreed to take on Duncan. I am happy to be able to do something to help my old friend. He is now thirty-one and has never married—how sad.

When I Move to Newman's Row

June 16, 1669 — Newman's Row, Lincoln's Inn Fields

We've done it: the Larks, the chickens, the dogs, the ducks, Jezebel, Grandfather, Molly, and me—quite a brood when you see us all together; good thing we have an enormous back garden opening onto the open fields. We left our furnishings behind on the king's instruction. Bagnigge Wells is to be used as our country home. Charles has promised that we will visit often. I feel terribly decadent having two houses but also bereft. Bagnigge Wells is *mine*. I found it, bought it, furnished it, and love it. A house I receive as a gift, however beautiful, will never feel as inviolably safe to me. The little house is still there, I remind myself. I can always go back.

When we arrived in town, exhausted and dirty and expecting a half-renovated empty house, we found that the king had ordered the decoration and supply of my suite of rooms! My private closet is a pale sage green, trimmed in alabaster white, with a delicate painted chaise covered in soft green damask with a beautiful tulipwood desk, and my bedroom is done in pinks and creams. In the gilt-edged wardrobe I found rows of new gowns, crisp white chemises, gauzy petticoats, whalebone corsets (watered silk!), and delicate slippers in all colours—all in my size and to my taste. I sat down on the bed, stunned at the magnitude of his gift.

"Like it?" a voice behind me asked.

I turned to see the king, standing in the doorway, beaming. I could not answer him but ran straight into his open arms.

"So beautiful," I said into his chest.

"As are you, my love." He laughed, pulling me into the great pink feather-bed.

Later—nine p.m. (my new bedroom)

"But can you afford it?" I asked him later as we were sitting up devouring the supper Mrs. Lark had brought: a tray of canary wine, cold chicken, fresh salad, and potatoes roasted with rosemary. Charles loves to be generous, but too often it is not within his budget.

He laughed. "Why, how practical you are, my darling. What kind of question is that to put to your king?"

"A very pertinent one," I persisted.

"True," he conceded. "My budget is limited, but I can afford to furnish and renovate a small London house—just not London itself. But soon I will not be relying on Parliament for my funding." He meant the Dover Treaty—not signed and still a long way off.

"Will King Louis be generous?" I ventured.

"My cousin Louis is shrewd and knows he has to offer considerable terms to tempt me into Catholicism," Charles said solemnly.

I instinctively looked around to make sure no one had heard. The king laughed. "You think there are Protestant spies lurking under the bed? By the way, before I forget, de Croissy, the new French ambassador, is stopping by tomorrow morning. Would you ask Mrs. Lark to make some of her yellow butter cakes?"

"He's coming *here*?"

"Why not? We shall have a little court in Newman's Row."

I thought of my untrained, noisy servants banging up and down the stairs, my utterly unfinished building site of a house, and my indulged, unruly menagerie. "We shall certainly have an informal court in Newman's Row." I giggled. "State visits to my house, good God."

Even later—four a.m. (moonlight)

"Come and see the best part," the king said, waking me in the night and handing me my robe. "Slippers, too—it is chilly." We crept up the backstairs in our nightclothes, trailed by the sleepy dogs. He led me up through the house, past the servants' bedrooms, and up a little crooked attic stairway.

Lifting up a hatch, he handed me up to a rooftop beyond. It was an English garden in miniature, with potted orange trees, climbing roses, pink cabbage roses, larkspur, sweet-william, white lilac, and an ivied trellis railing running along the perimeter.

"Charles!"

"Here." He tugged my hand, too impatient to let me discover his magical garden myself. "Look."

It was a telescope, protected by a tiny three-sided wooden gazebo. We spent the rest of the night looking at the starlit sky.

Undated—Newman's Row

Mrs. Chiffinch told me this morning that the queen knows of this house. We were in the morning room discussing colours and fabrics for the bedrooms when she abruptly delivered this news.

"But she is not angry," Mrs. Chiffinch reassured me, seeing my horrified expression. "She has come to understand that there will always be some woman, and it is easier for her if it is you."

"But I was her friend," I said miserably, setting down the heavy book of fabric swatches.

"Yes, you were, and you behaved badly in that respect, but of all of them, you are the only one who does not urge him to divorce the queen. Unlike Castlemaine, your ambitions stop at his heart. You love him for his own sake, and she of all women can understand that."

Later (Dusk)

I am shaken. I had not expected sympathy. She is right. I do not want to destroy his marriage. She is the queen, as I could never be. There is room for us both.

June 20, 1669—Official Notations for Privy Council Meeting on This Day to Be Entered into the Log-book

Notations taken by Secretary of State Henry Bennet, Earl of Arlington

A sad day for the House of Stuart, Her Grace the Dowager Queen Henrietta Maria has died in her sleep at Colombes in her native country of France. The court will go into deep mourning as of this afternoon. Necessary cloth has been ordered for the public buildings; all royal domestics will be issued black livery. Parliament has approved funds for public mourning.

Letters of condolence arrived from King Louis of France and his queen.

There is some concern that the Monsieur, Phillippe Duc d'Orléans, will claim the late queen's possessions on behalf of his wife Princesse Henriette-Anne, who has just borne another daughter. Nothing as yet has been decided. There is also the question of the grain of laudanum that Dr. Vallot, physician to the French royal family, administered to help Queen Henrietta Maria sleep that night. The Dowager Queen had previously refused the draught, claiming that such things did not agree with her constitution. When she was yet unable to sleep, she consented. King Louis XIV has ordered a full enquiry into this matter and will send his findings to our Council directly.

Nothing further to report.
Secretary of State Henry Bennet, Earl of Arlington

June 25, 1669— Newman's Row

"To the left, Lark," Charles instructed. "Tie it just there."

We were in the back garden training pink climbing roses to grow over the new curved arbour gate that Grandfather, Charles, and Lark had just finished building.

"About Madame's letter," said Monsieur de Croissy, the new French ambassador who was pacing about the garden, trying to draw the king into conversation.

"And then if we start the other batch growing from this side, Your Majesty?" Lark asked, holding up a pretty vine. "It should knit together by summer's end."

"Very good!" the king said enthusiastically, his bare hands covered in fresh dirt. "What do you say, sir?" he asked Grandfather, who was sitting in the cool shade of the peach tree. "Another slimmer trellis over the garden door?"

I looked up from my bed of creamy cabbage roses to watch the king working so happily in the company of my family.

"Lark!" Mrs. Lark called from the kitchen door. "Oh, begging your pardon, Your Majesty," she said, upon seeing the king. "I just finished a fresh pitcher of sweet lemon water; it's a new recipe, with honey and touch of mint, and I was going to test it out on Mr. Lark."

"You must try it out on us, Mrs. Lark! It sounds delicious!" the king said, wiping his hands on a clean cloth.

"With some butter cakes," Mrs. Lark determined. "With lemon-sugar icing." She was already heading back into the house.

She returned and, spreading out a snowy cloth, laid out a pretty afternoon collation of cakes, cold coffee, and sweet citrus juices. We ate in the slanting sun and talked of this and that: the law banning blood transfusions in France, the newest plays, the stylish new cutaway jackets, and the next shipment of imported lace—everything but government, politics, and the king's family.

June 27, 1669— Newman's Row (hot)

Charles is spending most of his days here. He does not care to publicly mourn with the court. He is quiet and thoughtful but not sad. It was a complicated affection, he tells me. He does not miss her but regrets that he did not heed his sister's pleas and visit their ailing Mother. "I was not at the deathbed of either of my parents," he told me, "but then my father did not die in a bed." He picked up a Venetian glass ball and held it up to the afternoon sun. "Did you know I sent a blank letter? Just my signature and nothing else."

"Blank letter?"

"To Cromwell, from the Hague. Any terms. I left it blank to show that I would sign my name to *any* terms that would spare my father's life." He looked at the blue glass ball in his hand as if he was surprised to find it there.

When I asked about his mother, his description was, at best, unflattering: "She was opinionated, stubborn, and nothing I did pleased her. She has been determined to be miserable every day since the death of my father." He broke off, hearing his escaping bitterness. This was a man who had trained himself to experience only the sweet side of everything. "But, my God . . . ," he said thoughtfully, as he looked out the window to the meadow beyond, "did she love him."

Every so often he breaks the quiet with random anecdotes pulled from his past: how she charged him per meal during their penniless exile, how she fed his dogs free of charge, how she passionately loved her husband but never understood her adopted country. He replays his life over and over.

He worries for his sister, now the last member of his immediate family left in France, and is forever urging her to visit, although having just risen from childbed, she cannot. Her grief for her mother is genuine. "There is no one Minette could not love, including our mam," he said after reading her letter. I just sit by him and stay quiet: It is all I can do.

Note—I asked Rose to sew some mourning clothes for me and the staff, and she has already sent over a stunning black striped satin gown: black on black, very elegant.

June 28, 1669—Bagnigge Wells

Charles and I have returned to the quiet of the country. He was loath to go to one of his official residences for fear of all the fuss and ceremony, so we slipped away here. The Larks accompanied us, and each day we take all the dogs, a duck or two if they are inclined, and Molly on a long walk by the river.

Charles is teaching me to fish, although I try not to catch any—it seems cruel. Charles is much preoccupied with his sister's well-being and happiness and, I suspect, with the brewing treaty betwixt the two countries. I do not try to divert him but let him know that I am here at the end of the path.

June 30, 1669—Official Notations for Privy Council Meeting on this Day to Be Entered into the Log-book

Notations taken by Secretary of State Henry Bennet, Earl of Arlington

The king's instinct was correct and the Monsieur did indeed try to claim the late queen's goods—particularly her jewels—for his wife. But the Madame, with the support of King Louis, insisted that what rightfully belonged to England should be returned to the English Crown, and so the queen's jewels and effects will be sent here.

The king instructed the Council to issue an invitation for the Madame to bring them herself, as a guest of the English Crown, but she has formally refused.

Nothing further to report.
Secretary of State Henry Arlington, Earl of Arlington

August 19

Clean linen again this month. Hold still. Trust. Hope. Another month, and I tell him.

When I Share a Joy

September 12, 1669 — Bagnigge Wells (still hot!)

"This won't work if you stay on the bank, Nell!" Charles called out, lazily floating in the shady water. Ruby and Scandalous looked at me in alarm, concerned that if I go in, they might be required to jump in and rescue me. Charles's spaniels, all accustomed to water sports, flung themselves into the water with abandon.

"Sit, stay," I told them. "But how does it *work*?" I asked, buying time on hard ground and watching the dogs swim round their master.

"Out! Out!" He herded them onto the bank. "Well, we are largely composed of humours that float, and so, on the whole, *we* float."

I put my bare toe into the river. It felt cold, but then *he* looked warm, and the dogs, now shaking off the water and stretching out in the sunshine, looked warm, and so it must *be* warm. "On the whole?" I asked sceptically. "Ruby, sit." I did not want her going in the water.

"Well, the odd man here or there doesn't float, but most do. In any case I am right here to save you. Just go, all at once! No hesitation! One, two, three! There's my brave girl!" he whooped as I ungracefully tumbled in on my bottom.

I rose, sputtering, to the surface, shocked by the cold—it was *not* warm at all. Laughing, he caught me in his arms and held me securely as I caught my breath. It was an exhilarating feeling: the chilly weightlessness after the bright day's warmth. Just then Molly jumped in after me and paddled in circles around us. This was too much for the dogs, and they all began to bark, alarming Molly, who only paddled faster.

"Now, kick your legs and move your arms like this—that's it!" he cheered, as I began to gently propel myself through the water with Molly on one side and Charles on the other. The three of us splashed about happily and then lay on the sunstriped lawn to dry. I can swim!

Later

"Is that safe?" I asked him tentatively. He was lying on his back, enjoying the golden summer evening light. "For a woman, I mean."

"Well, you're a woman and you're safe," he answered without opening his eyes.

"Suppose a woman were in a more *delicate* condition?"

"And what kind of condition might that be?" he asked softly, propping himself up on one elbow to look down at me.

Tuesday, October 1, 1669 — Church Street, Windsor

The queen is in residence, and I just can't stay in the castle—well, *won't* is a better word. *Refuse* is an even better word. Barbara Castlemaine and her brood are also lodged in the castle while Nunsuch is being renovated (again), another excellent reason to live here. This house is matchbox charming and set back on a quiet lane. Charles has hired a full staff, including two coachman, cook, cook-maid, housekeeper, housemaid, lady's maid, scullery maid, laundry-maid, porter, two footmen, kitchen gardener, flower gardener, and errand boy. The Larks stayed in London to supervise the decoration and look after the animals; Jezebel got up to all kinds of wickedness and has had a family. Grandfather and Mr. Lark have had to build a larger shed for them.

This house is tall but slim and will not hold such a large staff, so I have packed some of them off to London to help ready the house in Newman's Row, which is *still* under renovation and showing no sins of being finished anytime soon. Charles drew up wonderful plans for modernising the kitchens, widening the stairway, raising the door frames, breaking through walls to combine small rooms into larger ones and even installing an indoor water closet, but I fear that we will never see the end of the construction and I will be doomed to live forever in a cloud of sawdust. We have *still* not chosen colours or furnishings for any of the reception rooms, despite Mrs. Lark's pestering. I want green (verdant and peaceful), and she wants gold (ornate and gaudy); we are at an impasse. Grandfather and Mr. Lark are enjoying the building process enormously and spend hours poring over the plans and debating at length all the technical logistics of this wild endeavour.

Meanwhile, without the distraction of the stage, I am growing increasingly restless. I understand that Charles is determined that I should not overdo it, but at this rate I will have nothing *to* do. With the exception of his obsessive but warranted care of the queen during her many unsuccessful pregnancies, I have never heard of his expressing such vivid concern when his women are with child, and this is his ninth child! He has not even been to my bed in the last week, saying I need my rest. I hope there are no court beauties up there luring him back at night.

Later—Church Street (two o'clock in the morning)

The queen just left. I read these words and cannot quite believe them.

Tonight:

At eleven o'clock, after Charles had returned to the castle, Jerome arrived with a note from the queen requesting a brief audience. Stunned, I quickly agreed. She arrived within a few minutes, leaving me little time to remove all traces of Charles from the sitting room: his books, maps, boots, clocks, and his velvet hat with the crimson plume . . .

"Your Majesty." I curtsied deeply. She was smaller than I remembered.

"Mrs. Gwyn," she said, refusing the proffered chair, her back willow-wand straight. "I understand you are carrying my husband's child."

I nodded, startled by her directness and moved by her great courage.

"And will you be seeking . . . placement?" Her voice had lost none of its rich Portuguese lilt.

"At court?" In spite of myself, I giggled at the ludicrous thought.

She smiled at my response, visibly relaxing. "It is rumoured that you have requested a place in my household, and after a royal birth. . . . It has happened . . . before." Her mouth turned up in a sardonic smile. In a gesture of impulsive sweetness, she reached out, taking my hand in her own. "I knew it to be false, but I wanted to be sure. It did not sound like you. While you have caused me tremendous hurt, Ellen"—she paused, searching for the right words—"you have never been cruel."

I squeezed her tiny hand. "Your Majesty . . ." How to ask forgiveness? She shook her head, my unspoken apology running off her like a raindrop. Her eyes met mine in absolute understanding. She left without another word, lightly climbing into the waiting coach.

I will not tell anyone of her visit. I know she would prefer it, and I very much want to please this brave little woman.

When We Disagree

October 3, 1669—Church Street, Windsor

I have just returned from a tense walk with Charles through Home Park, which is rapidly returning to its pre-war beauty, I am told. It was a walk with a specific purpose, I discovered soon after we set out.

"Hmmm." Charles uncharacteristically cleared his throat. "As you will not be returning to the stage—"

"What?"

"Ellen, you must see that it is impossible to be the mother of my natural child and an *actress,*" he said tersely, his eyes focusing somewhere above my head.

"Charles, I was an actress when you met me, an actress when you took me into your bed, and I am still an actress now that I am carrying your child." I felt panic rising in my throat. I had been down this utterly dependent, unhappy, landmarkless road before.

"You must not upset yourself, my darling. As I said, it is impossible and not worth arguing over . . . especially now, when—"

"It would make me unhappy," I said bluntly, stopping on the path and sitting heavily down in the cold grass. "Is that not worth arguing over?"

"What is it?" he asked, looking down at me in alarm. "Are you ill? Do you have pain?"

"I am *unhappy.* I just told you. Weren't you listening?"

He set his mouth in a grim line and did not respond.

Note—Again! He left after supper again! I wore my new creamy silk gown—very *décolleté* and meant to be irresistible, but obviously isn't as he left without even going upstairs! He said he would not be able to overcome the temptation if he slept here. "Why are you so busy overcoming temptation?" I asked him, settling onto his lap.

"Your health, my love," he said lightly, setting me down in an armchair and moving across the room. "Good night, sweetheart," he said, pulling the door shut behind him.

Rubbish my health! I will ask Teddy what is going on. He and Tom arrive tomorrow to entertain the court.

October 4, 1669 — Church Street

"Nope, no one, just you," Teddy said, leaning back in the midday sun. We were seated in the garden amongst the last of the fragrant summer roses.

"No one?" Ruby rolled over in my lap for her afternoon sleep.

"Be careful, she is getting so fat," Teddy observed, frowning at my pudgy dog. "If you keep feeding her—"

"Teddy! There is truly no one who has caught his eye? Frances? Is she back?" I feared Frances's hold on him.

"No! She is off with her lumpy husband, twittering away in other pastures, thank God." Frances irritates Teddy as well. "Honestly, just the queen."

"And no one is trying to catch his eye?" I asked hopefully.

Teddy looked at me disdainfully and did not bother even to answer that.

"Right, sorry." This court is stacked ten deep with pretty young women hurling themselves at the king.

"They've been imitating you, this last crop. Some wear their hair like you, some wear breeches, some laugh overloudly." I pinched him at that. "What? You do! But when you do it, it is genuine and enchanting, and we love it and he loves it. I meant to tell you, Jemimah Sandwich said a couple of the latest bunch even tried to tint their hair red—came out a kind of awful carroty orange. Too bad."

"So what is he doing when he is not with me? I can't be there all the time, and since we came to Windsor I haven't had the energy to be there at all." I leaned forward in my garden chair, eager to pry information out of my observant friend.

"Do? Tennis, swimming, riding, a lot of hunting lately, but I suspect he told you that. The poor gamekeepers are going to have to go by night and kidnap stags from other forests and bring them here so the king can hunt them—he's killed so many. Jemimah says she will never eat venison again after this season, she's had so much of it. Oh, and his children are about and he has been much with them—but I expect he told you that, too."

I nodded. "Castlemaine around much?" I asked, attempting to sound casual. I knew it was she who had been spreading rumours of my request for a place in the queen's household.

"Barbara doesn't really interest him anymore; only her children interest him. I know she wormed her way back in by perpetually renovating her houses and making them uninhabitable construction zones, but of course he sees through that," Teddy said, stretching out his long legs. "I think she frankly gets on his nerves at this point, and she is loud and vulgar and is losing her looks at a terrifying rate. I give you permission to shoot me should I ever get that fat," he pronounced, closing his eyes.

I giggled and smelled the fading roses and watched the dying summer butterflies swirl around my friend.

Later

Teddy just left to head up to the castle dressed in all his masculine finery—his feminine finery is far more *de luxe,* but he does what he can. I am feeling too sleepy to go. If there is no one else charming him, then why does he not sleep here?

October 5, 1669— Church Street, Windsor

I did not attend the evening of cards in James York's suite last night—yet another evening I was too exhausted to attend. Too exhausted and too puffy. It feels as if I shall never leave this house again. Teddy says that Hart has arrived to be with Castlemaine, and I find the whole affair too incongrously bothersome to witness. To bring her new lover, who is my old lover, to her old lover's house—while I, his new lover, am here—ludicrous.

In any case I was too irritated to see anyone. A note arrived from Charles this morning and has left me feeling on edge all day. Jerome gave me a rueful smile as he handed me the little envelope with the great gold seal. I asked Lucy, the new chambermaid, to take him through to the kitchen for some breakfast and sat down to read.

DELIVERED BY HAND TO CHURCH STREET, WINDSOR

Ellen,

You are to receive a generous allowance from the Privy Purse, subject to increase at regular intervals, and if your expenditures should exceed this sum, you are to promptly send the receipts to Mr. Bab May, the Keeper of the Privy Purse. The deed to Newman's Row shall be signed over to you, and a permanent legal pension will be drawn up after your confinement and the birth of our child.

So you see, my love, there is no need for you to return to the stage. You will be well provided for. I have arranged everything. I hope this sets your mind at ease. There now, you see, there was no need to quarrel.

I love you and am your,
Charles

A contract, then? If I am to receive a salary, he must believe that I am for hire, and if I am for hire, then I am a . . . No. I am *not* for hire. Gifts, yes. Salary, no. King or no king.

Three p.m.

A draft for a staggering sum arrived this afternoon along with a curt note from Mr. May, all inside a hideously gaudy envelope with a fat ornate seal. I find him an insubstantial yet sourish sort of person and am well aware that he favours Castlemaine, regardless of her dismissal in this ridiculous horse race for the king's heart. She plays on his love of finery and wild, risky living and plies him with extravagant compliments and hints of undreamed of favours yet to come—absurd. All the while she has her sly fingers in the Privy Purse. Castlemaine is a mother five times over and ought to let go of her vixeny, compulsive flirting. It is unbecoming.

I have decided to put the whole matter out of my head for the moment, as I can see there will be no changing Charles's mind at present, nor any reason for me to give ground. In fact, I've a good mind to write to Tom and ensure my billing for the autumn season.

Note—Teddy says the rumours have begun. My absence has been noticed, and everyone can guess the cause.

October 7, 1669— Church Street, Windsor

Rose is here visiting me while her husband is away in the Cinque Ports in Jemmy Monmouth's bloated retinue, and this morning she and I sat in my cheery yellow closet sketching designs for new dresses.

"Ivory taffeta, striped with palest cream, will be lovely for evening. And if we order a cream hat with matching veil from London today, Madame Sophie should be able to have them here by next week," Rose said, looking at her diary. She takes her dress-making very seriously, and once she has promised, she is careful to deliver on the appointed day.

"Ivory?" I asked, looking at her design. "I'm not sure wheaty colours will do much for me. Perhaps a bolder shade . . ."

"Yes, but your skin is peachy from the sun—you've obviously not been wearing your bonnet—so ivory will suit for evening: very pretty by candle-light, and more stylish than a dark colour," she overruled. "Do you still have the gold slippers with the embroidered butterflies?"

"No, I got them wet," I said distractedly. I was looking for the right time to tell her my news—particularly as it would affect the dresses she was designing. This might not be the best season for *stripes*. I would look like a circus tent, and we would certainly need more material for the winter gowns once I was showing.

"Rose . . ." This was proving more difficult than I thought.

"Ellen, the way you go through slippers! You used to be able to make one pair last for two years!"

"Well, they were made of sterner stuff. Rose . . ."

"What about the green slippers edged in silver lace for the pink gown? No, the green may be too dark. You need *something* to temper that dress—if only I had known it was going to be such a *bright* pink."

"Yes, that sounds perfect. Rose . . ."

"And a grey feathered hat for your new black walking gown? Something fluffy and grey will offset that dress—otherwise it's a bit severe.

"Rose . . ."

"But on rainy days only, you must be sure to wear it on rainy days—not the pastel gowns you are always dragging through the mud, Ellen. Grey is lovely in the rain."

This wasn't going to work.

Later— Three p.m. (over warm chocolate and toast)

"Rose! I had thought this would be welcome news—a bastard, of course, but welcome!"

"It is happy! I am happy!" Her brown eyes grew bright with tears.

"You don't *look* happy." I was watching her pace about the room—window to chaise, chaise to window.

"I just wish . . . Oh, Ellen." She dropped heavily onto the tufted armchair and began picking at the fraying fabric—the dogs are destroying that chair. "I worry that I won't ever, can't ever . . ." Her words dissolved into sobs.

"Of course you can, Rose; it just takes time," I said, sounding trite. I felt selfish; I'd had no idea she wanted a child so badly.

"You don't understand, Ellen . . . the things we did to get rid of them. We couldn't, we just *couldn't* have them."

I looked at her, horrified. "You mean you . . . on purpose? How?"

She took a deep steadying breath. "Lots of ways: herbs, emetics, purgatives, if you caught it early enough . . . and if you didn't, then you just . . . well, you just *had* to. Everyone did it. So many times. And now, when I want one so much, I can't."

"Rose, you will," I said, kneeling beside her and trying to sound confident. I brushed her loose curls off her face.

"No, I won't. I can't. And it is right. A punishment," she said dully, blowing her nose.

"No, you can't be punished for something you did when you were little more than a child yourself." I was surprised at the conviction in my voice—inwardly, I grieved for her and was hurt that she had not *told* me.

"Yes, you can," she said flatly. "You can always be punished." There was no doubt in her voice, only regret.

Later

Charles came for supper, and it was a forced, awkward affair. I did not bring it up. He did not bring it up. He returned to sleep in the castle. London tomorrow.

> *To Lord John Wilmot, Earl of Rochester, Le Marais, Paris*
> *From Mrs. Ellen Gwyn, Newman's Row, London*
> *Dearest Johnny,*
>   *Please do not take it amiss that I write so seldom. You are ever in my thoughts and are missed, by me, by the king, by everyone. Charles loves you—you must know that—but is saddened by your wildness. You are exiled out of exasperation and not anger. He does not understand the blackness at the bottom of you. Nor do I. All I can do is love you with all the light I possess. I hope you are well, my dearest. Your lovely wife has not been to town, but I have heard from Savile that she is well at Adderbury. I am glad of it. We are all waiting for you to come home.*
>   *Dearest, what do I do? The king bids me to leave the stage, and I do not know how. It is not that the stage is my heart, for he is my heart, but the stage is my courage. I do not know how to enter the world as myself without it. He loves me, and*

I fear I am impossibly ordinary without the magic that happens in the dark of that great room. It will be my undoing, and he cannot and will not understand it.

I am ever and ever your,

Ellen

October 31, 1669— Newman's Row (All Gallows Eve)

Ghosts are abroad tonight as the legends go. I feel I am becoming one of them. After a blazing row I have yielded to the king's wishes and have accepted no roles this season—a truce, for now. I am writing this in the little curved window-seat in my bedroom. The fire has died down and the house is asleep, but I cannot stop running over and over tonight's exchange with the king.

"I will not have it!" Charles roared, knocking a small blue vase off the mantel. It rolled on the carpet, scattering the spaniels, but did not break. He did not notice, and I did not move to pick it up. This was truly the first time I had ever seen him lose his temper. "I would sooner shut down the theatre, both theatres, all theatres!" He struggled for patience and took a long breath. When he spoke, his voice had a cool sharpness, like a winter blade. "I gave the theatre patents, and I can revoke them just as easily," he menaced. I found his quiet malice more devastating than his hot rage.

I believed him and shuddered to think of my friends disbanded and Tom ruined. I shifted Ruby onto my lap in the yellow silk armchair. Think! Think! No. There was no recourse, and I must accept, but try as I might I could not make my lips form the words. No sound came, and so I closed my mouth like a goldfish.

"Ellen, don't you see," he said, kneeling in front of me on the thick carpet. "If anything happened to you . . . last time you survived, but this time, what if . . ."

"How did you know?" I asked, astonished. "How did you even know there was a last time?" Only a handful of people ever knew there was a baby. Teddy, Tom, Mother, Rose, Hugh, Cook . . .

"Barbara."

"Barbara!" I had not expected that answer. I slowly puzzled it together:

Hart must have told Barbara Castlemaine, and Barbara told the king—it was just the kind of juicy unfortunate sort of story she would be eager to pass on. But Hart . . . How could he? How could he discuss something so private and so painful with that horrible woman?

"She told me out of concern," he said solicitously, guessing my thoughts.

I rolled my eyes. Barbara Castlemaine only concerned herself with one person. Why? Why would she tell him? She said it to keep him out of my bed! I turned quickly to face Charles, still kneeling on the rug. "Did *she* suggest we sleep apart until after the baby is born?"

"Well, no, yes . . . in a way, but not a suggestion, really, more of a caution. She has, after all, had five children."

"And did you stay away from her bed during all those pregnancies?"

"No, naturally not, but then she was saying how delicate you are, and then she told me about your baby—your baby baptised Elizabeth."

I drew my breath in sharply, stunned that Hart would share such a detail, and squeezed my eyes shut against the answering bright white pain. Charles took my hands gently, as if they were as fragile as robin's eggs.

"Barbara told me that you nearly died when you lost that baby," he said simply. "That was enough for me . . . nothing would make me risk you. It matters not at all what else she said."

"Oh, Charles," It was not our child he worried for—his concern was for *me*. I immediately softened towards him. "I wouldn't do anything to endanger myself or the baby. It was a carriage accident. It could happen to anyone."

"I couldn't bear it, Ellen," he whispered, holding me tightly. "Please, for me. I just couldn't bear it."

"I won't," I promised. "Not while I am carrying our child, I won't."

November 1, 1669—All Souls' Day

I lit a candle, as I do every year, for my dead: Father, Great-Aunt Margaret, Theo, lost baby Elizabeth . . .

Monday—Theatre Royal, London

I have become an unpleasant person. Tom and Teddy are disappointed, and I find I cannot discuss my distress with them. I roam reasonlessly about the theatre. I feel without anchor or purpose. I feel jealousy born of idleness and am snapping at everyone. I harbour undeserved and unbridled anger for Hart, who is currently enjoying a short country holiday.

All I have is Charles and our baby, who does not even exist yet. I am riddled with envy for his wife, his children, his ministers . . . He is to be my whole life, but I am only to be a small part of his. I rage at the unfairness. I feel diminished, less, as if I am dissolving a little more each day. "Go back," my heart whispers. But I promised.

Barbara is gone; Moll is vanquished; I suppose I am now *maîtresse en titre*, but no one refers to me as such. As always, I remain Ellen. But I am less Ellen than I ever was before.

November 22, 1669— Newman's Row (early frosty morning)

Charles went off to St. James's Park for his morning constitutional, and I was left amongst the familiar debris: coffee cups, news sheets, dog bones, a forgotten tennis racquet, a book by Thucydides left face-down with the spine broken, papers and more papers, and half dismantled clocks. I must remember to tell Mrs. Lark not to disturb the pieces of this particular clock, or Charles will be cross—he has been working on it for two days.

I took myself downstairs so that the chambermaids could tidy up and roamed from room to room. The building work is nearly finished, and I could hear the carpenters, Mr. Lark, and Grandfather up on the second floor discussing plumbing for the new water closet. The broad books of fabric samples and paint colours and furniture designs were all lying out on the dining room table, where we left them last night. So far we have decided on periwinkle blue, pale gold, and creams for the formal drawing room—but have yet to order the furniture—and luscious reds for Charles's closet, for which we have ordered two deep armchairs, a bookshelf, a writing table, and a chaise longue. I am too superstitious to design the nursery yet, and Charles agrees.

I was too agitated to think about furniture and wandered out onto the front steps—yes, scandalous: a pregnant, unmarried actress and chief mistress of the King of England lounging about her front stoop in her dressing-gown. I squinted into the morning sunshine and saw Aphra come hurrying down the street. I raised my hand in greeting. She would not be shocked by such immodesty.

"You'll freeze!" she scolded. "Inside, inside!" she said, herding me back into the house.

The dogs heard sounds of intruders and began to bark, setting off Molly, who is nearly full grown and makes a sort of nasally croaking squawk. I led Aphra though the noisy animals into my small downstairs sitting room (one of the few furnished rooms on the ground floor). I rang the bell for coffee and victuals, as Aphra shed her light coat and pulled off her stylish black hat.

"Like it? Madame Sophie. Lady Herbert sent it back, and so she sold it to me for half off."

I giggled at my friend's ever-unabashed economising.

"My dear, I hope I don't offend, but you look dreadful. Sort of grey and unloved. Is something the matter?"

Trust Aphra to recognise a sickness of soul rather than body.

"Is it the king?"

I shook my head no.

"Your mother?"

My wild drunken mother perversely appealed to Aphra's sense of female independence. Again, I shook my head. "I'm just not myself. I've been foul to everyone. I have agreed to give up the stage, and it grieves me in a way that I do not understand."

"Why should you not understand it?" she said briskly. "Of course you are grieved. You carved out a shiny sliver of life for yourself—just you—and now you must give it up and become someone else." She shrugged dismissively. "Your sparkle came from your secret, Ellen. When we are young, very young, if we are lucky, we believe that we are guaranteed a special place in the world, all our own. It is only when we find out that there is no such place unless we scratch it out with our own hands that our lights begin to dim."

"My secret?" I asked, not following.

"You were yourself by your own right. However much it may have looked like you were in someone's possession. That was your great secret. That is why you sparkled beyond all others. You were free."

After Aphra had gone I mulled over what she had said. It is a grief, I thought. A grief for having lost something I did not care to lose. He prefers me not to act . . . but must I give up my theatre altogether? The performance is but a small part. I quickly wrote a note to Tom.

November 26, 1669 — Newman's Row, London (sunny after days of rain)

"Wrap up, Ellen; it is chilly," Grandfather said, standing at the door of the church. In fact, it was not cold but a balmy autumn day, warmed with remembered summer. Dutifully, I pulled my green muffler around me.

"You do realise that I have six months to go?" I teased affectionately. Grandfather is also terrified I will miscarry again and run into danger.

"And step carefully here," he said, leading me over a shallow puddle. Grandfather loves me with a steady discipline that underpins all he does.

I rolled my eyes. Am I to be treated like spun marzipan until May? *Yes,* his look tells me.

When we returned home, I tore open Tom's note, waiting in the silver dish:

> To Mrs. Ellen Gwyn
> Newman's Row, London
> My dear Ellen,
>   Of course! I should welcome your insight into all facets of our theatre. Shall we begin today? Twelfth Night *is proving a bear, and I would love your assistance. Let me know what time is convenient, and I will come with the set designer and stage*

manager if I may. I will send the script over to you directly. My groom is waiting for
your reply.

Affectionately your,
Tom

Thank God. Tom sent over several scripts for me to read through. I am res-
cued. He is coming over later with Mr. Fuller and Mr. Booth. I have also asked
Rose to come to discuss set, costumes, and casting for *Twelfth Night*. The
familiar rhythm of rehearsal and performance will steady and soothe me. I am
at home in the midst of that chaos. I feel the brilliance of activity coming on.

Later

They just left after a heated discussion and a lovely supper of roasted meats
and fresh salad. Becka is to play Maria, and Nan is to play Viola. Lizzie will
take Olivia, and in a fit of malice, I suggested Hart play Malvolio, complete
with yellow hose. I feel appeased, as it is a part he loathes. I am renewed
and painted in bright colours once more.

To Mrs. Eleanor Gwyn, Newman's Row, London
From Lord John Wilmot, Earl of Rochester, in Paris
December 10, 1669
Ellen,

Accede to his wishes until after the baby and then return. It would be somewhat
disastrous if you were to insist on the stage and then have a mishap. Undoing the king's
child is not like undoing a private citizen, to put it crudely. Be sure to come back,
Ellen. You are all my firelight, my dear, and I would be in darkness without you.

Paris is dull, and I am dull with it. I miss myself dreadfully, how selfish. Tell
Rose I shall bring her back lovely French fabric, and I won a pair of very pretty
shoes of Babs Chatillon the other day—they shall go to Teddy. Savile has asked for
the most outrageously expensive snuff, and I shall lie and tell him I could not find
it anywhere. Etheredge is being pompous and has requested books. You will get the
prize, my darling—as ever, my whole heart.

Johnny Rochester

Saturday, December 15 — Newman's Row

It happened. It was bound to. Hart could not go on skulking about the theatre indefinitely, and I? I needed to know why. This afternoon:

After dropping off a pile of costumes in the dress-maker's room (it was particularly galling to hand over my costumes, and the roles they accompanied, to the Marshall sisters) I heard Hart humming in his private tiring room. He only hums when he is alone. Without hesitating, I pushed open the slim wooden door to find him halfway through his afternoon shave.

"Ellen!" He quickly wiped the comically foamy shaving cream from his chin with a worn blue cloth.

Having impulsively rushed into this confrontation, I found I was unsure of what I wanted to say. No. I balled my fists in renewed purpose. "Why?" I demanded in a low wolfish growl. Was that really my voice? "Why tell her?" I knew he would understand me. I braced myself for his inevitable rage and useless explanations and then, hating myself for it, I suddenly began to weep, the tears coursing down my face like a soft spring rain.

"Ellen," he said quietly, "I should not have told her. Castlemaine is not a woman to understand such a thing, and I regret it. Forgive me."

Caught off guard, I reached out for a nearby chair to steady myself. Instantly, he was at my side, gently helping me to sit down, pressing a clean handkerchief into my wet palm. "I hadn't thought you would be sorry," I said, bewildered and stating the obvious.

"Yes." He laughed, still holding my hand. "Yes, I can see that."

"Why, Hart?" I asked earnestly. I was determined to know. "Something so private, so personal? Why tell her my secret?" And then I heard it: *my* secret, not *our* secret. My daughter, to be named Rose. His daughter, Elizabeth, for his mother. Our daughter. When had she become mine?

"Because I cannot forget her," he said, looking away, his voice catching, tearing. "As I cannot forget you."

Without a word I kissed his hand, still closed around mine, and rose to go. He roughly stood and returned to the washstand. He did not turn as the door closed. I know we will never speak of it again. It is all I can do for him.

Monday, December 20 — Theatre Royal

Sitting in on *Twelfth Night* rehearsals. Hart passed me in the wings without a word.

December 26, 1669 — Newman's Row (snow!)

We celebrated our Christmas tonight as Charles had to spend yesterday divided between Christmas festivities with his children (Chiffinch says he bought each of his daughters a compass and his sons new saddles) and the official court Christmas feast with his queen. Tonight is just for us. Mrs. Lark made her buttery yellow cakes with sugared lemon icing, while Mr. Lark and Grandfather decorated the banisters with lengths of evergreen. Rose and I hung a ball of mistletoe in my bedroom doorway—we can no longer close the door, but no matter. After supper and hot mulled wine we curled up on the sofa by the fire and opened our presents. Charles handed me a slim gilt-edged printed card wrapped in a golden ribbon:

A FAREWELL PERFORMANCE
BY MRS. ELLEN GWYN

A performance sponsored by the King of England

I turned to Charles. "Sponsored?"

"Yes, costumes, sets, and a lovely party afterwards at Chatelin's."

"Charles!"

"I could not think of any gift that would please you more. It will be a lovely good-bye, my dear."

"Good-bye for now," I added.

January 15, 1670— Newman's Row

Charles told me this evening that the queen is planning to attend my performance. He was clearly surprised and pleased by this news. I am delighted but not surprised. She is a woman with a rare capacity to forgive, and I am honoured.

When I Make My Last Entrance

LONDON GAZETTE

Sunday, February 13, 1670

Most Deservedly Called London's Best and Brilliant Broadsheet

The Social Notebook
Volume 400
Ambrose Pink's social observations du jour

Darlings,

By order of His Majesty, our dearest divine Nelly will return to us for one bright night. What he hath plucked he hath returned for one glittering evening. Cherish it, my petals! They will say in years to come: "I was there at that beautiful moment when a beautiful girl left her beautiful stage."

And in addition, you will be treated to the creamiest *de la crème:* Dryden will write, Lacy will dance, Ned will sing, and *naturellement, le roi* will watch! And then, poof! Our darling girl will be gone, and she will be missed, for she has been most loved, and may I say, it is never been more deservedly so.

À bientôt!
Ever your eyes and ears,
Your bated and breathy,
Ambrose Pink, Esq.

February 14—St. Valentine's Day, Will's Coffee-house

"You must know him, Ellen," Teddy said from behind his news sheet. I could hear him chewing his toasted gingerbread.

"Or her," Peg said, buttering her toast.

She is in town for my farewell performance—farewell . . . until after the baby performance—I keep stipulating. No one believes me, and everyone is sure I will fall so in love with my baby that I will give up all thoughts of the theatre. "Look how you are with your goose," Teddy keeps saying, as if that explains everything.

"Sounds like a man's writing to me," Teddy said, not bothering to offer any proof whatsoever.

"But . . . ," Peg interrupted.

"Peg, how many women do you know named 'Ambrose,'" Tom asked witheringly, not looking up from his sketches. He is finding it impossible to fit all of the distinguished guests attending this gala into appropriately distinguished boxes.

"It is not her *real* name, naturally," Peg said, dropping crumbs on her silk dress. "The language is too . . . I don't know . . . *floral* to be a *real* man."

"Men can be *floral*," Teddy insisted. "I can be a veritable bouquet. In any case, it was a lovely thing for *him* to write—whoever *he* may be," Teddy said sincerely. We looked at him in surprise. He is usually vitriolic about Pink's column. I wonder . . .

"But he called you 'Ned.' You hate being called 'Ned,'" Peg said.

"Well, obviously I hated that part." Teddy grimaced. "Ellen? Is the king your valentine?" he asked, changing the subject.

"*Now* he is. I had a false start. I woke up and saw Francis, the king's groom, first. I got straight back into bed and tried again," I said, rolling my eyes.

"Rupert always leaves a blindfold beside the bed, and then I have to go stumbling around the castle looking for him. It's an *old* castle, and the floors are *not* level. I never make it through unscathed," Peg said, showing us her scraped elbow.

"But then he gives you something delicious to make up, I see," purred Teddy, eyeing Peg's new ruby bracelet.

"Oh dear," said Tom in a small voice. "Cecilia usually reminds me . . . oh dear."

"You forgot?" Teddy asked, astonished. "I do not even *like* my wife, but I still send something," Teddy scolded, pouring more coffee.

"What did the king give you, Ellen?" Peg asked.

"I don't know," I said, looking at my miniature gold timepiece (a New Year's gift from Charles). Oh dear, I was going to be late. "I'm off to meet him at Newman's Row now." I slung on my coat. At six months, I was starting to feel unwieldy. I said quick good-byes and then hurried out the door for home.

The king, Buckingham, Buckhurst, Sedley, Rose, Grandfather, the Larks, and most of the household staff were waiting on the front steps when I arrived. "Has something happened?" I called, surprised to see them standing in the frosty air. A small crowd of onlookers had also gathered at the end of my street. My house has become something of a destination, and often people lurk there in the hope of catching a glimpse of the king. Today, their hopes were rewarded and then some; half the court seemed to be standing on my front stoop.

"Nothing has happened; we are just impatient. You are four minutes late," the meticulously punctual monarch reprimanded, snapping shut his timepiece. "If you had come in this"—he clapped his hands, grinning broadly—"you would have been on time." Cook and Johnston came tearing around the corner carrying a beautiful japanned sedan chair between them. "Good St. Valentine's Day, sweetheart." The king beamed, and everyone gathered on the steps began to cheer.

"Wait, wait!" Teddy panted from down the street.

I turned, surprised to see the little bunch I had just left at breakfast had followed me home. "Teddy—"

"You left so quickly," Tom said, reaching us and doubling over with exhaustion. "We hadn't paid the bill or put on our coats or anything. We had to run to catch up."

"Well, now that you are all here," said the king, descending the steps and encircling me in his arms, "what do you think?"

"It is beautiful. Just beautiful," I said, looking at the stylish contraption.

"Rose and I picked the emerald green seat coverings," Peg said proudly. Rose came down the steps and hugged me as well.

"Your little feet will grace our ground no more," trilled Buckhurst over-dramatically, his cheeks pinked with the cold.

"Try it out!" Teddy called, as the king helped me into the boxy interior. With that, Johnston and Cook took up the long handles and off we went, bouncing down the street. It took a few moments for them to match their strides and for me to regain my balance, but eventually I was able to turn to see the group of beloved faces waving good-bye. I blew them a theatrical kiss from the window and settled down to enjoy the bumpy ride.

Nine p.m., Newman's Row

"You truly like it, sweetheart?"

We were settled into our bed, under the quilted satin coverlets. At last, Charles is happy to sleep here, despite his concerns.

"I love it," I said, dropping a kiss on his nose. "Nothing could make me happier."

"Nothing?" he asked archly.

I shook my head firmly. "Nothing."

"Not even this?" he asked softly, pulling out a light, wrapped box from beside the bed. "Open it." He smiled and put the box into my hands.

I gently unbound the grosgrain ribbon and stripped away the thin tissue. Inside was a long, ruffled christening robe. The creamy satin ran through my fingers like water.

"It was used for my brother Henry and my sister."

"Minette?"

He nodded. The favourites. I knew how much he still missed Henry. I fell into his arms. There was nothing to say.

February 16, 1670 — Theatre Royal

I no longer walk anywhere. "It certainly makes me more conspicuous," I confided to Teddy after the morning rehearsal for my farewell event. Today, I will rehearse the new monologue Dryden has written for me. I was hoping he would not have too many script changes.

"Nothing wrong with conspicuous," Teddy said, smiling. I had caught him this morning in a pretty pink walking frock, alighting from Lady Jemimah's open carriage.

"Ellen, would you look at this," Dryden said, hurrying over to me, his hat plumes bobbing as he waved the newest playbill aloft.

By Order of His Majesty

Mrs. Nelly Gwyn's Farewell Performance

"If you wanted inconspicuous, you have chosen the wrong profession, my lamb." Teddy giggled.

"And the wrong lover," Dryden added fondly.

Note—Hart has unexpectedly left for Hill House. "I don't think he could face saying good-bye," Tom said wisely.

March 1, 1670 — Theatre Royal, backstage (My farewell Performance!)

"You are sure you are up to this?" Charles asked for the millionth time.

I kissed him in response. "I love the stage, Charles. It makes me happy. Of course I am up to it."

"But you feel well? The baby feels well?" Charles asked, rubbing my back; my back has been cramping lately.

"Your Majesty." Tom bowed, flustered. "You'd best be in your box, sire, as we are about to begin."

"I issued the patent on this theatre. You will begin when I choose," the king said in an uncharacteristically imperious tone. Tom looked instantly shamefaced and dropped into a deep court bow and began to stutter.

I giggled at that. "He is jesting, Tom. Do stop scraping."

The king pealed with laughter. Tom came up from his bow to see the king's merry face. "I, uh, we can start whenever you wish . . . ," he said, looking from me to the king.

"I will get to my box now, Tom. We will start when *Ellen* is ready," Charles said generously, hugging me close.

The king released me and went up to his seat, and Tom hurried off to talk to Mr. Booth, the stage manager and Keeper of the Prompt Book for the evening. He would record this, my last night on the stage. I could sense the house quieting around me. I put my hand on my belly and curved around my baby growing inside me. Closing my eyes, I felt the absolute precise calm born of being in the correct place at the correct time. Stepping forward, I gathered up my many Ellens, like a fisherman pulling in a net, and held them to me for this moment.

Take a breath. Count three. Curtain up. *Now.*

Epilogue

Dear Aunt Rose,

The funeral is set for Thursday. (King James has offered to send a royal coach for you.) Archbishop Tenison has agreed to give the sermon, and Mother's great friend Mr. Edward Kynaston of the King's Theatre has promised to help choose the music. She asked to be buried in St. Martin in the Fields. I think if she couldn't be buried with Father at Westminster Abbey, she wanted to rest nearby. She always said that music sounded sweeter in St. Martin in the Fields than anywhere else in England. She left the rector a generous bequest and asked that I ensure the bells of that church ring for her every Thursday. I know you and I will be comforted to hear those bells.

I am trying to abide by her wishes and remember her present happiness. When we realised she would not recover from this last apoplexy, she was anxious to assure us of her joy in rejoining Father and my sweet brother, James. Just yesterday she laughed that it was best that she hurried, as she would not want Father running off with any angels in her absence. How like her to make us laugh at such a time.

My stepmother, Queen Catherine, now in Portugal, sent a beautiful letter, reminding me of her deep affection for my mother. I think they understood each other as well as two people can. People cry out to me now when they see Mother's crested coach. They throw flowers and bestow good wishes upon me wherever I go. It has been a bit awkward when I am with my half-brothers and -sisters, as their mothers were less popular, to put it discreetly. I suppose I am only now, at seventeen, beginning to realise how rare a person can inspire such devotion.

Would you have the last of her roses at Pall Mall cut and brought to the church early on Thursday morning? She will like that—to be buried beneath flowers they planted together.

Charles Beauclerk, Duke of St. Albans,
Son of King Charles II and Ellen Gwyn

Author's Note

Gwyn Family

In 1679 old Madam Gwyn drowned in a puddle near Chelsea. Charles Hart, Charles Buckhurst, George Buckingham, Johnny Rochester, and all the Merry Gang turned out for her funeral. After her husband's death, Rose Gwyn lived on an allowance provided by King Charles II. She never bore children.

The Theatre

John Wilmot, Earl of Rochester, died at age thirty-three, debilitated by alcoholism and syphilis. He died after reconciling with King Charles II. Rochester remained a close friend of Nell's to the end of his life. Aphra Behn became the first prominent female playwright on the English stage, dedicating her play *The Feign'd Courtesan* to her dear friend Ellen Guin. Virginia Woolf wrote in *A Room of One's Own*, "All women together ought to let flowers fall upon the tomb of Aphra Behn . . . for it was she who earned them the right to speak their minds."

Edward Kynaston, whom Peyps called "the loveliest lady that I ever saw in my life," retired from the stage in 1699 after a successful career playing both male and female roles. Thomas Killigrew retired from the stage in 1677, leaving his company to be mismanaged by his two sons, Henry and

Charles. Charles Hart left the stage in 1682 and died at his home in Middlesex less than a year later. Peg Hughes eventually married Prince Rupert and bore him a daughter, Ruperta. It was said that Prince Rupert hoped his daughter would marry Nell's son, but Prince Rupert died before this came to pass. Dryden died in 1700 after writing some of the most famous poetry of his age and is buried next to Geoffrey Chaucer in Poet's Corner in Westminster Abbey.

The Court

James (Jemmy), Duke of Monmouth, declared himself the legitimate king after the death of his father and led an unsuccessful rebellion against his uncle King James II. His uncle ordered his execution in the summer of 1685. The unpopular King James II was deposed in 1688. Henriette-Anne (Minette), Duchesse d'Orléans, died suddenly at St. Cloud in 1670, two weeks after returning from England. It was rumored at the time that she had been poisoned by her husband. Minette's Treaty of Dover was successful, and King Charles II fulfilled his promise to declare himself a Catholic, although he waited until his deathbed to do so. Although they remained childless, King Charles II refused to divorce Queen Catherine of Braganza and she returned to her native Portugal only after her husband's death.

Nell and Charles

After giving birth to the king's son Charles Beauclerk, Duke of St. Albans, in May 1670 Nell returned to the stage to appear in Dryden's *Conquest of Granada* before retiring from the theatre permanently. James, her second son, died in Paris at the age of eight. Nell's love affair with Charles II thrived until his death in February 1685. Among his last recorded words was the entreaty to "let not poor Nelly starve." On his deathbed he gave Nell's son Charles the ring his father had given Bishop Juxon moments before his execution.

Nell remained faithful to Charles to the end of her life, reportedly saying she would not "let a dog lie where the deer hath lain." Nell survived Charles by only two years and died at age thirty-seven—it was said of a broken heart.

While I invented much of Nell's daily life, the major events I describe are rooted in fact. All of the central characters and the majority of the peripheral characters really lived. The happenings in London, the court, the weather, the recipes, the remedies, the medical advancements, and the theatre are also historically based, as is much of the gossip (as much as gossip can be). A lunatic did predict the end of the world, a comet did appear just before the plague, and it did become customary at that time to bless someone who sneezes.

Some of the unlikelier elements are also true, such as Rochester's destruction of the king's sundial and Queen Catherine's discovery of Nell's slipper in her husband's bedroom. Of all of her husband's mistresses, Nell is the only one she befriended. It is interesting to note that Queen Catherine of Braganza is credited with introducing tea to England. Nell's "three Charleses" are also accurate. She began her affair with Charles Hart (who was in his mid-thirties) at the age of fourteen and then abruptly took up with Charles Buckhurst and moved to Epsom before beginning her long affair with Charles II in approximately 1668. Charles II would have been thirty-eight at the time and Nell would have been eighteen. These age gaps would not have startled a seventeenth century observer; as these were considered reasonable liaisons in the seventeenth century, I chose not to evaluate them through my twenty-first-century lens. Nell was forthright about her personal history and did in fact refer to King Charles as her Charles III.

For anyone wishing to read further on the subject, I recommend Charles Beauclerk's wonderful work *Nell Gwyn: Mistress to a King,* a comprehensive biography of his endearingly illustrious ancestor. I also urge anyone interested in the period to read Antonia Fraser's magnificent biography *King Charles II.*

I should mention the several variations of Nell's name I use throughout the story. Although history remembers her as Nell, in the few places she signed her name Nell often used the initials "E.G." or "Ellen," and Aphra Behn dedicated her play to "Ellen Guin." One historical fact I chose to dispute was Nell's purported illiteracy. I find it difficult to believe that an actress who was required to learn up to three scripts in a week and was an intimate of both the king and the great writers of her age could have been unable to read.

Nell is still remembered today as the orange girl who captured the heart of the king.

Acknowledgments

My ever patient, laconic, wonderful, wonderful mother, who is part of every word of this book, told me that happiness is feeling like you are in the right place at the right time doing the right thing with the right people. This book has been an adventure in happy. There have been lucky accidents; fortunate coincidences; and, at each turning, unbelievable kindness.

I would like to thank:

Meredith Bryan, Eve Ensler, Chris Evatt, Candice Fuhrman, Sandra Gulland, Jainee McCarroll, Shael Norris, Sharon Kay Penman, Leslie Silbert, and especially: Dr. Sarah Carpenter, Dr. Roger Savage, and Dr. Olga Taxidou.

In London:

Kaleem Aftab, David Babani, Alex Kerr, David Milner, Charlotte Phillips, and Dan Pirrie; the boys: Jack Brough, Jamie Deeks, Dan Johnston, and Ewen Macintosh, who stood in the street outside the flat, cheering as I went off to my first agent meeting and have been cheering every moment since; Adriana Paice, Sadie Speers, and Aron Rollin for quietly understanding it all.

In Kauai, New York, and Los Angeles:

Consuelo Costin and Rafael Feldman; Tamee De Silva; Robert Dickstein; Benji, Terri, and Teddy Garfinkle; Dr. Hunter, Sally Moore, and Dr. Deborah Barbour; David Katz; Julie and Koko Kanealii; Max Miles; Neal, Melissa, and Koa Norman; Matt Nicholson for the first page and Naomi Nicholson for her beautiful photographs; Michelle Masuoka; Angela Pycha; Chris Reiner and Koah Viercutter; Amber Sky Stevenson; Edelle Sher;

Stuart and Maria Sher; Tora and Kirk Smart; Megan Wong; and especially my wonderful students: Amber and Chloe Garfinkle, Ely Smart, and Wyatt Miles, for every day making me remember the wonder of words.

In particular I would like to thank: Gaylen and Mike Tracy for their unending kindness; Chad Deal and Wendy Devore for being my family and keeping my room ready; Matt Pycha and Amber Naea for more than I could ever say.

I would like to thank my brilliant agent, Alexandra Machinist; my fantastic editors, Danielle Friedman and Trish Todd. Thank you all for believing in Nell. Stacy Creamer, Martha Schwartz, Cherlynne Li, Renata DiBiase, Alessandra Preziosi, Marcia Burch, and everyone at Simon & Schuster, who took such beautiful care of this book; David Hansen, who helped me to find Rory Friedman, who helped me to find the wonderful Tamar Rydzinski; and Noah Sher, who helped me to find it all.

I would like to thank Philippa Gregory, who with extraordinary grace and generosity took such time to encourage and help me, and has been so truly kind. Thank you.

And my family: Nicky, Tina, and my mother and father. You make everything better, sillier, stronger, safer, funnier, happier, and infinitely more valuable. I love you so much. Thank you.

Exit the Actress

It is seventeenth-century London: England is at peace, Charles II has been restored to the throne, and young Ellen Gwyn has a decision to make. Does she obey her mother and follow her sister Rose into the *demi-monde* of prostitution or does she risk all and chart her own course? Ellen, better known to history as "Nell," defies her family and becomes an orange girl, selling fruit at Covent Garden's famous Theatre Royal. Her risk brings speedy rewards, and at the theatre she soon rises to become the most popular actress in London.

Outrageous, bright, and brimming with wit, beauty, and grace, she charms all who meet her, quickly befriending poet laureate John Dryden; playwright Aphra Behn; famed libertine Johnny, Earl of Rochester; and the last of the cross-dressing actors, Edward Kynaston. She is courted by men named Charles: leading actor Charles Hart; wealthy, young wit Lord Charles Buckhurst; and finally the most famous Charles of all, the king.

Weaving back and forth from the theatre to the court to the backstreets of Drury Lane, *Exit the Actress* follows Ellen, by means of her fictionalized journal entries, letters from the royal family, playbills, recipes, and many other creative and comprehensive documents. It chronicles this engaging and delightful heroine's meteoric rise from humble orange seller to beloved royal mistress as she rises and falls in the high-stakes game of intrigue that constantly surrounds the king she loves.

For Discussion

1. Throughout the novel Ellen comes back to the idea of there being multiple Ellens. The last instance of this occurs in the final chapter when she writes, "Stepping forward, I gathered up my many Ellens, like a fisherman pulling in a net, and held them to me for this moment." What do you think she means by her "many Ellens"? How many can you identify, and what are the defining characteristics of each one?

2. In a shocking moment early in the novel, a very young Ellen sees her sister Rose being groped in public, which leads to an even more shocking revelation when Rose says, "You think [Mother] did not *ask* me to be here?" While Ellen is determined not to live her sister's life, this certainly seems like her mother's plan for her. Why do you think Ellen is able to escape her fate and Rose is not? Do you think Ellen eventually succeeds in rescuing Rose from her life of prostitution, or is it too little too late?

3. Who do you think writes under the *nom du plume* Ambrose Pink? Do you think one of the main characters doubles as the gossip column writer, or is it someone we are never introduced to? Is Ambrose Pink a man or a woman?

4. Ellen's relationship with Charles Hart was hardly a casual affair. Hart seems deeply in love with her and showers her with gifts and affection. Why do you think she is never able to completely fall in love with him? If their child had survived, do you think their relationship would have suffered as it did?

5. "The game is afoot," says Lord Buckingham, as he makes up his mind to place Ellen as the next *maîtresse en titre*. Lord Buckingham has many reasons for choosing her, but he makes it clear that he expects her to help increase his standing with the king and perhaps, more

important, to push his cousin Lady Castlemaine out of favor. As Buckingham notes, "Her bright, whorish light is going out." Do you think Ellen could have become one of the king's mistresses without Lord Buckingham's help? To what extent do you think she understands her relationship with the king to be a "game"?

6. Lord Buckhurst pursues Ellen in a manner that is persistent but hardly romantic. He first offers to pay her one hundred pounds a year to be his mistress, and then he declares in a letter: "I have decided. You are to be mine." Why do you think she still chooses to run off with him and the rest of the "merry mob"? Should she have left Buckhurst earlier than she did, or was she right in trying to save face by not coming back into public life immediately?

7. Ellen's attitude toward the queen is a fascinating combination of admiration and pity. Do you think she betrays the queen to the same degree the other mistresses do, or does Ellen redeem herself because of her seemingly unique approach to the affair?

8. John Dryden and Aphra Behn both play prominent roles in the novel and help to place it not only in a historical but also in Ellen's artistic context. Allusions are made to many of their plays and poems throughout. Discuss Ellen's prowess as an actress and comedienne in their works. What parts of her personality allow her to excel onstage and why do you think she is so beloved by the patrons of the theatre? What modern actresses would you compare her to?

9. While Lady Castlemaine plays the villainess throughout the novel, there is no denying that she was a very powerful woman. Her fertility was legendary; and the money, titles, and property she received from the king were enough to last her several lifetimes. Nevertheless, she seems sad as the novel progresses, and she ultimately loses the fight to remain as the king's mistress once her looks have faded. In what ways is she similar to Ellen and how is she different? Do you think in her role in Charles's life she was even more important than the queen at times?

10. Charles II's letters to his sister Minette, the Madame of France, are brilliant glimpses into the kind of ruler he was. They show vulnerability, indecision at times, and ultimately a playfulness and levity that seem to define his reign. Discuss some of their correspondence. Do you think Minette ever offered a piece of bad advice? How much influence do you think she had over her older brother?

11. Johnny Rochester provides comic relief throughout the novel, but he also serves as a confidant to both Ellen and Charles. Though he is wittier than most and very well liked, his destructive streak eventually forces his exile. Ellen remains a loyal friend until the end, writing in her final letter to him, "[Charles does] not understand the blackness at the bottom of you. . . . All I can do is love you with all the light I possess." What do you think of Johnny Rochester? Why do you think his darker moments are so painful for the king and Ellen to endure? And why do you think he and Ellen get along so well?

12. It is very important to Ellen that she owns her own property and pays for it herself, resulting in her purchase of Bagnigge House. Later, she also accepts a house at Newman's Row from the king. Why do you think she insists on purchasing her own property but then eventually accepts the Newman's Row residence? Does this undermine her independent spirit in any way, or would she simply have been foolish to continue to shun the benefits of being the king's mistress?

A Conversation with Priya Parmar

Did you choose the court of Charles II as the setting for your novel, or was the character of Ellen Gwyn your primary interest and the court simply came with her? Did you consider any other of Charles II's mistresses as a focal point?

Ellen was the first woman I encountered while researching my doctorate, and she caught my interest and refused to let go. I was fascinated by her contradictions. She was a woman working in the raciest profession, in the raciest court in Europe, but she was known to be utterly faithful to her lovers. She was described by Samuel Peyps as "a mad, mad girl," but she moved easily in the most exclusive literary and sophisticated social circles of her day. She was small boned and red-haired at a time when voluptuous dark beauty was the ideal. I wrote about the Restoration London because that is where Ellen lives.

How did you come up with the fantastic idea of telling the story through letters, playbills, diary entries, and other historical documents? How accurately does the format you wrote in reflect the findings of the research you did to write the novel?

I really like primary documents. With respect to history, I am most interested in contradictory paper trails—the conflicting perceptions, misconceptions, jealousies, petty likes, dislikes, beliefs, and lies—that are the ingredients of what cook into hard, historical fact. Telling the story this way allows me to let characters speak for themselves and explore the roots of misunderstandings, legends, reputations, and rumours.

Ellen herself left very little in the way of documentation. What we mostly have from her are enormous bills for dresses and shoes and a will that displays her extraordinary generosity. The *London Gazette* existed, but Ambrose's column is fictional. Similarly, the playbills reflect the company at the time, but it is often difficult to guess who would have been cast in each role. The recipes are patterned after authentic dishes, and the tone of the letters between Charles and Minette is inspired by existing correspondence. I tried to create their singularly easy relationship within a difficult, uneasy family. Some of the small details—such as the barge for Minette, the gift of sealing wax, and even Charles's ending a letter by being called off to dance—are entirely accurate.

As a first-time novelist, what drew you to the genre of historical fiction? Does the historical context that your novel is placed in enhance your imaginative facilities or hinder them?

I have always loved reading historical fiction. I love reunderstanding an event or period through a fictional character. I am fascinated by the specifics of history: the small, everyday earmarks of a time that feel so foreign to us now.

It was wonderful to write inside a historical frame. It offered a way into the characters. I could easily imagine Ellen's walk in her cumbersome skirts and contrast it with the lissome freedom she must have felt dancing in breeches. There are the rooted in the facts we know about her, and then there is all the fun, creative space in between. For instance, I know that Ellen ran off with Charles Sackville, ostensibly leaving the stage for good. Shortly after, she returned to the Theatre Royal and, according to Samuel Pepys, played parts that did not quite suit her. Why? It was hugely fun to construct a plot congruent with her fictional character that would explain such a series of events.

Are the recipes from the *Lady's Household Companion* real? They are such a great touch and add a practical aspect to the lives of the seventeenth-century characters. Have you tried any of them yourself?

They are real, but I am a nightmare in the kitchen! My meringues were pancake flat and my macaroons tasted like salt. I tried making snow cream, but it turned out looking like runny whipped cream from a can. I am sure that someone more adept in the kitchen would fare much better than I!

I can guarantee your readers are dying to know if Ambrose Pink is a man or a woman and who he or she was. Was the character based on an actual gossip writer from the era, or was he an imaginative conceit?

Ambrose is entirely fictional, but all the gossip is based on real events of the day. There were writers chronicling the lives of celebrities such as Ellen, Lady Castlemaine, and Peg. Much like today, the public wanted to know all about their beauty routines, diet, and personal life.

I assumed Ambrose *was* an outside character, and it was only halfway through writing the novel that I realized he was someone I knew—Teddy. He is positioned to understand all the overlapping circles of her life: the court, the theatre, and London itself and he loves Ellen dearly. He was so much fun to write.

Did your past work as a dramaturge on Broadway and in the West End of London help in the research and writing of this novel? How do you think theatre culture has changed since the seventeenth century and what are some of the most striking similarities?

I loved being in the theatre. There is something exciting and electric when the cast is backstage and the audience is coming in. The air crackles and the actors are on the edge of a moment, and then the lights dim and they jump. It is thrilling. I think it would have been hard for me to understand the controlled, organized chaos that is a performance without that experience.

The theatre was a rough and rowdy place in the seventeenth century. It was a noisy dialogue between the audience and the actors, and it was not uncommon for a popular scene to be repeated three or four times at the audience's request. This was an exciting era for theatre. Extensive stage machinery and set construction was becoming more common, and theatre took on an aspect of spectacle. Audiences came to expect a higher production value and were vocal if disappointed. That is the essential difference: there was no protective balm of politeness as there is now. It was an interactive and sometimes brutal experience.

Do you read historical fiction as well as write it? What are you reading right now? Are there any particular writers who have inspired or influenced your style?

My mother taught me how to write. She has always encouraged me to look at why a line works and to see the vertebrae of good writing wherever I find it, whether it is on a shampoo bottle or in a Jane Austen novel. I hear her voice in my head as I pare down a line or find the footstep of a phrase. Her constant question is "Do you need that word?" Usually when she asks that, I don't!

In terms of literary influence I love the economy, heft, and precision of poetry. It is such a marvelous combination of tangential evocation and steely discipline. I love the way poetry stretches the capability of a word or punctuation mark. W. H. Auden, Czeslaw Milosz, Constantine Cavafy, and Pablo Neruda are some of my favorites.

Are you currently working on any other works of historical fiction? Will you continue to set your novels in the seventeenth century, or will you delve into a different era altogether?

I am currently working on my second historical novel, which takes place in London during the First World War. I hope to return to the seventeenth century someday, as I truly love it, but for now I am riding on omnibuses through leafy squares, summering in Sussex, and hoping this war will be over by Christmas.

Enhance Your Book Club

1. The novel contains several wonderful little snippets from the *Lady's Household Companion*. Try a few of them out with your book club. Perhaps the Remedy for the Sickened Body would be a good place to start:

   > *Make up a pot of lemon posset. [Don't worry; it's a hot milk-based drink . . . not as bad as it sounds.]*
   > *Thicken it with the yolks of six eggs.*
   > *Sweeten it with sugar and kindness.*

   Does it work? How much kindness did you put in? If you are feeling a little less adventurous, try the recipe for French Macaroons on page 65. Afterwards, relax by whipping together some of the Venetian Ceruse described on page 54 (but don't use white lead!) and kicking your feet up. Remember not to smile or laugh after applying it, though, so as not to create any creases.

2. To get your book club into a seventeenth-century mood, read aloud some of the timeless poems by two prominent figures in the life of Ellen Gwyn: John Dryden and Aphra Behn. Poetryfoundation.org has a wonderful collection of poems from both writers as well as excellent biographies and further reading suggestions. For Dryden, try reading one of his shorter light poems such as "Marriage a-la Mode," or "You charm'd me not with that fair face." As an introduction to Behn, dip into a poem called "The Willing Mistress." Could she have drawn any inspiration from Ellen?

3. Did you know that the British monarchy has its own website? There are profiles going all the way back to the first official king of England, Athelstan, who died in 939. This site has a great profile of Charles II as well as of his father, Charles I; and it features a collection of royal

portraits to show you what they looked like. Check it out at www
.royal.gov.uk. Find out if Charles was really as reckless with his money
as he seems in the novel. Did he ever officially convert to Catholicism
as he promised his cousin Louis XIV of France? As you delve into the
history of the seventeenth-century monarchs, you will begin to recog-
nize a lot of names from the novel!